ENCOUNTER
WITH A VAMPIRE!

I arrived at Guilty Pleasures a little after midnight. Jean-Claude was standing at the bottom of the steps. He was leaning against the wall, utterly still. If he was breathing, I couldn't see it. The wind blew the lace on his shirt. A lock of black hair trailed across the smooth paleness of his cheek.

"You smell of other people's blood, ma petite."

I smiled at him, sweetly. "It was no one you knew. . . ."

Ace Books by Laurell K. Hamilton

GUILTY PLEASURES
THE LAUGHING CORPSE
CIRCUS OF THE DAMNED

GUILTY PLEASURES

LAURELL K. HAMILTON

ACE BOOKS, NEW YORK

This book is an Ace original edition,
and has never been previously published.

GUILTY PLEASURES

An Ace Book / published by arrangement with
the author

PRINTING HISTORY
Ace edition / October 1993

ISBN: 0-441-30483-4

ACE®
Ace Books are published by The Berkley Publishing Group,
200 Madison Avenue, New York, NY 10016.
ACE and the "A" design
are trademarks belonging to Charter Communications, Inc.

PRINTED IN THE UNITED STATES OF AMERICA

10 9 8 7 6 5 4

To Gary W. Hamilton, my husband,
who doesn't like scary things,
but who read this book anyway.

ACKNOWLEDGMENTS

Carl Nassau and Gary Chehowski for introducing me to the wide world of guns. Ricia Mainhardt, my agent, who believed in me. Deborah Millitello for enthusiasm above and beyond the call of duty. M. C. Sumner, new friend and valuable critic. Mary-Dale Amison, who has an eye for the small details that get by the rest of us. And to all the rest of the Alternate Historians who came in too late to critique this book: Janni Lee Simner, Marella Sands, and Robert K. Sheaf. Thanks for the cake, Bob. And to everyone who attended my reading at Archon 14.

1

Willie McCoy had been a jerk before he died. His being dead didn't change that. He sat across from me, wearing a loud plaid sport jacket. The polyester pants were primary Crayola green. His short, black hair was slicked back from a thin, triangular face. He had always reminded me of a bit player in a gangster movie. The kind that sells information, runs errands, and is expendable.

Of course now that Willie was a vampire, the expendable part didn't count anymore. But he was still selling information and running errands. No, death hadn't changed him much. But just in case, I avoided looking directly into his eyes. It was standard policy for dealing with vampires. He was a slime bucket, but now he was an undead slime bucket. It was a new category for me.

We sat in the quiet air-conditioned hush of my office. The powder blue walls, which Bert, my boss, thought would be soothing, made the room feel cold.

"Mind if I smoke?" he asked.

"Yes," I said, "I do."

"Damn, you aren't gonna make this easy, are you?"

I looked directly at him for a moment. His eyes were still brown. He caught me looking, and I looked down at my desk.

Willie laughed, a wheezing snicker of a sound. The laugh hadn't changed. "Geez, I love it. You're afraid of me."

"Not afraid, just cautious."

"You don't have to admit it. I can smell the fear on you, almost like somethin' touching my face, my brain. You're afraid of me, 'cause I'm a vampire."

I shrugged; what could I say? How do you lie to someone who can smell your fear? "Why are you here, Willie?"

"Geez, I wish I had a smoke." The skin began to jump at the corner of his mouth.

"I didn't think vampires had nervous twitches."

His hand went up, almost touched it. He smiled, flashing fangs. "Some things don't change."

I wanted to ask him, what does change? How does it feel to be dead? I knew other vampires, but Willie was the first I had known before and after death. It was a peculiar feeling. "What do you want?"

"Hey, I'm here to give you money. To become a client."

I glanced up at him, avoiding his eyes. His tie tack caught the overhead lights. Real gold. Willie had never had anything like that before. He was doing all right for a dead man. "I raise the dead for a living, no pun intended. Why would a vampire need a zombie raised?"

He shook his head, two quick jerks to either side. "No, no voodoo stuff. I wanna hire you to investigate some murders."

"I am not a private investigator."

"But you got one of 'em on retainer to your outfit."

I nodded. "You could just hire Ms. Sims directly. You don't have to go through me for that."

Again that jerky head shake. "But she don't know about vampires the way you do."

I sighed. "Can we cut to the chase here, Willie? I have to leave"—I glanced at the wall clock—"in fifteen minutes. I don't like to leave a client waiting alone in a cemetery. They tend to get jumpy."

He laughed. I found the snickery laugh comforting, even with the fangs. Surely vampires should have rich, melodious laughs. "I'll bet they do. I'll just bet they do." His face sobered suddenly, as if a hand had wiped his laughter away.

I felt fear like a jerk in the pit of my stomach. Vampires could change movements like clicking a switch. If he could do that, what else could he do?

"You know about the vampires that are getting wasted over in the District?"

He made it a question, so I answered. "I'm familiar with them." Four vampires had been slaughtered in the new vampire club district. Their hearts had been torn out, their heads cut off.

"You still working with the cops?"

"I am still on retainer with the new task force."

He laughed again. "Yeah, the spook squad. Underbudgeted and undermanned, right."

"You've described most of the police work in this town."

"Maybe, but the cops feel like you do, Anita. What's one more dead vampire? New laws don't change that."

It had only been two years since Addison v. Clark. The court case gave us a revised version of what life was, and what death wasn't. Vampirism was legal in the good ol' U. S. of A. We were one of the few countries to acknowledge them. The immigration people were having fits trying to keep foreign vampires from immigrating in, well, flocks.

All sorts of questions were being fought out in court. Did heirs have to give back their inheritance? Were you widowed if your spouse became undead? Was it murder to slay a vampire? There was even a movement to give them the vote. Times were a-changing.

I stared at the vampire in front of me and shrugged. Did I really believe, what was one more dead vampire? Maybe. "If you believe I feel that way, why come to me at all?"

"Because you're the best at what you do. We need the best."

It was the first time he had said "we." "Who are you working for, Willie?"

He smiled then, a close secretive smile, like he knew something I should know. "Never you mind that. Money's real good. We want somebody who knows the night life to be looking into these murders."

"I've seen the bodies, Willie. I gave my opinions to the police."

"What'd you think?" He leaned forward in the chair, small hands flat on my desk. His fingernails were pale, almost white, bloodless.

"I gave a full report to the police." I stared up at him, almost looking him in the eye.

"Won't even give me that, will ya?"

"I am not at liberty to discuss police business with you."

"I told 'em you wouldn't go for this."

"Go for what? You haven't told me a damn thing."

"We want you to investigate the vampire killings, find out who's, or what's, doing it. We'll pay you three times your normal fee."

I shook my head. That explained why Bert, the greedy son of a gun, had set up this meeting. He knew how I felt about vampires, but my contract forced me to at least meet with any client that had given Bert a retainer. My boss would do anything for money. Problem was he thought I should, too. Bert and I would be having a "talk" very soon.

I stood. "The police are looking into it. I am already giving them all the help I can. In a way I am already working on the case. Save your money."

He sat staring up at me, very still. It was not that lifeless immobility of the long dead, but it was a shadow of it.

Fear ran up my spine and into my throat. I fought an urge to draw my crucifix out of my shirt and drive him from my office. Somehow throwing a client out using a holy item seemed less than professional. So I just stood there, waiting for him to move.

"Why won't you help us?"

"I have clients to meet, Willie. I'm sorry that I can't help you."

"Won't help, you mean."

I nodded. "Have it your way." I walked around the desk to show him to the door.

He moved with a liquid quickness that Willie had never had, but I saw him move and was one step back from his reaching hand. "I'm not just another pretty face to fall for mind tricks."

"You saw me move."

"I heard you move. You're the new dead, Willie. Vampire or not, you've got a lot to learn."

He was frowning at me, hand still half-extended towards me. "Maybe, but no human could a stepped outta reach like that." He stepped up close to me, plaid jacket nearly brushing against me. Pressed together like that, we were nearly the same height— short. His eyes were on a perfect level with mine. I stared as hard as I could at his shoulder.

It took everything I had not to step back from him. But dammit, undead or not, he was Willie McCoy. I wasn't going to give him the satisfaction.

He said, "You ain't human, any more than I am."

I moved to open the door. I hadn't stepped away from him. I had stepped away to open the door. I tried convincing the sweat along my spine that there was a difference. The cold feeling in my stomach wasn't fooled either.

"I really have to be going now. Thank you for thinking of Animators, Inc." I gave him my best professional smile, empty of meaning as a light bulb, but dazzling.

He paused in the open doorway. "Why won't you work for us? I gotta tell 'em something when I go back."

I wasn't sure, but there was something like fear in his voice. Would he get in trouble for failing? I felt sorry for him and knew it was stupid. He was the undead, for heaven's sake, but he stood looking at me, and he was still Willie, with his funny coats and small nervous hands.

"Tell them, whoever they are, that I don't work for vampires."

"A firm rule?" Again he made it sound like a question.

"Concrete."

There was a flash of something on his face, the old Willie peeking through. It was almost pity. "I wish you hadn't said that, Anita. These people don't like anybody telling 'em no."

"I think you've overstayed your welcome. I don't like to be threatened."

"It ain't a threat, Anita. It's the truth." He straightened his tie, fondling the new gold tie tack, squared his thin shoulders and walked out.

I closed the door behind him and leaned against it. My knees felt weak. But there wasn't time for me to sit here and shake. Mrs. Grundick was probably already at the cemetery. She would be standing there with her little black purse and her grown sons, waiting for me to raise her husband from the dead. There was a mystery of two very different wills. It was either years of court costs and arguments, or raise Albert Grundick from the dead and ask.

Everything I needed was in my car, even the chickens. I drew the silver crucifix free of my blouse and let it hang in full view. I have several guns, and I know how to use them. I keep a 9 mm Browning Hi-Power in my desk. The gun weighed a little over two pounds, silver-plated bullets and all. Silver won't kill a vampire, but it can discourage them. It forces them to have to heal the wounds, almost human slow. I wiped my sweaty palms on my skirt and went out.

Craig, our night secretary, was typing furiously at the computer keyboard. His eyes widened as I walked over the thick carpeting. Maybe it was the cross swinging on its long chain. Maybe it was the shoulder rig tight across my back, and the gun out in plain sight. He didn't mention either. Smart man.

I put my nice little corduroy jacket over it all. The jacket didn't lie flat over the gun, but that was okay. I doubted the Grundicks and their lawyers would notice.

2

I had gotten to see the sun rise as I drove home that morning. I hate sunrises. They mean I've overscheduled myself and worked all bloody night. St. Louis has more trees edging its highways than any other city I have driven through. I could almost admit the trees looked nice in the first light of dawn, almost. My apartment always looks depressingly white and cheerful in morning sunlight. The walls are the same vanilla ice cream white as every apartment I've ever seen. The carpeting is a nice shade of grey, preferable to that dog poop brown that is more common.

The apartment is a roomy one-bedroom. I am told it has a nice view of the park next door. You couldn't prove it by me. If I had my choice, there would be no windows. I get by with heavy drapes that turn the brightest day to cool twilight.

I switched the radio on low to drown the small noises of my day-living neighbors. Sleep sucked me under to the soft music of Chopin. A minute later the phone rang.

I lay there for a minute, cursing myself for forgetting to turn on the answering machine. Maybe if I ignored it? Five rings later I gave in. "Hello."

"Oh, I'm sorry. Did I wake you?"

It was a woman I didn't know. If it was a salesperson I was going to become violent. "Who is this?" I blinked at the bedside clock. It was eight. I'd had nearly two hours of sleep. Yippee.

"I'm Monica Vespucci." She said it like it should explain everything. It didn't.

"Yes." I tried to sound helpful, encouraging. I think it came out as a growl.

"Oh, my, uh. I'm the Monica that works with Catherine Maison."

I huddled around the receiver and tried to think. I don't think really well on two hours of sleep. Catherine was a good friend, a name I knew. She had probably mentioned this woman to me, but for the life of me, I couldn't place her. "Sure, Monica, yes. What do you want?" It sounded rude, even to me. "I'm sorry if I don't sound too good. I got off work at six."

"My god, you mean you've only had two hours of sleep. Do you want to shoot me, or what?"

I didn't answer the question. I'm not that rude. "Did you want something, Monica?"

"Sure, yes. I'm throwing a surprise bachelorette party for Catherine. You know she gets married next month."

I nodded, remembered she couldn't see me, and mumbled, "I'm in the wedding."

"Oh, sure, I knew that. Pretty dresses for the bridesmaids, don't you think?"

Actually, the last thing I wanted to spend a hundred and twenty dollars on was a long pink formal with puffy sleeves, but it was Catherine's wedding. "What about the bachelorette party?"

"Oh, I'm rambling, aren't I? And you just desperate for sleep."

I wondered if screaming at her would make her go away any faster. Naw, she'd probably cry. "What do you want, please, Monica?"

"Well, I know it's short notice, but everything just sort of slipped up on me. I meant to call you a week ago, but I just never got around to it."

This I believed. "Go on."

"The bachelorette party is tonight. Catherine says you don't drink, so I was wondering if you could be designated driver."

I just lay there for a minute, wondering how mad to get, and if it would do me any good. Maybe if I'd been more awake, I wouldn't have said what I was thinking. "Don't you think this is awfully short notice, since you want me to drive?"

"I know. I'm so sorry. I'm just so scattered lately. Catherine told me you usually have either Friday or Saturday night off. Is Friday not your night off this week?"

As a matter of fact it was, but I didn't really want to give up my only night off to this airhead on the other end of the phone. "I do have the night off."

"Great! I'll give you directions, and you can pick us up after work. Is that okay?"

It wasn't, but what else could I say. "That's fine."

"Pencil and paper?"

"You said you worked with Catherine, right?" I was actually beginning to remember Monica.

"Why, yes."

"I know where Catherine works. I don't need directions."

"Oh, how silly of me, of course. Then we'll see you about five. Dress up, but no heels. We may be dancing tonight."

I hate to dance. "Sure, see you then."

"See you tonight."

The phone went dead in my ear. I turned on the answering machine and cuddled back under the sheets. Monica worked with Catherine, that made her a lawyer. That was a frightening thought. Maybe she was one of those people who was only organized at work. Naw.

It occurred to me then, when it was too late, that I could just have refused the invitation. Damn. I was quick today. Oh, well, how bad could it be? Watching strangers get blitzed out of their minds. If I was lucky, maybe someone would throw up in my car.

I had the strangest dreams once I got back to sleep. All about this woman I didn't know, a coconut cream pie, and Willie McCoy's funeral.

3

Monica Vespucci was wearing a button that said, "Vampires are People, too." It was not a promising beginning to the evening. Her white blouse was silk with a high, flared collar framing a dark, health-club tan. Her hair was short and expertly cut; her makeup, perfect.

The button should have tipped me off to what kind of bachelorette party she'd planned. Some days I'm just slow to catch on.

I was wearing black jeans, knee-high boots, and a crimson blouse. My hair was made to order for the outfit, black curling just over the shoulders of the red blouse. The solid, nearly black-brown of my eyes matches the hair. Only the skin stands out, too pale, Germanic against the Latin darkness. A very ex-boyfriend once described me as a little china doll. He meant it as a compliment. I didn't take it that way. There are reasons why I don't date much.

The blouse was long-sleeved to hide the knife sheath on my right wrist and the scars on my left arm. I had left my gun locked in the trunk of my car. I didn't think the bachelorette party would get that out of hand.

"I'm so sorry that I put off planning this to the last minute, Catherine. That's why there's only three of us. Everybody else had plans," Monica said.

"Imagine that, people having plans for Friday night," I said.

Monica stared at me as if trying to decide whether I was joking or not.

Catherine gave me a warning glare. I gave them both my best angelic smile. Monica smiled back. Catherine wasn't fooled.

Monica began dancing down the sidewalk, happy as a drunken clam. She had had only two drinks with dinner. It was a bad sign.

"Be nice," Catherine whispered.

"What did I say?"

"Anita." Her voice sounded like my father's used to sound when I'd stayed out too late.

I sighed. "You're just no fun tonight."

"I plan to be a lot of fun tonight." She stretched her arms skyward. She still wore the crumpled remains of her business suit. The wind blew her long, copper-colored hair. I've never been able to decide if Catherine would be prettier if she cut her hair, so you'd notice the face first, or if the hair was what made her pretty.

"If I have to give up one of my few free nights, then I am going to enjoy myself—immensely," she said.

There was a kind of fierceness to the last word. I stared up at her. "You are not planning to get falling-down drunk, are you?"

"Maybe." She looked smug.

Catherine knew I didn't approve of, or rather, didn't understand drinking. I didn't like having my inhibitions lowered. If I was going to cut loose, I wanted to be in control of just how loose I got.

We had left my car in a parking lot two blocks back. The one with the wrought-iron fence around it. There wasn't much parking down by the river. The narrow brick roads and ancient sidewalks had been designed for horses, not automobiles. The streets had been fresh-washed by a summer thunderstorm that had come and gone while we ate dinner. The first stars glittered overhead, like diamonds trapped in velvet.

Monica yelled, "Hurry up, slowpokes."

Catherine looked at me and grinned. The next thing I knew, she was running towards Monica.

"Oh, for heaven's sake," I muttered. Maybe if I'd had drinks with dinner, I'd have run, too, but I doubted it.

"Don't be an old stick in the mud," Catherine called back.

Stick in the mud? I caught up to them walking. Monica was giggling. Somehow I had known she would be. Catherine and she were leaning against each other laughing. I suspected they might be laughing at me.

Monica calmed enough to fake an ominous stage whisper. "Do you know what lies around this corner?"

As a matter of fact, I did. The last vampire killing had been only four blocks from here. We were in what the vampires called "the District." Humans called it the Riverfront, or Blood Square, depending on if they were being rude or not.

"Guilty Pleasures," I said.

"Oh, pooh, you spoiled the surprise."

"What's Guilty Pleasures?" Catherine asked.

Monica giggled. "Oh, goodie, the surprise isn't spoiled after all." She put her arm through Catherine's. "You are going to love this, I promise you."

Maybe Catherine would; I knew I wouldn't, but I followed them around the corner anyway. The sign was a wonderful swirling neon the color of heart blood. The symbolism was not lost on me.

We went up three broad steps, and there was a vampire standing in front of the propped-open door. He had a black crew cut and small, pale eyes. His massive shoulders threatened to rip the tight black t-shirt he wore. Wasn't pumping iron redundant after you died?

Even standing on the threshold I could hear the busy hum of voices, laughter, music. That rich, murmurous sound of many people in a small space, determined to have a good time.

The vampire stood beside the door, very still. There was still a movement to him, an aliveness, for lack of a better term. He couldn't have been dead more than twenty years, if that. In the dark he looked almost human, even to me. He had fed already tonight. His skin was flushed and healthy. He looked damn near rosy-cheeked. A meal of fresh blood will do that to you.

Monica squeezed his arm. "Ooo, feel that muscle."

He grinned, flashing fangs. Catherine gasped. He grinned wider. "Buzz here is an old friend, aren't you, Buzz?"

Buzz the vampire? Surely not.

But he nodded. "Go on in, Monica. Your table is waiting."

Table? What kind of clout did Monica have? Guilty Pleasures was one of the hottest clubs in the District, and they did not take reservations.

There was a large sign on the door. "No crosses, crucifixes, or other holy items allowed inside." I read the sign and walked past it. I had no intention of getting rid of my cross.

A rich, melodious voice floated around us. "Anita, how good of you to come."

The voice belonged to Jean-Claude, club owner and master vampire. He looked like a vampire was supposed to look. Softly curling hair tangled with the high white lace of an antique shirt.

Lace spilled over pale, long-fingered hands. The shirt hung open, giving a glimpse of lean bare chest framed by more frothy lace. Most men couldn't have worn a shirt like that. The vampire made it seem utterly masculine.

"You two know each other?" Monica sounded surprised.

"Oh, yes," Jean-Claude said. "Ms. Blake and I have met before."

"I've been helping the police work cases on the Riverfront."

"She is their vampire expert." He made the last word soft and warm and vaguely obscene.

Monica giggled. Catherine was staring at Jean-Claude, eyes wide and innocent. I touched her arm, and she jerked as if waking from a dream. I didn't bother to whisper because I knew he would have heard me anyway. "Important safety tip—never look a vampire in the eye."

She nodded. The first hint of fear showed in her face.

"I would never harm such a lovely young woman." He took Catherine's hand and raised it to his mouth. A mere brush of lips. Catherine blushed.

He kissed Monica's hand as well. He looked at me and laughed. "Do not worry, my little animator. I will not touch you. That would be cheating."

He moved to stand next to me. I stared fixedly at his chest. There was a burn scar almost hidden in the lace. The burn was in the shape of a cross. How many decades ago had someone shoved a cross into his flesh?

"Just as you having a cross would be an unfair advantage."

What could I say? In a way he was right.

It was a shame that it wasn't merely the shape of a cross that hurt a vampire. Jean-Claude would have been in deep shit. Unfortunately, the cross had to be blessed, and backed up by faith. An atheist waving a cross at a vampire was a truly pitiful sight.

He breathed my name like a whisper against my skin. "Anita, what are you thinking?"

The voice was so damn soothing. I wanted to look up and see what face went with such words. Jean-Claude had been intrigued by my partial immunity to him. That and the cross-shaped burn scar on my arm. He found the scar amusing. Every time we met, he did his best to bespell me, and I did my best to ignore him. I had won up until now.

"You never objected to me carrying a cross before."

"You were on police business then; now you are not."

I stared at his chest and wondered if the lace was as soft as it looked; probably not.

"Are you so insecure in your own powers, little animator? Do you believe that all your resistance to me resides in that piece of silver around your neck?"

I didn't believe that, but I knew it helped. Jean-Claude was a self-admitted two hundred and five years old. A vampire gains a lot of power in two centuries. He was suggesting I was a coward. I was not.

I reached up to unfasten the chain. He stepped away from me and turned his back. The cross spilled silver into my hands. A blonde human woman appeared beside me. She handed me a check stub and took the cross. Nice, a holy item check girl.

I felt suddenly underdressed without my cross. I slept and showered in it.

Jean-Claude stepped close again. "You will not resist the show tonight, Anita. Someone will enthrall you."

"No," I said. But it's hard to be tough when you're staring at someone's chest. You really need eye contact to play tough, but that was a no-no.

He laughed. The sound seemed to rub over my skin, like the brush of fur. Warm and feeling ever so slightly of death.

Monica grabbed my arm. "You're going to love this, I promise you."

"Yes," Jean-Claude said. "It will be a night you will never forget."

"Is that a threat?"

He laughed again, that warm awful sound. "This is a place of pleasure, Anita, not violence."

Monica was pulling at my arm. "Hurry, the entertainment's about to begin."

"Entertainment?" Catherine asked.

I had to smile. "Welcome to the world's only vampire strip club, Catherine."

"You are joking."

"Scout's honor." I glanced back at the door; I don't know why. Jean-Claude stood utterly still, no sense of anything, as if he were not there at all. Then he moved, one pale hand raised to his lips. He blew me a kiss across the room. The night's entertainment had begun.

4

Our table was nearly bumping up against the stage. The room was full of liquor and laughter, and a few faked screams as the vampire waiters moved around the tables. There was an undercurrent of fear. That peculiar terror that you get on roller coasters and at horror movies. Safe terror.

The lights went out. Screams echoed through the room, high and shrill. Real fear for an instant. Jean-Claude's voice came out of the darkness. "Welcome to Guilty Pleasures. We are here to serve you. To make your most evil thought come true."

His voice was silken whispers in the small hours of night. Damn, he was good.

"Have you ever wondered what it would be like to feel my breath upon your skin? My lips along your neck. The hard brush of teeth. The sweet, sharp pain of fangs. Your heart beating frantically against my chest. Your blood flowing into my veins. Sharing yourself. Giving me life. Knowing that I truly could not live without you, all of you."

Perhaps it was the intimacy of darkness; whatever, I felt as if his voice was speaking just for me, to me. I was his chosen, his special one. No, that wasn't right. Every woman in the club felt the same. We were all his chosen. And perhaps there was more truth in that than in anything else.

"Our first gentleman tonight shares your fantasy. He wanted to know how the sweetest of kisses would feel. He has gone before you to tell you that it is wondrous." He let silence fill the darkness, until my own heartbeat sounded loud. "Phillip is with us tonight."

Monica whispered, "Phillip!" A collective gasp ran through the audience, then a soft chanting began. "Phillip, Phillip . . ." The sound rose around us in the dark like a prayer.

The lights began to come up like at the end of a movie. A figure stood in the center of the stage. A white t-shirt hugged his upper

14

body; not a muscleman, but well built. Not too much of a good thing. A black leather jacket, tight jeans and boots completed the outfit. He could have walked off any street. His thick, brown hair was long enough to sweep his shoulders.

Music drifted into the twilit silence. The man swayed to the sounds, hips rotating ever so slightly. He began to slip out of the leather jacket, moving almost in slow motion. The soft music began to have a pulse. A pulse that his body moved with, swaying. The jacket slid to the stage. He stared out at the audience for a minute, letting us see what there was to see. Scars hugged the bend of each arm, until the skin had formed white mounds of scar tissue.

I swallowed hard. I wasn't sure what was about to happen, but I was betting I wasn't going to like it.

He swept back his long hair from his face with both hands. He swayed and strutted around the edge of the stage. He stood near our table, looking down at us. His neck looked like a junkie's arm.

I had to look away. All those neat little bite marks, neat little scars. I glanced up and found Catherine staring at her lap. Monica was leaning forward in her chair, lips half-parted.

He grabbed the t-shirt with strong hands and pulled. It peeled away from his chest, ripping. Screams from the audience. A few of them called his name. He smiled. The smile was dazzling, brilliant, melt-in-your-mouth sexy.

There was scar tissue on his smooth, bare chest: white scars, pinkish scars, new scars, old scars. I just sat staring with my mouth open.

Catherine whispered, "Dear God!"

"He's wonderful, isn't he?" Monica asked.

I glanced at her. Her flared collar had slipped, exposing two neat puncture wounds, fairly old, almost scars. Sweet Jesus.

The music burst into a pulsing violence. He danced, swaying, gyrating, throwing the strength of his body into every move. There was a white mass of scars over his left collarbone, ragged and vicious. My stomach tightened. A vampire had torn through his collarbone, ripped at him like a dog with a piece of meat. I knew, because I had a similar scar. I had a lot of similar scars.

Dollar bills appeared in hands like mushrooms after a rain. Monica was waving her money like a flag. I didn't want Phillip at our table. I had to lean into Monica to be heard over the noise.

"Monica, please, don't bring him over here."

Even as she turned to look at me, I knew it was too late. Phillip of the many scars was standing on the stage, looking down at us. I stared up into his very human eyes.

I could see the pulse in Monica's throat. She licked her lips; her eyes were enormous. She stuffed the money down the front of his pants.

Her hands traced his scars like nervous butterflies. She leaned her face close to his stomach and began kissing his scars, leaving red lipstick prints behind. He knelt as she kissed him, forcing her mouth higher and higher up his chest.

He knelt, and she pressed lips to his face. He brushed his hair back from his neck, as if he knew what she wanted. She licked the newest bite scar, tongue small and pink, like a cat. I heard her breath go out in a trembling sigh. She bit him, mouth locking over the wound. Phillip jerked with pain, or just surprise. Her jaws tightened, her throat worked. She was sucking the wound.

I looked across the table at Catherine. She was staring at them, face blank with astonishment.

The crowd was going wild, screaming and waving money. Phillip pulled away from Monica and moved on to another table. Monica slumped forward, head collapsing into her lap, arms limp at her side.

Had she fainted? I reached out to touch her shoulder and realized I didn't want to touch her. I gripped her shoulder gently. She moved, turning her head to look at me. Her eyes held that lazy fullness that sex gives. Her mouth looked pale with most of the lipstick worn away. She hadn't fainted; she was basking in the afterglow.

I drew back from her, rubbing my hand against my jeans. My palms were sweating.

Phillip was back on the stage. He had stopped dancing. He was just standing there. Monica had left a small round mark on his neck.

I felt the first stirrings of an old mind, flowing over the crowd. Catherine asked, "What's happening?"

"It's all right," Monica said. She was sitting upright in her chair, eyes still half-closed. She licked her lips and stretched, hands over her head.

Catherine turned to me. "Anita, what is it?"

"Vampire," I said.

Fear flashed on her face, but it didn't last. I watched the fear fade under the weight of the vampire's mind. She turned slowly to stare at Phillip as he waited on the stage. Catherine was in no danger. This mass hypnosis was not personal, and not permanent.

The vampire wasn't as old as Jean-Claude, nor as good. I sat there feeling the press and flow of over a hundred years of power, and it wasn't enough. I felt him move up through the tables. He had gone to a lot of trouble to make sure the poor humans wouldn't see him come. He would simply appear in their midst, like magic.

You don't get to surprise vampires often. I turned to watch the vampire walk towards the stage. Every human face I saw was enraptured, turned blindly to the stage, waiting. The vampire was tall with high cheekbones, model-perfect, sculpted. He was too masculine to be beautiful, and too perfect to be real.

He strode through the tables wearing a proverbial vampire outfit, black tux and white gloves. He stopped one table away from me, to stare. He held the audience in the palm of his mind, helpless and waiting. But there I sat staring at him, though not at his eyes.

His body stiffened, surprised. There's nothing like ruining the calm of a hundred-year-old vampire to boost a girl's morale.

I looked past him to see Jean-Claude. He was staring at me. I saluted him with my drink. He acknowledged it with a nod of his head.

The tall vampire was standing beside Phillip. Phillip's eyes were as blank as any human's. The spell or whatever drifted away. With a thought he awoke the audience, and they gasped. Magic.

Jean-Claude's voice filled the sudden silence. "This is Robert. Welcome him to our stage."

The crowd went wild, applauding and screaming. Catherine was applauding along with everyone else. Apparently, she was impressed.

The music changed again, pulsing and throbbing in the air, almost painfully loud. Robert the vampire began to dance. He moved with a careful violence, pumping to the music. He threw his white gloves into the audience. One landed at my feet. I left it there.

Monica said, "Pick it up."

I shook my head.

Another woman leaned over from another table. Her breath smelled like whiskey. "You don't want it?"

I shook my head.

She got up, I suppose to get the glove. Monica beat her to it. The woman sat down, looking unhappy.

The vampire had stripped, showing a smooth expanse of chest. He dropped to the stage and did fingertip push-ups. The audience went wild. I wasn't impressed. I knew he could bench press a car, if he wanted to. What's a few push-ups compared to that?

He began to dance around Phillip. Phillip turned to face him, arms outspread, slightly crouched, as if he were ready for an attack. They began circling each other. The music softened until it was only a soft underscoring to the movements on stage.

The vampire began to move closer to Phillip. Phillip moved as if trying to run from the stage. The vampire was suddenly there, blocking his escape.

I hadn't seen him move. The vampire had just appeared in front of the man. I hadn't seen him move. Fear drove all the air from my body in an icy rush. I hadn't felt the mind trick, but it had happened.

Jean-Claude was standing only two tables away. He raised one pale hand in a salute to me. The bastard had been in my mind, and I hadn't known it. The audience gasped, and I looked back to the stage.

They were both kneeling; the vampire had one of Phillip's arms pinned behind his back. One hand gripped Phillip's long hair, pulling his neck back at a painful angle.

Phillip's eyes were wide and terrified. The vampire hadn't put him under. He wasn't under! He was aware and scared. Dear God. He was panting, his chest rising and falling in short gasps.

The vampire looked out at the audience and hissed, fangs flashing in the lights. The hiss turned the beautiful face to something bestial. His hunger rode out over the crowd. His need so intense, it made my stomach cramp.

No, I would not feel this with him. I dug fingernails into the palm of my hand and concentrated. The feeling faded. Pain helped. I opened my shaking fingers and found four half-moons that slowly filled with blood. The hunger beat around me, filling the crowd, but not me, not me.

I pressed a napkin to my hand and tried to look inconspicuous.

The vampire drew back his head.

"No," I whispered.

The vampire struck, teeth sinking into flesh. Phillip shrieked, and it echoed in the club. The music died abruptly. No one moved. You could have dropped a pin.

Soft, moist sucking sounds filled the silence. Phillip began to moan, high in his throat. Over and over again, small helpless sounds.

I looked out at the crowd. They were with the vampire, feeling his hunger, his need, feeling him feed. Maybe sharing Phillip's terror, I didn't know. I was apart from it, and glad.

The vampire stood, letting Phillip fall to the stage, limp, unmoving. I stood without meaning to. The man's scarred back convulsed in a deep, shattering breath, as if he were fighting back from death. And maybe he was.

He was alive. I sat back down. My knees felt weak. Sweat covered my palms and stung the cuts on my hand. He was alive, and he enjoyed it. I wouldn't have believed it if someone had told me. I would have called them a liar.

A vampire junkie. Surely to God, I'd seen everything now.

Jean-Claude whispered, "Who wants a kiss?"

No one moved for a heartbeat; then hands, holding money, raised here and there. Not many, but a few. Most people looked confused, as if they had woken from a bad dream. Monica was holding money up.

Phillip lay where he had been dropped, chest rising and falling.

Robert the vampire came to Monica. She tucked money down his pants. He pressed his bloody, fanged mouth to her lips. The kiss was long and deep, full of probing tongues. They were tasting each other.

The vampire drew away from Monica. Her hands at his neck tried to draw him back, but he pulled away. He turned to me. I shook my head and showed him empty hands. No money here, folks.

He grabbed for me, snake-quick. No time to think. My chair crashed to the floor. I was standing, just out of reach. No ordinary human could have seen him coming. The jig, as they say, was up.

A buzz of voices raised through the audience as they tried to figure out what had happened. Just your friendly neighborhood animator, folks, nothing to get excited about. The vampire was still staring at me.

Jean-Claude was suddenly beside me, and I hadn't seen him come. "Are you all right, Anita?"

His voice held things that the words didn't even hint at. Promises whispered in darkened rooms, under cool sheets. He sucked me under, rolled my mind like a wino after money, and it felt good. Crash—Shrill—Noise thundered through my mind, chased the vampire out, held him at bay.

My beeper had gone off. I blinked and staggered against our table. He reached out to steady me. "Don't touch me," I said.

He smiled. "Of course."

I pushed the button on my beeper to silence it. Thank you God, that I hung the beeper on my waistband instead of stuffing it in a purse. I might never have heard it otherwise. I called from the phone at the bar. The police wanted my expertise at the Hillcrest Cemetery. I had to work on my night off. Yippee, and I meant it.

I offered to take Catherine with me, but she wanted to stay. Whatever else you can say about vampires, they are fascinating. It went with the job description, like drinking blood and working nights. It was her choice.

I promised to come back in time to drive them home. Then I picked up my cross from the holy item check girl and slipped it inside my shirt.

Jean-Claude was standing by the door. He said, "I almost had you, my little animator."

I glanced at his face and quickly down. "Almost doesn't count, you blood-sucking bastard."

Jean-Claude threw back his head and laughed. His laughter followed me out into the night, like velvet rubbing along my spine.

5

The coffin lay on its side. A white scar of claw marks ran down the dark varnish. The pale blue lining, imitation silk, was sliced and gouged. One bloody handprint showed plainly; it could almost have been human. All that was left of the older corpse was a shredded brown suit, a finger bone gnawed clean and a scrap of scalp. The man had been blond.

A second body lay perhaps five feet away. The man's clothes were shredded. His chest had been ripped open, ribs cracked like eggshells. Most of his internal organs were gone, leaving his body cavity like a hollowed-out log. Only his face was untouched. Pale eyes stared impossibly wide up into the summer stars.

I was glad it was dark. My night vision is good, but darkness steals color. All the blood was black. The man's body was lost in the shadows of the trees. I didn't have to see him, unless I walked up to him. I had done that. I had measured the bite marks with my trusty tape measure. With my little plastic gloves I had searched the corpse over, looking for clues. There weren't any.

I could do anything I wanted to the scene of the crime. It had already been videotaped and snapped from every possible angle. I was always the last "expert" called in. The ambulance was waiting to take the bodies away, once I was finished.

I was about finished. I knew what had killed the man. Ghouls. I had narrowed the search down to a particular kind of undead. Bully for me. The coroner could have told them that.

I was beginning to sweat inside the coverall I had put on to protect my clothes. The coverall was originally for vampire stakings, but I had started using it at crime scenes. There were black stains at the knees and down the legs. There had been so much blood in the grass. Thank you, dear God, that I didn't have to see this in broad daylight.

I don't know why seeing something like this in daylight makes it worse, but I'm more likely to dream about a daylight scene. The blood is always so red and brown and thick.

Night softens it, makes it less real. I appreciated that.

I unzipped the front of my coverall, letting it gape open around my clothes. The wind blew against me, amazingly cool. The air smelled of rain. Another thunderstorm was moving this way.

The yellow police tape was wrapped around tree trunks, strung through bushes. One yellow loop went around the stone feet of an angel. The tape flapped and cracked in the growing wind. Sergeant Rudolf Storr lifted the tape and walked towards me.

He was six-eight and built like a wrestler. He had a brisk, striding walk. His close-cropped black hair left his ears bare. Dolph was the head of the newest task force, the spook squad. Officially, it was the Regional Preternatural Investigation Team, R-P-I-T, pronounced rip it. It handled all supernatural-related crime. It wasn't exactly a step up for his career. Willie McCoy had been right; the task force was a half-hearted effort to placate the press and the liberals.

Dolph had pissed somebody off, or he wouldn't have been here. But Dolph, being Dolph, was determined to do the best job he could. He was like a force of nature. He didn't yell, he was just there, and things got done because of it.

"Well," he said.

That's Dolph, a man of many words. "It was a ghoul attack."

"And."

I shrugged. "And there are no ghouls in this cemetery."

He stared down at me, face carefully neutral. He was good at that, didn't like to influence his people. "You just said it was a ghoul attack."

"Yes, but they came from somewhere outside the cemetery."

"So?"

"I have never known of any ghouls to travel this far outside their own cemetery." I stared at him, trying to see if he understood what I was saying.

"Tell me about ghouls, Anita." He had his trusty little notebook out, pen poised and ready.

"This cemetery is still holy ground. Cemeteries that have ghoul infestations are usually very old or have satanic or certain voodoo rites performed in them. The evil sort of uses up the blessing, until the ground becomes unholy. Once that happens, ghouls either move in or rise from the graves. No one's sure exactly which."

"Wait, what do you mean, that no one knows?"

"Basically."

He shook his head, staring at the notes he'd made, frowning. "Explain."

"Vampires are made by other vampires. Zombies are raised from the grave by an animator or voodoo priest. Ghouls, as far as we know, just crawl out of their graves on their own. There are theories that very evil people become ghouls. I don't buy that. There was a theory for a while that people bitten by a supernatural being, wereanimal, vampire, whatever, would become a ghoul. But I've seen whole cemeteries emptied, every corpse a ghoul. No way they were all attacked by supernatural forces while alive."

"All right, we don't know where ghouls come from. What do we know?"

"Ghouls don't rot like zombies. They retain their form more like vampires. They are more than animal intelligent, but not by much. They are cowards and won't attack a person unless she is hurt or unconscious."

"They sure as hell attacked the groundskeeper."

"He could have been knocked unconscious somehow."

"How?"

"Someone would have had to knock him out."

"Is that likely?"

"No, ghouls don't work with humans, or any other undead. A zombie will obey orders, vampires have their own thoughts. Ghouls are like pack animals, wolves maybe, but a lot more dangerous. They wouldn't be able to understand working with someone. If you're not a ghoul, you're either meat or something to hide from."

"Then what happened here?"

"Dolph, these ghouls traveled quite a distance to reach this cemetery. There isn't another one for miles. Ghouls don't travel like that. So maybe, just maybe, they attacked the caretaker when he came to scare them off. They should have run from him; maybe they didn't."

"Could it be something, or someone, pretending to be ghouls?"

"Maybe, but I doubt it. Whoever it was, they ate that man. A human might do that, but a human couldn't tear the body apart like that. They just don't have the strength."

"Vampire?"

"Vampires don't eat meat."

"Zombies?"

"Maybe. There are rare cases where zombies go a little crazy and start attacking people. They seem to crave flesh. If they don't get it, they'll start to decay."

"I thought zombies always decayed."

"Flesh-eating zombies last a lot longer than normal. There's one case of a woman who is still human-looking after three years."

"They let her go around eating people?"

I smiled. "They feed her raw meat. I believe the article said lamb was preferred."

"Article?"

"Every career has its professional journal, Dolph."

"What's it called?"

I shrugged. "*The Animator*; what else?"

He actually smiled. "Okay. How likely is it that it's zombies?"

"Not very. Zombies don't run in packs unless they're ordered to."

"Even"—he checked his notes—"flesh-eating zombies?"

"There have only been three documented cases. All of them were solitary hunters."

"So, flesh-eating zombies, or a new kind of ghoul. That sum it up?"

I nodded. "Yeah."

"Okay, thanks. Sorry to interrupt your night off." He closed his notebook and looked at me. He was almost grinning. "The secretary said you were at a bachelorette party." He wiggled his eyebrows. "Hoochie coochie."

"Don't give me a hard time, Dolph."

"Wouldn't dream of it."

"Riiight," I said. "If you don't need me anymore, I'll be getting back."

"We're finished, for now. Call me if you think of anything else."

"Will do." I walked back to my car. The bloody plastic gloves were shoved into a garbage sack in the trunk. I debated on the coveralls and finally folded them on top of the garbage sack. I might be able to wear them one more time.

Dolph called out, "You be careful tonight, Anita. Wouldn't want you picking up anything."

I glared back at him. The rest of the men waved at me and called in unison, "We loove you."

"Gimme a break."

One called, "If I'd known you liked to see naked men, we could have worked something out."

"The stuff you got, Zerbrowski, I don't want to see."

Laughter, and someone grabbed him around the neck. "She got you, man . . . Give it up, she gets you every time."

I got into my car to the sound of masculine laughter, and one offer to be my "luv" slave. It was probably Zerbrowski.

6

I arrived back at Guilty Pleasures a little after midnight. Jean-Claude was standing at the bottom of the steps. He was leaning against the wall, utterly still. If he was breathing, I couldn't see it. The wind blew the lace on his shirt. A lock of black hair trailed across the smooth paleness of his cheek.

"You smell of other people's blood, ma petite."

I smiled at him, sweetly. "It was no one you knew."

His voice when it came was low and dark, full of a quiet rage. It slithered across my skin, like a cold wind. "Have you been killing vampires, my little animator?"

"No." I whispered it, my voice suddenly hoarse. I had never heard his voice like that.

"They call you The Executioner, did you know that?"

"Yes." He had done nothing to threaten me, yet nothing at that moment would have forced me to pass him. They might as well have barred the door.

"How many kills do you have to your credit?"

I didn't like this conversation. It wasn't going to end anywhere I wanted to be. I knew one master vampire who could smell lies. I didn't understand Jean-Claude's mood, but I wasn't about to lie to him. "Fourteen."

"And you call us murderers."

I just stared at him, not sure what he wanted me to say.

Buzz the vampire came down the steps. He stared from Jean-Claude to me, then took up his post by the door, huge arms crossed over his chest.

Jean-Claude asked, "Did you have a nice break?"

"Yes, thank you, master."

The master vampire smiled. "I've told you before, Buzz, don't call me master."

"Yes, M-M . . . Jean-Claude."

26

The vampire gave his wondrous, nearly touchable laugh. "Come, Anita, let us go inside where it is warmer."

It was over eighty degrees on the sidewalk. I didn't know what in the world he was talking about. I didn't know what we'd been talking about for the last few minutes.

Jean-Claude walked up the steps. I watched him disappear inside. I stood staring at the door, not wanting to go inside. Something was wrong, and I didn't know what.

"You going inside?" Buzz asked.

"I don't suppose you'd go inside, and ask Monica and the red-haired woman she's with to come outside?"

He smiled, flashing fang. It's the mark of the new dead that they flash their fangs around. They like the shock effect. "Can't leave my post. I just had a break."

"Thought you'd say something like that."

He grinned at me.

I went into the twilit dark of the club. The holy item check girl was waiting for me at the door. I gave her my cross. She gave me a check stub. It wasn't a fair trade. Jean-Claude was nowhere in sight.

Catherine was on the stage. She was standing motionless, eyes wide. Her face had that open, fragile look that faces get when they sleep, like a child's face. Her long, copper-colored hair glistened in the lights. I knew a deep trance when I saw it.

"Catherine." I breathed her name and ran towards her. Monica was sitting at our table, watching me come. There was an awful, knowing smile on her face.

I was almost to the stage when a vampire appeared behind Catherine. He didn't walk out from behind the curtain, he just bloody appeared behind her. For the first time I understood what humans must see. Magic.

The vampire stared at me. His hair was golden silk, his skin ivory, eyes like drowning pools. I closed my eyes and shook my head. This couldn't be happening. No one was that beautiful.

His voice was almost ordinary after the face, but it was a command. "Call her."

I opened my eyes to find the audience staring at me. I glanced at Catherine's blank face and knew what would happen, but like any ignorant client I had to try. "Catherine, Catherine, can you hear me?"

She never moved; only the faintest of movements showed her breathing. She was alive, but for how long? The vampire had gotten to her, deep trance. That meant he could call her anytime, anywhere, and she would come. From this moment on, her life belonged to him. Whenever he wanted it.

"Catherine, please!" There was nothing I could do, the damage was done. Dammit, I should never have left her here, never!

The vampire touched her shoulder. She blinked and stared around, surprised, scared. She gave a nervous laugh. "What happened?"

The vampire raised her hand to his lips. "You are now under my power, my lovely one."

She laughed again, not understanding that he had told her the absolute truth. He led her to the edge of the stage, and two waiters helped her back to her seat. "I feel fuzzy," she said.

Monica patted her hand. "You were great."

"What did I do?"

"I'll tell you later. The show's not over yet." She stared at me when she said the last.

I already knew I was in trouble. The vampire on the stage was staring at me. It was like weight against my skin. His will, force, personality, whatever it was, beat against me. I could feel it like a pulsing wind. The skin on my arms crawled with it.

"I am Aubrey," the vampire said. "Give me your name."

My mouth was suddenly dry, but my name was not important. He could have that. "Anita."

"Anita. How pretty."

My knees sort of buckled and spilled me into a chair. Monica was staring at me, eyes enormous and eager.

"Come, Anita, join me on the stage." His voice wasn't as good as Jean-Claude's, it just wasn't. There was no texture to it, but the mind behind the voice was like nothing I had ever felt. It was ancient, terribly ancient. The force of his mind made my bones ache.

"Come."

I kept shaking my head, over and over. It was all I could do. No words, no real thoughts, but I knew I could not get out of this chair. If I came to him now, he would have power over me just as he did Catherine. Sweat soaked through the back of my blouse.

"Come to me, now!"

I was standing, and I didn't remember doing it. Dear God, help me! "No!" I dug my fingernails into the palm of my hand. I tore my own skin and welcomed the pain. I could breathe again.

His mind receded like the ocean pulling back. I felt light-headed, empty. I slumped against the table. One of the vampire waiters was at my side. "Don't fight him. He gets angry if you fight him."

I pushed him away. "If I don't fight him, he'll own me!"

The waiter looked almost human, one of the new dead. There was a look on his face. It was fear.

I called to the thing on the stage, "I'll come to the stage if you don't force me."

Monica gasped. I ignored her. Nothing mattered but getting through the next few moments.

"Then by all means, come," the vampire said.

I stood away from the table and found I could stand without falling. Point for me. I could even walk. Two points for me. I stared at the hard, polished floor. If I concentrated just on walking I would be all right. The first step of the stage came into view. I glanced up.

Aubrey was standing in the center of the stage. He wasn't trying to call me. He stood perfectly still. It was like he wasn't there at all; he was a terrible nothingness. I could feel his stillness like a pulse in my head. I think he could have stood in plain sight, and unless he wanted me to, I would never have seen him.

"Come." Not a voice, but a sound inside my head. "Come to me."

I tried to move back and couldn't. My pulse thundered into my throat. I couldn't breathe. I was choking! I stood with the force of his mind twisting against me.

"Don't fight me!" He screamed in my head.

Someone was screaming, wordlessly, and it was me. If I stopped fighting, it would be so easy, like drowning after you stop struggling. A peaceful way to die. No, no. "No." My voice sounded strange, even to me.

"What?" he asked. His voice held surprise.

"No," I said, and I looked up at him. I met his eyes with the weight of all those centuries pulsing down. Whatever it was that made me an animator, that helped me raise the dead, it was there now. I met the eyes and stood still.

He smiled then, a slow spreading of lips. "Then I will come to you."

"Please, please, don't." I could not step back. His mind held me like velvet steel. It was everything I could do not to move forward. Not to run to meet him.

He stopped, with our bodies almost touching. His eyes were a solid, perfect brown, bottomless, endless. I looked away from his face. Sweat trickled down my forehead.

"You smell of fear, Anita."

His cool hand traced the edge of my cheek. I started to shake and couldn't stop. His fingers pulled gently through the waves of my hair. "How can you face me this way?"

He breathed along my face, warm as silk. His breath slid to my neck, warm and close. He drew a deep, shuddering breath. His hunger pulsed against my skin. My stomach cramped with his need. He hissed at the audience, and they squealed in terror. He was going to do it.

Terror came in a blinding rush of adrenaline. I pushed away from him. I fell to the stage and scrambled away on hands and knees.

An arm grabbed me around the waist, lifting. I screamed, striking backwards with my elbow. It thudded home, and I heard him gasp, but the arm tightened. Tightened until it was crushing me.

I tore at my sleeve. Cloth ripped. He threw me onto my back. He was crouched over me, face twisted with hunger. His lips curled back from his teeth, fangs glistening.

Someone moved onto the stage, one of the waiters. The vampire hissed at him, spittle running down his chin. There was nothing human left.

It came for me in a blinding rush of speed and hunger. I pressed the silver knife over his heart. A trickle of blood glistened down his chest. He snarled at me, fangs gnashing like a dog on the end of a chain. I screamed.

Terror had washed his power away. There was nothing left but fear. He lunged for me and drove the point of the knife into his skin. Blood began to drip over my hand and onto my blouse. His blood.

Jean-Claude was suddenly there. "Aubrey, let her go."

The vampire growled deep and low in his throat. It was an animal sound.

My voice was high and thin with fear; I sounded like a little girl. "Get him off me, or I'll kill him!"

The vampire reared back, fangs slashing his own lips. "Get him off me!"

Jean-Claude began to speak softly in French. Even when I couldn't understand the language his voice was like velvet, soothing. Jean-Claude knelt by us, speaking softly. The vampire growled and lashed out, grabbing Jean-Claude's wrist.

He gasped, and it sounded like pain.

Should I kill him? Could I plunge the knife home before he tore out my throat? How fast was he? My mind seemed to be working incredibly fast. There was an illusion that I had all the time in the world to decide and act.

I felt the vampire's weight heavier against my legs. His voice sounded hoarse, but calm. "May I get up now?"

His face was human again, pleasant, handsome, but the illusion didn't work anymore. I had seen him unmasked, and that image would always stay with me. "Get off me, slowly."

He smiled then, a slow confident spread of lips. He moved off me, human-slow. Jean-Claude waved him back until he stood near the curtain.

"Are you all right, ma petite?"

I stared at the bloody silver knife and shook my head. "I don't know."

"I did not mean for this to happen." He helped me sit up, and I let him. The room had fallen silent. The audience knew something had gone wrong. They had seen the truth behind the charming mask. There were a lot of pale, frightened faces out there.

My right sleeve hung torn where I ripped it to get the knife.

"Please, put away the knife," Jean-Claude said.

I stared at him, and for the first time I looked him in the eyes and felt nothing. Nothing but emptiness.

"My word of honor that you will leave this place in safety. Put the knife away."

It took me three tries to slide the knife into its sheath, my hands were trembling so badly. Jean-Claude smiled at me, tight-lipped. "Now, we will get off this stage." He helped me stand. I would have fallen if his arm hadn't caught me. He kept a tight grip on my left hand; the lace on his sleeve brushed my skin. The lace wasn't soft at all.

Jean-Claude held his other hand out to Aubrey. I tried to pull away, and he whispered, "No fear, I will protect you, I swear it."

I believed him, I don't know why, maybe because I had no one else to believe. He led Aubrey and me to the front of the stage. His rich voice caressed the crowd. "We hope you enjoyed our little melodrama. It was very realistic, wasn't it?"

The audience shifted uncomfortably, fear plain in their faces.

He smiled out at them and dropped Aubrey's hand. He unbuttoned my sleeve and pushed it back, exposing the burn scar. The cross was dark against my skin. The audience was silent, still not understanding. Jean-Claude pulled the lace away from his chest, exposing his own cross-shaped burn.

There was a moment of stunned silence, then applause thundered around the room. Screams and shouts, and whistles roared around us.

They thought I was a vampire, and it had all been an act. I stared at Jean-Claude's smiling face and the matching scars: his chest, my arm.

Jean-Claude's hand pulled me down into a bow. As the applause finally began to fade, Jean-Claude whispered, "We need to talk, Anita. Your friend Catherine's life depends on your actions."

I met his eyes and said, "I killed the things that gave me this scar."

He smiled broadly, showing just a hint of fang. "What a lovely coincidence. So did I."

7

Jean-Claude led us through the curtains at the back of the stage. Another vampire stripper was waiting to go on. He was dressed like a gladiator, complete with metal breastplate and short sword. "Talk about an act that's hard to follow. Shit." He jerked the curtain open and stalked through.

Catherine came through, her face so pale her freckles stood out like brown ink spots. I wondered if I looked as pale? Naw. I didn't have the skin tone for it.

"My God, are you all right?" she asked.

I stepped carefully over a line of cables that snaked across the backstage floor and leaned against the wall. I began to relearn how to breathe. "I'm fine," I lied.

"Anita, what is going on? What was that stuff on stage? You aren't a vampire any more than I am."

Aubrey made a silent hiss behind her back, fangs straining, making his lips bleed. His shoulders shook with silent laughter.

Catherine gripped my arm. "Anita?"

I hugged her, and she hugged me back. I would not let her die like this. I would not let it happen. She pulled away from me and stared into my face. "Talk to me."

"Shall we talk in my office?" Jean-Claude asked.

"Catherine doesn't need to come."

Aubrey strolled closer. He seemed to glimmer in the twilight dark, like a jewel. "I think she should come. It does concern her— intimately." He licked his bloody lips, tongue pink and quick as a cat's.

"No, I want her out of this, any way I can get her out of it."

"Out of what? What are you talking about?"

Jean-Claude asked, "Is she likely to go to the police?"

"Go to the police about what?" Catherine asked, her voice getting louder with each question.

33

"If she did?"

"She would die," Jean-Claude said.

"Wait just a minute," Catherine said. "Are you threatening me?"

Catherine's face was gaining a lot of color. Anger did that to her. "She'll go to the police," I said.

"It is your choice."

"I'm sorry, Catherine, but it would be better for us all if you didn't remember any of this."

"That's it! We are leaving, now." She grabbed my hand, and I didn't stop her.

Aubrey moved up behind her. "Look at me, Catherine."

She stiffened. Her fingers dug into my hand; incredible tension vibrated down her muscles. She was fighting it. God, help her. But she didn't have any magic, or crucifixes. Strength of will was not enough, not against something like Aubrey.

Her hand fell away from my arm, fingers going limp all at once. Breath went out of her in a long, shuddering sigh. She stared at something just a little over my head, something I couldn't see.

I whispered, "Catherine, I'm sorry."

"Aubrey can wipe her memory of this night. She will think she drank too much, but that will not undo the damage."

"I know. The only thing that can break Aubrey's hold on her is his death."

"She will be dust in her grave before that happens."

I stared at him, at the blood stain on his shirt. I smiled a very careful smile.

"This little wound was luck and nothing more. Do not let it make you overconfident," Aubrey said.

Overconfident; now that was funny. I barely managed not to laugh. "I understand the threat, Jean-Claude. Either I do what you want or Aubrey finishes what he started with Catherine."

"You have grasped the situation, ma petite."

"Stop calling me that. What is it exactly that you want from me?"

"I believe Willie McCoy told you what we wanted."

"You want to hire me to check into the vampire murders?"

"Exactly."

"This," I motioned to Catherine's blank face, "was hardly necessary. You could have beaten me up, threatened my life, offered me more money. You could have done a lot of things before you did this."

He smiled, lips tight. "All that would have taken time. And let us be truthful. In the end you would still have refused us."

"Maybe."

"This way, you have no choice."

He had a point. "Okay, I'm on the case. Satisfied?"

"Very," Jean-Claude said, his voice very soft. "What of your friend?"

"I want her to go home in a cab. And I want some guarantees that old long-fang isn't going to kill her anyway."

Aubrey laughed, a rich sound that ended in a hysterical hissing. He was bent over, shaking with laughter. "Long-fang, I like that."

Jean-Claude glanced at the laughing vampire and said, "I will give you my word that she will not be harmed if you help us."

"No offense, but that's not enough."

"You doubt my word." His voice growled low and warm, angry.

"No, but you don't hold Aubrey's leash. Unless he answers to you, you can't guarantee his behavior."

Aubrey's laughter had softened to a few faint giggles. I had never heard a vampire giggle before. It wasn't a pleasant sound. The laughter died completely, and he straightened. "No one holds my leash, girl. I am my own master."

"Oh, get real. If you were over five hundred years old, and a master vampire, you'd have cleaned up the stage with me. As it was"—I flattened my hands palms up—"you didn't, which means you're very old but not your own master."

He growled low in his throat, face darkening with anger. "How dare you?"

"Think, Aubrey, she judged your age within fifty years. You are not a master vampire, and she knew that. We need her."

"She needs to learn some humility." He stalked towards me, body rigid with anger, hands clenching and unclenching in the air.

Jean-Claude stepped between us. "Nikolaos is expecting us to bring her, unharmed."

Aubrey hesitated. He snarled; his jaws snapped on empty air. The smack of his teeth biting together was a dull, angry sound.

They stared at each other. I could feel their wills straining through the air, like a distant wind. It made the skin at the back of my neck crawl. It was Aubrey who looked away, with an angry graceful blink. "I will not anger, my master." He emphasized "my," making it clear that Jean-Claude was not "his" master.

I swallowed hard twice, and it sounded loud. If they wanted me scared, they were doing a hell of a job. "Who is Nikolaos?"

Jean-Claude turned to look at me, his face calm and beautiful. "That question is not ours to answer."

"What is that supposed to mean?"

He smiled, lips curling carefully so no fang showed. "Let us put your friend in a cab, out of harm's way."

"What of Monica?"

He grinned then, fangs showing; he looked genuinely amused. "Are you worried for her safety?"

It hit me then—the impromptu bachelorette party, there only being the three of us. "She was the lure to get Catherine and me down here."

He nodded, once down, once up.

I wanted to go back out and smash Monica's face in. The more I thought about the idea, the better it sounded. As if by magic, she parted the curtains and came back. I smiled at her, and it felt good.

She hesitated, glancing from me to Jean-Claude and back. "Is everything going according to plan?"

I walked towards her. Jean-Claude grabbed my arm. "Do not harm her, Anita. She is under our protection."

"I swear to you that I will not lay a finger on her tonight. I just want to tell her something."

He released my arm, slowly, like he wasn't sure it was a good idea. I stepped next to Monica, until our bodies almost touched. I whispered into her face, "If anything happens to Catherine, I will see you dead."

She smirked at me, confident in her protectors. "They will bring me back as one of them."

I felt my head shake, a little to the right, a little to the left, a slow precise movement. "I will cut out your heart." I was still smiling, I couldn't seem to stop. "Then I will burn it and scatter the ashes in the river. Do you understand me?"

She swallowed audibly. Her health-club tan looked a little green. She nodded, staring at me like I was the bogey man.

I think she believed I'd do it. Peachy keen. I hate to waste a really good threat.

8

I watched Catherine's cab vanish around the corner. She never turned, or waved, or spoke. She would wake tomorrow with vague memories. Just a night out with the girls.

I would like to have thought she was out of it, safe, but I knew better. The air smelled thickly of rain. The street lights glistened off the sidewalk. The air was almost too thick to breathe. St. Louis in the summer. Peachy.

"Shall we go?" Jean-Claude asked.

He stood, white shirt gleaming in the dark. If the humidity bothered him, it didn't show. Aubrey stood in the shadows near the door. The only light on him was the crimson neon of the club sign. He grinned at me, face painted red, body lost in shadows.

"It's a little too contrived, Aubrey," I said.

His grin wavered. "What do you mean?"

"You look like a B-movie Dracula."

He flowed down the steps, with that easy perfection that only the really old ones have. The street light showed his face tight, hands balled into fists.

Jean-Claude stepped in front of him and spoke low, voice a soothing whisper. Aubrey turned away with a jerky shrug and began to glide up the street.

Jean-Claude turned to me. "If you continue to taunt him, there will come a point from which I cannot bring him back. And you will die."

"I thought your job was to keep me alive for this Nikolaos."

He frowned. "It is, but I will not die to defend you. Do you understand that?"

"I do now."

"Good. Shall we go?" He gestured down the sidewalk, in the direction Aubrey had gone.

"We're going to walk?"

"It is not far." He held his hand out to me.

I stared at it and shook my head.

"It is necessary, Anita. I would not ask it otherwise."

"How is it necessary?"

"This night must remain secret from the police, Anita. Hold my hand, play the besotted human with her vampire lover. It will explain the blood on your blouse. It will explain where we are going, and why."

His hand hung there, pale and slender. There was no tremor to the fingers, no movement, as if he could stand there offering me his hand forever. And maybe he could.

I took his hand. His long fingers curved over the back of my hand. We began walking, his hand very still in mine. I could feel the pulse in my hand against his skin. His pulse began to speed up to match mine. I could feel his blood flow like a second heart.

"Have you fed tonight?" my voice sounded soft.

"Can you not tell?"

"I can never tell with you."

I saw him smile out of the corner of my eye. "I am flattered."

"You never answered my question."

"No," he said.

"No, you haven't answered me, or no, you haven't fed?"

He turned his head to me, as we walked. Sweat gleamed on his upper lip. "What do you think, ma petite?" His voice was the softest of whispers.

I jerked my hand, tried to get away, even though I knew it was silly, and wouldn't work. His hand convulsed around mine, squeezed until I gasped. He wasn't even trying hard.

"Do not struggle against me, Anita." His tongue slid across his upper lip. "Struggling is—exciting."

"Why didn't you feed earlier?"

"I was ordered not to."

"Why?"

He didn't answer me. Rain began to patter down. Light and cool.

"Why?" I repeated.

"I don't know." His voice was nearly lost in the soft fall of rain. If it had been anyone else I would have said he was afraid.

The hotel was tall and thin, and made of real brick. The sign out front glowed blue and said, "Vacancy." There was no other sign. Nothing to tell you what the place was called, or even what it was. Just vacancy.

Rain glistened in Jean-Claude's hair, like black diamonds. My top was sticking to my body. The blood had begun to wash away. Cold water was just the thing for a fresh blood stain.

A police car eased around the corner. I tensed. Jean-Claude jerked me against him. I put my palm against his chest, to keep our bodies from touching. His heart thudded under my hand.

The police car was going very slowly. A spotlight began to search the shadows. They swept the District regularly. It was bad for tourism if the tourists got wasted by our biggest attractions.

Jean-Claude grabbed my chin and turned me to look at him. I tried to pull away, but his fingers dug into my chin. "Don't fight me!"

"I won't look in your eyes!"

"My word that I will not try to bespell you. For this night you may look into my eyes with safety. I swear it." He glanced at the police car, still moving towards us. "If the police are brought into this, I cannot promise what will happen to your friend."

I forced myself to relax in his arms, letting my body ease against his. My heartbeat sounded loud, as if I had been running. Then I realized it wasn't my heart I was hearing. Jean-Claude's pulse was throbbing through my body. I could hear it, feel it, almost squeeze it in my hand. I stared up at his face. His eyes were the darkest blue I had ever seen, perfect as a midnight sky. They were dark and alive, but there was no sense of drowning, no pull. They were just eyes.

His face leaned towards me. He whispered, "I swear."

He was going to kiss me. I didn't want him to. But I didn't want the police to stop and question us. I didn't want to explain the blood stains, the torn blouse. His lips hesitated over my mouth. His heartbeat was loud in my head, his pulse was racing, and my breathing was ragged with his need.

His lips were silk, his tongue a quick wetness. I tried to pull back and found his hand at the back of my neck, pressing my mouth against his.

The police spotlight swept over us. I relaxed against Jean-Claude, letting him kiss me. Our mouths pressed together. My tongue found the smooth hardness of fangs. I pulled away, and he let me. He pressed my face against his chest, one arm like steel against my back, pressing me against him. He was trembling, and it wasn't from the rain.

His breathing was ragged, his heart jumping under his skin against my cheek. The slick roughness of his burn scar touched my face.

His hunger poured over me in a violent wave, like heat. He had been sheltering me from it, until now. "Jean-Claude!" I didn't try to keep the fear out of my voice.

"Hush." A shudder ran through his body. His breath escaped in a loud sigh. He released me so abruptly, I stumbled.

He walked away from me to lean against a parked car. He raised his face up into the rain. I could still feel his heartbeat. I had never been so aware of my own pulse, the blood flowing through my veins. I hugged myself, shivering in the hot rain.

The police car had vanished into the streetlight darkness. After perhaps five minutes Jean-Claude stood. I could no longer feel his heartbeat. My own pulse was slow and regular. Whatever had happened was over.

He walked past me and called over his shoulder. "Come, Nikolaos awaits us inside."

I followed him through the door. He did not try to take my hand. In fact he stayed out of reach, and I trailed after him through a small square lobby. A human man sat behind the front desk. He glanced up from the magazine he was reading. His eyes flicked to Jean-Claude and back to me. He leered at me.

I glared back. He shrugged and turned back to his magazine. Jean-Claude moved swiftly up the stairs, not waiting for me. He didn't even look back. Maybe he could hear me walking behind him, or maybe he didn't care if I followed.

I guess we weren't pretending to be lovers anymore. Fancy that. I would almost have said the master vampire didn't trust himself around me.

There was a long hallway with doors on either side. Jean-Claude was halfway through one of those doors. I walked towards it. I refused to hurry. They could damn well wait.

The room held a bed, a nightstand with a lamp, and three vampires: Aubrey, Jean-Claude, and a strange female vampire. Aubrey was standing in the far corner, near the window. He was smiling at me. Jean-Claude stood near the door. The female vampire reclined on the bed. She looked like a vampire should. Long, straight, black hair fell around her shoulders. Her dress was full-skirted and black. She wore high black boots with three-inch heels.

"Look into my eyes," she said.

I glanced at her, before I could stop myself, then stared down at the floor.

She laughed, and it had the same quality of touch that Jean-Claude's did. A sound that you could feel with your hands.

"Close the door, Aubrey," she said. Her r's were thick with some accent that I couldn't place.

Aubrey brushed past me as he closed the door. He stayed in back of me, where I couldn't see him. I moved to stand with my back to the only empty wall, so I could see all of them, for what good it would do me.

"Afraid?" Aubrey asked.

"Still bleeding?" I asked.

He crossed his arms over the blood stain on his shirt. "We shall see who is bleeding come dawn."

"Aubrey, do not be childish." The vampire on the bed stood. Her heels clicked against the bare floor. She stalked around me, and I fought an urge to turn and keep her in sight. She laughed again, as if she knew it.

"You wish me to guarantee your friend's safety?" she asked. She had gone back to sink gracefully onto the bed. The bare, dingy room seemed somehow worse with her sitting there in her two-hundred-dollar leather boots.

"No," I said.

"That is what you asked, Anita," Jean-Claude said.

"I said that I wanted guarantees from Aubrey's master."

"You are speaking with my master, girl."

"No, I am not." The room was suddenly very still. I could hear something scrambling inside the wall. I had to look up to make sure the vampires were still in the room. They were all utterly still, like statues, no sense of movement or breathing, or life. They were all so damn old, but none of them were old enough to be Nikolaos.

"I am Nikolaos," the female said, her voice coaxing and breathing through the room. I wanted to believe her, but I didn't.

"No," I said. "You are not Aubrey's master." I risked a glance into her eyes. They were black and widened in surprise when I looked at them. "You are very old, and very good, but you are not old enough or strong enough to be Aubrey's master."

Jean-Claude said, "I told you she would see through it."

"Silence!"

"The game is over, Theresa. She knows."

"Only because you have told her."

"Tell them how you knew, Anita."

I shrugged. "She feels wrong. She just isn't old enough. There is more of a sense of power from Aubrey than from her. That isn't right."

"Do you still insist on speaking with our master?" the woman asked.

"I still want guarantees on my friend's safety." I glanced through the room, at each of them. "And I am getting tired of stupid little games."

Aubrey was suddenly moving towards me. The world slowed. There was no time for fear. I tried to back away, knowing there was nowhere to go.

Jean-Claude rushed him, hands reaching. He wouldn't make it in time.

Aubrey's hand came out of nowhere and caught me in the shoulder. The blow knocked all the air from my body and sent me flying backwards. My back slammed into the wall. My head hit a moment later, hard. The world went grey. I slid down the wall. I couldn't breathe. Tiny white shapes danced over the greyness. The world began to go black. I slid to the floor. It didn't hurt; nothing hurt. I struggled to breathe until my chest burned, and darkness took everything away.

9

Voices floated through the darkness. Dreams. "We shouldn't have moved her."

"Did you want to disobey Nikolaos?"

"I helped bring her here, did I not?" It was a man's voice.

"Yes," a woman said.

I lay there with my eyes closed. I wasn't dreaming. I remembered Aubrey's hand coming from nowhere. It had been an open backhand slap. If he had closed his fist . . . but he hadn't. I was alive.

"Anita, are you awake?"

I opened my eyes. Light speared into my head. I closed my eyes against the light and the pain, but the pain stayed. I turned my head, and that was a mistake. The pain was a nauseating ache. It felt like the bones in my head were trying to slide off. I raised hands to cover my eyes and groaned.

"Anita, are you all right?"

Why do people always ask you that when the answer is obviously no? I spoke in a whisper, not sure how it would feel to talk. It didn't feel too bad. "Just peachy keen."

"What?" This from the woman.

"I think she is being sarcastic," Jean-Claude said. He sounded relieved. "She can't be hurt too badly if she is making jokes."

I wasn't sure about the hurt too badly part. Nausea flowed in waves, from head to stomach, instead of the other way around. I was betting I had a concussion. The question was, how bad?

"Can you move, Anita?"

"No," I whispered.

"Let me rephrase. If I help you, can you sit up?"

I swallowed, trying to breathe through the pain and nausea. "Maybe."

Hands curved under my shoulders. The bones in my head

started sliding forward as he lifted. I gasped and swallowed. "I'm going to be sick."

I rolled over on all fours. The movement was too rapid. The pain was a whirl of light and darkness. My stomach heaved. Vomit burned up my throat. My head was exploding.

Jean-Claude held me around the waist, one cool hand on my forehead, holding the bones of my head in place. His voice held me, a soothing sheet against my skin. He was speaking French, very softly. I didn't understand a word of it, and didn't need to. His voice held me, rocked me, took some of the pain.

He cradled me against his chest, and I was too weak to protest. The pain had been screaming through my head; now it was distant, a throbbing ache. It still felt obscene to turn my head, as if my head were sliding apart, but the pain was different, bearable.

He wiped my face and mouth with a damp cloth. "Do you feel better now?" he asked.

"Yes." I didn't understand where the pain had gone.

Theresa said, "Jean-Claude, what have you done?"

"Nikolaos wishes her to be aware and well for this visit. You saw her. She needs a hospital, not more tormenting."

"So you helped her." The vampire's voice sounded amused. "Nikolaos will not be pleased."

I felt him shrug. "I did what was necessary."

I could open my eyes without squinting or increasing the pain. We were in a dungeon; there was no other word for it. Thick stone walls enclosed a square room, perhaps twenty by twenty feet. Steps led up to a barred, wooden door. There were even chains set in the walls. Torches guttered along the walls. The only thing missing was a rack and a black-hooded torturer, one with big, beefy arms, and a tattoo that said "I love Mom." Yeah, that would have made it perfect.

I was feeling better, much better. I shouldn't have been recovering this quickly. I had been hurt before, badly. It didn't just fade, not like this.

"Can you sit unaided?" Jean-Claude asked.

Surprisingly, the answer was yes. I sat with my back to the wall. The pain was still there, but it just didn't hurt as much. Jean-Claude got a bucket from near the stairs and washed it over the floor. There was a very modern drain in the middle of the floor.

Theresa stood staring at me, hands on hips. "You certainly are recovering quickly." Her voice held amusement, and something else I couldn't define.

"The pain, the nausea, it's almost gone. How?"

She smirked, lips curling. "You'll have to ask Jean-Claude that. It's his doing, not mine."

"Because you could not have done it." There was a warm edge of anger to his voice.

Her face paled. "I would not have, regardless."

"What are you talking about?" I asked.

Jean-Claude looked at me, beautiful face unreadable. His dark eyes stared into mine. They were still just eyes.

"Go on, master vampire, tell her. See how grateful she is."

Jean-Claude stared at me, watching my face. "You are badly hurt, a concussion. But Nikolaos will not let us take you to a hospital until this . . . interview is over with. I feared you would die or be unable to . . . function." I had never heard his voice so uncertain. "So I shared my life-force with you."

I started to shake my head. Big mistake. I pressed hands to my forehead. "I don't understand."

He spread his hands wide. "I do not have the words."

"Oh, allow me," Theresa said. "He has taken the first step to making you a human servant."

"No." I was still having trouble thinking clearly, but I knew that wasn't right. "He didn't try to trick me with his mind, or eyes. He didn't bite me."

"I don't mean one of those pathetic half-creatures that have a few bites and do our bidding. I mean a permanent human servant, one that will never be bitten, never be hurt. One that will age almost as slowly as we do."

I still didn't understand. Perhaps it showed in my face because Jean-Claude said, "I took your pain and gave you some of my . . . stamina."

"Are you experiencing my pain, then?"

"No, the pain is gone. I have made you a little harder to hurt."

I still wasn't taking it all in, or maybe it was just beyond me. "I don't understand."

"Listen, woman, he has shared with you what we consider a great gift to be given only to people who have proven themselves invaluable."

I stared at Jean-Claude. "Does this mean I am in your power somehow?"

"Just the opposite," Theresa said, "you are now immune to his glance, his voice, his mind. You will serve him out of willingness, nothing more. You see what he has done."

I stared into her black eyes. They were just eyes.

She nodded. "Now you begin to understand. As an animator you had partial immunity to our gaze. Now you have almost complete immunity." She gave an abrupt barking laugh. "Nikolaos is going to destroy you both." With that she stalked up the stairs, the heels of her boots smacking against the stone. She left the door open behind her.

Jean-Claude had come to stand over me. His face was unreadable.

"Why?" I asked.

He just stared down at me. His hair had dried in unruly curls around his face. He was still beautiful, but the hair made him seem more real.

"Why?"

He smiled then, and there were tired lines near his eyes. "If you died, our master would have punished us. Aubrey is already suffering for his . . . indiscretion."

He turned and walked up the stairs. He moved up the steps like a cat, all boneless, liquid grace.

He paused at the door and glanced back at me. "Someone will come for you when Nikolaos decides it is time." He closed the door, and I heard it latch and lock. His voice floated through the bars, rich, almost bubbling with laughter, "And perhaps, because I liked you." His laughter was bitter, like broken glass.

10

I had to check the locked door. Rattle it, poke at the lock, as if I knew how to pick locks. See if any bars were loose, though I could never have squeezed through the small window anyway.

I checked the door because I could not resist it. It was the same urge that made you rattle your trunk after you locked your keys inside.

I have been on the wrong side of a lot of locked doors. Not a one of them had just opened for me, but there was always a first time. Yeah, I should live so long. Scratch that; bad phrase.

A sound brought me back to the cell and its seeping, damp walls. A rat scurried against the far wall. Another peered around the edge of the steps, whiskers twitching. I guess you can't have a dungeon without rats, but I would have been willing to give it a try.

Something else pattered around the edge of the steps; in the torchlight I thought it was a dog. It wasn't. A rat the size of a German shepherd sat up on its sleek black haunches. It stared at me, huge paws tucked close to its furry chest. It cocked one large, black button eye at me. Lips drew back from yellowed teeth. The incisors were five inches long, blunt-edged daggers.

I yelled, "Jean-Claude!"

The air filled with high-pitched squeals, echoing, as if they were running up a tunnel. I stepped to the far edge of the stairs. And I saw it. A tunnel cut into the wall, almost man-high. Rats poured out of the tunnel in a thick, furry wave, squealing and biting. They flowed out and began to cover the floor.

"Jean-Claude!" I beat on the door, jerked at the bars, everything I had done before. It was useless. I wasn't getting out. I kicked the door and screamed, "Dammit!" The sound echoed against the stone walls and almost drowned out the sound of thousands of scrambling claws.

"They will not come for you until we are finished."

I froze, hands still on the door. I turned, slowly. The voice had come from inside the cell. The floor writhed and twisted with furry little bodies. High-pitched squeals, the thick brush of fur, the clatter of thousands of tiny claws filled the room. Thousands of them, thousands.

Four giant rats sat like mountains in the writhing furry tide. One of them stared at me with black button eyes. There was nothing ratlike in the stare. I had never seen wererats before, but I was betting that I was seeing them now.

One figure stood, legs half-bent. It was man-size, with a narrow, ratlike face. A huge naked tail curved around its bent legs like thick fleshy rope. It—no, he, definitely he—extended a clawed hand. "Come down and join us, human." The voice sounded thick, almost furry, with an edge of whine to it. Each word precise and a little wrong. Rats' lips are not made for talking.

I was not coming down the steps. No way. I could taste my heart in my throat. I knew a man who survived a werewolf attack, nearly died, and didn't become a werewolf. I know another man who was barely scratched and became a weretiger. Odds were, if I was so much as scratched, in a month's time I would be playing fur-face, complete with black button eyes and yellowish fangs. Dear God.

"Come down, human. Come down and play."

I swallowed hard. It felt like I was trying to swallow my heart. "I don't think so."

It gave a hissing laugh. "We could come up and fetch you." He strode through the lesser rats, and they parted for him frantically, leaping on top of each other to avoid his touch. He stood at the edge of the steps, looking up at me. His fur was almost a honey-brown color, streaked with blond. "If we force you off the steps, you won't like it much."

I swallowed hard. I believed him. I went for my knife and found the sheath empty. Of course, the vampires had taken it. Dammit.

"Come down, human, come down and play."

"If you want me, you're going to have to come get me."

He curled his tail through his hands, stroking it. One clawed hand ran through the fur of his belly, and stroked lower. I stared very hard at his face, and he laughed at me.

"Fetch her."

Two of the dog-size rats moved towards the stairs. A small rat squealed and rolled under their feet. It gave a high, piteous shriek, then nothing. It twitched until the other rats covered it. Tiny bones snapped. Nothing would go to waste.

I pressed against the door, as if I could sink through it. The two rats crept up the steps, sleek well-fed animals. But there was no animal in the eyes. Whatever was there was human, intelligent.

"Wait, wait."

The rats hesitated.

The ratman said, "Yes?"

I swallowed audibly. "What do you want?"

"Nikolaos asked that we entertain you while you wait."

"That doesn't answer my question. What do you want me to do? What do you want?"

Lips curled back from yellowed teeth. It looked like a snarl, but I think it was a smile. "Come down to us, human. Touch us, let us touch you. Let us teach you the joys of fur and teeth." He rubbed claws through the fur of his thighs. It drew my attention to him, between his legs. I looked away, and heat rushed up my skin. I was blushing. Dammit!

My voice came out almost steady. "Is that supposed to be impressive?" I asked.

He froze for an instant, then snarled, "Get her down here!"

Great, Anita, antagonize him. Imply that his equipment is a little undersized.

His hissing laugh ran up my skin in cold waves. "We are going to have fun tonight. I can tell."

The giant rats came up the steps, muscles working under fur, whiskers thick as wire, wriggling furiously. I pressed my back against the door and began to slide down the wood. "Please, please don't." My voice sounded high and frightened, and I hated it.

"We've broken you so soon; how very sad," the ratman said.

The two giant rats were almost on me. I braced my back against the door, knees tucked up, heels planted, the rest of the foot slightly raised. A claw touched my leg, I flinched, but I waited. It had to be right. Please, God, don't let them draw blood. Whiskers scraped along my face, the weight of fur on top of me.

I kicked out, both feet hitting solidly in the rat. It raised onto its hind legs and toppled backwards. It tittered, tail lashing. I threw myself forward and smashed it in the chest. The rat tumbled over the edge.

The second rat crouched, making a sound low in its throat. I watched its muscles bunch, and I went down to one knee and braced. If it leaped on me standing, I'd go over the edge. I was only inches from the drop.

It leaped. I dropped flat to the floor and rolled. I shoved feet and one hand into the warmth of its body and helped it along. The rat plummeted over me and out of sight. I heard the frightened shrieks as it fell. The sound was a thick "thumpth." Satisfying. I doubted either of them were dead. But it was the best I could do.

I stood, putting my back to the door again. The ratman wasn't smiling anymore. I smiled at him sweetly, my best angelic smile. He didn't seem impressed.

He made a motion like parting air, smooth. The lesser rats flowed forward with his hand. A creeping brown tide of furry little bodies began to boil up the steps.

I might be able to get a few of them, but not all of them. If he wanted them to, they'd eat me alive, one tiny crimson bite at a time.

Rats flowed around my feet, scrambling and arguing. Tiny bodies bumped against my boots. One stretched itself thin, reaching up to grab the edge of my boot. I kicked it off. It fell squealing over the edge.

The giant rats had dragged one of their injured friends off to one side. The rat wasn't moving. The other I had thrown off was limping.

A rat leaped upward, claws hooked in my blouse. It hung there, claws trapped in the cloth. I could feel its weight over my breast. I grabbed it around its middle. Teeth sank into my hand until they met, grinding skin, missing bone. I screamed, jerking the rat away from me. It dangled from my hand like an obscene earring. Blood ran down its fur. Another rat leaped on my blouse.

The ratman was smiling.

A rat was climbing for my face. I grabbed it by the tail and pulled it away. I yelled, "Are you afraid to come yourself? Are you afraid of me?" My voice was thin with panic, but I said it. "Your friends are injured doing something you're afraid to do. Is that it? Is it?"

The giant rats were staring from me to the ratman. He glanced at them. "I am not afraid of a human."

"Then come up, take me yourself, if you can." The rat on my hand dropped away in a spout of blood. The skin between thumb and forefinger was ripped apart.

The lesser rats hesitated, staring wildly around. One was half-way up my jeans. It dropped to the floor.

"I am not afraid."

"Prove it." My voice sounded a little steadier, maybe about nine years old instead of five.

The giant rats were staring at him, intent, judging, waiting. He made that same cutting-air motion in reverse. The rats squeaked and stood on hind legs staring around, as if they couldn't believe it, but they began to pour down the stairs the way they had come.

I leaned into the door, knees weak, cradling the bitten hand against my chest. The ratman began to creep up the stairs. He moved easily on the balls of his elongated feet, strong clawed toes digging into the stone.

Lycanthropes are stronger and faster than humans. No mind tricks, no sleight of hand, they are just better. I would not be able to surprise the wererat, as I had the first. I doubted he would grow angry enough to be stupid, but one could always hope. I was hurt, unarmed, and outmatched. If I couldn't get him to make a mistake, I was in deep shit.

A long, pink tongue curved over his teeth. "Fresh blood," he said. He drew in a loud breath of air. "You stink of fear, human. Blood and fear, smells like dinner to me." The tongue flicked out and he laughed at me.

I slid my uninjured hand behind my back, as if reaching for something. "Come closer, ratman, and we'll see how you like silver."

The ratman hesitated, frozen, half-crouched on the top step. "You have no silver."

"Want to bet your life on it?"

His clawed hands clutched each other. One of the large rats squeaked something. He snarled down at it. "I am not afraid!"

If they egged him on, my bluff wasn't going to work. "You saw what I did to your friends. That was without a weapon." My voice sounded low and sure of itself. Good for me.

He eyed me out of one large patent-leather eye. His fur glistened in the torchlight as if freshly washed. He gave a small jump and was on the landing, just out of reach.

"I've never seen a blond rat before," I said. Anything to fill the silence, anything to keep him from taking that one last step. Surely Jean-Claude would come back for me soon. I laughed then, abrupt and half-choked.

The ratman froze, staring at me. "Why are you laughing?" His voice held just a hint of unease. Good.

"I was hoping that the vampires would come for me soon and save me. You've got to admit that's funny."

He didn't seem to think it was funny. A lot of people don't get my jokes. If I was less secure, I'd think my jokes weren't funny. Naw.

I moved my hand behind my back, still pretending that there was a knife in it. One of the giant rats squealed, and even to me it sounded derisive. He would never live it down if I bluffed him. I might not live it down if I didn't.

Most people, when confronted with a wererat, freeze or panic. I'd had time to get used to the idea. I wasn't going to fade away if he touched me. There was one possible solution where I could save myself. If I was wrong, he was going to kill me. My stomach turned a sharp flip-flop, and I had to swallow hard. Better dead than furry. If he attacked me, I'd just as soon he killed me. Rats were not my top choice for being a lycanthrope. If your luck was bad, the smallest scratch could infect you.

If I was quick and lucky, I could go to a hospital and be treated. Sort of like rabies. Of course sometimes the inoculations worked, and sometimes they gave you lycanthropy.

He wrapped his long, naked tail through his clawed hands. "You ever been had by a were?"

I wasn't sure if he was talking sex or as a meal. Neither sounded pleasant. He was going to work up to it, get himself brave, then he'd come for me, when he was ready. I wanted him to come when I was ready.

I chose sex and said, "You haven't got what it takes, ratman."

He stiffened, hand sliding down his body, claws combing fur. "We'll see who has what, human."

"Is this the only way you get any sex, forcing yourself on someone? Are you as ugly in human form as you are right now?"

He hissed at me, mouth wide, teeth bared. A sound rose out of his body, deep and high, a whining growl. I'd never heard a sound like it before. It rose up and down and filled the room with violent, hissing echoes. His shoulders crouched.

I held my breath. I had pissed him off. Now we would see if my plan worked, or if he killed me. He leaped forward. I dropped to the floor, but he was ready for it. Incredible speed and he was on me, snarling, claws reaching, screaming in my face.

I bunched my legs against my chest, or he would have been on top of me. He put one claw-hand on my knees and began to push. I tucked arms over my knees, fighting him. It was like fighting steel that moved. He screamed again, high and hissing, spittle raining on me. He went up on his knees to get a better angle at forcing my legs down. I kicked outward, everything I had. He saw it coming and tried to move back, but both feet hit him square between the legs. The impact lifted him off his knees, and he collapsed to the landing, claws scrambling on the stone. He was making a high, whining, breathy sound. He couldn't seem to get enough air.

A second ratman came scrambling through the tunnel, and rats ran everywhere, squeaking and squealing. I just sat there on the landing as far away from the writhing blond ratman as I could get. I stared at the new ratman, feeling tired and angry.

Dammit, it should have worked. The bad guys weren't allowed reinforcements when I was already outnumbered. This one's fur was black, jet absolute black. He wore a pair of jean cutoffs over his slightly bent legs. He motioned, smooth and out from his body.

I swallowed my heart, pulse thudding. My skin crawled with the memory of small bodies sliding over me. My hand throbbed where the rat had bitten me. They'd tear me apart. "Jean-Claude!"

The rats moved, a flowing brownish tide, away from the stairs. The rats ran squeaking and shrilling into the tunnel. All I could do was stare.

The giant rats hissed at him, gesturing with noses and paws at the fallen giant rat. "She was defending herself. What were you doing?" The ratman's voice was low and deep, slurred only around the edges. If I had closed my eyes, I might have said it was human.

I didn't close my eyes. The giant rats left, crouch-dragging their still unconscious friend. He wasn't dead, but he was hurt. One giant rat glanced up at me as the others vanished into the tunnel. Its empty black eye glared at me, promised me painful things if we ever met again.

The blond ratman had stopped writhing and was lying very still, panting, hands cradling himself. The new ratman said, "I told you never to come here."

The first ratman struggled to sit up. The movement seemed to hurt. "The master called and I obeyed."

"I am your king. You obey me." The black-furred rat began to stride up the stairs, tail lashing angrily, almost catlike.

I stood and put the cell door at my back for the umpteenth time that night.

The hurt ratman said, "You are only our king until you die. If you stand against the master, that will be soon. She is powerful, more powerful than you." His voice still sounded weak, thready, but he was recovering. Anger will do that to you.

The rat king leaped, a black blur in motion. He jerked the ratman off his feet, holding him with slightly bent elbows, feet dangling off the ground. He held him close to his face. "I am your king, and you will obey me or I will kill you." Clawed hands dug into the blond ratman's throat, until he scrambled for air. The rat king tossed the ratman down the stairs. He fell tumbling and nearly boneless.

He glared up from the bottom in a painful, gasping heap. The hatred in his eyes would have lit a bonfire.

"Are you all right?" the new ratman asked.

It took me a minute to realize he was speaking to me. I nodded. Apparently I was being rescued, not that I had need of it. Of course not. "Thank you."

"I did not come to save you," he said. "I have forbidden my people to hunt for the vampire. That is why I came."

"Well, I know where I rate, somewhere above a flea. Thank you anyway. Whatever your motives."

He nodded. "You are welcome."

I noticed a burn scar on his left forearm. It was the shape of a crude crown. Someone had branded him. "Wouldn't it be easier just to carry around a crown and scepter?"

He glanced down at his arm, then gave that rat smile, teeth bare. "This leaves my hands free."

I looked up into his eyes to see if he was teasing me, and I couldn't tell. You try reading rat faces.

"What do the vampires want with you?" he asked.

"They want me to work for them."

"Do it. They'll hurt you if you don't."

"Like they'll hurt you if you keep the rats away?"

He shrugged, an awkward motion. "Nikolaos thinks she is queen of the rats because that is her animal to call. We are not merely rats, but men, and we have a choice. I have a choice."

"Do what she wants, and she won't hurt you," I said.

Again that smile. "I give good advice. I do not always take it."

"Me either," I said.

He stared at me out of one black eye, then turned towards the door. "They are coming."

I knew who "they" were. The party was over. The vampires were coming. The rat king sprang down the stairs and scooped up the fallen ratman. He tossed him over his shoulder as if it were no effort, then he was gone, running for the tunnel, fast, fast as a mouse surprised by the kitchen light. A dark blur.

I heard heels clicking down the hallway, and I stepped away from the door. It opened, and Theresa stood on the landing. She stared down at me and the empty room, hands on hips, mouth squeezed tight. "Where are they?"

I held up my wounded hand. "They did their part, then they left."

"They weren't supposed to leave," she said. Theresa made an exasperated sound low in her throat. "It was that rat king of theirs, wasn't it?"

I shrugged. "They left; I don't know why."

"So calm, so unafraid. Didn't the rats frighten you?"

I shrugged again. When something works, stay with it.

"They were not supposed to draw blood." She stared at me. "Are you going to shape shift next full moon?" Her voice held a hint of curiosity. Curiosity killed the vampire. One could always hope.

"No," I said, and I left it at that. No explanation. If she really wanted one, she could just beat me against the wall until I told her what she wanted to hear. She wouldn't even break a sweat. Of course, Aubrey was being punished for hurting me.

Her eyes narrowed as she studied me. "The rats were supposed to frighten you, animator. They don't seem to have done their job."

"Maybe I don't frighten that easily." I met her eyes without any effort. They were just eyes.

Theresa grinned at me suddenly, flashing fang. "Nikolaos will find something that frightens you, animator. For fear is power." She whispered the last as if afraid to say it too loud.

What did vampires fear? Did visions of sharpened stakes and garlic haunt them, or were there worse things? How do you frighten the dead?

"Walk in front of me, animator. Go meet your master."

"Isn't Nikolaos your master as well, Theresa?"

She stared at me, face blank, as if the laughter had been an illusion. Her eyes were cold and dark. The rats' eyes had held more personality. "Before the night is out, animator, Nikolaos will be everyone's master."

I shook my head. "I don't think so."

"Jean-Claude's power has made you foolish."

"No," I said, "it isn't that."

"Then what, mortal?"

"I would rather die than be a vampire's flunky."

Theresa never blinked, only nodded, very slowly. "You may get your wish."

The hair at the back of my neck crawled. I could meet her gaze, but evil has a certain feel to it. A neck-ruffling, throat-tightening feeling that tightens your gut. I have felt it around humans as well. You don't have to be undead to be evil. But it helps.

I walked in front of her. Theresa's boots clicked sharp echoes from the hallway. Maybe it was only my fear talking, but I felt her staring at me, like an ice cube sliding down my spine.

11

The room was huge, like a warehouse, but the walls were solid, massive stone. I kept waiting for Bela Lugosi to sweep around the corner in his cape. What was sitting against one wall was almost as good.

She had been about twelve or thirteen when she died. Small, half-formed breasts showed under a long flimsy dress. It was pale blue and looked warm against the total whiteness of her skin. She had been pale when alive; as a vampire she was ghostly. Her hair was that shining white-blonde that some children have before their hair darkens to brown. This hair would never grow dark.

Nikolaos sat in a carved wooden chair. Her feet did not quite touch the floor.

A male vampire moved to lean on the chair arm. His skin was a strange shade of brownish ivory. He leaned over and whispered in Nikolaos's ear.

She laughed, and it was the sound of chimes or bells. A lovely, calculated sound. Theresa went to the girl in the chair, and stood behind it, hands trailing in the long white-blonde hair.

A human male came to stand to the right of her chair. Back against the wall, hands clasped at his side. He stared straight ahead, face blank, spine rigid. He was nearly perfectly bald, face narrow, eyes dark. Most men don't look good without hair. This one did. He was handsome but had the air of a man who didn't care much about that. I wanted to call him a soldier, though I didn't know why.

Another man came to lean against Theresa. His hair was a sandy blond, cut short. His face was strange, not good-looking, but not ugly, a face you would remember. A face that might become lovely if you looked at it long enough. His eyes were a pale greenish color.

He wasn't a vampire, but I might have been hasty calling him human.

Jean-Claude came last to stand to the left of the chair. He touched no one, and even standing with them, he was apart from them.

"Well," I said, "all we need is the theme from *Dracula, Prince of Darkness*, and we'll be all set."

Her voice was like her laugh, high and harmless. Planned innocence. "You think you are funny, don't you?"

I shrugged. "It comes and goes."

She smiled at me. No fang showed. She looked so human, eyes sparkling with humor, face rounded and pleasant. See how harmless I am, just a pretty child. Right.

The black vampire whispered in her ear again. She laughed, so high and clear you could have bottled it.

"Do you practice the laugh, or is it natural talent? Naw, I'm betting you practice."

Jean-Claude's face twisted. I wasn't sure if he was trying not to laugh, or not to frown. Maybe both. I affected some people that way.

The laughter seeped out of her face, very human, until only her eyes sparkled. There was nothing funny about the look in those twinkling eyes. It was the sort of look that cats give small birds.

Her voice lilted at the end of each word, a Shirley Temple affectation. "You are either very brave, or very stupid."

"You really need at least one dimple to go with the voice."

Jean-Claude said softly, "I'm betting on stupid."

I glanced at him and then back at the ghoulie pack. "What I am is tired, hurt, angry, and scared. I would very much like to get the show over with, and get down to business."

"I am beginning to see why Aubrey lost his temper." Her voice was dry, humorless. The lilting sing-song was dripping away like melting ice.

"Do you know how old I am?"

I stared at her and shook my head.

"I thought you said she was good, Jean-Claude." She said his name like she was angry with him.

"She is good."

"Tell me how old I am." Her voice was cold, an angry grownup's voice.

"I can't. I don't know why, but I can't."

"How old is Theresa?"

I stared at the dark-haired vampire, remembering the weight of her in my mind. She was laughing at me. "A hundred, maybe hundred and fifty, no more."

Her face was unreadable, carved marble, as she asked, "Why, no more?"

"That's how old she feels."

"Feels?"

"In my head, she feels a certain . . . degree of power." I always hated to explain this part aloud. It always sounded mystical. It wasn't. I knew vampires the way some people knew horses, or cars. It was a knack. It was practice. I didn't think Nikolaos would enjoy being compared to a horse, or car, so I kept my mouth shut. See, not stupid after all.

"Look at me, human. Look into my eyes." Her voice was still bland, with none of that commanding power that Jean-Claude had.

Geez, look into my eyes. You'd think the city's master vampire could be more original. But I didn't say it out loud. Her eyes were blue, or grey, or both. Her gaze was like a weight pressing against my skin. If I put my hands up, I almost expected to be able to push something away. I had never felt any vampire's gaze like that.

But I could meet her eyes. Somehow, I knew that wasn't supposed to happen.

The soldier standing to her right was looking at me, as if I'd finally done something interesting.

Nikolaos stood. She moved a little in front of her entourage. She would only come to my collarbone, which made her short. She stood there for a moment, looking ethereal and lovely like a painting. No sense of life but a thing of lovely lines and careful color.

She stood there without moving and opened her mind to me. It felt like she had opened a door that had been locked. Her mind crashed against mine, and I staggered. Thoughts ripped into me like knives, steel-edged dreams. Fleeting bits of her mind danced in my head; where they touched I was numbed, hurt.

I was on my knees, and I didn't remember falling. I was cold, so cold. There was nothing for me. I was an insignificant thing, beside that mind. How could I think to call myself an equal? How could I do anything but crawl to her and beg to be forgiven? My insolence was intolerable.

I began to crawl to her, on hands and knees. It seemed like the right thing to do. I had to beg her forgiveness. I needed to be forgiven. How else did you approach a goddess but on bended knee?

No. Something was wrong. But what? I should ask the goddess to forgive me. I should worship her, do anything she asked. No. No.

"No." I whispered it. "No."

"Come to me, my child." Her voice was like spring after a long winter. It opened me up inside. It made me feel warm and welcome.

She held out pale arms to me. The goddess would let me embrace her. Wondrous. Why was I cowering on the floor? Why didn't I run to her?

"No." I slammed my hands into the stone. It stung, but not enough. "No!" I smashed my fist into the floor. My whole arm tingled and went numb. "NO!" I pounded my fists into the rock over and over until they bled. Pain was sharp, real, mine. I screamed, "Get out of my mind! You bitch!"

I crouched on the floor, panting, cradling my hands against my stomach. My pulse was jumping in my throat. I couldn't breathe past it. Anger washed through me, clean and sharp-edged. It chased the last shadow of Nikolaos's mind away.

I glared up at her. Anger, and behind that terror. Nikolaos had washed over my mind like the ocean in a seashell, filled me up and emptied me out. She might have to drive me crazy to break me, but she could do it if she wanted to. And there wasn't a damn thing I could do to protect myself.

She stared down at me and laughed, that wondrous wind chime of a laugh. "Oh, we have found something the animator fears. Yes, we have." Her voice was lilting and pleasant. A child bride again.

Nikolaos knelt in front of me, sweeping the sky-blue dress under her knees. Ladylike. She bent at the waist so she could look me in the eyes. "How old am I, animator?"

I was starting to shake with reaction, shock. My teeth chattered like I was freezing to death, and maybe I was. My voice squeezed out between my teeth and the tight jerk of my jaw. "A thousand," I said. "Maybe more."

"You were right, Jean-Claude. She is good." She pressed her face nearly into mine. I wanted to push her away, but more than anything, I didn't want her to touch me.

She laughed again, high and wild, heartrendingly pure. If I hadn't been hurting so badly, I might have cried, or spit in her face.

"Good, animator, we understand each other. You do what we want, or I will peel your mind away like the layers of an onion." She breathed against my face, voice dropping to a whisper. A child's whisper with an edge of giggling to it. "You do believe I can do that, don't you?"

I believed.

12

I wanted to spit in that smooth, pale face, but I was afraid of what she would do to me. A drop of sweat ran slowly down my face. I wanted to promise her anything, anything, if she would never touch me again. Nikolaos didn't have to bespell me; all she had had to do was terrify me. The fear would control me. It was what she was counting on. I could not let that happen.

"Get . . . out . . . of . . . my . . . face," I said.

She laughed. Her breath was warm and smelled like peppermint. Breath mints. But underneath the clean, modern smell, very faint, was the scent of fresh blood. Old death. Recent murder.

I wasn't shivering anymore. I said, "Your breath smells like blood."

She jerked back, a hand going to her lips. It was such a human gesture that I laughed. Her dress brushed my face as she stood. One small, slippered foot kicked me in the chest.

The force tumbled me backwards, sharp pain, no air. For the second time that night, I couldn't breathe. I lay flat on my stomach, gasping, swallowing past the pain. I hadn't heard anything break. Something should have broken.

The voice thudded over me, hot enough to scald. "Get her out of here before I kill her myself."

The pain faded to a sharp ache. Air burned going down. My chest was tight, like I'd swallowed lead.

"Stay where you are, Jean."

Jean-Claude was standing away from the wall, halfway to me. Nikolaos commanded him to stillness with one small, pale hand.

"Can you hear me, animator?"

"Yes." My voice was strangled. I couldn't get enough air to talk.

"Did I break something?" Her voice rose upward like a small bird.

I coughed, trying to clear my throat, but it hurt. I huddled around my chest while the ache faded. "No."

"Pity. But I suppose that would have slowed things down, or made you useless to us." She seemed to think about the last as if that had had possibilities. What would they have done to me if something had been broken? I didn't want to know.

"The police are aware of only four vampire murders. There have been six more."

I breathed in carefully. "Why not tell the police?"

"My dear animator, there are many among us who do not trust the human laws. We know how equal human justice is for the undead." She smiled, and again there should have been a dimple. "Jean-Claude was the fifth most powerful vampire in this city. Now he is the third."

I stared up at her, waiting for her to laugh, to say it was a joke. She continued to smile, the same exact smile, like a piece of wax. Were they playing me for a fool? "Something has killed two master vampires? Stronger than"—I had to swallow before continuing—"Jean-Claude?"

Her smile widened, flashing a distinct glimpse of fang. "You do grasp the situation quickly. I will give you that. And perhaps that will make Jean-Claude's punishment less—severe. He recommended you to us, did you know that?"

I shook my head and glanced at him. He had not moved, not even to breathe. Only his eyes looked at me. Dark blue like midnight skies, almost fever-bright. He hadn't fed yet. Why wouldn't she let him feed?

"Why is he being punished?"

"Are you worried about him?" Her voice held a mockery of surprise. "My, my, my, aren't you angry that he brought you into this?"

I stared at him for a moment. I knew then what I saw in his eyes. It was fear. He was afraid of Nikolaos. And I knew if I had any ally in this room, it was him. Fear will bind you closer than love, or hate, and it works a hell of a lot quicker. "No," I said.

"No, no." She minced the word, crying it up and down, a child's imitation. "Fine." Her voice was suddenly lower, grown-up, shimmering with heat, angry. "We will give you a gift, animator. We have a witness to the second murder. He saw Lucas die. He will tell you everything he saw, won't he, Zachary?" She smiled at the sandy-haired man.

Zachary nodded. He stepped from around the chair and swept a low bow towards me. His lips were too thin for his face, his smile crooked. Yet, the ice-green eyes stayed with me. I had seen that face before, but where?

He strode to a small door. I hadn't seen it before. It was hidden in the flickering shadows of the torches, but still I should have noticed. I glanced at Nikolaos, and she nodded at me, a smile curving her lips.

She had hidden the door from me without me knowing it. I tried to stand, pushing myself up with my hands. Mistake. I gasped and stood as quickly as I dared. The hands were already stiff with bruises and scrapes. If I lived until morning, I was going to be one sore puppy.

Zachary opened the door with a flourish, like a magician drawing a curtain. A man stood in the door. He was dressed in the remains of a business suit. A slender figure, a little thick around the middle, too many beers, too little exercise. He was maybe thirty.

"Come," Zachary said.

The man moved out into the room. His eyes were round with fear. A pinkie ring winked in the firelight. He stank of fear and death.

He was still tanned, eyes still full. He could pass for human better than any vampire in the room, but he was more a corpse than any of them. It was just a matter of time. I raised the dead for a living. I knew a zombie when I saw one.

"Do you remember Nikolaos?" Zachary asked.

The zombie's human eyes grew large, and the color drained from his face. Damn, he looked human. "Yes."

"You will answer Nikolaos's questions, do you understand that?"

"I understand." His forehead wrinkled as if he were concentrating on something, something he couldn't quite remember.

"He would not answer our questions before. Would you?" Nikolaos said.

The zombie shook its head, eyes staring at her with a sort of fearful fascination. Birds must look at snakes that way.

"We tortured him, but he was most stubborn. Then before we could continue our work, he hung himself. We really should have taken his belt away." She sounded wistful, pouty.

The zombie was staring at her. "I . . . hung myself. I don't understand. I . . ."

"He doesn't know?" I asked.

Zachary smiled. "No, he doesn't. Isn't it fabulous? You know how hard it is to make one so human, that he forgets he has died."

I knew. It meant somebody had a lot of power. Zachary was staring at the confused undead like he was a work of art. Precious. "You raised him?" I asked.

Nikolaos said, "Did you not recognize a fellow animator?" She laughed, lightly, a breeze of far-off bells.

I glanced at Zachary's face. He was staring at me, eyes memorizing me. Face blank, with a thread of something making the skin under one eye jump. Anger, fear? Then he smiled at me, brilliant, echoing. Again there was that shock of recognition.

"Ask your question, Nikolaos. He has to answer now."

"Is that true?" she asked me.

I hesitated, surprised that she had turned to me. "Yes."

"Who killed the vampire, Lucas?"

He stared at her, face crumbling. His breathing was shallow and too fast.

"Why doesn't he answer me?"

"The question is too complex," Zachary explained. "He may not remember who Lucas is."

"Then you ask him the questions, and I expect him to answer." Her voice was warm with threat.

Zachary turned with a flourish, spreading arms wide. "Ladies and gentlemen, behold, the undead." He grinned at his own joke. No one else even smiled. I didn't get it either.

"Did you see a vampire murdered?"

The zombie nodded. "Yes."

"How was he murdered?"

"Heart torn out, head cut off." His voice was paper-thin with fear.

"Who tore out his heart?"

The zombie started to shake his head over and over, quick, jerky movements. "Don't know, don't know."

"Ask him what killed the vampire," I said.

Zachary shot me a look. His eyes were green glass. Bones stood out in his face. Rage sculpted him into a skeleton with canvas skin.

"This is my zombie, my business!"

"Zachary," Nikolaos said.

He turned to her, movements stiff.

"It is a good question. A reasonable question." Her voice was low, calm. No one was fooled. Hell must be full of voices like that. Deadly, but oh so reasonable.

"Ask her question, Zachary."

He turned back to the zombie, hands balled into fists. I didn't understand where the anger was coming from. "What killed the vampire?"

"Don't understand." The voice held a knife's edge of panic.

"What sort of creature tore out the heart? Was it a human?"

"No."

"Was it another vampire?"

"No."

This was why zombies still didn't do well in court. You had to lead them by the hand, so to speak, to get answers. Lawyers accused you of leading the witness. Which was true, but it didn't mean the zombie was lying.

"Then what killed the vampire?"

Again that head shaking, back and forth, back and forth. He opened his mouth, but no sound came out. He seemed to be choking on the words, as if someone had stuffed paper down his throat. "Can't!"

"What do you mean, can't?" Zachary screamed it at him and slapped him across the face. The zombie threw up its arms to cover its head. "You . . . will . . . answer . . . me." Each word was punctuated with a slap.

The zombie fell to its knees and started to cry. "Can't!"

"Answer me, damn you!" He kicked the zombie, and it collapsed to the ground, rolling into a tight ball.

"Stop it." I walked towards them. "Stop it!"

He kicked the zombie one last time and turned on me. "It's my zombie! I can do what I want with him."

"That used to be a human being. It deserves more respect than this." I knelt by the crying zombie. I felt Zachary looming over me.

Nickolaos said, "Leave her alone, for now."

He stood there like an angry shadow pressing over my back. I touched the zombie's arm. It flinched. "It's all right. I'm not going to hurt you." Not going to hurt you. He had killed himself to escape. But not even the grave was sanctuary enough. Before tonight I would have said no animator would have raised the dead for such a purpose. Sometimes the world is a worse place than I want to know about.

I had to peel the zombie's hands from his face, then turn the face up to stare at me. One look was enough. Dark eyes were incredibly wide, fear, such fear. A thin line of spittle oozed from his mouth.

I shook my head and stood. "You've broken him."

"Damn right. No damn zombie is going to make a fool of me. He'll answer the questions."

I whirled to stare at the man's angry eyes. "Don't you understand? You've broken his mind."

"Zombies don't have minds."

"That's right, they don't. All they have, and for a very short time, is the memory of what they were. If you treat them well, they can retain their personalities for maybe a week, a little more, but this . . ." I pointed at the zombie, then spoke to Nikolaos. "Ill treatment will speed the process. Shock will destroy it."

"What are you saying, animator?"

"This sadist"—I jabbed a thumb at Zachary—"has destroyed the zombie's mind. It won't be answering any more questions. Not for anyone, not ever."

Nikolaos turned like a pale storm. Her eyes were blue glass. Her words filled the room with a soft burning. "You arrogant . . ." A tremor ran through her body, from small, slippered feet to long white-blonde hair. I waited for the wooden chair to catch fire and blaze from the fine heat of her anger.

The anger stripped away the child puppet. Bones stood out against white paper skin. Hands grabbed at the air, clawed and straining. One hand dug into the arm of her chair. The wood whined, then cracked. The sound echoed against the stone walls. Her voice burned along our skin. "Get out of here before I kill you. Take the woman and see her safely back to her car. If you fail me again, large or small, I will tear your throat out, and my children will bathe in a shower of your blood."

Nicely graphic; a little melodramatic, but nicely graphic. I didn't say it out loud. Hell, I wasn't even breathing. Any movement might attract her. All she needed was an excuse.

Zachary seemed to sense it as well. He bowed, eyes never leaving her face. Then without a word he turned and began to walk towards the small door. His movements were unhurried, as if death wasn't staring holes in his back. He paused at the open door and made a motion as if to escort me through the door. I glanced at Jean-Claude, still standing where she had left him. I had not asked about Catherine's safety; there had been no opportunity. Things were happening too fast. I opened my mouth; maybe Jean-Claude guessed.

He silenced me with a wave of a slender, pale hand. The hand seemed as white as the lace on his shirt. His eye sockets were filled with blue flame. The long, black hair floated around his suddenly death-pale face. His humanity was folding away. His power flared across my skin, raising the hairs on my arms. I hugged myself, staring at the creature that had been Jean-Claude.

"Run!" He screamed it at me, voice slashing into me. I should have been bleeding from it. I hesitated and caught sight of Nikolaos. She was levitating, ever so slowly, upward. Milkweed hair danced around her skeleton head. She raised a clawed hand. Bones and veins were caught in the amber of her skin.

Jean-Claude whirled, claw-hand slashing out at me. Something slammed me into the wall and half out the door. Zachary caught my arm and pulled me through.

I twisted free of him. The door thudded closed in my face. I whispered, "Sweet Jesus."

Zachary was at the foot of a narrow stairway, leading up. He held his hand out to me. His face was slick with sweat. "Please!" He fluttered his hand at me like a trapped bird.

A smell oozed from under the door. It was the smell of rotting corpses. The smell of bloated bodies, of skin cracked and ripening in the sun, of blood slowed and rotting in quiet veins. I gagged and backed away.

"Oh, God," Zachary whispered. He put one hand over his mouth and nose, the other still held out to me.

I ignored his hand but stood beside him on the stairs. He opened his mouth to say something, but the door creaked. The wood shook and hammered, like a giant wind was beating against it. Wind whooshed from under the door. My hair streamed in a tornado wind. We backed up a few steps while the heavy wooden door fluttered and kicked against a wind that couldn't be there. A storm indoors? The sick smell of rotting flesh bled into the wind. We looked at each other. There was that moment of recognition of us against them, or it. We turned and started running like we were attached by wires.

There couldn't be a storm behind that door. There couldn't be a wind chasing us up the narrow stone stairs. There were no rotting corpses in that room. Or were there? God, I didn't want to know. I did not want to know.

13

An explosion ripped up the stairs. The wind smashed us down like toys. The door had blown. I scrambled on all fours trying to get away, just get away. Zachary got to his feet, dragging me up by one arm. We ran.

There was a howling from behind us, out of sight. The wind roared up behind us. My hair streamed over my face, blinding me. Zachary's hand grabbed mine and held on. The walls were smooth, the stairs slick stone, there was nothing to hold on to. We flattened ourselves against the stairs and hung onto each other.

"Anita." Jean-Claude's velvet voice whispered. "Anita." I fought to look up into the wind, blinking to see. There was nothing there. "Anita." The wind was calling my name. "Anita." Something glimmered, blue fire. Two points of blue flame, hung on the wind. Eyes—were those Jean-Claude's eyes? Was he dead?

The blue flames began to float downward. The wind didn't touch them. I screamed, "Zachary!" But the sound was swallowed in the roar of the wind. Did he see it, too, or was I going crazy?

The blue flames came lower and lower, and suddenly I didn't want it to touch me, just as suddenly I knew that was what it was going to do. Something told me that that would be a very bad thing.

I tore loose from Zachary. He screamed something at me, but the wind roared and screeched between the narrow walls like a roller coaster gone mad. There was no other sound. I started to crawl up the stairs, wind beating against me, trying to crush me down. There was one other sound, Jean-Claude's voice in my head. "Forgive me."

The blue lights were suddenly in front of my face. I flattened myself against a wall, hitting at the fire. My hands passed through the burning. It wasn't there.

I screamed, "Leave me alone!"

The fire melted through my hands like they weren't there, and into my eyes. The world was blue glass, silent, nothing, blue ice. A whisper: "Run, run." I was sitting on the stairs again, blinking into the wind. Zachary was staring at me.

The wind stopped like someone had turned a switch. The silence was deafening. My breath was coming in short gasps. I had no pulse. I couldn't feel my heartbeat. All I could hear was my breathing, too loud, too shallow. I finally knew what they meant by breathless with fear.

Zachary's voice was hoarse and too loud in the silence. I think he was whispering, but it came out like a shout. "Your eyes, they glowed blue!"

I whispered, "Hush, shhh." I didn't understand why, but someone must not hear what he had just said, must not know what had happened. My life depended on it. There was no more whispering in my head, but the last bit of advice had been good. Run. Running sounded very good.

The silence was dangerous. It meant the fight was over, and the winner could turn its attention to other things. I did not want to be one of those things.

I stood and offered a hand to Zachary. He looked puzzled but took it, standing. I pulled him up the steps and started running. I had to get away, had to, or I would die in this place, tonight, now. I knew that with a surety that left no room for questions, no time for hesitation. I was running for my life. I would die, if Nikolaos saw me now. I would die.

And I would never know why.

Either Zachary felt the panic too, or he thought I knew something he didn't, because he ran with me. When one of us stumbled, the other pulled him, or her, to their feet, and we ran. We ran until acid burned the muscles in my legs, and my chest squeezed into a hard ache for lack of air.

This was why I jogged, so I could run like hell when something was chasing me. Thinner thighs was not incentive enough. But this was, running when you had to, running for your life. The silence was heavy, almost touchable. It seemed to flow up the stairs, as if searching for something. The silence chased us as surely as the wind had.

The trouble with running up stairs, if you've ever had a knee injury, is that you can't do it forever. Give me a flat surface, and

I can run for hours. Put me on an incline, and my knees give me fits. It started as an ache, but it didn't take long to become a sharp, grinding pain. Each step began to scream up my leg, until the entire leg pulsed with it.

The knee began to pop as it moved, an audible sound. That was a bad sign. The knee was threatening to go out on me. If it popped out of joint, I'd be crippled here on the stairs with the silence breathing around me. Nikolaos would find me and kill me. Why was I so sure of that? No answer, but I knew it, knew it with every pull of air. I didn't argue with the feeling.

I slowed and rested on the steps, stretching out the muscles in my legs. Refusing to gasp as the muscles on my bad leg twitched. I would stretch it out and feel better. The pain wouldn't go away, I'd abused it too much for that, but I would be able to walk without the knee betraying me.

Zachary collapsed on the stairs, obviously not a jogger. His muscles would tighten up if he didn't keep moving. Maybe he knew that. Maybe he didn't care.

I stretched my arms against the wall until my shoulders stretched out. Just something familiar to do while I waited for the knee to calm down. Something to do, while I listened for—what? Something heavy and sliding, something ancient, long dead.

Sounds from above, higher up the stairs. I froze pressed against the wall, palms flat against the cool stone. What now? What more? Surely, to God, it would be dawn soon.

Zachary stood and turned to face up the stairs. I stood with my back to the wall, so I could see up as well as down. I didn't want something sneaking up on me from below while I was looking upstairs. I wanted my gun. It was locked in my trunk, where it was doing me a hell of a lot of good.

We were standing just below a landing, a turn in the stairs. There have been times when I wished I could see around corners. This was one of them. The scrape of cloth against stone, the rub of shoes.

The man who walked around the corner was human, surprise, surprise. His neck was even unmarked. Cotton-white hair was shaved close to his head. The muscles in his neck bulged. His biceps were bigger around than my waist. My waist is kinda small, but his arms were still, ah, impressive. He was at least six-three, and there wasn't enough fat on him to grease a cake pan.

His eyes were the crystalline paleness of January skies, a distant, icy, blue. He was also the first bodybuilder I'd ever seen who didn't have a tan. All that rippling muscle was done in white, like Moby Dick. A black mesh tank top showed off every inch of his massive chest. Black jogging shorts flared around the swell of his legs. He had had to cut them up the sides to slip them over the rock bulge of his thighs.

I whispered, "Jesus, how much do you bench press?"

He smiled, close-lipped. He spoke with the barest movement of lips, never giving a glimpse of his incisors. "Four hundred."

I gave a low whistle. And said what he wanted me to say: "Impressive."

He smiled, careful not to show teeth. He was trying to play the vampire. Such a careful act being wasted on me. Should I tell him that he screamed human? Naw, he might break me over his thigh like kindling.

"This is Winter," Zachary said. The name was too perfect to be real, like a 1940s movie star.

"What is happening?" he asked.

"Our master and Jean-Claude are fighting," Zachary said.

He drew a deep, sighing breath. His eyes widened just a bit. "Jean-Claude?" He made it sound like a question.

Zachary nodded and smiled. "Yes, he's been holding out."

"Who are you?" he asked.

I hesitated; Zachary shrugged. "Anita Blake."

He smiled then, flashing nice normal teeth at last. "You're The Executioner?"

"Yes."

He laughed. The sound echoed between the stone walls. The silence seemed to tighten around us. The laughter stopped abruptly, a dew of sweat on his lip. Winter felt it and feared it. His voice came low, almost a whisper, as if he was afraid of being overheard. "You aren't big enough to be The Executioner."

I shrugged. "It disappoints me, too, sometimes."

He smiled, almost laughed again, but swallowed it. His eyes were shiny.

"Let's all get out of here," Zachary said.

I was with him.

"I was sent to check on Nikolaos," Winter said.

The silence pulsed with the name. A bead of sweat dripped down his face. Important safety tip: never say the name of an angry master vampire when they are within "hearing" distance.

"She can take care of herself," Zachary whispered, but the sound echoed anyway.

"Nooo," I said.

Zachary glared at me and I shrugged. Sometimes I just can't help myself.

Winter stared at me, face as impersonal as carved marble; only his eyes trembled. Mr. Macho. "Come," he said. He turned without waiting to see if we would follow. We followed.

I would have followed him anywhere as long as he went upstairs. All I knew was that nothing, absolutely nothing, could get me back down those stairs. Not willingly. Of course, there are always other options. I glanced up at Winter's broad back. Yeah, if you don't want to do it willingly, there are always other options.

14

The stairs opened into a square chamber. An electric bulb dangled from the ceiling. I had never thought one dim electric light could be beautiful, but it was. A sign that we were leaving the underground chamber of horrors behind and approaching the real world. I was ready to go home.

There were two doors leading out of the stone room, one straight ahead and one to the right. Music floated through the one in front of us. High, bright circus music. The door opened, and the music boiled around us. There was a glimpse of bright colors and hundreds of people milling about. A sign flashed, "Fun house." A carnival midway, inside a building. I knew where I was. Circus of the Damned.

The city's most powerful vampires slept under the Circus. It was something to remember.

The door started to shut, dimming the music, cutting off the bright signs. I looked into the eyes of a teenage girl, who was straining to see around the doorway. The door clicked shut.

A man leaned against the door. He was tall and slender, dressed like a riverboat gambler. Royal purple coat, lace at the neck and down the front, straight black pants and boots. A straight-brimmed hat shaded his face, and a gold mask covered everything but his mouth and chin. Dark eyes stared at me through the gold mask.

His tongue danced over his lips and teeth: fangs, a vampire. Why didn't that surprise me?

"I was afraid I would miss you, Executioner." His voice had a Southern thickness.

Winter moved to stand between us. The vampire laughed, a rich barking sound. "The muscle man here thinks he can protect you. Shall I tear him to pieces to prove him wrong?"

"That won't be necessary," I said. Zachary moved up to stand beside me.

"Do you recognize my voice?" the vampire asked.

I shook my head.

"It has been two years. I didn't know until this business came up that you were The Executioner. I thought you died."

"Can we cut to the chase here? Who are you and what do you want?"

"So eager, so impatient, so human." He raised gloved hands and took off his hat. Short, auburn hair framed the gold mask.

"Please don't do this," Zachary said. "The master has ordered me to see the woman safely to her car."

"I don't intend to harm a hair on her head—tonight." The gloves lifted the mask away. The left side of the face was scarred, pitted, melted away. Only his brown eye was still whole and alive, rolling in a circle of pinkish-white scar tissue. Acid burns look like that. Except it hadn't been acid. It had been Holy Water.

I remembered his body pinning me to the ground. His teeth tearing at my arm while I tried to keep him off my throat. The clean sharp snap of bone where he bit through. My screams. His hand forcing my head back. Him rearing to strike. Helpless. He missed the neck; I never knew why. Teeth sank around my collarbone, snapped it. He lapped up my blood like a cat with cream. I lay under his weight listening to him lap up my blood. The broken bones didn't hurt yet; shock. I was beginning not to hurt, not to be afraid. I was beginning to die.

My right hand reached out in the grass and touched something smooth—glass. A vial of Holy Water that had been thrown out of my bag, scattered by the half-human servants. The vampire never looked at me. His face was pressed over the wound. His tongue was exploring the hole he'd made. His teeth grated along the naked bone, and I screamed.

He laughed into my shoulder, laughed while he killed me. I flicked the lid open on the vial and splashed his face. Flesh boiled. His skin popped and bubbled. He knelt over me, clutching his face and shrieking.

I thought he had been trapped in the house when it burned down. I had wanted him dead, wished him dead. I had wished that memory away, pushed it back. Now here he stood, my favorite nightmare come to life.

"What, no scream of horror? No gasp of fright? You disappoint me, Executioner. Don't you admire your own handiwork?"

My voice came out strangled, hushed. "I thought you died."

"Now ya know different. And now I know you're alive, too. How cosy."

He smiled, and the muscles on his scarred cheek pulled the smile to one side, making it a grimace. Even vampires can't heal everything. "Eternity, Executioner, eternity like this." He caressed the scars with a gloved hand.

"What do you want?"

"Be brave, little girl, be brave as you want to be. I can feel your fear. I want to see the scars I gave you, see that you remember me, like I remember you."

"I remember you."

"Scars, girl, show me the scars."

"I show you the scars, then what?"

"Then you go home, or wherever you're going. The master has given strict orders you are not be harmed until after you do your job for us."

"Then?"

He smiled, a broad glistening expanse of teeth. "Then, I hunt you down, and I pay you back for this." He touched his face. "Come, girl, don't be shy, I seen it all before. I tasted your blood. Show me the scars, and the muscle man won't have to die proving how strong he is."

I glanced at Winter. Massive fists were crossed over his chest. His spine nearly vibrated with readiness. The vampire was right; Winter would die trying. I pushed the ripped sleeve above the elbow. A mound of scar tissue decorated the bend in my arm; scars dribbled down from it, like liquid, crisscrossing and flowing down the outer edge of my arm. The cross-shaped burn took up the only clear space on the inside of my forearm.

"I didn't think you'd ever use that arm again, after the way I tore into it."

"Physical therapy is a wonderful thing."

"Ain't no physical therapy gonna help me."

"No," I said. The first button was missing on my blouse. One more and I spread my shirt back to expose the collarbone. Scars ridged it, crawled over it. It looked real attractive in a bathing suit.

"Good," the vampire said. "You smell like cold sweat when you think of me, little girl. I was hoping I haunted you the way you haunted me."

"There is a difference, you know."

"And what might that be?"

"You were trying to kill me. I was defending myself."

"And why had you come to our house? To put stakes through our hearts. You came to our house to kill us. We didn't go hunting for you."

"But you did go hunting for twenty-three other people. That's a lot of people. Your group had to be stopped."

"Who appointed you God? Who made you our executioner?"

I took a deep breath. It was steady, didn't tremble. Brownie point for me. "The police."

"Bah." He spit on the floor. Very appealing. "You work real hard, girl. You find the murderer, then we'll finish up."

"May I go now?"

"By all means. You're safe tonight, because the master says so, but that will change."

Zachary said, "Out the side door." He walked nearly backwards watching the vampire as we moved away. Winter stayed behind, guarding our backs. Idiot.

Zachary opened the door. The night was hot and sticky. Summer wind slapped against my face, humid, and close, and beautiful.

The vampire called, "Remember the name Valentine, 'cause you'll be hearing from me."

Zachary and I walked out the door. It clanged shut behind us. There was no handle on the outside, no way to open it. A one way ticket, out. Out sounded just fine.

We started to walk. "You got a gun with silver bullets in it?" he asked.

"Yes."

"I'd start carrying it if I were you."

"Silver bullets won't kill him."

"But it'll slow him down."

"Yeah." We walked for a few minutes in silence. The warm summer night seemed to slide around us, hold us in sticky, curious hands.

"What I need is a shotgun."

He looked at me. "You going to carry a shotgun with you day after day?"

"Sawed off, it would fit under a coat."

"In the middle of a Missouri summer, you'd melt. Why not a machine gun, or a flamethrower, while you're at it?"

"Machine gun has too wide a spread range. You may hit innocent people. Flamethrower's bulky. Messy, too."

He stopped me with a hand on my shoulder. "You've used a flamethrower on vampires before?"

"No, but I saw it used."

"My god." He stared off into space for a moment, then asked, "Did it work?"

"Like a charm; messy, though. And it burned the house down around us. I thought it was a little extreme."

"I'll bet." We started walking again. "You must hate vampires."

"I don't hate them."

"Then why do you kill them?"

"Because it's my job, and I'm good at it." We turned a corner, and I could see the parking lot where I had left my car. It seemed like I had parked my car days ago. My watch said hours. It was a little like jet lag, but instead of crossing time zones, you crossed events. So many traumatic events and your time sense screws up. Too much happening in too short a space of time.

"I'm your daytime contact. If you need anything, or want to give a message, here's my number." He shoved a matchbook into my hand.

I glanced at the matchbook. It read "Circus of the Damned" bleeding red onto a shiny black background. I shoved it in my jeans pocket.

My gun was lying there in my trunk. I slipped into the shoulder rig, not caring that I had no jacket to cover it. A gun out in plain sight attracts attention, but most people leave you alone. They often even start running, clearing a path before you. It made chases very convenient.

Zachary waited until I was sitting in my car. He leaned into the open door. "It can't just be a job, Anita. There's got to be a better reason than that."

I glanced down at my lap and started the car. I looked up into his pale eyes. "I'm afraid of them. It is a very natural human trait to destroy that which frightens us."

"Most people spend their lives avoiding things they fear. You run after them. That's crazy."

He had a point. I closed the door and left him standing in the hot dark. I raised the dead and laid the undead to rest. It was what I did. Who I was. If I ever started questioning my motives, I would stop killing vampires. Simple as that.

I wasn't questioning my motives tonight, so I was still a vampire slayer, still the name they had given me. I was The Executioner.

15

Dawn slid across the sky like a curtain of light. The morning star glittered like a diamond chip against the easy flow of light.

I had seen two sunrises in as many days. I was beginning to feel grumpy. The trick would be to decide whom to be grumpy at, and what to do about it. Right now all I wanted was to sleep. The rest could wait, would have to wait. I had been running on fear, adrenaline, and stubbornness for hours. In the quiet hush of the car I could feel my body. It was not happy.

It hurt to grip the wheel, hurt to turn it. The bloody scrapes on my hands looked a lot worse than they were, I hoped. My whole body felt stiff. Everybody underrates bruises. They hurt. They would hurt a lot more after I slept on them. There is nothing like waking up the morning after a good beating. It's like a hangover that covers your entire body.

The corridor of my apartment building was hushed. The whir of the air conditioner breathed in the silence. I could almost feel all the people asleep behind the doors. I had an urge to press my ear to one of the doors and see if I could hear my neighbors breathing. So quiet. The hour after dawn is the most private of all. It is a time to be alone and enjoy the silence.

The only hour more hushed is three a.m. and I am not a fan of three a.m.

I had my keys in my hand, had almost touched the door, when I realized it was ajar. A tiny crack, almost closed, but not. I moved to the right of the door and pressed my back against the wall. Had they heard the keys jingling? Who was inside? Adrenaline was flowing like fine champagne. I was alert to every shadow, the way the light fell. My body was in emergency mode, and I hoped to God I didn't need it.

I drew my gun and leaned against the wall. Now what? There was no sound from inside the apartment, nothing. It could be

80

more vampires, but it was nearly true dawn. It wouldn't be vampires. Who else would break into my apartment? I took a deep breath and let it out. I didn't know. Didn't have the faintest idea. You'd think I'd get used to not knowing what the hell is going on, but I never do. It just makes me grumpy, and a little scared.

I had several choices. I could leave and call the police, not a bad choice. But what could they do that I couldn't, except walk in and get killed in my place? That was unacceptable. I could wait in the corridor until whoever it was got curious. That could take a while, and the apartment might be empty. I'd feel pretty stupid standing out here for hours, gun trained on an empty apartment. I was tired, and I wanted to go to bed. Dammit!

I could always just go in, gun blazing. Naw. I could push the door open and be lying on the floor and shoot anyone inside. If they had a gun. If there was anyone inside.

The smart thing would be to outwait them, but I was tired. The adrenaline rush was fading under the frustration of too many choices. There comes a point when you just get tired. I didn't think I could stand out here in the air-conditioned silence and stay alert. I wouldn't fall asleep standing up, but it was a thought. And another hour would see my neighbors up and about, maybe caught in the crossfire. Unacceptable. Whatever was going to happen needed to happen now.

Decision made. Good. Nothing like fear to wash your mind clean. I moved as far from the door as I could and crossed over, gun trained on the door. I moved along the left-hand wall towards the hinge side of the door. It opened in. Just give it a push flat against the wall; simple. Right.

I crouched down on one knee, my shoulders hunched as if I could draw my head down like a turtle. I was betting that any gun would hit above me, chest-high. Crouched down, I was a lot shorter than chest-high.

I shoved the door open with my left hand and hugged the doorsill. It worked like a charm. My gun was pointing at the bad guy's chest. Except his hands were already in the air, and he was smiling at me.

"Don't shoot," he said. "It's Edward."

I knelt there staring at him; anger rose like a warm tide. "You bastard. You knew I was out here."

He steepled his fingers. "I heard the keys."

I stood, eyes searching the room. Edward had moved my white overstuffed chair to face the door. Nothing else seemed to be moved.

"I assure you, Anita, I am quite alone."

"That I believe. Why didn't you call out to me?"

"I wanted to see if you were still good. I could have blown you away when you hesitated in front of the door, with your keys jingling so nicely."

I shut the door behind me and locked it, though truthfully with Edward inside I might have been safer locking myself out rather than in. He was not an imposing man, not frightening, if you didn't know him. He was five-eight, slender, blond, blue-eyed, charming. But if I was The Executioner, he was Death itself. He was the person I had seen use a flamethrower.

I had worked with him before, and heaven knows you felt safe with him. He carried more firepower than Rambo, but he was a little too careless of innocent bystanders. He began life as a hit man. That much the police knew. I think humans became too easy so he switched to vampires and lycanthropes. And I knew that if a time came where it was more expedient to kill me than to be my "friend," he would do it. Edward had no conscience. It made him the perfect killer.

"I've been up all bloody night, Edward. I'm not in the mood for your games."

"How hurt are you?"

I shrugged and winced. "The hands are sore, bruises mostly. I'm all right."

"Your night secretary said you were out at a bachelorette party." He grinned at me, eyes sparkling. "It must have been some party."

"I ran into a vampire you might know."

He raised his yellow eyebrows and made a silent "Oh" with his lips.

"Remember the house you nearly roasted down around us?"

"About two years ago. We killed six vampires, and two human servants."

I walked past him and flopped onto the couch. "We missed one."

"No, we didn't." His voice was very precise. Edward at his most dangerous.

I looked at the carefully cut back of his head. "Trust me on this one, Edward. He damn near killed me tonight." Which was a partial truth, also known as a lie. If the vampires didn't want me to tell the police, they certainly didn't want Death to know. Edward was a whole lot more dangerous to them than the police.

"What one?"

"The one who nearly tore me to pieces. He calls himself Valentine. He's still wearing the acid scars I gave him."

"Holy Water?"

"Yeah."

Edward came to sit beside me on the couch. He kept to one end, a careful distance. "Tell me." His eyes were intense on my face.

I looked away. "There isn't much left to tell."

"You're lying, Anita. Why?"

I stared at him, anger coming in a rush. I hate to be caught in a lie. "There have been some vampires murdered down along the river. How long have you been in town, Edward?"

He smiled then, though at what I wasn't sure. "Not long. I heard a rumor that you got to meet the city's head vampire tonight."

I couldn't stop it. My mouth fell open; the surprise was too much to hide. "How the hell do you know that?"

He gave a graceful shrug. "I have my sources."

"No vampire would talk to you, not willingly."

Again that shrug that said everything and nothing at all.

"What have you done tonight, Edward?"

"What have *you* done tonight, Anita?"

Touché, Mexican standoff, whatever. "Why have you come to me then? What do you want?"

"I want the location of the master vampire. The daytime resting place."

I had recovered enough so that my face was bland, no surprise here. "How would I know that?"

"Do you know?"

"No." I stood up. "I'm tired, and I want to go to bed. If there's nothing else?"

He stood, too, still smiling, like he knew I had lied. "I'll be in touch. If you do happen to run across the information I need . . ." He let the sentence trail off and started for the door.

"Edward."

He half-turned to me.

"Do you have a sawed-off shotgun?"

His eyebrows went up again. "I could get one for you."

"I'd pay."

"No, a gift."

"I can't tell you."

"But you do know?"

"Edward . . ."

"How deep are you in, Anita?"

"Eye level and sinking fast."

"I could help you."

"I know."

"Would helping you allow me to kill more vampires?"

"Maybe."

He grinned at me, brilliant, heart-stopping. The grin was his very best harmless good ol' boy smile. I could never decide whether the smile was real or just another mask. Would the real Edward please stand up? Probably not.

"I enjoy hunting vampires. Let me in on it if you can."

"I will."

He paused with a hand on the doorknob. "I hope I have more luck with my other sources than I did with you."

"What happens if you can't find the location from someone else?"

"Why, I come back."

"And?"

"And you will tell me what I want to know. Won't you?" He was still grinning at me, charming, boyish. He was also talking about torturing me if he had to.

I swallowed, hard. "Give me a few days, Edward, and I might have your information."

"Good. I'll bring the shotgun later today. If you're not home, I'll leave it on the kitchen table."

I didn't ask how he'd get inside if I wasn't home. He would only have smiled or laughed. Locks weren't much of a deterrent to Edward. "Thank you. For the shotgun, I mean."

"My pleasure, Anita. Until tomorrow." He stepped out the door, and it closed behind him.

Great. Vampires, now Edward. The day was about fifteen minutes old. Not a very promising beginning. I locked the door, for what good it would do me, and went to bed. The Browning Hi-Power was in its second home, a modified holster strapped to the headboard of my bed. The crucifix was cool metal around my neck. I was as safe as I was going to be and almost too tired to care.

I took one more thing to bed with me, a stuffed toy penguin named Sigmund. I don't sleep with him often, just every once in a while after someone tries to kill me. Everyone has their weaknesses. Some people smoke. I collect stuffed penguins. If you won't tell, I won't.

16

I stood in the huge stone room where Nikolaos had sat. Only the wooden chair remained, empty, alone. A coffin sat on the floor to one side. Torchlight gleamed off the polished wood. A breeze eased through the room. The torches wavered and threw huge black shadows on the walls. The shadows seemed to move independent of the light. The longer I looked at them, the more I was sure the shadows were too dark, too thick.

I could taste my heart in my throat. My pulse was hammering in my head. I couldn't breathe. Then I realized I was hearing a second heartbeat, like an echo. "Jean-Claude?" The shadows cried, "Jean-Claude," in high whining voices.

I knelt by the coffin and gripped the lid. It was all one piece, and raised on smooth oiled hinges. Blood poured down the sides of the coffin. The blood poured over my legs, splashed on my arms. I screamed and stood, covered in blood. It was still warm. "Jean-Claude!"

A pale hand raised out of the blood, spasmed, and collapsed against the side of the coffin. Jean-Claude's face floated to the top. My hand was reaching out. His heart was fluttering in my head, but he was dead. He was dead! His hand was icy wax. His eyes flew open. The dead hand grabbed my wrist.

"No!" I tried to pull my hand free. I went down on my knees in the cooling blood and screamed, "Let me go!"

He sat up. He was covered in blood. The white shirt dripped with it, like a bloody rag.

"No!"

He pulled my arm closer to him, and pulled me with it. I braced one hand on the coffin. I would not go to him. I would not go! He bent over my arm, mouth wide, fangs reaching. His heart beat against the shadows like thunder. "Jean-Claude, no!"

He looked up at me, just before he struck. "I had no choice." Blood began to drip down his face from his hair, until his face was a bloody mask. Fangs sank into my arm. I screamed, and woke sitting straight up in bed.

The doorbell was buzzing. I scrambled out of bed, forgetting. I gasped. I had moved too fast for the beating I'd had last night. I ached all over in places I couldn't possibly be bruised. My hands were stiff with dried blood. They felt arthritic.

The doorbell was buzzing continuously as if someone was leaning against it. Whoever it was, was going to get a hug for waking me up. I was sleeping in an oversized shirt. Pulling last night's jeans on was my version of a robe.

I put Sigmund the stuffed penguin back with all the rest. The stuffed toys sat on a small loveseat against the far wall, under the window. Penguins lined the floor around it like a plump fuzzy tide.

It hurt to move. It even felt tight when I breathed. I yelled, "I'm coming." It occurred to me, halfway to the door, that it might be someone unfriendly. I padded back into the bedroom and got my gun. My hand felt stiff and awkward around it. I should have cleaned and bandaged the hands last night. Oh, well.

I knelt behind the chair Edward had moved in front of the door and called, "Who is it?"

"It's Ronnie, Anita. We're supposed to work out this morning."

It was Saturday. I had forgotten. It was always amazing how ordinary life was, even while people were trying to hurt you. I felt like Ronnie should know about last night. Something so extraordinary should touch all my life, but it didn't work that way. When I'd been in the hospital with my arm in traction and tubes running all through me, my stepmother had complained that I wasn't married yet. She's worried that I will be an old maid at the ripe age of twenty-four. Judith is not what you would call a liberated woman.

My family does not cope well with what I do, the chances I take, the injuries. So they ignore it as best they can. Except for my sixteen-year-old stepbrother. Josh thinks I'm cool, neat, whatever word they're using now.

Veronica Sims is different. She's my friend, and she understands. Ronnie is a private detective. We take turns visiting each other in the hospital.

I opened the door and let her in, gun limp at my side. She took it all in and said, "Shit, you look awful."

I smiled. "Well, at least I look like I feel."

She came in and dropped her gym bag in front of the chair. "Can you tell me what happened?" Not a demand, a question. Ronnie understood that not everything could be shared.

"Sorry that I won't be able to work out today."

"Looks like you had all the workout you can handle. Go soak those hands in the sink. I'll make coffee. Okay?"

I nodded and regretted it. Aspirins, aspirins sounded real good right now. I stopped just before I went into the bathroom. "Ronnie?"

"Yes." She stood there in my small kitchen, a measuring cup of fresh coffee beans in one hand. She was five-nine. Sometimes, I forget how tall that is. It amazes people that we can run together. The trick is I set the pace, and I push myself. It's a very good workout.

"I think I have some bagels in the fridge. Could you pop them in the microwave with some cheese?"

She stared at me. "I've known you for three years, and this is the first time I've ever heard you ask for food before ten o'clock."

"Listen, if it's too much trouble, forget it."

"It isn't that, and you know it."

"Sorry. I'm just tired."

"Go doctor yourself, then you can tell me about it. Okay?"

"Yeah." Soaking the hands did not make them feel better. It felt like I was peeling the skin off my fingers. I patted them dry and rubbed Neosporin ointment over the scrapes. "A topical antibacterial," the label read. By the time I finished all the Band-Aids, I looked like a pinkish-tan version of the mummy's hand.

My back was a mass of dark bruises. My ribs were decorated in putrid purple. There wasn't much I could do about it, except hope the aspirin kicked in. Well, there was one thing I could do—move. Stretching exercises would limber the body and give me movement without pain, sort of. The stretching itself would feel like torture. I'd do it later. I needed to eat first.

I was starving. Usually, the thought of eating before ten made me nauseous. This morning I wanted food, needed food. Very weird. Maybe it was stress.

The smell of bagels and melting cheese made my stomach ripple. The smell of fresh brewed coffee made me want to chew the couch.

I scarfed down two bagels and three cups of coffee while Ronnie sat across from me, sipping her first cup. I looked up and found her watching me. Her grey eyes were staring at me. I'd seen her look at suspects like that. "What?" I asked.

She shrugged. "Nothing. Can you catch your breath and tell me about last night?"

I nodded, and it didn't hurt as much. Aspirin, nature's gift to modern man. I told her, from Monica's call to my meeting with Valentine. I didn't tell her that it all took place at the Circus of the Damned. That was very dangerous information to have right now. And I left out the blue lights on the stairs, the sound of Jean-Claude's voice in my head. Something told me that was dangerous information, too. I've learned to trust my instincts, so I left it out.

Ronnie's good, she looked at me, and said, "Is that everything?"

"Yes." An easy lie, simple, one word. I don't think Ronnie bought it.

"Okay." She took a sip of coffee. "What do you want me to do?"

"Ask around. You have access to the hate groups. Like Humans Against Vampires, The League of Human Voters, the usual. See if any of them might be involved with the murders. I can't go near them." I smiled. "After all, animators are one of the groups they hate."

"But you do kill vampires."

"Yeah, but I also raise zombies. Too weird for the hardcore bigot."

"All right. I'll check out HAV and the rest. Anything else?"

I thought about it and shook my head, almost no pain at all. "Not that I can think of. Just be very careful. I don't want to endanger you the way I did Catherine."

"That wasn't your fault."

"Right."

"It isn't your fault, none of this is."

"Tell that to Catherine and her fiancé if things go bad."

"Anita, dammit, these creatures are using you. They want you discouraged and frightened, so they can control you. If you let the guilt mess with your head, you're going to get killed."

"Well, gee, Ronnie, just what I wanted to hear. If this is your version of a pep talk, I'll skip the rally."

"You don't need cheering up. You need a good shaking."

"Thanks, I already had one last night."

"Anita, listen to me." She was staring at me, eyes intense, her face searching mine, trying to see if I was really hearing her. "You've done all you can for Catherine. I want you to concentrate on keeping yourself alive. You're ass-deep in enemies. Don't get sidetracked."

She was right. Do what you can and move on. Catherine was out of it, for now. It was the best I could do. "Ass-deep in enemies, but ankle-deep in friends."

She grinned. "Maybe it'll even out."

I cradled the coffee in my bandaged hands. Warmth radiated through the cup. "I'm scared."

"Which proves you aren't as stupid as you look."

"Gee, thanks a lot."

"You're welcome." She raised her coffee cup in a salute. "To Anita Blake, animator, vampire slayer, and good friend. Watch your back."

I clinked my cup against hers. "You watch yours, too. Being my friend right now may not be the healthiest of avocations."

"Since when was that a news bulletin?"

Unfortunately, she had a point.

17

I had two choices after Ronnie left: I could go back to sleep, not a bad idea; or I could start solving the case that everyone was so eager for me to work on. I could get by on four hours sleep, for a while. I could not last nearly as long if Aubrey tore my throat out. Guess I would go to work.

It is hard to wear a gun in St. Louis in the summertime. Shoulder or hip holster, you have the same problem. If you wear a jacket to cover the gun, you melt in the heat. If you keep the gun in your purse, you get killed, because no woman can find anything in her purse in under twelve minutes. It is a rule.

No one had been shooting at me yet; I was encouraged by that. But I had also been kidnapped and nearly killed. I did not plan on it happening again without a fight. I could bench press a hundred pounds, not bad, not bad at all. But when you only weigh a hundred and six, it puts you at a disadvantage. I would bet on me against any human bad guy my size. Trouble was, there just weren't many bad guys my size. And vampires, well, unless I could bench press trucks, I was outclassed. So a gun.

I finally settled on a less than professional look. The t-shirt was oversize, hitting me at mid-thigh. It billowed around me. The only thing that saved it was the picture on the front, penguins playing beach volleyball, complete with kiddie penguins making sand castles to one side. I like penguins. I had bought the shirt to sleep in and never planned to wear it where people could see me. As long as the fashion police didn't see me, I was safe.

I looped a belt through a pair of black shorts for my inside-the-pant holster. It was an Uncle Mike's Sidekick and I was very fond of it, but it was not for the Browning. I had a second gun for comfort and concealability: a Firestar, a compact little 9mm with a seven-shot magazine.

White jogging socks, with tasteful blue stripes that matched the blue leather piping on my white Nikes, completed the outfit. It made me look and feel about sixteen, an awkward sixteen, but when I turned to the mirror there was no hint of the gun on my belt. The shirt fell out and around it, invisible.

My upper body is slender, petite if you will, muscular and not bad to look at. Unfortunately, my legs are about five inches too short to ever be America's ideal legs. I will never have skinny thighs, nor anything short of muscular calves. The outfit emphasized my legs and hid everything else, but I had my gun and I wouldn't melt in the heat. Compromise is an imperfect art.

My crucifix hung inside my shirt, but I added a small charm bracelet to my left wrist. Three small crosses dangled from the silver chain. My scars also were in plain sight, but in the summer I try to pretend they aren't there. I cannot face the thought of wearing long sleeves in hundred-degree weather with hundred-percent humidity. My arms would fall off. The scars really aren't the first thing you notice with my arms bare. Really.

Animators, Inc., had new offices. We'd been here only three months. There was a psychologist's office across from us, nothing less than a hundred an hour; a plastic surgeon down the hall; two lawyers; one marriage counselor, and a real estate company. Four years ago Animators, Inc., had worked out of a spare room above a garage. Business was good.

Most of that good luck was due to Bert Vaughn, our boss. He was a businessman, a showman, a moneymaker, a scalawag, and a borderline cheat. Nothing illegal, not really, but . . . Most people choose to think of themselves as white hats, good guys. A few people wear black hats and enjoy it. Grey was Bert's color. Sometimes I think if you cut him, he'd bleed green, fresh-minted money.

He had turned what was an unusual talent, an embarrassing curse, or a religious experience, raising the dead, into a profitable business. We animators had the talent, but Bert knew how to make it pay. It was hard to argue with that. But I was going to try.

The reception room's wallpaper is pale, pale green with small oriental designs done in greens and browns. The carpet is thick and soft green, too pale to be grass, but it tries. Plants are everywhere.

A *Ficus benjium* grows to the right of the door, slender as a willow with small leather green leaves. It nearly curls around the chair in front of its pot. A second tree grows in the far corner, tall and straight with the stiff spiky tops of palm trees—*Dracaena marginta*. Or that's what it says on the tags tied to the spindly trunks. Both trees brush the ceiling. Dozens of smaller plants are pushed and potted in every spare corner of the soft green room.

Bert thinks the pastel green is soothing, and the plants give it that homey touch. I think it looks like an unhappy marriage between a mortuary and a plant shop.

Mary, our day secretary, is over fifty. How much over is her own business. Her hair is short and does not move in the wind. A carton of hair spray sees to that. Mary is not into the natural look. She has two grown sons and four grandchildren. She gave me her best professional smile as I came through the door. "May I help . . . Oh, Anita, I didn't think you were due in until five."

"I'm not, but I need to speak to Bert and get some things from my office."

She frowned down at her appointment book, our appointment book. "Well, Jamison is in your office right now with a client." There are only three offices in our little area. One belongs to Bert, and the other two rotate between the rest of us. Most of our work is done in the field, or rather the graveyard, so we never really need our offices all at the same time. It worked like time-sharing a condo.

"How long will the client be?"

Mary glanced down at her notes. "It's a mother whose son is thinking about joining the Church of Eternal Life."

"Is Jamison trying to talk him into it or out of it?"

"Anita!" Mary scolded me, but it was the truth. The Church of Eternal Life was the vampire church. The first church in history that could guarantee you eternal life, and prove it. No waiting around. No mystery. Just eternity on a silver platter. Most people don't believe in their immortal souls anymore. It isn't popular to worry about Heaven and Hell, and whether you are an absolutely good person. So the Church was gaining followers all over the place. If you didn't believe that it destroyed your soul, what did you have to lose? Daylight. Food. Not much to give up.

It was the soul part that bothered me. My immortal soul is not for sale, not even for eternity. You see, I knew vampires could die. I had proved it. No one seemed curious as to what happened to a vampire's soul when it died. Could you be a good vampire and go to Heaven? Somehow that didn't quite work for me.

"Is Bert with a client, too?"

She glanced once more at the appointment book. "No, he's free." She looked up and smiled, as if she was pleased to be able to help me. Maybe she was.

It is true that Bert took the smallest of the three offices. The walls are a soft pastel blue, the carpet two colors darker. Bert thinks it soothes the clients. I think it's like standing inside a blue ice cube.

Bert didn't match the small blue office. There is nothing small about Bert. Six-four, broad shoulders, a college athlete's figure getting a little soft around the middle. His white hair is close-cut over small ears. A boater's tan forces his pale eyes and hair into sharp contrast. His eyes are a nearly colorless grey, like dirty window glass. You have to work very hard to make dirty grey eyes shine, but they were shining now. Bert was practically beaming at me. It was a bad sign.

"Anita, what a pleasant surprise. Have a sit." He waved a business envelope at me. "We got the check today."

"Check?" I asked.

"For looking into the vampire murders."

I had forgotten. I had forgotten that somewhere in all this I had been promised money. It seemed ridiculous, obscene, that Nikolaos would make everything better with money. From the look on Bert's face, a lot of money.

"How much?"

"Ten thousand dollars." He stretched each word out, making it last.

"It isn't enough."

He laughed. "Anita, getting greedy in your old age. I thought that was my job."

"It isn't enough for Catherine's life, or mine."

His grin wilted slightly. His eyes looked wary, as if I was about to tell him there was no Easter Bunny. I could almost hear him wondering if he would have to return the check.

"What are you talking about, Anita?"

I told him, with a few minor revisions. No "Circus of the Damned." No blue fire. No first vampire mark.

When I got to the part about Aubrey smashing me into the wall, he said, "You are kidding."

"Want to see the bruises?"

I finished the story and watched his solemn, square face. His large, blunt-fingered hands were folded on his desk. The check was lying beside him atop his neat pile of manila folders. His face was attentive, concerned. Empathy never worked well on Bert's face. I could always see the wheels moving. The angles calculating.

"Don't worry, Bert, you can cash the check."

"Now, Anita, that wasn't . . ."

"Save it."

"Anita, truly I would never purposefully endanger you."

I laughed. "Bull."

"Anita!" He looked shocked, small eyes widening, one hand touching his chest. Mr. Sincerity.

"I'm not buying, so save the bullshit for clients. I know you too well."

He smiled then. It was his only genuine smile. The real Bert Vaughn please stand up. His eyes gleamed but not with warmth, more with pleasure. There is something measuring, obscenely knowledgeable, about Bert's smile. As if he knew the darkest thing you had ever done and would gladly keep silent—for a price.

There was something a little frightening about a man who knew he was not a nice person and didn't give a damn. It went against everything America holds dear. We are taught above all else to be nice, to be liked, to be popular. A person who has set aside all that is a maverick and a potentially dangerous human being.

"What can Animators, Inc., do to help?"

"I've already got Ronnie working on some things. I think the fewer people involved, the fewer people in danger."

"You always were a humanitarian."

"Unlike some people I could mention."

"I had no idea what they wanted."

"No, but you knew how I felt about vampires."

He gave me a smile that said, "I know your secret, I know your darkest dreams." That was Bert. Budding blackmailer.

I smiled back at him, friendly. "If you ever send me a vampire client again without running it by me first, I'll quit."

"And go where?"

"I'll take my client list with me, Bert. Who is the one that does the radio interviews? Who did the articles focus on? You made sure it was me, Bert. You thought I was the most marketable of all of us. The most harmless-looking, the most appealing. Like a puppy at the pound. When people call Animators, Inc., who do they ask for?"

His smile was gone, eyes like winter ice. "You wouldn't make it without me."

"The question is, would you make it without me?"

"I'd make it."

"So would I."

We stared at each other for a long space of moments. Neither of us was willing to look away, to blink first. Bert started to smile, still staring into my eyes. The edges of a smile began to tug at my mouth. We laughed together and that was that.

"All right, Anita, no more vampires."

I stood. "Thank you."

"Would you really quit?" His face was all laughing sincerity, a tasteful, pleasant mask.

"I don't believe in idle threats, Bert. You know that."

"Yes," he said, "I know that. I honestly didn't know this job would endanger your life."

"Would it have made a difference?"

He thought about it for a minute, then laughed. "No, but I would have charged more."

"You keep making money, Bert. That's what you're good at."

"Amen."

I left him so he could fondle the check in privacy. Maybe chuckle over it. It was blood money, no pun intended. Somehow, I didn't think that bothered Bert. It bothered me.

18

The door to the other office opened. A tall, blonde woman stepped through. She was somewhere between forty and fifty. Tailored golden pants encircled a slender waist. A sleeveless blouse the color of an eggshell exposed tanned arms, a gold Rolex watch, and a wedding band encircled with diamonds. The rock in the engagement ring must have weighed a pound. I bet she hadn't even blinked when Jamison talked price.

The boy that followed her was also slender and blond. He looked about fifteen, but I knew he had to be at least eighteen. Legally, you cannot join the Church of Eternal Life unless you are of age. He couldn't drink legally yet, but he could choose to die and live forever. Funny, how that didn't make much sense to me.

Jamison brought up the rear, smiling, solicitous. He was talking softly to the boy as he walked them towards the door.

I got a business card out of my purse. I held it out towards the woman. She looked at it, then at me. Her gaze slid over me from top to bottom. She didn't seem impressed; maybe it was the shirt. "Yes," she said.

Breeding. It takes real breeding to make a person feel like shit with one word. Of course, it didn't bother me. No, the great golden goddess did not make me feel small and grubby. Right. "The number on this card is for a man who specializes in vampire cults. He's good."

"I do not want my son brainwashed."

I managed a smile. Raymond Fields was my vampire cult expert, and he didn't do brainwashing. He did do truth, no matter how unpleasant. "Mr. Fields will give you the potential down side of vampirism," I said.

"I believe Mr. Clarke has given us all the information we need."

97

I raised my arm near her face. "I didn't get these scars playing touch football. Please, take the card. Call him, or not. It's up to you."

She was a little pale under her expert makeup. Her eyes were a little wide, staring at my arm. "Vampires did this?" Her voice was small and breathy, almost human.

"Yes," I said.

Jamison took her elbow. "Mrs. Franks, I see you've met our resident vampire slayer."

She looked at him, then back at me. Her careful face was beginning to crumble. She licked her lips and turned back to me. "Really." She was recovering quickly; she sounded superior again.

I shrugged. What could I say? I pressed the card into her manicured hand, and Jamison tactfully took it from her and pocketed it. But she had let him. What could I do? Nothing. I had tried. Period. Over. But I stared at her son. His face was incredibly young.

I remembered when eighteen was grown-up. I had thought I knew everything. I was about twenty-one when I figured out I knew dip-wad. I still knew nothing, but I tried real hard. Sometimes, that is the best you can do. Maybe the best anyone can do. Boy, Miss Cynical in the morning.

Jamison was ushering them towards the door. I caught a few sentences. "She was trying to kill them. They merely defended themselves."

Yeah, that's me, hit person for the undead. Scourge of the graveyard. Right. I left Jamison to his half-truths and went into the office. I still needed the files. Life goes on, at least for me. I couldn't stop seeing the boy's face, the wide eyes. His face had been all golden tan, baby smooth. Shouldn't you at least have to shave before you can kill yourself?

I shook my head as if I could shake the boy's face away. It almost worked. I was kneeling with the folders in my hands when Jamison came in the office. He shut the door behind him. I had thought he might.

His skin was the color of dark honey, his eyes pale green; long, tight curls framed his face. The hair was almost auburn. Jamison was the first green-eyed, red-haired black man I had ever met. He was slender, lean, not the thinness of exercise but of lucky genetics. Jamison's idea of a workout was lifting shot glasses at a good party.

"Don't ever do that again," he said.

"Do what?" I stood with the files clasped to my chest.

He shook his head and almost smiled, but it was an angry smile, a flash of small white teeth. "Don't be a smart ass."

"Sorry," I said.

"Bullshit, you're not sorry."

"About trying to give Fields's card to the woman, no. I'm not sorry. I'd do it again."

"I don't like to be undermined in front of my clients."

I shrugged.

"I mean it, Anita. Don't ever do that again."

I wanted to ask him, or what, but I didn't. "You aren't qualified to counsel people about whether or not they become the undead."

"Bert thinks I am."

"Bert would take money for a hit on the Pope if he thought he could get away with it."

Jamison smiled, then frowned at me, then couldn't help himself and smiled again. "You do have a way with words."

"Thanks."

"Don't undermine me with clients, okay?"

"I promise never to interfere when you are discussing raising the dead."

"That isn't good enough," he said.

"It's the best you're going to get. You are not qualified to counsel people. It's wrong."

"Little Miss Perfect. You murder people for money. You're nothing but a damned assassin."

I took a deep breath, and let it out. I would not fight with him today. "I execute criminals with the full blessing of the law."

"Yeah, but you enjoy it. You get your jollies by pounding in the stakes. You can't go a fucking week without bathing in someone's blood."

I just stared at him. "Do you really believe that?" I asked.

He wouldn't look at me but finally said, "I don't know."

"Poor little vampires, poor misunderstood creatures. Right? The one who branded me slaughtered twenty-three people before the courts would give me the go-ahead." I yanked my shirt down to expose the collarbone scar. "This vampire had killed ten people. He specialized in little boys, said their meat was most tender. He's not dead, Jamison. He got away. But he found me last night and threatened my life."

"You don't understand them."

"No!" I shoved a finger in his chest. "You don't understand them."

He glared down at me, nostrils flaring, breath coming in warm gasps. I stepped back. I shouldn't have touched him; that was against the rules. You never touch anyone in a fight unless you want violence.

"I'm sorry, Jamison." I don't know if he understood what I was apologizing for. He didn't say anything.

As I walked past him, he asked, "What are the files for?"

I hesitated, but he knew the files as well as I did. He'd know what was missing. "The vampire murders."

We turned towards each other at the same moment. Staring. "You took the money?" he asked.

That stopped me. "You knew about it?"

He nodded. "Bert tried to get them to hire me in your place. They wouldn't go for it."

"And after all the good PR you've given them."

"I told Bert you wouldn't do it. That you wouldn't work for vampires."

His slightly up-tilted eyes were studying my face, searching, trying to squeeze some truth out. I ignored him, my face a pleasant blankness. "Money talks, Jamison, even to me."

"You don't give a damn about money."

"Awful shortsighted of me, isn't it?" I said.

"I always thought so. You didn't do it for money." A statement. "What was it?"

I didn't want Jamison in on this. He thought vampires were fanged people. And they were very careful to keep him on the nice, clean fringes. He never got his hands dirty, so he could afford to pretend or ignore, or even lie to himself. I had gotten dirty once too often. Lying to yourself was a good way to die. "Look, Jamison, we don't agree on vampires, but anything that can kill vampires could make meat pies out of human beings. I want to catch the maniac before he, she, or it, does just that."

It wasn't a bad lie, as lies go. It was even plausible. He blinked at me. Whether he believed me or not would depend on how much he needed to believe me. How much he needed his world to stay safe and clean. He nodded, once, very slowly. "You think you can catch something the master vampires can't catch?"

"They seem to think so." I opened the door and he followed me out. Maybe he would have asked more questions, maybe not, but a voice interrupted.

"Anita, are you ready to go?"

We both turned, and I must have looked as puzzled as Jamison. I wasn't meeting anyone.

There was a man sitting in one of the lobby chairs, half-lost in the jungle plants. I didn't recognize him at first. Thick brown hair, cut short, stretched back from a very nice face. Black sunglasses hid the eyes. He turned his head and spoiled the illusion of short hair. A thick ponytail curled over his collar. He was wearing a blue denim jacket with the collar up. A blood-red tank top set off his tan. He stood slowly, smiled, and removed his glasses.

It was Phillip of the many scars. I hadn't recognized him with his clothes on. There was a bandage on the side of his neck, mostly hidden by the jacket collar. "We need to talk," he said.

I closed my mouth and tried to look reasonably intelligent. "Phillip, I didn't expect to see you so soon."

Jamison was looking from one to the other of us. He was frowning. Suspicious. Mary was sitting, chin leaning on her hands, enjoying the show.

The silence was damn awkward. Phillip put a hand out to Jamison. I mumbled. "Jamison Clarke, this is Phillip . . . a friend." The moment I said it, I wanted to take it back. "Friend" is what people call their lovers. Beats the heck out of significant other.

Jamison smiled broadly. "So, you're Anita's . . . friend." He said the last word slowly, rolling it around on his tongue.

Mary made a hubba-hubba motion with one hand. Phillip saw it and flashed her a dazzling melt-your-libido smile. She blushed.

"Well, we have to go now. Come along, Phillip." I grabbed his arm and began pulling him towards the door.

"Nice to meet you, Phillip," Jamison said. "I'll be sure to mention you to all the rest of the guys who work here. I'm sure they'd love to meet you sometime."

Jamison was really enjoying himself. "We're very busy right now, Jamison. Maybe some other time," I said.

"Sure, sure," he said.

Jamison walked us to the door and held it for us. He grinned at us as we walked down the hallway, arm in arm. Fudge buckets. I had to let the smirking little creep think I had a lover. Good grief. And he would tell everyone. Phillip slid his arm around my waist, and I fought an urge to push him away. We were pretending, right, right. I felt him hesitate as his hand brushed the gun on my belt.

We met one of the real estate agents in the hall. She said hello to me but stared at Phillip. He smiled at her. When we passed her and were waiting for the elevator, I glanced back. Sure enough, she was watching his backside as we walked away.

I had to admit it was a nice backside. She caught me looking at her and hurriedly turned away.

"Defending my honor," Phillip asked.

I pushed away from him and punched the elevator button. "What are you doing here?"

"Jean-Claude didn't come back last night. Do you know why?"

"I didn't do away with him, if that's what you're implying."

The doors opened. Phillip leaned against them, holding them open with his body and one arm. The smile he flashed me was full of potential, a little evil, a lot of sex. Did I really want to be alone in an elevator with him? Probably not, but I was armed. He, as far as I could tell, was not.

I walked under his arm without having to duck. The doors hushed behind us. We were alone. He leaned into one corner, arms crossed over his chest, staring at me from behind black lenses.

"Do you always do that?" I asked.

A slight smile. "Do what?"

"Pose."

He stiffened just a little, then relaxed against the wall. "Natural talent."

I shook my head. "Uh-huh." I stared at the flickering floor numbers.

"Is Jean-Claude all right?"

I glanced at him and didn't know what to say. The elevator stopped. We got out. "You didn't answer me," he said softly.

I sighed. It was too long a story. "It's almost noon. I'll tell you what I can over lunch."

He grinned. "Trying to pick me up, Ms. Blake?"

I smiled before I could stop myself. "You wish."

"Maybe," he said.

"Flirtatious little thing, aren't you?"

"Most women like it."

"I would like it better if I didn't think you'd flirt with my ninety-year-old grandmother the same way you're flirting with me now."

He coughed back a laugh. "You don't have a very high opinion of me."

"I am a very judgmental person. It's one of my faults."

He laughed again, a nice sound. "Maybe I can hear about the rest of your faults after you've told me where Jean-Claude is."

"I don't think so."

"Why not?"

I stopped just in front of the glass doors that led out into the street. "Because I saw you last night. I know what you are, and I know how you get your kicks."

His hand reached out and brushed my shoulder. "I get my kicks a lot of different ways."

I frowned at his hand, and it moved away. "Save it, Phillip. I'm not buying."

"Maybe by the end of lunch you will be."

I sighed. I had met men like Phillip before, handsome men who are accustomed to women drooling over them. He wasn't trying to seduce me; he just wanted me to admit that I found him attractive. If I didn't admit it, he would keep pestering me. "I give up; you win."

"What do I win?" he asked.

"You're wonderful, you're gorgeous. You are one of the best-looking men I have ever seen. From the soles of your boots, the length of your skin-tight jeans, to the flat, rippling plains of your stomach, to the sculpted line of your jaw, you are beautiful. Now can we go to lunch and cut the nonsense?"

He lowered his sunglasses just enough to see over the top of them. He stared at me like that for several minutes, then raised the glasses back in place. "You pick the restaurant." He said it flat, no teasing.

I wondered if I had offended him. I wondered if I cared.

19

The heat outside the doors was solid, a wall of damp warmth that melded to your skin like plastic wrap. "You're going to melt wearing that jacket," I said.

"Most people object to the scars."

I unfolded my arms from around the folders and extended my left arm. The scar glistened in the sunlight, shinier than the other skin. "I won't tell if you won't."

He slipped off his sunglasses and stared at me. I couldn't read his face. All I knew was that something was going on behind those big brown eyes. His voice was soft. "Is that your only bite scar?"

"No," I said.

His hands convulsed into fists, neck jerking, as if he'd had a jolt of electricity. A tremor ran up his arms into his shoulders, along his spine. He rotated his neck, as if to get rid of it. He slipped the black lenses back on his face, his eyes anonymous. The jacket came off. The scars at the bend of his arms were pale against his tan. The collarbone scar peeked from under the edges of the tank top. He had a nice neck, thick but not muscled, a stretch of smooth, tanned skin. I counted four sets of bites on that flawless skin. That was just the right side. The left was hidden by a bandage.

"I can put the jacket back on," he said.

I had been staring at him. "No, it's just . . ."

"What?"

"It's none of my business."

"Ask anyway."

"Why do you do what you do?"

He smiled, but it was twisted, a wry smile. "That is a very personal question."

"You did say ask anyway." I glanced across the street. "I usually go to Mabel's, but we might be seen."

"Ashamed of me?" His voice held a harsh edge to it, like sand-paper. His eyes were hidden, but his jaw muscles were clenched.

"It isn't that," I said. "You are the one who came into the office, pretending to be my 'friend'. If we go some place I'm known, we'll have to continue the charade."

"There are women who would pay to have me escort them."

"I know, I saw them last night at the club."

"True, but the point is still that you're ashamed to be seen with me. Because of this." His hand touched his neck, tentatively, deli-cate as a bird.

I got the distinct impression I had hurt his feelings. That didn't bother me, not really. But I knew what it was like to be differ-ent. I knew what it was like to be an embarrassment to people who should have known better. I knew better. It wasn't Phillip's feelings but the principle of the thing. "Let's go."

"Where to?"

"To Mabel's."

"Thank you," he said. He rewarded me with one of those bril-liant smiles. If I had been less professional, it might have melted me into my socks. There was a tinge of evil to it, a lot of sex, but under that was a little boy peeking out, an uncertain little boy. That was it. That was the attraction. Nothing is more appealing than a handsome man who is also uncertain of himself.

It appeals not only to the woman in us all, but the mother. A dangerous combination. Luckily, I was immune. Sure. Besides, I had seen Phillip's idea of sex. He was definitely not my type.

Mabel's is a cafeteria, but the food is wonderful and reasonably priced. On weekdays the place is filled to the brim with suits and business skirts, thin little briefcases, and manila file folders. On Saturdays it was nearly deserted.

Beatrice smiled at me from behind the steaming food. She was tall and plump with brown hair and a tired face. Her pink uniform didn't fit well through the shoulders, and the hairnet made her face look too long. But she always smiled, and we always spoke.

"Hi, Beatrice." And without waiting to be asked, "This is Phillip."

"Hi, Phillip," she said.

He gave her a smile every bit as dazzling as he had given the real estate agent. She flushed, averted her eyes, and giggled. I hadn't known Beatrice could do that. Did she notice the scars? Did it matter to her?

It was too hot for meat loaf, but I ordered it anyway. It was always moist and the catsup sauce just tangy enough. I even got dessert, which I almost never do. I was starving. We managed to pay and find a table without Phillip flirting with anyone else. A major accomplishment.

"What has happened to Jean-Claude?" he asked.

"One more minute." I said grace over my food. He was staring at me when I looked up. We ate, and I told him an edited version of last night. Mostly, I told him about Jean-Claude and Nikolaos and the punishment.

He had stopped eating by the time I finished. He was staring over my head, at nothing that I could see. "Phillip?" I asked.

He shook his head and looked at me. "She could kill him."

"I got the impression she was just going to punish him. Do you know what that would be?"

He nodded, voice soft, saying, "She traps them in coffins and uses crosses to hold them inside. Aubrey disappeared for three months. When I saw him again, he was like he is now. Crazy."

I shivered. Would Jean-Claude go crazy? I picked up my fork and found myself halfway through a piece of blackberry pie. I hate blackberries. Damn, I treat myself to pie and get the wrong kind. What was the matter with me? The taste was still warm and thick in my mouth. I took a big swig of Coke to wash it down. The Coke didn't help much.

"What are you going to do?" he asked.

I pushed the half-eaten pie away and opened one of the folders. The first victim, one Maurice no last name, had lived with a woman named Rebecca Miles. They had cohabited for five years. "Cohabited" sounded better than "shacked up." "I'll talk to friends and lovers of the dead vampires."

"I might know the names."

I stared at him, debating. I didn't want to share information with him because I knew good ol' Phillip was the daytime eyes and ears of the undead. Yet, when I had talked to Rebecca Miles in the company of the police, she had told us zip. I didn't have time to wade through crap. I needed information and fast. Nikolaos wanted results. And what Nikolaos wanted, Nikolaos damn well better get.

"Rebecca Miles," I said.

"I know her. She was Maurice's—property." He shrugged an apology at the word, but he let it stand. And I wondered what he meant by it. "Where do we go first?" he asked.

"Nowhere. I don't want a civilian along while I work."

"I might be able to help."

"No offense, you look strong and maybe even quick, but that isn't enough. Do you know how to fight? Do you carry a gun?"

"No gun, but I can handle myself."

I doubted that. Most people don't react well to violence. It freezes them. There are a handful of seconds where the body hesitates, the mind doesn't understand. Those few seconds can get you killed. The only way to kill the hesitation is practice. Violence has to become a part of your thinking. It makes you cautious, suspicious as hell, and lengthens your life expectancy. Phillip was familiar with violence, but only as the victim. I didn't need a professional victim tagging along. Yet, I needed information from people who wouldn't want to talk to me. They might talk to Phillip.

I didn't expect to run into a gun battle in broad daylight. Nor did I really expect anyone to jump me, at least not today. I've been wrong before but . . . If Phillip could help me, I saw no harm in it. As long as he didn't flash that smile at the wrong time and get molested by nuns, we would be safe.

"If someone threatens me, can you stay out of it and let me do my job, or would you charge in and try to save me?" I asked.

"Oh," he said. He stared down at his drink for a few minutes. "I don't know."

Brownie point for him. Most people would have lied. "Then I'd rather you didn't come."

"How are you going to convince Rebecca you work for the master vampire of this city? The Executioner working for vampires?"

It sounded ridiculous even to me. "I don't know."

He smiled. "Then it's settled. I'll come along and help calm the waters."

"I didn't agree to that."

"You didn't say no, either."

He had a point. I sipped my Coke and looked at his smug face for perhaps a minute. He said nothing, only stared back. His face was neutral, no challenge to it. There was no contest of egos as with Bert. "Let's go," I said.

We stood. I left a tip. We went off in search of clues.

20

Rebecca Miles lived in South City's Dogtown. The streets were all named for states: Texas, Mississippi, Indiana. The building was blind, most of the windows boarded up. The grass was tall as an elephant's eye, but not half so beautiful. A block over were expensive rehabs full of yuppies and politicians. There were no yuppies on Rebecca's block.

Her apartment was on a long, narrow corridor. There was no air conditioning in the hallway, and the heat was like chest-high fur, thick and warm. One dim light bulb gleamed over the threadbare carpeting. In places the off-green walls were patched with white plaster, but it was clean. The smell of pine-scented Lysol was thick and almost nauseating in the small, dark hallway. You could probably have eaten off the carpeting if you had wanted to, but you would have gotten fuzzies in your mouth. No amount of Lysol would get rid of carpet fuzzies.

As we had discussed in the car, Phillip knocked on the door. The idea was that he would calm any misgivings she might have about The Executioner coming into her humble abode. It took fifteen minutes of knocking and waiting before we heard someone moving around behind the door.

The door opened as far as the chain would allow. I couldn't see who answered the door. A woman's voice, thick with sleep, said, "Phillip, what are you doing here?"

"Can I come in for a few minutes?" he asked. I couldn't see his face, but I would have bet everything I owned that he was flashing her one of his infamous smiles.

"Sure; sorry, you woke me up." The door closed, and the chain rattled. The door reopened, wide. I still couldn't see around Phillip. So I guess Rebecca didn't see me either.

Phillip walked in, and I followed behind him before the door could close. The apartment was ovenlike, a gasping, stranded-fish heat. The darkness should have made it cooler, but instead made it claustrophobic. Sweat trickled down my face.

Rebecca Miles stood holding onto the door. She was thin, with lifeless dark hair falling straight to her shoulders. High cheekbones clung to the skin of her face. She was nearly overwhelmed by the white robe she wore. Delicate was the phrase, fragile. Small, dark eyes blinked at me. It was dim in the apartment, thick drapes cutting out the light. She had only seen me once, shortly after Maurice's death.

"Did you bring a friend?" she asked. She shut the door, and we were in near darkness.

"Yes," Phillip said. "This is Anita Blake . . ."

Her voice came out small and choked. "The Executioner?"

"Yes, but . . ."

She opened her small mouth and shrieked. She threw herself at me, hands clawing and slapping. I braced and covered my face with my forearms. She fought like a girl, all open-handed slaps, scratches, and flailing arms. I grabbed her wrist and used her own momentum to pull her past me. She stumbled to her knees with a little help. I had her right arm in a joint lock. It puts pressure on the elbow, it hurts, and a little extra push will snap the arm. Most people don't fight well after you break their arm at the elbow.

I didn't want to break the woman's arm. I didn't want to hurt her at all. There were two bloody scratches on my arm where she had gotten me. I guess I was lucky she hadn't had a gun.

She tried to move, and I pressed on the arm. I felt her tremble. Her breath was coming in huge gasps. "You can't kill him! You can't! Please, please don't." She started to cry, thin shoulders shaking inside the too-big robe. I stood there, holding her arm, causing her pain.

I released her arm, slowly, and stepped back out of reach. I hoped she didn't attack again. I didn't want to hurt her, and I didn't want her to hurt me. The scratches were beginning to sting.

Rebecca Miles wasn't going to try again. She huddled against the door, thin, starved hands locked around her knees. She sobbed, gasping for air, "You . . . can't . . . kill him. Please!" She started to rock back and forth, hugging herself tight as if she might shatter, like weak glass.

Jesus, some days I hate my job. "Talk to her, Phillip. Tell her we didn't come here to hurt anyone."

Phillip knelt beside her. He kept his hands at his sides as he talked to her. I didn't hear what he said. Her shuddering sobs floated after me through a right-hand doorway. It led into the bedroom.

A coffin sat beside the bed, dark wood, maybe cherry, varnished until it gleamed in the twilit dark. She thought I came to kill her lover. Jesus.

The bathroom was small and cluttered. I hit the light switch, and the harsh yellow light was not kind. Her makeup was scattered around the cracked sink like casualties. The tub was nearly rotted with rust. I found what I hoped was a clean washrag and ran cold water over it. The water that trickled out was the color of weak coffee. The pipes shuddered and clanked and whined. The water finally ran clear. It felt good on my hands, but I didn't splash any on my neck or face. It would have been cool, but the bathroom was dirty. I couldn't use the water, not if I didn't have to. I looked up as I squeezed the rag out. The mirror was shattered, a spiderweb of cracks. It gave me my face back in broken pieces.

I didn't look in the mirror again. I walked back past the coffin and hesitated. I had an urge to knock on the smooth wood. Anybody home? I didn't do it. For all I knew, someone might have knocked back.

Phillip had the woman on the couch. She was leaning against him, boneless, panting, but the crying had almost stopped. She flinched when she saw me. I tried not to look menacing, something I'm good at, and handed the rag to Phillip. "Wipe her face and put it against the back of her neck; it'll help."

He did what I asked, and she sat there with the damp rag against her neck, staring at me. Her eyes were wide, a lot of white showing. She shivered.

I found the light switch, and harsh light flooded the room. One look at the room and I wanted to turn the light off again, but I didn't. I thought Rebecca might attack me again if I sat beside her, or maybe she'd have a complete breakdown. Wouldn't that be pretty? The only chair was lopsided and had yellowed stuffing bulging out one side. I decided to stand.

Phillip looked up at me. His sunglasses were hooked over the front of his tank top. His eyes were wide and careful, as if he didn't want me to know what he was thinking. One tanned arm was wrapped around her shoulders, protective. I felt like a bully.

"I told her why we are here. I told her you wouldn't hurt Jack."

"The coffin?" I smiled. I couldn't help it. He was a "jack in the box."

"Yes," Phillip said. He stared at me as if grinning were not appropriate.

It wasn't, so I stopped, but it was something of an effort.

I nodded. If Rebecca wanted to shack up with vampires, that was her business. It certainly wasn't police business.

"Go on, Rebecca. She's trying to help us," Phillip said.

"Why?" she asked.

It was a good question. I had scared her and made her cry. I answered her question. "The master of the city made me an offer I couldn't refuse."

She stared at me, studying my face, like she was committing me to memory. "I don't believe you," she said.

I shrugged. That's what you get for telling the truth. Someone calls you a liar. Most people will accept a likely lie to an unlikely truth. In fact, they prefer it.

"How could any vampire threaten The Executioner?" she asked.

I sighed. "I'm not the bogeyman, Rebecca. Have you ever met the master of the city?"

"No."

"Then you'll have to trust me. I am scared shitless of the master. Anybody in their right mind would be."

She still looked unconvinced, but she started talking. Her small, tight voice told the same story she'd told the police. Bland and useless as a new-minted penny.

"Rebecca, I am trying to catch the person, or thing, that killed your boyfriend. Please help me."

Phillip hugged her. "Tell her what you told me."

She glanced at him, then back at me. She sucked her lower lip in and scraped it with her upper teeth, thoughtful. She took a deep, shaky breath. "We were at a freak party that night."

I blinked, then tried to sound reasonably intelligent. "I know a freak is someone who likes vampires. Is a freak party what I think it is?"

Phillip was the one who nodded. "I go to them a lot." He wouldn't look at me while he said it. "You can have a vampire almost any way you want it. And they can have you." He darted a glance at my face, then down again. Maybe he didn't like what he saw.

I tried to keep my face blank, but I wasn't having much luck. A freak party, dear God. But it was somewhere to start. "Did anything special happen at the party?" I asked.

She blinked at me, face blank, as if she didn't understand. I tried again. "Did anything out of the ordinary happen at the freak party?" When in doubt, change your vocabulary.

She stared down into her lap and shook her head. Long, dark hair trailed over her face like a thin curtain.

"Did Maurice have any enemies that you know of?"

Rebecca shook her head without even looking up. I glimpsed her eyes through her hair like a frightened rabbit staring out from behind a bush. Did she have more information, or had I used her up? If I pushed she'd break, shatter, and maybe a clue would come spilling out, then again, maybe not. Her hands were tangled in her lap, white-knuckled. They trembled ever so slightly. How badly did I want to know? Not that badly. I let it go. Anita Blake, humanitarian.

Phillip tucked Rebecca in bed, while I waited in the living room. I half-expected to hear giggling or some sound that said he was working his charm. There was nothing but the quiet murmur of voices and the cool rustle of sheets. When he came out of the bedroom, his face was serious, solemn. He slipped his glasses back on and hit the light switch. The room was a thick, hot darkness. I heard him move in the ovenlike blackness. A rustle of jeans, a scrape of boot. I fumbled for the doorknob, found it, flung it open.

Pale light spilled in. Phillip was standing, staring at me, eyes hidden. His body was relaxed, easy, but somehow I could feel his hostility. We were no longer playing friends. I wasn't sure if he was angry with me for some reason, or himself, or fate. When you end up with a life like Rebecca's, there should be someone to blame.

"That could have been me," he said.

I looked at him. "But it wasn't."

He spread his arms wide, flexing. "But it could be."

I didn't know what to say to that. What could I say? There but for the grace of God go you? I doubted God had much to do with Phillip's world.

Phillip made sure the door locked behind us, then said, "I know at least two other murdered vampires were regulars on the party circuit."

My stomach tightened, a little flutter of excitement. "Do you think the rest of the . . . victims could be freak aficionados?"

He shrugged. "I can find out." His face was still closed to me, blank. Something had turned off his switch. Maybe it was Rebecca Miles's small, starved hands. I know it hadn't done a lot for me.

Could I trust him to find out? Would he tell me the truth? Would it endanger him? No answers, just more questions, but at least the questions were getting better. Freak parties. A common thread, a real live clue. Hot dog.

21

Inside my car I turned the air conditioning on full blast. Sweat chilled on my skin, jelling in place. I turned the air down before I got a headache from the temperature change.

Phillip sat as far away from me as he could get. His body was half-turned, as much as the seat belt would allow, towards the window. His eyes behind their sunglasses stared out and away. Phillip didn't want to talk about what had just happened. How did I know that? Anita the mind reader. No, just Anita the not so stupid.

His whole body was hunched in upon itself. If I hadn't known better, I'd have said he was in pain. Come to think of it, maybe he was.

I had just bullied a very fragile human being. It hadn't felt very good, but it beat the heck out of knocking her senseless. I had not hurt her physically. Why didn't I believe that? Now, I was going to question Phillip because he had given me a clue. The proverbial lead. I couldn't let it go.

"Phillip?" I asked.

His shoulders tightened, but he continued to stare out the window.

"Phillip, I need to know about the freak parties."

"Drop me at the club."

"Guilty Pleasures?" I asked. Brilliant repartee, that's me.

He nodded, still turned away.

"Don't you need to pick up your car?"

"I don't drive," he said. "Monica dropped me off at your office."

"Did she now?" I felt the anger, instantaneous and warm.

He turned then, stared at me, face blank, eyes hidden. "Why are you so angry at her? She just got you to the club, that's all."

I shrugged.

"Why?" His voice was tired, human, normal.

I wouldn't have answered the teasing flirt, but this person was real. Real people deserve answers. "She's human, and she betrayed other humans to nonhumans," I said.

"And that's a worse crime than Jean-Claude choosing you to be our champion?"

"Jean-Claude is a vampire. You expect treachery from vampires."

"You do. I do not."

"Rebecca Miles looks like a person who's been betrayed."

He flinched.

Great Anita, just great, let's emotionally abuse everyone we meet today. But it was true.

He had turned back to the window, and I had to fill the pained silence. "Vampires are not human. Their loyalty, first and foremost, must be to their own kind. I understand that. Monica betrayed her own kind. She also betrayed a friend. That is unforgivable."

He twisted to look at me. I wished I could see his eyes. "So if someone was your friend, you would do anything for them?"

I thought about that as we drove down 70 East. Anything? That was a tall order. Almost anything? Yes. "Almost anything," I said.

"So loyalty and friendship are very important to you?"

"Yes."

"Because you believe Monica betrayed both of those things, it makes it a worse crime than anything the vampires did?"

I shifted in the seat, not happy with the way the conversation was going. I am not a big one for personal analysis. I know who I am and what I do, and that's usually enough. Not always, but most of the time. "Not anything; I don't believe in many absolutes. But, if you want a short version, yes, that's why I'm angry at Monica."

He nodded, as if that were the answer he wanted. "She's afraid of you; did you know that?"

I smiled, and it wasn't a very nice smile. I could feel the edges curl up with a dark sort of satisfaction. "I hope the little bitch is sweating it out, big time."

"She is," he said. His voice was very quiet.

I glanced at him, then quickly back to the road. I had a feeling he didn't approve of my scaring Monica. Of course, that was his problem. I was quite pleased with the results.

We were getting close to the Riverfront turnoff. He had still not answered my question. In fact, he had very nicely avoided it. "Tell me about freak parties, Phillip."

"Did you really threaten to cut out Monica's heart?"

"Yes. Are you going to tell me about the parties or not?"

"Would you really do it? Cut out her heart, I mean?"

"You answer my question, I'll answer yours." I turned the car onto the narrow brick roads of the Riverfront. Two more blocks and we would be at Guilty Pleasures.

"I told you what the parties are like. I've stopped going the last few months."

I glanced at him again. I wanted to ask why. So I did. "Why?"

"Damn, you do ask personal questions, don't you?"

"I didn't mean it to be."

I thought he wasn't going to answer the question, but he did. "I got tired of being passed around. I didn't want to end up like Rebecca, or worse."

I wanted to ask what was worse, but I let it go. I try not to be cruel, just persistent. There are days when the difference is pretty damn slight. "If you find out that all the vampires went to freak parties, call me."

"Then what?" he asked.

"I need to go to a party." I parked in front of Guilty Pleasures. The neon was quiet, a dim ghost of its nighttime self. The place looked closed.

"You don't want to go to a party, Anita."

"I'm trying to solve a crime, Phillip. If I don't, my friend dies. And I have no illusions about what the master will do to me if I fail. A quick death would be the best I could hope for."

He shivered. "Yeah, yeah." He unbuckled the seat belt and rubbed his hands along his arms, as if he were cold. "You never answered my question about Monica," he said.

"You never really told me about the parties."

He looked down, staring at the tops of his thighs. "There's one tonight. If you have to go, I'll take you." He turned to me, arms still hugging his elbows. "The parties are always at a different location. When I find out where, how do I get in touch with you?"

"Leave a message on my answering machine, my home number." I got a business card out of my purse and wrote my home phone number on the back. He got his jean jacket out of the back seat and stuffed the card into a pocket. He opened the door, and the heat washed into the chill, air-conditioned car like the breath of a dragon.

He leaned into the car, one arm on the roof, one on the door. "Now, answer my question. Would you really cut out Monica's heart, so she couldn't come back as a vampire?"

I stared into the blackness of his sunglasses and said, "Yes."

"Remind me never to piss you off." He took a deep breath. "You'll need to wear something that shows off your scars tonight. Buy something if you don't have it." He hesitated, then asked, "Are you as good at being a friend as you are an enemy?"

I took a deep breath and let it out. What could I say? "You don't want me for an enemy, Phillip. I make a much better friend."

"Yeah, I'll bet you do." He closed the door and walked up to the club door. He knocked, and a few moments later the door opened. I got a glimpse of a pale figure opening the door. It couldn't be a vampire, could it? The door closed before I could see much. Vampires could not come out in daylight. That was a rule. But until last night I had known vampires could not fly. So much for what I knew.

Whoever it was had been expecting Phillip. I pulled away from the curb. Why had they sent him at his flirtatious best? Had he been sent to charm me? Or was he the only human they could get at short notice? The only daytime member of their little club. Except for Monica. And I wasn't real fond of her right now. That was just dandy with me.

I didn't think Phillip was lying about the freak parties, but what did I know about Phillip? He stripped at Guilty Pleasures, not exactly a character reference. He was a vampire junkie, better and better. Was all that pain an act? Was he luring me someplace, just as Monica had?

I didn't know. And I needed to know. There was one place I could go that might have the answers. The only place in the District where I was truly welcome. Dead Dave's, a nice bar that served a mean hamburger. The proprietor was an ex-cop who had been kicked off the force for being dead. Picky, picky. Dave liked to help out, but he resented the prejudice of his former comrades. So he talked to me. And I talked to the police. It was a nice little arrangement that let Dave be pissed off at the police and still help them.

It made me nearly invaluable to the police. Since I was on retainer, that pleased Bert to no end.

It being daytime, Dead Dave was tucked in his coffin, but Luther would be there. Luther was the daytime manager and bartender. He was one of the few people in the District who didn't have much to do with vampires, except for the fact that he worked for one. Life is never perfect.

I actually found a parking place not far from Dave's. Daytime parking is a lot more open in the District. When the Riverfront used to be human-owned businesses, there was never any parking on a weekend, day or night. It was one of the few positives of the new vampire laws. That and the tourism.

St. Louis was a real hot spot for vampire watchers. The only place better was New York, but we had a lower crime rate. There was a gang that had gone all vampire in New York. They had spread to Los Angeles and tried to spread here. The police found the first recruits chopped into bite-size pieces.

Our vampire community prides itself on being mainstream. A vampire gang would be bad publicity, so they took care of it. I admired the efficiency of it but wished they had done it differently. I had had nightmares for weeks about walls that bled and dismembered arms that crawled along the floor all by themselves. We never did find the heads.

22

Dead Dave's is all dark glass and glowing beer signs. At night the front windows look like some sort of modern art, featuring brand names. In the daylight everything is muted. Bars are sort of like vampires; they are at their best after dark. There is something tired and wistful about a daytime bar.

The air conditioning was up full blast, like the inside of a freezer. It was almost a physical jolt after the skin-melting heat outside. I stood just inside the door and waited for my eyes to adjust to the twilight interior. Why are all bars so damn dark, like caves, places to hide? The air smelled of stale cigarettes no matter when you came in, as if years of smoke had settled into the upholstery, like aromatic ghosts.

Two guys in business suits were settled at the farthest booth from the door. They were eating and had manila folders spread across the table top. Working on a Saturday. Just like me, well, maybe not just like me. I was betting that no one had threatened to tear their throats out. Of course, I could be wrong, but I doubted it. I was betting the worst threat they had had this week was lack of job security. Ah, the good old days.

There was a man crouched on a bar stool, nursing a tall drink. His face was already slack, his movements very slow and precise, as if he were afraid he'd spill something. Drunk at one-thirty in the afternoon; not a good sign for him. But it wasn't my business. You can't save everybody. In fact, there are days when I think you can't save anyone. Each person has to save himself first, then you can move in and help. I have found this philosophy does not work during a gun battle, or a knife fight either. Outside of that it works just fine.

Luther was polishing glasses with a very clean white towel. He looked up when I slipped up on the bar stool. He nodded, a cigarette dangling from his thick lips. Luther is large, nay, fat. There is no other word for it, but it is hard fat, rock-solid, almost a kind of muscle. His hands are huge-knuckled and as big as my face. Of course, my face is small. He is a very dark black man, nearly purplish black, like mahogany. The creamy chocolate of his eyes is yellow-edged from too much cigarette smoke. I don't think I have ever seen Luther without a cig clasped between his lips. He is overweight, chain-smokes, and the grey in his hair marks him as over fifty, yet he's never sick. Good genetics, I guess.

"What'll it be, Anita?" His voice matched his body, deep and gravelly.

"The usual."

He poured me a short glass of orange juice. Vitamins. We pretended it was a screwdriver, so my penchant for sobriety wouldn't give the bar a bad name. Who wants to get drunk when there are teetotalers in the crowd? And why in the world would I keep coming to a bar if I didn't drink?

I sipped my fake screwdriver and said, "I need some info."

"Figured that. Whatcha need?"

"I need information on a man named Phillip, dances at Guilty Pleasures."

One thick eyebrow raised. "Vamp?"

I shook my head. "Vampire junkie."

He took a big drag on his cig, making the end glow like a live coal. He blew a huge puff of smoke politely away from me. "Whatcha want to know about him?"

"Is he trustworthy?"

He stared at me for a heartbeat, then he grinned. "Trustworthy? Hell, Anita, he's a junkie. Don't matter what he's strung out on, drugs, liquor, sex, vampires, no diff. No junkie is trustworthy, you know that."

I nodded. I did know that, but what could I do? "I have to trust him, Luther. He's all I got."

"Damn, girl, you are moving in the wrong circles."

I smiled. Luther was the only person I let call me girl. All women were "girl," all men "fella." "I need to know if you've heard anything really bad about him," I said.

"What are you up to?" he asked.

"I can't say. I'd share it if I could, or if I thought it would do any good."

He studied me for a moment, cig dribbling ash onto the countertop. He wiped up the ash absentmindedly with his clear white towel. "Okay, Anita, you've earned the right to say no, this once, but next time you better have something to share."

I smiled. "Cross my heart."

He just shook his head and pulled a fresh cigarette out of the pack he always kept behind the bar. He took one last drag of the nearly burned cig, then clasped the fresh one between his lips. He put the glowing orange end of the old cig against the fresh white tip and sucked air. The paper and tobacco caught, flared orange-red, and he stubbed out the old cig in the already full ashtray he carried with him from place to place, like a teddy bear.

"I know they got a dancer down at the club that is a freak. He does the party circuit and is reeeal popular with a certain sort of vamp." Luther shrugged, a massive movement like mountains hiccuping. "Don't have no dirt on him, 'cept he's a junkie, and he does the circuit. Shit, Anita, that's bad enough. Sounds like someone to stay away from."

"I would if I could." It was my turn to shrug. "But you haven't heard anything else about him?"

He thought for a moment, sucking on his new cigarette. "No, not a word. He ain't a big player in the district. He's a professional victim. Most of the talk is about the predators down here, not the sheep." He frowned. "Just a minute. I got something, an idea." He thought very carefully for a few minutes, then smiled broadly. "Yeah, got some news on a predator. Vamp calls himself Valentine, wears a mask. He been bragging that he did ol' Phillip the first time."

"So," I said.

"Not the first time he was a junkie, girl, the first time period. Valentine claims he jumped the boy when he was small, did him good. Claims ol' Phillip liked it so much that's why he's a junkie."

"Dear God." I remembered the nightmares, the reality, of Valentine. What would it have been like to have been small when it happened? What would it have done to me?

"You know Valentine?" Luther asked.

I nodded. "Yeah. He ever say how old Phillip was when the attack took place?"

He shook his head. "No, but word is anything over twelve is too old for Valentine, 'less it's revenge. He's a real big one for revenge. Word is if the master didn't keep him in line, he'd be damn dangerous."

"You bet your sweet ass he's dangerous."

"You know him." It wasn't a question.

I looked up at Luther. "I need to know where Valentine stays during the day."

"That's two bits of information for nuthin'. I don't think so."

"He wears a mask because I doused him with Holy Water about two years ago. Until last night I thought he was dead, and he thought the same about me. He's going to kill me, if he can."

"You awful hard to kill, Anita."

"There's a first time, Luther, and that's all it takes."

"I hear that." He started polishing already clean glasses. "I don't know. Word gets out we giving you daytime resting places, it could go bad for us. They could burn this place to the ground with us inside."

"You're right. I don't have a right to ask." But I sat there on the bar stool, staring at him, willing him to give me what I needed. Risk your life for me old buddy ol' pal, I'd do the same for you. Riiight.

"If you could swear you wouldn't use the info to kill him, I could tell you," Luther said.

"It'd be a lie."

"You got a warrant to kill him?" he asked.

"Not active, but I could get one."

"Would you wait for it?"

"It's illegal to kill a vampire without a court order of execution," I said.

He stared at me. "That ain't the question. Would you jump the gun to make sure of the kill?"

"Might."

He shook his head. "You gonna be up on charges one of these days, girl. Murder is a serious rap."

I shrugged. "Beats getting your throat torn out."

He blinked. "Well, now." He didn't seem to know what to say, so he polished a sparkling glass over and over in his big hands. "I'll have to ask Dave. If he says it's okay, you can have it."

I finished my orange juice and paid up, a little heavy on the tip to keep things aboveboard. Dave would never admit he helped me because of my tie with the police, so money had to exchange hands, even if it wasn't nearly what the information was worth. "Thanks, Luther."

"Word on the street is that you met the master last night. That true?"

"You know about that before or after the fact?" I asked.

He looked pained. "Anita, we woulda told you if we'd known, gratis."

I nodded. "Sorry, Luther, it's been a rough few nights."

"I'll bet. So the rumor's true?"

What could I say? Deny it? A lot of people seemed to know. I guess you can't even trust the dead to keep a secret. "Maybe." I might as well have said yes, because I didn't say no. Luther understood the game. He nodded. "What did they want with you?"

"Can't say."

"Mmm . . . uh. Okay, Anita, you be damn careful. You might wanta get some help, if there's anybody you can trust."

Trust? It wasn't lack of trust. "There may be only two ways out of this mess, Luther. Death would be my choice. A quick death would be best, but I doubt I'll get the chance if things go bad. What friend am I supposed to drag into that?"

His round, dark face stared at me. "I don't have no answers, girl. I wish I did."

"So do I."

The phone rang. Luther answered it. He looked at me and carried the phone down on its long cord. "For you," he said.

I cradled the phone against my cheek. "Yes."

"It's Ronnie." Her voice was suppressed excitement, a kid on Christmas morning.

My stomach tightened. "You have something?"

"There is a rumor going around Humans Against Vampires. A death squad designed to wipe the vampires off the face of the earth."

"You have proof, a witness?"

"Not yet."

I sighed before I could stop myself.

"Come on, Anita, this is good news."

I cupped my hand over the phone and whispered, "I can't take a rumor about HAV to the master. The vampires would slaughter them. A lot of innocent people would get killed, and we're not even sure that HAV is really behind the murders."

"All right, all right," Ronnie said. "I'll have something more concrete by tomorrow, I promise. Bribe or threat, I'll get the information."

"Thanks, Ronnie."

"What are friends for? Besides, Bert's going to have to pay for overtime and bribes. I always love the look of pain when he has to part with money."

I grinned into the phone. "Me, too."

"What are you doing tonight?"

"Going to a party."

"What?"

I explained as briefly as I could. After a long silence she said, "That is very freaky."

I agreed with her. "You keep working your end, I'll try from this side. Maybe we'll meet in the middle."

"It'd be nice to think so." Her voice sounded warm, almost angry.

"What's wrong?"

"You're going in without backup, aren't you?" she asked.

"You're alone," I said.

"But I'm not surrounded by vampires and freakazoids."

"If you're at HAV headquarters, that last is debatable."

"Don't be cute. You know what I mean."

"Yes, Ronnie, I know what you mean. You are the only friend I have who can handle herself." I shrugged, realized she couldn't see it, and said, "Anybody else would be like Catherine, sheep among wolves, and you know it."

"What about another animator?"

"Who? Jamison thinks vampires are nifty. Bert talks a good game, but he doesn't endanger his lily white ass. Charles is a good enough corpse-raiser, but he's squeamish, and he's got a four-year-old kid. Manny doesn't hunt vampires anymore. He spent four months in the hospital being put back together after his last hunt."

"If I remember correctly, you were in the hospital, too," she said.

"A broken arm and a busted collarbone were my worst injuries, Ronnie. Manny almost died. Besides, he's got a wife and four kids."

Manny had been the animator who trained me. He taught me how to raise the dead, and how to slay vampires. Though admittedly I had expanded on Manny's teachings. He was a traditionalist, a stake-and-garlic man. He had carried a gun, but as backup, not as a primary tool. If modern technology will allow me to take out a vampire from a distance, rather than straddling its waist and pounding a stake through its heart, heh, why not?

Two years ago, Rosita, Manny's wife, had come to me and begged me not to endanger her husband anymore. Fifty-two was too old to hunt vampires, she had said. What would happen to her and the children? Somehow I had gotten all the blame, like a mother whose favorite child had been led astray by the neighborhood ruffians. She had made me swear before God that I would never again ask Manny to join me on a hunt. If she hadn't cried, I would have held out, refused. Crying was damned unfair in a fight. Once a person started to cry, you couldn't talk anymore. You suddenly just wanted them to stop crying, stop hurting, stop making you feel like the biggest scum-bucket in the world. Anything to stop the tears.

Ronnie was quiet on the other end of the phone. "All right, but you be careful."

"Careful as a virgin on her wedding night, I promise."

She laughed. "You are incorrigible."

"Everybody tells me that," I said.

"Watch your back."

"You do the same."

"I will." She hung up. The phone buzzed dead in my hands.

"Good news?" Luther asked.

"Yeah." Humans Against Vampires had a death squad. Maybe. But maybe was better than what I'd had before. Look, folks, nothing up my sleeves, nothing in my pockets, no idea in hell what I was doing. Just blundering around trying to track down a killer that has taken out two master vampires. If I was on the right track, I'd attract attention soon. Which meant someone might try to kill me. Wouldn't that be fun?

I would need clothes that showed off my vampire scars and allowed me to hide weapons. It would not be an easy combination to find.

I would have to spend the afternoon shopping. I hate to shop. I consider it one of life's necessary evils, like brussels sprouts and high-heeled shoes. Of course, it beat the heck out of having my life threatened by vampires. But wait; we could go shopping now and be threatened by vampires in the evening. A perfect way to spend a Saturday night.

23

I transferred all the smaller bags into one big bag, to leave one hand free for my gun. You'd be amazed what a nice target you make juggling two armloads of shopping bags. First drop the bags—that is, if one of the handles isn't tangled over your wrist—then reach for your gun, pull, aim, fire. By the time you do all that, the bad guy has shot you twice and is walking away humming Dixie between his teeth.

I had been downright paranoid all afternoon, aware of everyone near me. Was I being followed? Had that man looked too long at me? Was that woman wearing a scarf around her neck because she had bite marks?

By the time I went for the car, my neck and shoulders were knotted into one painful ache. The most frightening thing I'd seen all afternoon had been the prices on the designer clothing.

The world was still bright blue and heat-soaked when I went for my car. It's easy to forget the passage of time in a mall. It is air conditioned, climate controlled, a private world where nothing real touches you. Disneyland for shopaholics.

I shut my packages in the trunk and watched the sky darken. I knew what fear felt like, a leaden balloon in the pit of your gut. A nice, quiet dread.

I shrugged to loosen my shoulders. Rotated my neck until it popped. Better, but still tight. I needed some aspirin. I had eaten in the mall, something I almost never did. The moment I smelled the food stalls, I had gone for them, starved.

The pizza had tasted like thin cardboard with imitation tomato paste spread over it. The cheese had been rubbery and tasteless. Yum, yum, mall food. Truth is, I love Corn Dog on a Stick and Mrs. Field's Cookies.

I got one piece of pizza with just cheese, the way I like it, but one piece with everything. I hate mushrooms and green peppers.

Sausage belongs on the breakfast table, not on pizza. I didn't know which bothered me more; that I ordered it in the first place, or that I had eaten half of it before I realized what I was doing. I was craving food that I normally hated. Why? One more question without an answer. Why did this one scare me?

My neighbor, Mrs. Pringle, was walking her dog back and forth on the grass in front of our apartment building. I parked and unloaded my one overstuffed bag from the trunk.

Mrs. Pringle is over sixty, nearly six feet tall, stretched too thin with age. Her faded blue eyes are bright and curious behind silver-rimmed glasses. Her dog Custard is a Pomeranian. He looks like a golden dandelion fluff with cat feet.

Mrs. Pringle waved at me, and I was trapped. I smiled and walked over to them. Custard began jumping up on me, like he had springs in his tiny legs. He looked like a wind-up toy. His yapping was frequent and insistent, joyous.

Custard knows I don't like him, and in his twisted doggy mind he is determined to win me over. Or maybe he just knows it irritates me. Whatever.

"Anita, you naughty girl, why didn't you tell me you had a beau?" Mrs. Pringle asked.

I frowned. "A beau?"

"A boyfriend," she said.

I didn't know what in the world she was talking about. "What do you mean?"

"Be coy if you wish, but when a young woman gives her apartment key to a man, it means something."

That lead balloon in my gut floated up a few inches. "Did you see someone going in my apartment today?" I worked very hard at keeping my face and voice casual.

"Yes, your nice young man. Very handsome."

I wanted to ask what he looked like, but if he was my boyfriend with a key to my apartment, I should know. I couldn't ask. Very handsome—could it be Phillip? But why? "When did he stop by?"

"Oh, around two this afternoon. I was just coming out to walk Custard as he was going in."

"Did you see him leave?"

She was staring at me a little too hard. "No. Anita, was he not supposed to be in your home? Did I let a burglar get away?"

"No." I managed a smile and almost a whole laugh. "I just didn't expect him today, that's all. If you see anyone going into my apartment, just let them. I'll have friends going in and out for a few days."

Her eyes had narrowed; her delicate-boned hands were very still. Even Custard was sitting in the grass, panting up at me. "Anita Blake," she said, and I was reminded that she was a retired schoolteacher, it was that kind of voice. "What are you up to?"

"Nothing, really. I've just never given my key to a man before, and I'm a little unsure about it. Jittery." I gave her my best wide-eyed innocent look. I resisted the urge to bat my eyes, but everything else was working.

She crossed her arms over her stomach. I don't think she believed me. "If you are that nervous about this young man, then he is not the right one for you. If he was, you wouldn't be jittery."

I felt light with relief. She believed. "You're probably right. Thank you for the advice. I may even take it." I felt so good, I patted Custard on top of his furry little head.

I heard Mrs. Pringle say as I walked away, "Now, Custard, do your business and let's go upstairs."

For the second time in the same day I might have an intruder in my apartment. I walked down the hushed corridor and drew my gun. A door opened. A man and two children walked out. I slipped my gun and my hand in the shopping bag, pretending to search for something. I listened to their footsteps echo down the stairs.

I couldn't just sit out here with a gun. Someone would call the police. Everybody was home from work, eating dinner, reading the paper, playing with the kids. Suburban America was awake and alert. You could not walk through it with a gun drawn.

I carried the shopping bag in my left hand in front of me, gun and right hand still inside it. If worse came to worse, I'd shoot through the bag. I walked two doors past my apartment and dug my keys out of my purse. I sat the shopping bag against the wall and transferred the gun to my left hand. I could shoot left-handed, not as well, but it would have to do. I held the gun parallel to my thigh and hoped nobody would come the wrong way down the hall and see it. I knelt by the door, keys cupped in my right hand, quiet, not jingling this time. I learn fast.

I held the gun in front of my chest and inserted the keys. The lock clicked. I flinched and waited for gunshots or noise, or something. Nothing. I slipped the keys into my pocket and switched the gun back to my right hand. With just my wrist and part of my arm in front of the door, I turned the knob and pushed, hard.

The door swung back and banged against the far wall, nobody there. No gunshots at the door. Silence.

I was crouched by the doorjamb, gun straight out, scanning the room. There was no one to see. The chair, still facing the door, was empty this time. I would almost have been relieved to see Edward.

Footsteps pounded up the stairs at the end of the hall. I had to make a decision. I reached my left hand back and got the shopping bag, never taking eyes or gun from the apartment. I scrambled inside, shoving the bag ahead of me. I shoved the door closed, still crouched by the floor.

The aquarium heater clicked, then whirred, and I jumped. Sweat was oozing down my spine. The brave vampire slayer. If they could only see me now. The apartment felt empty. There was no one here but me, but just in case, I searched in closets, under beds. Playing Dirty Harry as I slammed doors and flattened myself against walls. I felt like a fool, but I would have been a bigger fool to have trusted the apartment was empty and been wrong.

There was a shotgun on the kitchen table, along with two boxes of ammo. A sheet of white typing paper lay under it. In neat, black letters, it said, "Anita, you have twenty-four hours."

I stared at the note, reread it. Edward had been here. I don't think I breathed for a minute. I was picturing my neighbor chatting with Edward. If Mrs. Pringle had hesitated at his lie, showed fear, would he have killed her?

I didn't know. I just didn't know. Dammit! I was like a plague. Everyone around me was in danger, but what could I do?

When in doubt, take a deep breath and keep moving. A philosophy I have lived by for years. I've heard worse, really.

The note meant I had twenty-four hours before Edward came for the location of Nikolaos' daytime retreat. If I didn't give it to him, I would have to kill him. I might not be able to do that.

I told Ronnie we were professionals, but if Edward was a professional, then I was an amateur. And so was Ronnie.

Heavy damn sigh. I had to get dressed for the party. There just wasn't time to worry about Edward. I had other problems tonight.

My answering machine was blinking, and I switched it on. Ronnie's voice first, telling me what she had already told me about HAV. Evidently, she had called here first before contacting me at Dave's bar. Then, "Anita, this is Phillip. I know the location for the party. Pick me up in front of Guilty Pleasures at six-thirty. Bye."

The machine clicked, whirred, and was silent. I had two hours to dress and be there. Plenty of time. My average time for makeup is fifteen minutes. Hair takes less, because all I do is run a brush through it. Presto, I'm presentable.

I don't wear makeup often, so when I do, I always feel like it's too dark, too fake. But I always get compliments on it, like, "Why don't you wear eye shadow more often? It really brings out your eyes," or my favorite, "You look so much better in makeup." All the above implies that without makeup, you look like a candidate for the spinster farm.

One piece of makeup I don't use is base. I can't imagine smearing cake over my whole face. I own one bottle of clear nail polish, but it isn't for my fingers, it's for my panty hose. If I wear a pair of hose once without snagging them, I have had a very good day.

I stood in front of the full-length mirror in the bedroom. The top slipped over my head with one thin strap. There was no back; it tied across the small of my back in a cute little bow. I could have done without the bow, but otherwise it wasn't too bad. The top slipped into the black skirt, complete, dresslike without a break. The tan bandages on my hands clashed with the dress. Oh, well. The skirt was full and swirled when I moved. It had pockets.

Through those pockets were two thigh sheaths complete with silver knives. All I had to do was slip my hands in and come out with a weapon. Neat. Sweat is an interesting thing when you're wearing a thigh sheath. I had not been able to figure out how to hide a gun on me. I don't care how many times you've seen women carry guns on a thigh holster on television, it is damn awkward. You walk like a duck with a wet diaper on.

Hose and high-heeled black satin pumps completed the outfit. I had owned the shoes and the weapons; everything else was new.

One other new item was a cute black purse with a thin strap that would hang across my shoulders, leaving my hands free. I stuffed my smaller gun, the Firestar, into it. I know, I know, by the time I dug the gun from the depths of the purse, the bad guys would be feasting on my flesh, but it was better than not having it at all.

I slipped my cross on, and the silver looked good against the black top. Unfortunately, I doubted the vampires would let me into the party wearing a blessed crucifix. Oh, well. I'd leave it in the car, along with the shotgun and ammo.

Edward had kindly left a box near the table. What I assumed he had brought the gun up in. What had he told Mrs. Pringle, that it was a present for me?

Edward had said twenty-four hours, but twenty-four hours from when? Would he be here at dawn, bright and early, to torture the information out of me? Naw, Edward didn't strike me as a morning person. I was safe until at least afternoon. Probably.

24

I slid into a no-parking zone in front of Guilty Pleasures. Phillip was leaning against the building, arms loose at his sides. He wore black leather pants. The thought of leather in this heat made my knees break out in heat rash. His shirt was black fishnet, which showed off both scars and tan. I don't know if it was the leather or the fishnet, but the word "sleazy" came to mind. He had passed over some invisible line, from flirt to hustler.

I tried to picture him at twelve. It didn't work. Whatever had been done to him, he was what he was, and that was what I had to deal with. I wasn't a psychiatrist who could afford to feel sorry for the poor unfortunate. Pity is an emotion that can get you killed. The only thing more dangerous is blind hate, and maybe love.

Phillip pushed away from the wall and walked towards the car. I unlocked his door, and he slid inside. He smelled of leather, expensive cologne, and faintly of sweat.

I pulled away from the curb. "Aggressive little outfit there, Phillip."

He turned to stare at me, face immobile, eyes hidden behind the same sunglasses he had worn earlier. He lounged in the seat, one leg bent and pressed against the door, the other spread wide, knee tucked up on the seat. "Take Seventy West." His voice was rough, almost hoarse.

There is that moment when you are alone with a man and you both realize it. Alone together, there are always possibilities in that. There is a nearly painful awareness of each other. It can lead to awkwardness, to sex, or to fear, depending on the man and the situation.

Well, we weren't having sex, you could make book on that. I glanced at Phillip, and he was still turned towards me, lips slightly parted. He'd taken off the sunglasses. His eyes were very brown and very close. What the hell was going on?

132

We were on the highway and up to speed. I concentrated on the cars around me, on driving, and tried to ignore him. But I could feel the weight of his gaze along my skin. It was almost a warmth.

He began to slide along the seat towards me. I was suddenly very aware of the sound of leather rubbing along the upholstery. A warm, animal sound. His arm slid across my shoulders, his chest leaning into me.

"What do you think you're doing, Phillip!"

"What's wrong?" He breathed along my neck. "Isn't this aggressive enough for you?"

I laughed; I couldn't help it. He stiffened beside me. "I didn't mean to insult you, Phillip. I just didn't picture fishnet and leather for tonight."

He stayed too close to me, pressing, warm, his voice still strange and rough. "What do you like then?"

I glanced at him, but he was too close. I was suddenly staring into his eyes from two inches away. His nearness ran through me like an electric shock. I turned back to the road. "Get on your side of the car, Phillip."

"What turns you," he whispered in my ear, "on?"

I'd had enough. "How old were you the first time Valentine attacked you?"

His whole body jerked, and he scooted away from me. "Damn you!" He sounded like he meant it.

"I'll make you a deal, Phillip. You don't have to answer my question, and I won't answer yours."

His voice came out choked and breathy. "When did you see Valentine? Is he going to be here tonight? They promised me he wouldn't be here tonight." His voice held a thick edge of panic. I had never heard such instant terror.

I didn't want to see Phillip afraid. I might start feeling sorry for him, and I couldn't afford that. Anita Blake, hard as nails, sure of herself, unaffected by crying men. Riiight. "I did not talk to Valentine about you, Phillip, I swear."

"Then how . . ." He stopped, and I glanced at him. He'd slid the sunglasses back in place. His face looked very tight and still behind his dark glasses. Fragile. Sort of ruined the image.

I couldn't stand it. "How did I find out what he did to you?"

He nodded.

"I paid money to find out about your background. It came up. I needed to know if I could trust you."

"Can you?"

"I don't know yet," I said.

He took several deep breaths. The first two trembled, but each breath was a little more solid, until finally he had it under control, for now. I thought of Rebecca Miles and her small, starved-looking hands.

"You can trust me, Anita. I won't betray you. I won't." His voice sounded lost, a little boy with all his illusions stripped away.

I couldn't stomp all over that lost child voice. But I knew and he knew that he would do anything the vampires wanted, anything, including betraying me. A bridge was rising over the highway, a tall latticework of grey metal. Trees hugged the road on either side. The summer sky was pale watery blue, washed out by the heat and the bright summer sun. The car bumped up on the bridge, and the Missouri River stretched away on either side. The air seemed open and distant over the rolling water. A pigeon fluttered onto the bridge, settling beside maybe a dozen others, all strutting and burring over the bridge.

I had actually seen seagulls on the river before, but you never saw one near the bridge, just pigeons. Maybe seagulls didn't like cars.

"Where are we going, Phillip?"

"What?"

I wanted to say, "Question too hard for you?" but I resisted. It would have been like picking on him. "We're across the river. What is our destination?"

"Take the Zumbehl exit and turn right."

I did what he said. Zumbehl veers to the right and spills you automatically to a turn lane. I sat at the light and turned on red when it was clear. There is a small gathering of stores to the left, then an apartment complex, then trees, almost a woods, houses tucked back in them. A nursing home is next and then a rather large cemetery. I always wondered what the people in the nursing home thought of living next door to a cemetery. Was it a ghoulish reminder, no pun intended? A convenience, just in case?

The cemetery had been there a lot longer than the nursing home. Some of the stones went back to the early 1800s. I always thought the developer must have been a closet sadist to put the windows staring out over the rolling tombstoned hills. Old age is enough of a reminder of what comes next. No visual aids are needed.

Zumbehl is lined with other things—video store, kids clothing boutique, a place that sold stained glass, gas stations, and a huge apartment complex proclaiming, "Sun Valley Lake." There actually was a lake large enough to sail on if you were very careful.

A few more blocks and we were in suburbia. Houses with tiny yards stuffed with huge trees lined the road. There was a hill that sloped downward. The speed limit was thirty. It was impossible to keep the car to thirty going down the hill without using brakes. Would there be a policeman at the bottom of the hill?

If he stopped us with Phillip in his little fishnet shirt, all nicely scarred, would he be suspicious? Where are you going, miss? I'm sorry, officer, we have this illegal party to go to, and we're running late. I used my brakes going down the hill. Of course, there was no policeman. If I had been speeding, he'd have been there. Murphy's law is the only true dependable in my life most of the time.

"It's the big house on the left. Just pull into the driveway," Phillip said.

The house was dark red brick, two, maybe three stories, lots of windows, at least two porches. Victorian American does still exist. The yard was large with a private forest of tall, ancient trees. The grass was too high, giving the place a deserted look. The drive was gravel and wound through the trees to a modern garage that had been designed to match the house and almost succeeded.

There were only two other cars here. I couldn't see into the garage; maybe there were more inside.

"Don't leave the main room with anyone but me. If you do, I can't help you," he said.

"Help me how?" I asked.

"This is our cover story. You are the reason I have missed so many meetings. I left hints that not only are we lovers, but I've been . . ." He spread his hands wide as if searching for a word. " . . . cultivating you, until I felt you were ready for a party."

"Cultivating me?" I turned off the car, and the silence settled between us. He was staring at me. Even behind the glasses I felt the weight of his gaze. The skin between my shoulders crawled.

"You are a reluctant survivor of a real attack, not a freak, or a junkie, but I've talked you into a party. That's the story."

"Have you ever done this for real?" I asked.

"You mean given them someone?"

"Yes," I said.

He gave a rough snort. "You don't think much of me, do you?"

What was I supposed to say, no? "If we're lovers, that means we have to play lovers all evening."

He smiled. This smile was different, anticipatory.

"You bastard."

He shrugged and rotated his neck as if his shoulders were tight. "I'm not going to throw you down on the floor and ravish you, if that's what you're worried about."

"I knew you wouldn't be doing that tonight." I was glad he didn't know I had weapons. Maybe I could surprise him tonight.

He frowned at me. "Follow my lead. If anything I do makes you uncomfortable, we'll discuss it." He smiled, dazzling, teeth white and even against his tan.

"No discussion. You'll just stop."

He shrugged. "You might blow our cover and get us killed."

The car was filling with heat. A bead of sweat dripped down his face. I opened my door and got out. The heat was like a second skin. Cicadas droned, a high, buzzing song far up in the trees. Cicadas and heat, ah, summer.

Phillip walked around the car, his boots crunching on the gravel. "You might want to leave the cross in the car," he said.

I had expected it, but I didn't have to like it. I put the crucifix into the glove compartment, crawling over the seat to do so. When I closed the door, my hand went to my neck. I wore the chain so much it only felt odd when I wasn't wearing it.

Phillip held out his hand, and after a moment I took it. The palm of his hand was cupped heat, slightly moist in the center.

The back door was shaded by a white lattice arch. A clematis vine grew thick on one side. Flowers as big as my hand spread purple to the tree-filtered sun. A woman was standing in the shadow of the door, hidden from neighbors and passing cars. She wore sheer black stockings held up by garter belts. A bra and matching panties, both royal purple, left most of her body pale and naked. She was wearing five-inch spikes that forced her legs to look long and slender.

"I'm overdressed," I whispered to Phillip.

"Maybe not for long," he breathed into my hair.

"Don't bet your life on it." I stared up at him as I said it and watched his face crumble into confusion. It didn't last long. The smile came, a soft curl of lips. The serpent must have smiled at

Eve like that. I have this nice, shiny apple for you. Want some candy, little girl?

Whatever Phillip thought he was selling, I wasn't buying. He hugged me around the waist, one hand playing along the scars on my arm, fingers digging into the scar tissue just a little. His breath went out in a quick sigh. Jesus, what had I gotten myself into?

The woman was smiling at me, but her large brown eyes were fixed on Phillip's hand where it played with my scar. Her tongue darted out to wet her lips. I saw her chest rise and fall.

"Come into my parlor, said the spider to the fly."

"What did you say?" Phillip asked.

I shook my head. He probably didn't know the poem anyway. I couldn't remember how it ended. I couldn't remember if the fly got away. My stomach was tight. When Phillip's hand brushed my naked back, I jumped.

The woman laughed, high and maybe a little drunk. I whispered the fly's words as I went up the steps, "Oh, no, no, to ask me is in vain for whoever goes up your winding stairs can ne'er come down again."

Ne'er come down again. It had a bad ring to it.

25

The woman pressed against the wall, so we could pass, and shut the door behind us. I kept waiting for her to lock it so we couldn't get away, but she didn't. I shoved Phillip's hand off my scars, and he wrapped himself around my waist and led me down a long narrow hall. The house was cool, air conditioning purring against the heat. A square archway opened into a room.

It was a living room with all that implies—a couch, love seat, two chairs, plants hanging in front of a bay window, afternoon shadows snaking across the carpeting. Homey. A man stood in the center of the room, a drink in his hand. He looked like he had just come from Leather 'R' Us. Leather bands criss-crossed his chest and arms, like Hollywood's idea of an oversexed gladiator.

I owed Phillip an apology. He'd dressed downright conservatively. The happy homemaker came up behind us in her royal purple lingerie and laid a hand on Phillip's arm. Her fingernails were painted dark purple, almost black. The nails scratched along his arm, leaving faint reddish tracks behind.

Phillip shivered beside me, his arm tightening around my waist. Was this his idea of fun? I hoped not.

A tall, black woman rose from the couch. Her rather plentiful breasts threatened to squeeze out of a black wire bra. A crimson skirt with more holes than cloth hung from the bra and moved as she walked, giving glimpses of dark flesh. I was betting she was naked under the skirt.

There were pinkish scars on one wrist and her neck. A baby junkie, new, almost fresh. She stalked around us, like we were for sale and she wanted to get a good look. Her hand brushed my back, and I stood away from Phillip, facing the woman.

"That scar on your back; what is it? It isn't vampire bites." Her voice was low for a woman, an alto tenor maybe.

"A sharp piece of wood was slammed into my back by a human servant." I didn't add that the sharp piece of wood had been one of the stakes I brought with me, or that I had killed the human servant later that same night.

"My name's Rochelle," she said.

"Anita."

The happy homemaker stepped up next to me, hand stroking over my arm. I stepped away from her, her fingers sliding over my skin. Her nails left little red lines on my arm. I resisted the urge to rub them. I was a tough-as-nails vampire slayer; scratches didn't bother me. The look in the woman's eyes did. She looked like she wondered what flavor I was and how long I'd last. I had never been looked at that way by another woman. I didn't like it much.

"I'm Madge. That's my husband Harvey," she said, pointing to Mr. Leather, who had moved to stand beside Rochelle. "Welcome to our home. Phillip has told us so much about you, Anita."

Harvey tried to come up behind me, but I stepped back towards the couch, so I could face him. They were trying to circle like sharks. Phillip was staring at me, hard. Right; I was supposed to be enjoying myself, not acting like they all had communicable diseases.

Which was the lesser evil? A sixty-four-thousand-dollar question if ever I heard one. Madge licked her lips, slowly, suggestively. Her eyes said she was thinking naughty things about me, and her. No way. Rochelle swished her skirt, exposing far too much thigh. I had been right. She was naked under the skirt. I'd die first.

That left Harvey. His small, blunt-fingered hands were playing with the leather-and-metal studding of the little kilt he wore. Fingers rubbing over and over the leather. Shit.

I flashed him my best professional smile, not seductive, but it was better than a frown. His eyes widened and he took a step towards me, hand reaching out towards my left arm. I took a deep breath and held it, smile freezing in place.

His fingers barely traced over the bend of my arm, tickling down the skin, until I shivered. Harvey took the shiver for an invitation and moved in closer, bodies almost touching. I put a hand on his chest to keep him from coming any closer. The hair on his chest was coarse and thick, black. I've never been a fan of hairy chests. Give me smooth any day. His arm began to encircle my back. I wasn't sure what to do. If I took a step back I was going to sit down on the couch, not a good idea. If I stepped forward I'd be stepping into him, pressed against all that leather and skin.

He smiled at me. "I've been dying to meet you."

He said "dying" like it was a dirty word, or an inside joke. The others laughed, all except Phillip. He took my arm and pulled me away from Harvey. I leaned into Phillip, even put my arms around his waist. I had never hugged anyone in a fishnet shirt before. It was an interesting sensation.

Phillip said, "Remember what I said."

"Sure, sure," Madge said. "She's yours, all yours, no sharing, no halfsies." She stalked over to him, swaying in her tight lace panties. With the heels on she could look him in the eye. "You can keep her safe from us for now, but when the big boys get here, you'll share. They'll make you share."

He stared at her until she looked away. "I brought her here, and I'll take her home," he said.

Madge raised an eyebrow. "You're going to fight them? Phillip, my boy, she must be a sweet piece of tail, but no bedwarmer is worth pissing off the big guys."

I stepped away from Phillip and put a hand flat against her stomach and pushed, just enough to make her back up. The heels made her balance bad, and she almost fell. "Let's get something straight," I said. "I am not a piece of anything, nor am I a bedwarmer."

Phillip said, "Anita . . ."

"My, my, she's got a temper. Wherever did you find her, Phillip?" Madge asked.

If there is anything I hate, it is being found amusing when I'm angry. I stepped up close to her, and she smiled down at me. "Did you know," I said, "that when you smile, you get deep wrinkles on either side of your mouth? You are over forty, aren't you?"

She drew a deep, gasping breath and stepped back from me. "You little bitch."

"Don't ever call me a piece of tail again, Madge, darling."

Rochelle was laughing silently, her considerable bosom shaking like dark brown jello. Harvey stood straight-faced. If he had so much as smiled, I think Madge would have hurt him. His eyes were very shiny, but there was no hint of a smile.

A door opened and closed down the hall, farther into the house.
A woman stepped into the room. She was around fifty, or maybe
a hard forty. Very blonde hair framed a plump face. Even money
the blonde came out of a bottle. Plump little hands glittered with
rings, real stones. A long, black negligee swept the floor, complete
with an open lace robe. The flat black of the negligee was kind
to her figure, but not kind enough. She was overweight and there
was no hiding it. She looked like a PTA member, a Girl Scout
leader, a cookie baker, someone's mother. And there she stood
in the doorway, staring at Phillip.

She let out a little squeal and came running towards him. I got
out of the way before I was crushed in the stampede. Phillip had
just enough time to brace himself before she flung her considerable weight into his arms. For a minute I thought he was going to
fall backwards into the floor with her on top, but his back straightened, his legs tensed, and he righted them both.

Strong Phillip, able to lift overweight nymphomaniacs with
both hands.

Harvey said, "This is Crystal."

Crystal was kissing Phillip's chest, chubby, homey little hands
trying to pull his shirt out of his pants so she could touch his bare
flesh. She was like a cheerful little puppy in heat.

Phillip was trying to discourage her without much success. He
gave me a long glance. And I remembered what he had said, that
he had stopped coming to these parties. Was this why? Crystal
and her like? Madge of the sharp fingernails? I had forced him
to bring me, but in doing so, I had forced him to bring himself.

If you thought of it that way, it was my fault Phillip was here.
Damn, I owed him.

I patted the woman's cheek, softly. She blinked at me, and I
wondered if she was nearsighted. "Crystal," I said. I smiled my
best angelic smile. "Crystal, I don't mean to be rude, but you're
pawing my date."

Her mouth fell open; her pale eyes bugged out. "Date," she
squeaked. "No one has dates at a party."

"Well, I'm new to the parties. I don't know the rules yet. But
where I come from, one woman does not grope another woman's
date. At least wait until I turn my back, okay?"

Crystal's lower lip trembled. Her eyes began to fill with tears.
I had been gentle, kind even, and she was still going to cry. What
was she doing here with these people?

Madge came and put her arm around Crystal and led the woman away. Madge was making soothing noises and patting her black silken arms.

Rochelle said, "Very cold." She walked away from me towards a liquor cabinet that was against one wall.

Harvey had also left, following Madge and Crystal without so much as a backwards glance.

You'd think I'd kicked a puppy. Phillip let out a long breath and set down on the couch. He clasped his hands in front of him, between his knees. I sat down next to him, tucking my skirt down over my legs.

"I don't think I can do this," he whispered.

I touched his arm. He was trembling, a constant shaking that I didn't like at all. I hadn't realized what it would cost him to come tonight, but I was beginning to find out.

"We can go," I said.

He turned very slowly and stared at me. "What do you mean?"

"I mean we can go."

"You'd leave now without finding out anything because I'm having problems?" he asked.

"Let's just say I like you better as the overconfident flirt. You keep acting like a real person, and you'll have me all confused. We can go if you can't handle it."

He took a deep breath and let it out, then shook himself like a dog coming out of water. "I can do it. If I have a choice, I can do it."

It was my turn to stare. "Why didn't you have a choice before?"

He looked away. "I just felt like I had to bring you if you wanted to come."

"No, dammit, that wasn't what you meant at all." I touched his face and forced him to look at me. "Someone gave you orders to come see me the other day, didn't they? It wasn't just to find out about Jean-Claude, was it?"

His eyes were wide, and I could feel his pulse under my fingers. "What are you afraid of, Phillip? Who's giving you orders?"

"Anita, please, I can't."

My hand dropped to my lap. "What are your orders, Phillip?"

He swallowed, and I watched his throat work. "I'm to keep you safe here, that's all." His pulse was jumping under the bruised bite in his neck. He licked his lips, not seductive, nervous. He was lying to me. The trick was, how much of a lie and what about?

I heard Madge's voice coming up the hall, all cheerful seduction. Such a good hostess. She escorted two people into the room. One was a woman with short auburn hair and too much eye makeup, like green chalk smeared above her eyes. The second was Edward, smiling, at his charming best, with his arm around Madge's bare waist. She gave a rich, throaty laugh as he whispered something to her.

I froze, for a second. It was so unexpected that I just froze. If he had pulled out a gun, he could have killed me while I sat with my mouth hanging open. What the hell was he doing here?

Madge led him and the woman towards the bar. He glanced back at me over her shoulder and gave me a delicate smile that left his blue eyes empty as a doll's.

I knew my twenty-four hours were not up. I knew that. Edward had decided to come looking for Nikolaos. Had he followed us? Had he listened to Phillip's message on my machine?

"What's wrong?" Phillip asked.

"What's wrong?" I said. "You are taking orders from somebody, probably a vampire . . ." I finished the statement silently in my head: And Death has just waltzed in the door to play freak while he searches for Nikolaos. There was only one reason Edward searched for a particular vampire. He meant to kill her, if he could.

The assassin might finally have met his match. I had thought I wanted to be around when Edward finally lost. I wanted to see what prey was too large for Death to conquer. I had seen this prey, up close and personal. If Edward and Nikolaos met and she even suspected that I had a hand in it . . . shit. Shit, shit, shit!

I should turn Edward in. He had threatened me, and he would carry it out. He would torture me to get information. What did I owe him? But I couldn't do it, wouldn't do it. A human being does not turn another human being over to the monsters. Not for any reason.

Monica had broken that rule, and I despised her for it. I think I was the closest thing Edward had to a real friend. A person who knows who and what you are and likes you anyway. I did like him, despite or because of what he was. Even though I knew he'd kill me if it worked out that way? Yes, even though. It didn't make much sense when you looked at it that way. But I couldn't worry about Edward's morality. The only person I had to face in the mirror was me. The only moral dilemma I could solve was my own.

I watched Edward play kissy-face with Madge. He was much better at role-playing than I was. He was also a much better liar.

I would not tell, and Edward had known I would not tell. In his own way, he knew me, too. He had bet his life on my integrity, and that pissed me off. I hate to be used. My virtue had become its own punishment.

But maybe, I didn't know how yet, I could use Edward the way he was using me. Perhaps I could use his lack of honor as he used my honor now.

It had possibilities.

26

The auburn-haired woman with Edward came over to the couch and slid into Phillip's lap. She giggled and wrapped her arms around his neck with a little kick of her feet. Her hands didn't wander lower, and she didn't try to undress him. The night was looking up. Edward followed behind the woman like a blond shadow. There was a drink in his hand and a suitably harmless smile on his face.

If I hadn't known him, I would never have looked at him and said, there, there is a dangerous man. Edward the Chameleon. He balanced on the couch arm at the woman's back, one hand rubbing her shoulder.

"Anita, this is Darlene," Phillip said.

I nodded. She giggled and kicked her little feet.

"This is Teddy. Isn't he scrumptious?"

Teddy? Scrumptious? I managed a smile, and Edward kissed the side of her neck. She snuggled against his chest, managing to wiggle in Phillip's lap at the same time. Coordination.

"Let me have a taste." Darlene sucked her lower lip under her teeth and drew it out slowly.

Phillip's breath trembled. He whispered, "Yes."

I didn't think I was going to like this.

Darlene cupped his arm in her hands and raised it to her mouth. She bestowed a delicate kiss over one of his scars, then she slid her legs down between his until she was kneeling at his feet, still holding his arm. The full skirt of her dress was bunched up around her waist, caught on his legs. She was wearing red lace panties and matching garters. Color coordination.

Phillip's face had gone slack. He was staring at her as she brought his arm towards her mouth. A small pink tongue licked his arm, quick, out, wet, gone. She glanced up at Phillip, eyes dark and full. She must have liked what she saw because she began to

145

lick his scars, one by one, delicate, a cat with cream. Her eyes never left his face.

Phillip shuddered; his spine spasmed. He closed his eyes and leaned his head back against the couch. Her hands went to his stomach. She gripped the fishnet and pulled. It slid out of his pants, and her hands stroked up bare chest.

He jerked, eyes wide, and caught her arms. He shook his head. "No, no." His voice sounded hoarse, too deep.

"You want me to stop?" Darlene asked. Her eyes were nearly closed, breath deep, lips full and waiting.

He was struggling to talk and make sense at the same time. "If we do this . . . that leaves Anita alone. Fair game. Her first party."

Darlene looked at me, maybe for the first time. "With scars like that?"

"Scars are from a real attack. I talked her into the party." He brought her hands out from under his shirt. "I can't desert her." His eyes seemed to be focusing again. "She doesn't know the rules."

Darlene leaned her head on his thigh. "Phillip, please, I've missed you."

"You know what they'd do to her."

"Teddy will keep her safe. He knows the rules."

I asked, "You've been to other parties?"

"Yes," Edward said. He held my gaze for several seconds while I tried to picture him at other parties. So this was where he got his information about the vampire world, through the freaks.

"No," Phillip said. He stood, bringing Darlene to her feet, still holding her forearms. "No," he said, and his voice sounded certain, confident. He released her and held out his hand to me. I took it. What else could I do?

His hand was sweating and warm. He strode out of the room, and I was forced to half-run in my heels to catch up with my hand.

He led me down the hall to the bathroom and we went in. He locked the door and leaned against it, sweat beaded on his face, eyes closed. I took back my hand, and he didn't fight me.

I looked around at the available seating and finally chose to sit on the edge of the bathtub. It wasn't comfortable, but it seemed the lesser of two evils. Phillip drew in great gulps of air and finally turned to the sink. He ran water loud and splashing, dipped his hands in, and covered his face again and again until he stood, water dripping down his face. Droplets caught in his eyelashes and hair. He blinked at himself in the mirror over the basin. He looked startled, wide-eyed.

The water was dripping down his neck and chest. I stood and handed him a towel from the rack. He didn't respond. I mopped up his chest with the soft, clean-smelling folds of the towel.

He finally took the towel and finished drying off. His hair was dark and wet around his face. There was no way to dry it out. "I did it," he said.

"Yes," I said, "you did it."

"I almost let her."

"But you didn't, Phillip. That's what counts."

He nodded, rapidly, head bobbing. "I guess so." He still seemed out of breath.

"We better be getting back to the party."

He nodded. But he stayed where he was, breathing too deep, like he couldn't get enough oxygen.

"Phillip, are you all right?" It was a stupid question, but I couldn't think of what else to say.

He nodded. Mr. Conversation.

"Do you want to leave?" I asked.

He looked at me then. "That's the second time you've offered that. Why?"

"Why what?"

"Why would you offer to let me out of my promise?"

I shrugged and rubbed my hands over my arms. "Because . . . because you seem to be in some kind of pain. Because you're a junkie trying to kick the habit, sort of, and I don't want to screw that up for you."

"That's a very . . . decent thing to offer." He said decent like he wasn't used to the word.

"Do you want to leave?"

"Yes," he said, "but we can't."

"You said that before. Why can't we?"

"I can't, Anita, I can't."

"Yes, you can. Who are you taking orders from, Phillip? Tell me. What is going on?" I was standing nearly touching him, spitting each word into his chest, looking up at his face. It is always hard to be tough when you have to look up to see someone's eyes. But I've been short all my life, and practice makes perfect.

His hand slid around my shoulders. I pushed away from him, and his hands locked behind my back. "Phillip, stop it."

I had my hands flat on his chest to keep our bodies from pressing together. His shirt was wet and cold. His heart was hammering in his chest. I swallowed hard and said, "Your shirt's wet."

He released me so suddenly, I stumbled back from him. He drew the shirt over his head in one fluid motion. Of course, he had a lot of practice in undressing himself. It would have been such a nice chest without the scars.

He took one step towards me. "Stop, right where you are," I said. "What is this sudden change of mood?"

"I like you; isn't that enough?"

I shook my head. "No, it isn't."

He dropped the shirt to the floor. I watched it fall like it was important. Two steps and he was beside me. Bathrooms are so small. I did the only thing I could think of—I stepped into the bathtub. Not very dignified in high heels, but I wasn't pressed up against Phillip's chest. Anything was an improvement.

"Somebody is watching us," he said.

I turned, slowly, like a bad horror movie. Twilight hung against the sheer drapes, and a face peered out of the coming dark. It was Harvey, Mr. Leather. The windows were too high for him to be standing on the ground. Was he standing on a box? Or maybe they had little platforms at all the windows, so you could watch the show.

I let Phillip help me out of the bathtub. I whispered, "Could he hear us?"

Phillip shook his head. His arms slid around my back again. "We are supposed to be lovers. Do you want Harvey to stop believing that?"

"This is blackmail."

He smiled, dazzling, hold it in your hand and stroke it, sexy. My stomach tightened. He bent down, and I didn't stop him. The kiss was everything advertised, full soft lips, a press of skin, a heated weight. His hands tightened across my bare back, fingers kneading the muscles along the spine until I relaxed against him.

He kissed the lobe of my ear, breath warm. Tongue flicked along the edge of my jaw. His mouth found the pulse in my throat, his tongue searching for it, as if he were melting through the skin. Teeth scraped over the beating of my neck. Teeth clamped down, tight, hurting.

I shoved him back, away. "Shit! You bit me."

His eyes were unfocused, dazed. A crimson drop stained his lower lip.

I touched a hand to my neck and came away with blood. "Damn you!"

He licked my blood off his mouth. "I think Harvey believes the performance. Now you're marked. You've got the proof of what you are and why you came." He took a deep, shaking breath. "I won't have to touch you again tonight. I'll see that no one else does either. I swear."

My neck was throbbing; a bite, a freaking bite! "Do you know how many germs are in the human mouth?"

He smiled at me, still a little unfocused. "No," he said.

I shoved him out of the way and dabbed water on the cut. It looked like what it was, human teeth. It wasn't a perfect set of bite marks, but it was close. "Damn you."

"We need to go out so you can hunt for clues." He had picked his shirt up from the floor and stood there, holding it at his side. Bare tanned chest, leather pants, lips full like he'd been sucking on something. Me. "You look like an ad for Rent A Gigolo," I said.

He shrugged. "Ready to go out?"

I was still touching the wound. I tried to be angry and couldn't. I was scared. Scared of Phillip and what he was, or wasn't. I hadn't expected it. Was he right? Would I be safe for the rest of the night? Or had he just wanted to see what I tasted like?

He opened the door and waited for me. I went out. As we walked back to the living room, I realized Phillip had distracted me from my question. Who was he working for? I still didn't know.

It was damn embarrassing that every time he took his shirt off, my brain went out to lunch. But no more; I had had my first and last kiss from Phillip of the many scars. From now on I would remain the tough-as-nails vampire slayer, not to be distracted by rippling muscles or nice eyes.

My fingers touched the bite mark. It hurt. No more Ms. Nice Guy. If Phillip came near me again, I was going to hurt him. Of course, knowing Phillip, he'd probably enjoy it.

27

Madge stopped us in the hall. Her hand started to go up to my throat. I grabbed her wrist. "Touchy, touchy," she said. "Didn't you like it? Don't tell me you've been with Phillip a month and he hasn't tasted you before?"

She pulled down the silky bra to expose the upper mound of her breast. There was a perfect set of bite marks in the pale flesh. "It's Phillip's trademark, didn't you know?"

"No," I said. I pushed past her and started to turn into the living room. A man I did not know fell at my feet. Crystal was on top of him, pinning him to the floor. He looked young and a little frightened. His eyes looked up past Crystal, to me. I thought he was going to ask for help, but she kissed him, sloppy and deep, like she was drinking him from the mouth down. His hands began to lift the silk folds of her skirt. Her thighs were incredibly white, like beached whales.

I turned abruptly and went for the door. My heels made an important-sounding clack on the hardwood floor. If I hadn't known better, I would have said it sounded like I was running. I was not running. I was just walking very fast.

Phillip caught up with me at the door. His hand pressed flat against it to keep me from opening it. I took a deep, steadying breath. I would not lose my temper, not yet.

"I'm sorry, Anita, but it's better this way. You're safe now, from the humans."

I looked up at him and shook my head. "You just don't get it. I need some air, Phillip. I'm not leaving for the night, if that's what you're afraid of."

"I'll go out with you."

"No. That would defeat the purpose, Phillip. Since you are one of the things I want to get away from."

He stepped back then, hand at his side. His eyes shut down,

guarded, hiding. Why had that hurt his feelings? I didn't know, and I didn't want to know.

I opened the door, and the heat fell around me like fur.

"It's dark," he said. "They'll be here soon. I can't help you if I'm not with you."

I stepped close to him and said in a near whisper, "Let's be honest, Phillip. I'm a whole lot better at protecting myself than you are. The first vampire that crooks its finger will have you for lunch."

His face started to crumble, and I didn't want to see it. "Dammit, Phillip, pull yourself together." I walked out onto the trellis-covered porch and resisted an urge to slam the door behind me. That would have been childish. I was feeling a little childish about now, but I'd save it. You never know when some childish rage may come in handy.

The cicadas and crickets filled the night. There was a wind pulling at the tops of the tall trees, but it never touched the ground. The air down here was as stale and close as plastic.

The heat felt good after the air-conditioned house. It was real and somehow cleansing. I touched the bite on my neck. I felt dirty, used, abused, angry, pissed off. I wasn't going to find anything out here. If someone or something was killing off vampires who did the freak circuit, it didn't seem to be such a bad idea.

Of course, whether I sympathized with the murderer was not the point. Nikolaos expected me to solve the crimes, and I damn well better do it.

I took a deep breath of the stiff air and felt the first stirrings of . . . power. It oozed through the trees like wind, but the touch of it didn't cool the skin. The hair at the back of my neck was trying to crawl down my spine. Whoever it was, they were powerful. And they were trying to raise the dead.

Despite the heat, we'd had a lot of rain, and my heels sank into the grass immediately. I ended up walking in a sort of tiptoe crouch, trying not to flounder in the soft earth.

The ground was littered with acorns. It was like walking on marbles. I fell against a tree trunk, catching myself painfully against the shoulder Aubrey had bruised so nicely.

A sharp bleating, high and panic-stricken, sounded. It was close. Was it a trick of the still air or was it really a goat bleating? The cry ended in a wet gurgle of sound, thick and bubbling. The trees ended, and the ground was clear and moon-silvered.

I slipped off one shoe and tried the ground. Damp, cool, but not too bad. I slipped off the other shoe, tucked them in one hand, and ran.

The back yard was huge, stretching out into the silvered dark. It spread empty, except for a wall of overgrown hedges, like small trees in the distance. I ran for the hedges. The grave had to be there; there was no other place for it to hide.

The actual ritual for raising the dead is a short one, as rituals go. The power poured out into the night and into the grave. It built in a slow, steady rise, a warm "magic." It tugged at my stomach and brought me to the hedges. They towered up, black in the moonlight, hopelessly overgrown. There was no way I was squeezing through them.

A man cried out. Then a woman: "Where is it? Where is the zombie you promised us?"

"It was too old!" The man's voice was thin with fear.

"You said chickens weren't enough, so we got you a goat to kill. But no zombie. I thought you were good at this."

I found a gate in the opposite side of the hedges. Metal, rusted, and crooked in its frame. It groaned, a metal scream, as I pushed it open. More than a dozen pairs of eyes turned to me. Pale faces, the utter stillness of the undead. Vampires. They stood among the ancient grave markers of the small family cemetery, waiting. Nothing waits as patiently as the dead.

One of the vampires nearest me was the black male from Nikolaos's lair. My pulse quickened, and I did a quick scan of the crowd. She wasn't here. Thank you, God.

The vampire smiled and said, "Did you come to watch . . . animator?" Had he almost said, "Executioner"? Was it a secret?

Whatever, he motioned the others back and let me see the show. Zachary lay on the ground. His shirt was damp with blood. You can't slit anything's throat without getting a little messy. Theresa was standing over him, hands on hips. She was dressed in black. The only skin showing was a strip of flesh down the middle, pale and almost luminous in the starlight. Theresa, Mistress of the Dark.

Her eyes flicked to me, a moment, then back to the man. "Well, Zach-a-ri, where is our zombie?"

He swallowed audibly. "It's too old. There isn't enough left."

"Only a hundred years old, animator. Are you so weak?"

He looked down at the ground. His fingers dug into the soft

earth. He glanced up at me, then quickly down. I didn't know what he was trying to tell me with that one glance. Fear? For me to run? A plea for help? What?

"What good is an animator who can't raise the dead?" Theresa asked. She dropped to her knees, suddenly beside him, hands touching his shoulders. Zachary flinched but didn't try to get away.

A ripple of almost-movement ran through the other vampires. I could feel the whole circle at my back tense. They were going to kill him. The fact that he couldn't raise the zombie was just an excuse, part of the game.

Theresa ripped his shirt down the back. It fluttered around his lower arms, still tucked into his waist. A collective sigh ran through the vampires.

There was a woven rope band around his right upper arm. Beads were worked into it. It was a gris-gris, a voodoo charm, but it wouldn't help him now. No matter what it was supposed to do, it wouldn't be enough.

Theresa did a stage whisper. "Maybe you're just fresh meat?"

The vampires began to move in, silent as wind in the grass.

I couldn't just watch. He was a fellow animator and a human being. I couldn't just let him die, not like this, not in front of me. "Wait," I said.

No one seemed to hear me. The vampires moved in, and I was losing sight of Zachary. If one bit him, the feeding frenzy would be on. I had seen that happen once. I would never get rid of the nightmares if I saw it again.

I raised my voice and hoped they listened. "Wait! Didn't he belong to Nikolaos? Didn't he call Nikolaos master?"

They hesitated, then parted for Theresa to stride through them until she faced me. "This is not your business." She stared at me, and I didn't avoid her gaze. One less thing to worry about.

"I'm making it my business," I said.

"Do you wish to join him?"

The vampires began to spread out from Zachary to encircle me as well. I let them. There wasn't much I could do about it anyway. Either I'd get us both out alive or I'd die, too, maybe, probably. Oh, well.

"I wish to speak with him, one professional to another," I said.

"Why?" she asked.

I stepped close to her, almost touching. Her anger was nearly palpable. I was making her look bad in front of the others, and I knew it, and she knew I knew it. I whispered, though some of the others would hear me, "Nikolaos gave orders for the man to die, but she wants me alive, Theresa. What would she do to you if I accidentally died here tonight?" I breathed the last words into her face. "Do you want to spend eternity locked in a cross-wrapped coffin?"

She snarled and jerked away from me as if I had scalded her. "Damn you, mortal, damn you to hell!" Her black hair crackled around her face, her hands gripped into claws. "Talk to him, for what good it will do you. He must raise this zombie, this zombie, or he is ours. So says Nikolaos."

"If he raises the zombie, then he goes free, unharmed?" I asked.

"Yes, but he cannot do it; he isn't strong enough."

"Which was what Nikolaos was counting on," I said.

Theresa smiled, a fierce tug of lips exposing fangs. "Yesss." She turned her back on me and strode through the other vampires. They parted for her like frightened pigeons. And I was standing up to her. Sometimes bravery and stupidity are almost interchangeable.

I knelt by Zachary. "Are you hurt?"

He shook his head. "I appreciate the gesture, but they're going to try to kill me tonight." He looked up at me, pale eyes searching my face. "There isn't anything you can do to stop them." He gave a thin smile. "Even you have your limits."

"We can raise this zombie if you'll trust me."

He frowned, then stared at me. I couldn't read his expression—puzzlement and something else. "Why?"

What could I say, that I couldn't just watch him die? He had watched a man be tortured and hadn't lifted a hand. I opted for the short reason. "Because I can't let them have you, if I can stop it."

"I don't understand you, Anita, I don't understand you at all."

"That makes two of us. Can you stand?"

He nodded. "What are you planning?"

"We're going to share our talent."

His eyes widened. "Shit, you can act as a focus?"

"I've done it twice before." Twice before with the same person.

Twice before with someone who had trained me as an animator. Never with a stranger.

His voice dropped to a bare whisper. "Are you sure you want to do this?"

"Save you?" I asked.

"Share your power," he said.

Theresa strode over to us in a swish of cloth. "Enough of this, animator. He can't do it, so he pays the price. Either leave now, or join us at our . . . feast."

"Are you having rare Who-roast-beast?" I asked.

"What are you talking about?"

"It's from Dr. Seuss, *How the Grinch Stole Christmas*. You know the part, 'And they'd Feast! Feast! Feast! Feast! They would feast on Who-pudding, and rare Who-roast-beast.' "

"You are crazy."

"So I've been told."

"Do you want to die?" she asked.

I stood up, very slowly, and felt something build in me. A sureness, an absolute certainty that she was not a danger to me. Stupid, but it was there, solid and real. "Someone may kill me before all this is over, Theresa"—I stepped into her, and she gave ground—"but it won't be you."

I could almost taste her pulse in my mouth. Was she afraid of me? Was I going crazy? I had just stood up to a hundred-year-old vampire, and she had backed down. I felt disoriented, almost dizzy, as if reality had moved and no one had warned me.

Theresa turned her back on me, hands balled into fists. "Raise the dead, animators, or by all the blood ever spilled, I'll kill you both."

I think she meant it. I shook myself like a dog coming out of deep water. I had a baker's dozen worth of vampires to pacify and a one-hundred-year-old corpse to raise. I could only handle a zillion problems at a time. A zillion and one was beyond me.

"Get up, Zachary," I said. "Time to go to work."

He stood. "I've never worked with a focus before. You'll have to tell me what to do."

"No problem," I said.

28

The goat lay on its side. The bare white of its spine glimmered in the moonlight. Blood still seeped into the ground from the gaping wound. Eyes were rolled and glazed, tongue lolling out of its mouth.

The older the zombie, the bigger the death needed. I knew that, and that was why I avoided older zombies when I could. At a hundred years the corpse was just so much dust. Maybe a few bone fragments if you were lucky. They re-formed to rise from the grave. If you had the power to do it.

Problem was, most animators couldn't raise the long-dead, a century and over. I could. I just didn't want to. Bert and I had had long discussions about my preferences. The older the zombie, the more we can charge. This was at least a twenty-thousand-dollar job. I doubted I'd get paid tonight, unless living 'til morning was payment enough. Yeah, I guess it was. Here's to seeing another dawn.

Zachary came to stand beside me. He had torn the remnants of his shirt off. He stood thin and pale beside me. His face was all shadows and white flesh, high cheekbones almost cavernous. "What next?" he asked.

The goat carcass was inside the blood circle he had traced earlier; good. "Bring everything we need into the circle."

He brought a long hunting knife and a pint jar full of pale faintly luminous ointment. I preferred a machete myself, but the knife was huge, with one jagged edge and a gleaming point. The knife was clean and sharp. He took good care of his tools. Brownie point for him.

"We can't kill the goat twice," he said. "What are we going to use?"

"Us," I said.

"What are you talking about?"

"We'll cut ourselves; fresh, live blood, as much as we're willing to give."

"The blood loss would leave you too weak to go on."

I shook my head. "We already have a blood circle, Zachary. We're just going to rewalk, not redraw it."

"I don't understand."

"I don't have time to explain metaphysics to you. Every injury is a small death. We'll give the circle a lesser death, and reactivate it."

He shook his head. "I still don't get it."

I took a deep breath, and then realized I couldn't explain it to him. It was like trying to explain the mechanics of breathing. You could break it down into steps, but that didn't tell you what it felt like to breathe. "I'll show you what I mean." If he didn't feel this part of the ritual, understand it without words, the rest wouldn't work anyway.

I held out my hand for the knife. He hesitated, then handed it to me, hilt first. The thing felt top-heavy, but then it wasn't designed for throwing. I took a deep breath and pressed the blade edge against my left arm, just below the cross burn. A quick down stroke, and blood welled up, dark and dripping. It stung, sharp and immediate. I let out the breath I'd been holding and handed the knife to Zachary.

He was staring from me to the knife.

"Do it, right arm, so we'll mirror each other," I said.

He nodded and made a quick slash across his right upper arm. His breath hissed, almost a gasp.

"Kneel with me." I knelt, and he followed me down, mirroring me as I asked. A man who could follow directions; not bad.

I bent my left arm at the elbow and raised it so the fingertips were head-high, elbow shoulder-high. He did the same. "We clasp hands and press the cuts together."

He hesitated, immobile.

"What's the matter?" I asked.

He shook his head, two quick shakes, and his hand wrapped around mine. His arm was longer than mine, but we managed.

His skin felt uncomfortably cool against mine. I glanced up at his face, but I couldn't read it. I had no idea what he was thinking. I took a deep, cleansing breath and began. "We give our blood to the earth. Life for death, death for life. Raise the dead to drink our blood. Let us feed them as they obey us."

His eyes did widen then; he understood. One hurdle down. I stood and drew him with me. I led him along the blood circle. I could feel it, like an electric current up my spine. I stared straight into his eyes. They were almost silver in the moonlight. We walked the circle and ended where we had begun, by the sacrifice.

We sat in the blood-soaked grass. I dabbed my right hand in the still-oozing blood of the goat's wound. I was forced to kneel to reach Zachary's face. I smeared blood over his forehead, down his cheeks. Smooth skin, the rub of new beard. I left a dark handprint over his heart.

The woven band was like a ring of darkness on his arm. I smeared blood along the beads, fingertips finding the soft brush of feathers worked into the string. The gris-gris needed blood, I could feel that, but not goat blood. I shrugged it away. Time to worry about Zachary's personal magic later.

He smeared blood on my face. Fingertips only, as if afraid to touch me. I could feel his hand shake as he traced my cheek. The blood was a cool wetness over my breast. Heart blood.

Zachary unscrewed the jar of homemade ointment. It was a pale off-white color with flecks of greenish light in it. The glowing flecks were graveyard mold.

I rubbed ointment over the blood smears. The skin soaked it up.

He brushed the cream on my face. It felt waxy, thick. I could smell the pine scent of rosemary for memory, cinnamon and cloves for preservation, sage for wisdom, and some sharp herb, maybe thyme, to bind it all together. There was too much cinnamon in it. The night suddenly smelled like apple pie.

We went together to smear ointment and blood on the tombstone. The name was only soft grooves in the marble. I traced them with my fingertips. Estelle Hewitt. Born 18 something, died 1866. There had been more writing below the date and name, but it was gone, beyond reading. Who had she been? I had never raised a zombie that I knew nothing about. It wasn't always a good idea, but then this whole thing wasn't a good idea.

Zachary stood at the foot of the grave. I stayed by the tombstone. It felt like an invisible cord was stretched between Zachary and me. We started the chant together, no questions needed. "Hear us, Estelle Hewitt. We call you from the grave. By blood, magic, and steel, we call you. Arise, Estelle, come to us, come to us."

His eyes met mine, and I felt a tug along the invisible line that bound us. He was powerful. Why hadn't he been able to do it alone?

"Estelle, Estelle, come to us. Waken, Estelle, arise and come to us." We called her name in ever-rising voices.

The earth shuddered. The goat slid to one side as the ground erupted, and a hand clutched for air. A second hand grabbed at nothing, and the earth began to pour the dead woman out.

It was then, only then, that I realized what was wrong, why he hadn't been able to raise her on his own. I now knew where I had seen him before. I had been at his funeral. There were so few animators that if anyone died, you went, period. Professional courtesy. I had glimpsed that angular face, rouged and painted. Somebody had done a bad job of making him up, I remembered thinking that at the time.

The zombie had almost pulled itself from the grave. It sat panting, legs still trapped in the ground.

Zachary and I stared at each other over the grave. All I could do was stare at him like an idiot. He was dead, but not a zombie, not anything I'd ever heard of. I would have bet my life he was human, and I may have done just that.

The woven band on his arm. The spell that hadn't been satisfied with goat's blood. What was he doing to stay "alive"?

I had heard rumors of gris-gris that could cheat death. Rumors, legends, fairy tales. But then again, maybe not.

Estelle Hewitt may have been pretty once, but a hundred years in the grave takes a lot out of a person. Her skin was an ugly greyish white, waxy, nearly expressionless, fake-looking. White gloves hid the hands, stained with grave dirt. The dress was white and lace-covered. I was betting on wedding finery. Dear God.

Black hair clung to her head in a bun, wisps of it tracing her nearly skeletal face. All the bones showed, as if the skin were clay molded over a framework. Her eyes were wild, dark, showing too much white. At least they hadn't dried out like shriveled grapes. I hated that.

Estelle sat by her grave and tried to gather her thoughts. It would take a while. Even the recently dead took a few minutes to orient themselves. A hundred years was a damn long time to be dead.

I walked around the grave, careful to stay within the circle. Zachary watched me come without a word. He hadn't been able to raise the corpse because he was a corpse. The recently dead he could still handle, but not long-dead. The dead calling the dead from the grave; there was something really wrong with that.

I stared up at him, watching him grip the knife. I knew his secret. Did Nikolaos? Did anyone? Yes, whoever had made the gris-gris knew, but who else? I squeezed the skin around the cut on my arm. I reached bloody fingers towards the gris-gris.

He caught my wrist, eyes wide. His breathing had quickened. "Not you."

"Then who?"

"People who won't be missed."

The zombie we had raised moved in a rustle of petticoats and hoops. It began crawling towards us.

"I should have let them kill you," I said.

He smiled then. "Can you kill the dead?"

I jerked my wrist free. "I do it all the time."

The zombie was scrambling at my legs. It felt like sticks digging at me. "Feed it yourself, you son of a bitch," I said.

He held his wrist down to it. The zombie grabbed for it, clumsy, eager. It sniffed his skin but released him untouched. "I don't think I can feed it, Anita."

Of course not; fresh, live blood was needed to close the ritual. Zachary was dead. He didn't qualify anymore. But I did.

"Damn you, Zachary, damn you."

He just stared at me.

The zombie was making a mewling sound low in her throat. Dear God. I offered her my bleeding left arm. Her stick-hands dug into my skin. Her mouth fastened over the wound, sucking. I fought the urge to jerk away. I had made the bargain, had chosen the ritual. I had no choice. I stared at Zachary while the thing fed on my blood. Our zombie, a joint venture. Dammit.

"How many people have you killed to keep yourself alive?" I asked.

"You don't want to know."

"How many!"

"Enough," he said.

I tensed, raising my arm, nearly lifting the zombie to her feet. She cried, a soft sound, like a newborn kitten. She released my arm so suddenly, she fell backwards. Blood dripped down her bony chin. Her teeth were stained with it. I couldn't look at it, any of it.

Zachary said, "The circle is open. The zombie is yours."

For a minute I thought he was talking to me; then I remembered the vampires. They had been huddled in the dark, so still and unmoving I had forgotten them. I was the only live thing in the whole damn place. I had to get out of there.

I picked up my shoes and walked out of the circle. The vampires made way for me. Theresa stopped me, blocking my path. "Why did you let it suck your blood? Zombies don't do that."

I shook my head. Why did I think it would be faster to explain than to fight about it? "The ritual had already gone wrong. We couldn't start over without another sacrifice. So I offered myself as the sacrifice."

She stared. "Yourself?"

"It was the best I could do, Theresa. Now get out of my way." I was tired and sick. I had to get out of there, now. Maybe she heard it in my voice. Maybe she was too eager to get to the zombie to mess with me. I don't know, but she moved aside. She was just gone, like the wind had swept her away. Let them play their mind games. I was going home.

There was a small scream from behind me. A short, strangled sound, as if the voice wasn't used to talking. I kept walking. The zombie screamed, human memories still there, enough for fear. I heard a rich laugh, a faint echo of Jean-Claude's. Where are you, Jean-Claude?

I glanced back once. The vampires were closing in. The zombie was stumbling from one side to the other, trying to run. But there was nowhere to go.

I stumbled through the crooked gate. A wind had finally come down out of the trees. Another scream sounded from behind the hedges. I ran, and I didn't look back.

29

I slipped on the damp grass. Hose are not made for running in.
I sat there, breathing, trying not to think. I had raised a zombie
to save another human being, who wasn't a human being. Now
the zombie I had raised was being tortured by vampires. Shit. The
night wasn't even half-over. I whispered, "What next?"

A voice answered, light as music. "Greetings, animator. You
seem to be having a full night."

Nikolaos was standing in the shadows of the trees. Willie
McCoy was with her, a little to one side, not quite beside her,
like a bodyguard or a servant. I was betting on servant.

"You seem agitated. What ever is the matter?" Her voice rose
in a lilting sing-song. The dangerous little girl had returned.

"Zachary raised the zombie. You can't use that as an excuse
to kill him." I laughed then, and it sounded abrupt and harsh
even to me. He was already dead. I didn't think she knew.
She couldn't read minds, only force the truth from them. I bet
Nikolaos had never thought to ask, "Are you alive, Zachary, or
a walking corpse?" I laughed and couldn't seem to stop.

"Anita, you all right?" Willie's voice was like his voice had
always been.

I nodded, trying to catch my breath. "I'm fine."

"I do not see the humor in the situation, animator." The
child voice was slipping, like a mask sliding down. "You
helped Zachary raise the zombie." She made it sound like an
accusation.

"Yes."

I heard movement over the grass. Willie's footsteps, and nothing else. I glanced up and saw Nikolaos moving towards me,
noiseless as a cat. She was smiling, a cute, harmless, model, beautiful child. No. Her face was a little long. The perfect child bride
wasn't perfect anymore. The closer she came, the more flaws

I could pick out. Was I seeing her the way she really looked? Was I?

"You are staring at me, animator." She laughed, high and wild, wind chimes in a storm. "As if you'd seen a ghost." She knelt, smoothing her slacks over her knees, as if they were a skirt. "Have you seen a ghost, animator? Have you seen something that frightened you? Or is it something else?" Her face was only an arm's length away.

I was holding my breath, fingers digging into the ground. Fear washed over me like a cool second skin. The face was so pleasant, smiling, encouraging. She really needed a dimple to go with it all. My voice was hoarse, and I had to cough to clear it. "I raised the zombie. I don't want it hurt."

"But it is only a zombie, animator. They have no real minds."

I just stared at that thin, pleasant face, afraid to look away from her, afraid to look at her. My chest was tight with the urge to run. "It was a human being. I don't want it tortured."

"They won't hurt it much. My little vampires will be disappointed. The dead cannot feed off the dead."

"Ghouls can. They feed off the dead."

"But what is a ghoul, animator? Is it truly dead?"

"Yes."

"Am I dead?" she asked.

"Yes."

"Are you sure?" She had a small scar near her upper lip. She must have gotten it before she died.

"I'm sure," I said.

She laughed then, a sound to bring a smile to your face and a song to your heart. My stomach jerked at the noise. I might never enjoy Shirley Temple movies again.

"I don't think you are sure in the least." She stood, one smooth motion. A thousand years of practice makes perfect.

"I want the zombie put back, now, tonight," I said.

"You are not in a position to want anything." The voice was cold, very adult. Children didn't know how to strip skin with their voice.

"I raised it. I don't want it tortured."

"Isn't that too bad?"

What else could I say? "Please."

She stared down at me. "Why is it so important to you?"

I didn't think I could explain it to her. "It just is."

"How important?" she asked.

"I don't know what you mean."

"What would you be willing to endure for your zombie?"

Fear settled into a cold lump in the pit of my gut. "I don't know what you mean."

"Yes, you do," she said.

I stood then, not that it would help. I was actually taller than she was. She was tiny, a delicate fairy of a child. Right. "What do you want?"

"Don't do it, Anita." Willie was standing away from us, as if afraid to come too close. He was smarter dead than he had been alive.

"Quiet, Willie." Her voice was conversational when she said it, no yelling, no threat. But Willie fell silent instantly, like a well-trained dog.

Maybe she caught my look. Whatever, she said, "I had Willie punished for failing to hire you that first time."

"Punished?"

"Surely, Phillip has told you about our methods?"

I nodded. "A cross-wrapped coffin."

She smiled, brilliant, cheery. The shadows leeched it into a leer. "Willie was very afraid that I would leave him in there for months, or even years."

"Vampires can't starve to death. I understand the principle." I added silently in my head: You bitch. I can only be terrified so long before I get angry. Anger feels better.

"You smell of fresh blood. Let me taste you, and I will see your zombie safe."

"Does taste mean bite?" I asked.

She laughed, sweet, heartrending. Bitch. "Yes, human, it means bite." She was suddenly beside me. I jerked back without thinking. She laughed again. "It seems Phillip has beaten me to it."

For a minute I couldn't think what she meant; then my hand went to the bite mark on my neck. I felt suddenly uneasy, like she'd caught me naked.

The laugh floated on the summer air. It was really beginning to get on my nerves.

"No tasting," I said.

"Then let me enter your mind again. That's a type of feeding."

I shook my head, too rapid, too many times. I'd die before I'd let her in my mind again. If I had the choice.

A scream sounded in the not so far distance. Estelle was finding her voice. I winced like I'd been slapped.

"Let me taste your blood, animator. No teeth." She flashed fang as she said the last. "You stand and make no move to stop me. I will taste the fresh wound on your neck. I won't feed on you."

"It's not bleeding anymore. It's clotted."

She smiled, oh so sweetly. "I'll lick it clean."

I swallowed hard. I didn't know if I could do it. Another scream sounded, high and lost. God.

Willie said, "Anita . . ."

"Silence, or risk my anger." Her voice growled low and dark.

Willie seemed to shrink in upon himself. His face was a white triangle under his black hair.

"It's all right, Willie. Don't get hurt on my account," I said.

He stared at me across the distance, a few yards; it might as well have been miles. Only the lost look on his face helped. Poor Willie. Poor me.

"What good is it going to do you if you're not feeding off me?" I asked.

"No good at all." She reached a small, pale hand towards me. "Of course, fear is a kind of substance." Cool fingers slid around my wrist. I flinched but didn't pull back. I was going to let her do this, wasn't I?

"Call it shadow feeding, human. Blood and fear are always precious, no matter how one obtains them." She stepped up to me. She exhaled against my skin, and I backed away. Only her hand on my wrist kept me close.

"Wait. I want the zombie freed now, first."

She just stared at me, then nodded slowly. "Very well." She stared past me, pale eyes seeing things that weren't there or that I couldn't see. I felt a tension through her hand, almost a jerk of electricity. "Theresa will chase them off and have the animator lay the zombie to rest."

"You did all that, just then?"

"Theresa is mine to command; didn't you know that?"

"Yeah, I guessed that." I had not known that any vampire could do telepathy. Of course, before last night I hadn't thought they could fly either. Oh, I was just learning all sorts of new things.

"How do I know you're not just telling me that?" I asked.

"You will just have to trust me."

Now that was almost funny. If she had a sense of humor, maybe we could work something out. Naw.

She pulled my wrist closer to her body and me with it. Her hand was like fleshy steel. I couldn't pry her hand off, not with anything short of a blowtorch. And I was all out of blowtorches.

The top of her head fitted under my chin. She had to rise on tiptoe to breathe on my neck. It should have ruined the menace. It didn't. Soft lips touched my neck. I jerked. She laughed against my skin, face pressed against me. I shivered and couldn't stop.

"I promise to be gentle." She laughed again, and I fought an urge to shove her away. I would have given almost anything to hit her, just once, hard. But I didn't want to die tonight. Besides, I'd made a deal.

"Poor darling, you're shaking." She laid a hand on my shoulder to steady herself. She brushed lips along the hollow of my neck. "Are you cold?"

"Cut the crap. Just do it!"

She stiffened against me. "Don't you want me to touch you?"

"No," I said. Was she crazy? Rhetorical question.

Her voice was very still. "Where is the scar on my face?"

I answered without thinking. "Near your mouth."

"And how," she hissed, "did you know that?"

My heart leaped into my throat. Oops. I had let her know her mind tricks weren't working, and they should have been.

Her hand dug into my shoulder. I made a small sound, but I didn't cry out. "What have you been doing, animator?"

I didn't have the faintest idea. Somehow, I doubted she'd believe that.

"Leave her alone!" Phillip came half-running through the trees. "You promised me you wouldn't hurt her tonight."

Nikolaos didn't even turn around. "Willie." Just his name, but like all good servants he knew what was wanted.

He stepped in front of Phillip, one arm straight out from his body. He was going to stiff-arm him. Phillip sidestepped the arm, brushing past.

Willie never had been much of a fighter. Strength wasn't enough if you had shit for balance.

Nikolaos touched my chin and turned my face back to hers. "Do not force me to hold your attention, animator. You wouldn't like the methods I would choose."

I swallowed audibly. She was probably right. "You have my full attention, honest." My voice came out as a hoarse whisper, fear squeezing it down. If I coughed to clear it, I'd cough in her face. Not a good idea.

I heard the rush of feet swishing through the grass. I fought the urge to look up and away from the vampire.

Nikolaos spun from me to face the footsteps. I saw her move, but it was still blurring speed. She was just suddenly facing the other way. Phillip was standing in front of her. Willie caught up to him and grabbed an arm, but didn't seem to know what to do with it.

Would it occur to Willie that he could just crush the man's arm? I doubted it.

It had occurred to Nikolaos. "Release him. If he wants to keep coming, let him." Her voice promised a great deal of pain.

Willie stepped back. Phillip just stood there, staring past her at me. "Are you all right, Anita?"

"Go back inside, Phillip. I appreciate the concern, but I made a bargain. She isn't going to bite me."

He shook his head. "You promised she wouldn't be harmed. You promised." He was talking to Nikolaos again, carefully not looking directly at her.

"And so she shall not be harmed. I keep my word, Phillip, most of the time."

"I'm all right, Phillip. Don't get hurt because of me," I said.

His face crumbled with confusion. He didn't seem to know what to do. His courage seemed to have spilled out on the grass. But he didn't back off. Big point for him. I would have backed off, maybe. Probably. Oh, hell, Phillip was being brave, and I didn't want to see him die because of it.

"Just go back, Phillip, please!"

"No," Nikolaos said. "If the little man is feeling brave, let him try."

Phillip's hands flexed, as if trying to grab on to something.

Nikolaos was suddenly beside him. I hadn't seen her move. Phillip still hadn't. He was staring where she had been. She kicked his legs out from under him. He fell to the grass, blinking up at her like she'd just appeared.

"Don't hurt him!" I said.

A pale little hand shot out, the barest touch. His whole body jerked backwards. He rolled on one side, blood staining his face.

"Nikolaos, please!" I said. I had actually taken two steps towards her. Voluntarily. I could always try for my gun. It wouldn't kill her, but it might give Phillip time to run away. If he would run.

Screams sounded from the direction of the house. A man's voice yelled, "Perverts!"

"What is it?" I asked.

Nikolaos answered, "The Church of Eternal Life has sent its congregation." She sounded mildly amused. "I must leave this little get-together." She whirled to me, leaving Phillip dazed on the grass. "How did you see my scar?" she asked.

"I don't know."

"Little liar. We will finish this later." And she was gone, running like a pale shadow under the trees. At least she hadn't flown away. I didn't think my wits could handle that tonight.

I knelt by Phillip. He was bleeding where she had hit him. "Can you hear me?"

"Yes." He managed to sit up. "We have to get out of here. The churchgoers are always armed."

I helped him to stand. "Do they invade the freak parties often?"

"Whenever they can," he said.

He seemed steady on his feet. Good, I could never have carried him far.

Willie said, "I know I don't have a right to ask, but I'll help you get to your car." He wiped his hands down his pants. "Can I catch a ride?"

I couldn't help it. I laughed. "Can't you just disappear like the rest of them?"

He shrugged. "Don't know how yet."

"Oh, Willie." I sighed. "Come on, let's get out of here."

He grinned at me. Being able to look him in the eyes made him seem almost human. Phillip didn't object to the vampire joining us. Why had I thought he would?

There were screams from the house. "Somebody's gonna call the cops," Willie said.

He was right. I'd never be able to explain it. I grabbed Phillip's hand and steadied myself while I put the high heels back on. "If I'd known we'd be running from crazed fanatics tonight, I'd have worn lower heels," I said.

I kept a grip on Phillip's arm to steady myself through the mine-field of acorns. This was not the time to twist an ankle.

We were almost to the gravel drive when three figures spilled out of the house. One held a club. The others were vampires. They didn't need a weapon. I opened my purse and got my gun out, held down at my side, hidden against my skirt. I gave Phillip the car keys. "Start the car; I'll cover our backs."

"I don't know how to drive," he said.

I had forgotten. "Shit!"

"I'll do it." Willie took the keys, and I let him.

One of the vampires rushed us, arms wide, hissing. Maybe he meant to scare us; maybe he meant to do us harm. I'd had enough for one night. I clicked off the safety, chambered a round and fired into the ground at his feet.

He hesitated, almost stumbled. "Bullets can't hurt me, human."

There was more movement under the trees. I didn't know if it was friend or foe, or if it made a hell of a lot of difference. The vampire kept coming. It was a residential neighborhood. Bullets can travel a great distance before they hit something. I couldn't take the chance.

I raised my arm, aimed, and fired. The bullet took him in the stomach. He jerked and sort of crumpled over the wound. His face held astonishment.

"Silver-plated bullets, fang-face."

Willie went for the car. Phillip hesitated between helping me and going.

"Go, Phillip, now."

The second vampire was trying to circle around. "Stop right where you are," I said. The vampire froze. "Anybody makes a threatening gesture, I'm going to put a bullet in their brain."

"It won't kill us," the second vampire said.

"No, but it won't do you a hell of a lot of good, either."

The human with the club inched forward. "Don't," I told him.

The car started. I didn't dare glance back at it. I stepped backwards, hoping I wouldn't trip in the damn high heels. If I fell, they'd rush me. If they rushed me, somebody was going to die.

"Come on, Anita, get in." It was Phillip, leaning out of the passenger side door.

"Scoot over." He did, and I slid into the seat. The human rushed us. "Drive, now!"

Willie spun gravel, and I slammed the door shut. I really didn't want to kill anyone tonight. The human was shielding his face from the gravel as we rushed down the driveway.

The car bounced wildly, nearly colliding with a tree. "Slow down; we're safe," I said.

Willie eased back on the gas. He grinned at me. "We made it."

"Yeah." I smiled back at him, but I wasn't so sure.

Blood was dripping down Phillip's face in a nice steady flow. He voiced my thoughts. "Safe, but for how long?" He sounded as tired as I felt.

I patted his arm. "Everything will be all right, Phillip."

He looked at me. His face seemed older than it had, tired. "You don't believe that any more than I do."

What could I say? He was right.

clicked on the safety of my gun and struggled into a seat belt.
Phillip slumped down into the seat, long legs spreadeagled on
either side of the floorboard hump. His eyes were closed.

"Where to?" Willie asked.

Good question. I wanted to go home and go to sleep, but . . .
"Phillip's face needs patching up."

"You wanna take him to a hospital?"

"I'm all right," Phillip said. His voice was low and strange.

"You aren't all right," I said.

He opened his eyes and turned to look at me. The blood had
run down his neck, a dark, glistening stream that shone in the
flashes of the streetlights. "You were hurt a lot worse last night,"
he said.

I looked away from him, out the window. I didn't know what
to say. "I'm all right now."

"I'll be all right, too."

I looked back at him. He was staring at me. I couldn't read the
expression on his face, and wanted to. "What are you thinking,
Phillip?"

He turned his head to stare straight ahead. His face was all sil-
houette and shadows. "That I stood up to the master. I did it. I did
it!" His voice held a fierce warmth with the last. Fierce pride.

"You were very brave," I said.

"I was, wasn't I?"

I smiled and nodded. "Yes."

"I hate ta interrupt you two, but I need ta know where to drive
this thing," Willie said.

"Drop me back at Guilty Pleasures," Phillip said.

"You should see a doc."

"They'll take care of me at the club."

"Ya sure?"

He nodded, then winced and turned to me. "You wanted to know who was giving me orders. It was Nikolaos. You were right. That first day. She wanted me to seduce you." He smiled. It didn't look right with the blood. "Guess I wasn't up to the job."

"Phillip . . ." I said.

"No, it's all right. You were right about me. I'm sick. No wonder you didn't want me."

I glanced over at Willie. He was concentrating on his driving as if his life depended on it. Damn, he was smarter dead than alive.

I took a deep breath and tried to decide what to say. "Phillip . . . The kiss before you . . . bit me." God, how did I say this? "It was nice."

He glanced at me, quick, then away. "You mean that?"

"Yes."

An awkward silence stretched through the car. No sound but the rush of pavement under the wheels. The night flashes of lights and the isolating darkness.

"Standing up to Nikolaos tonight was one of the bravest things I've ever seen anybody do. Also one of the stupidest," I said.

He laughed, abrupt and surprised.

"Don't ever do it again. I don't want your death on my hands."

"It was my choice," he said.

"No more heroics, okay?"

He glanced at me. "Would you be sorry if I died?"

"Yes."

"I guess that's something."

What did he want me to say? To confess undying love, or something silly like that? How about undying lust? Either one would be a lie. What did he want from me? I almost asked him, but I didn't. I wasn't that brave.

31

It was nearly three by the time I walked up the stairs to my apartment. All the bruises were aching. My knees, feet, and lower back were a nearly burning grind of pain from the high heels. I wanted a long, hot shower and bed. Maybe if I were lucky I could actually get eight uninterrupted hours of sleep. Of course, I wouldn't bet on it.

I got my keys in one hand and gun in the other. I held the gun at my side, just in case a neighbor should open his or her door unexpectedly. Nothing to fear, folks, just your friendly neighborhood animator. Right.

For the first time in far too long my door was just the way I left it: locked. Thank you, God. I was not in the mood to play cops and robbers this very early morning.

I kicked off my shoes just inside the door, then stumbled to the bedroom. The message light was blinking on my answering machine. I laid my gun on the bed, hit the play button, and started undressing.

"Hi, Anita, this is Ronnie. I got a meeting set up for tomorrow with the guy from HAV. My office, eleven o'clock. If the time is bad, leave a message on my machine, and I'll get back to you. Be careful."

Click, whirr, and Edward's voice came out of the machine. "The clock is ticking, Anita." Click.

Damn. "You like your little games, don't you, you son of a bitch?" I was getting grumpy, and I didn't know what I was going to do about Edward. Or Nikolaos, or Zachary, or Valentine, or Aubrey. I did know I wanted a shower. I could start there. Maybe I'd have a brilliant idea while I was scrubbing goat blood off my skin.

I locked the door to the bathroom and laid my gun on the top of the toilet. I was beginning to get a little paranoid. Or maybe realistic was a better word.

I turned the water on until it steamed, then stepped into it. I was no closer to solving the vampire murders now than I had been twenty-four hours ago.

Even if I solved the case, I still had problems. Aubrey and Valentine were going to kill me once Nikolaos removed her protection from me. Peachy. I wasn't even sure that Nikolaos herself didn't have ideas in that direction. Now, Zachary, he was killing people to feed his voodoo charm. I had heard of charms that demanded human sacrifice. Charms that gave you a whole lot less than immortality. Wealth, power, sex—the age-old wants. It was very specific blood—children, or virgins, or preadolescent boys, or little old ladies with blue hair and one wooden leg. All right, not that specific, but there had to be a pattern to it. A string of disappearances with similar victims. If Zachary had been simply leaving the bodies to be found, the newspapers would have picked up on it by now. Maybe.

He had to be stopped. If I hadn't interfered tonight, he would have been stopped. No good deed goes unpunished.

I leaned palms against the bathroom tile, letting the water wash down my back in nearly scalding rivulets. Okay, I had to kill Valentine before he killed me. I had a warrant for his death. It had never been revoked. Of course, I had to find him first.

Aubrey was dangerous, but at least he was out of the way until Nikolaos let him out of his trapped coffin.

I could just turn Zachary over to the police. Dolph would listen to me, but I didn't have a shred of proof. Hell, the magic was even something I'd never heard of. If I couldn't understand what Zachary was, how was I going to explain it to the police?

Nikolaos. Would she let me live if I solved the case? Or not? I didn't know.

Edward was coming to get me tomorrow evening. I either gave him Nikolaos or he took a piece of my hide. Knowing Edward, it would be a painful piece to lose. Maybe I could just give him the vampire. Just tell him what he wanted to know. And he fails to kill her, and she comes and gets me. The one thing I wanted to avoid, almost more than anything else, was Nikolaos coming to get me.

I dried off, ran a brush through my hair, and had to get something to eat. I tried to tell myself I was too tired to eat. My stomach didn't believe me.

It was four before I fell into bed. My cross was safely around my neck. The gun in its holster behind the head board. And, just for pure panic's sake, I slipped a knife between the mattress and box springs. I'd never get to it in time to do any good, but . . . Well, you never know.

I dreamed about Jean-Claude again. He was sitting at a table eating blackberries.

"Vampires don't eat solid food," I said.

"Exactly." He smiled and pushed the bowl of fruit towards me.

"I hate blackberries," I said.

"They were always my favorite. I hadn't tasted them in centuries." His face looked wistful.

I picked up the bowl. It was cool, almost cold. The blackberries were floating in blood. The bowl fell from my hands, slow, spilling blood on the table, more than it could ever have held. Blood dripped down the tabletop, onto the floor.

Jean-Claude stared at me over the bleeding table. His words came like a warm wind. "Nikolaos will kill us both. We must strike first, ma petite."

"What's this 'we' crap?"

He cupped pale hands in the flowing blood and held them out to me, like a cup. Blood dripped out from between his fingers. "Drink. It will make you strong."

I woke staring up into the darkness. "Damn you, Jean-Claude," I whispered. "What have you done to me?"

There was no answer from the dark, empty room. Thank goodness for small favors. The clock read six-oh-three a.m. I rolled over and snuggled back into the covers. The whir of air conditioning couldn't hide the sounds of one of my neighbors running water. I switched on the radio. Mozart's piano concerto in E flat filled the darkened room. It was really too lively to sleep to, but I wanted noise. My choice of noise.

I don't know if it was Mozart or I was just too tired; whatever, I went back to sleep. If I dreamed, I didn't remember it.

32

The alarm shrieked through my sleep. It sounded like a car alarm, hideously loud. I smashed my palm on the buttons. Mercifully, it shut off. I blinked at the clock through half-slit eyes. Nine a.m. Damn. I had forgotten to unset the alarm. I had time to get dressed and make church. I did not want to get up. I did not want to go to church. Surely, God would forgive me just this once.

Of course, I did need all the help I could get right now. Maybe I'd even have a revelation, and everything would fall into place. Don't laugh; it had happened before. Divine aid is not something I rely on, but every once in a while I think better at church.

When the world is full of vampires and bad guys, and a blessed cross may be all that stands between you and death, it puts church in a different light. So to speak.

I crawled out of bed, groaning. The phone rang. I sat on the edge of the bed, waiting for the answering machine to pick up. It did. "Anita, this is Sergeant Storr. We got another vampire murder."

I picked up the receiver. "Hi, Dolph."

"Good. Glad I caught you before church."

"Is it another dead vampire?"

"Mmhuh."

"Just like the others?" I asked.

"Seems to be. Need you to come down and take a look."

I nodded, realized he couldn't see it, and said, "Sure, when?"

"Right now."

I sighed. So much for church. They couldn't hold the body until noon, or after, just for little ol' me. "Give me the location. Wait, let me get a pen that works." I kept a notepad by the bed, but the pen had died without my knowing it. "Okay, shoot."

The location was only about a block from Circus of the Damned. "That's on the fringe of the District. None of the other murders have been that far away from the Riverfront."

"True," he said.

"What else is different about this one?"

"You'll see it when you get here."

Mr. Information. "Fine, I'll be there in half an hour."

"See you then." The phone went dead.

"Well, good morning to you to, Dolph," I said to the receiver. Maybe he wasn't a morning person either.

My hands were healing. I had taken the Band-Aids off last night because they were covered with goat blood. The scrapes were scabbing nicely, so I didn't bother with more Band-Aids.

One fat bandage covered the knife wound on my arm. I couldn't hurt my left arm anymore. I had run out of room. The bite mark on my neck was beginning to bruise. It looked like the world's worst hicky. If Zerbrowski saw it, I would never live it down. I put a Band-Aid on it. Now it looked like I was covering a vampire bite. Damn. I left it. Let people wonder. None of their business anyway.

I put a red polo shirt on, tucked into jeans. My Nikes, and a shoulder harness for my gun, and I was all set. My shoulder rig has a little pouch for extra ammo. I put fresh clips in it. Twenty-six bullets. Watch out, bad guys. Truth was, most firefights were finished before the first eight shots were gone. But there was always a first time.

I carried a bright yellow windbreaker over my arm. I'd put it on just in case the gun started making people nervous. I would be working with the police. They'd have their guns out in plain sight. Why couldn't I? Besides, I was tired of games. Let the bastards know I was armed and willing.

There are always too many people at a murder scene. Not the gawkers, the people who come to watch; you expect that. There is always something fascinating about someone else's death. But the place always swarms with police, mostly detectives with a sprinkling of uniforms. So many cops for one little murder.

There was even a news van, with a huge satellite antenna sticking out of its back like a giant ray gun from some 1940s science fiction movie. There would be more news vans, I was betting on that. I don't know how the police kept it quiet this long.

Vampire murders, gee whiz, sensationalism at its best. You don't even have to add anything to make it bizarre.

I kept the crowd between myself and the cameraman. A reporter with short blond hair and a stylish business suit was shoving a microphone in Dolph's face. As long as I stayed near the gruesome remains, I was safe. They might get me on film, but they wouldn't be able to show it on television. Good taste and all, you know.

I had a little plastic-enclosed card, complete with picture, that gave me access to police areas. I always felt like a junior G-man when I clipped it to my collar.

I was stopped at the yellow police banner by a vigilant uniform. He stared at my I. D. for several seconds, as if trying to decide whether I was kosher or not. Would he let me through the line, or would he call a detective over first?

I stood, hands at my sides, trying to look harmless. I'm actually very good at that. I can look downright cute. The uniform raised the tape and let me through. I resisted an urge to say, "Atta boy." I did say, "Thank you."

The body lay near a lamp pole. Legs were spreadeagled. One arm twisted under the body, probably broken. The center of the back was missing, as if someone had shoved a hand through the body and just scooped out the center. The heart would be gone, just like all the others.

Detective Clive Perry was standing by the body. He was a tall, slender, black man, and most recent member of the spook squad. He always seemed so soft-spoken and pleasant. I could never imagine Perry doing anything rude enough to piss someone off, but you didn't get assigned to the squad without a reason.

He looked up from his notebook. "Hi, Ms. Blake."

"Hello, Detective Perry."

He smiled. "Sergeant Storr said you'd be coming down."

"Is everyone else finished with the body?"

He nodded. "It's all yours."

A dark brown puddle of blood spread out from under the body. I knelt beside it. The blood had congealed to a tacky, gluelike consistency. Rigor mortis had come and gone, if there had been rigor mortis. Vampires didn't always react to "death" the way a human body did. It made judging the time of death harder. But that was the coroner's job, not mine.

The bright summer sun pressed down over the body. From the shape and the black pants suit, I was betting it was female. It was sort of hard to tell, lying on its stomach, chest caved in, and the head missing. The spine showed white and glistening. Blood had poured out of the neck like a broken bottle of red wine. The skin was torn, twisted. It looked like somebody had ripped the freaking head off.

I swallowed very hard. I hadn't thrown up on a murder victim in months. I stood up and put a little distance between myself and the body.

Could this have been done by a human being? No; maybe. Hell. If it was a human being, then they were trying very hard to make it look otherwise. No matter what a surface look revealed, the coroner always found knife marks on the body. The question was, did the knife marks come before or after death? Was it a human trying to look like a monster, or a monster trying to look like a human?

"Where's the head?" I asked.

"You sure you feel all right?"

I looked up at him. Did I look pale? "I'll be fine." Me, big, tough vampire slayer, no throw up at the sight of decapitated heads. Right.

Perry raised his eyebrows but was too polite to push the issue. He led me about eight feet down the sidewalk. Someone had thrown a plastic cover over the head. A second smaller pool of congealing blood oozed out from under the plastic.

Perry bent over and grasped the plastic. "You ready?"

I nodded, not trusting my voice. He lifted the plastic, like a curtain backdrop to what lay on the sidewalk.

Long, black hair flowed around a pale face. The hair was matted and sticky with blood. The face had been attractive but no more. The features were slack, almost doll-like in their unreality. My eyes saw it, but it took my brain a few seconds to register. "Shit!"

"What is it?"

I stood up, fast, and took two steps out into the street. Perry came to stand beside me. "Are you all right?"

I glanced back at the plastic with its grisly little lump. Was I all right? Good question. I could identify this body.

It was Theresa.

33

I arrived at Ronnie's office a few minutes before eleven. I paused with my hand on the doorknob. I couldn't shake the image of Theresa's head on the sidewalk. She had been cruel and had probably killed hundreds of humans. Why did I feel pity for her? Stupidity, I suppose. I took a deep breath and pushed the door inward.

Ronnie's office is full of windows. Light glares in from two sides, south and west. Which means in the afternoon the room is like a solar heater. No amount of air conditioning is going to overcome that much sunshine.

You can see the District from Ronnie's sunshiny windows. If you care to look.

Ronnie waved me through the door into the almost blinding glare of her office.

A delicate-looking woman was sitting in a chair across from the desk. She was Asian with shiny, black hair styled carefully back from her face. A royal purple jacket, which matched her tailored skirt, was folded neatly on the chair arm. A shiny, lavender blouse brought attention to the up-tilted eyes and the faint lavender shading on the lids and brow. Her ankles were crossed, hands folded in her lap. She looked cool in her lavender blouse, even in the sweltering sunshine.

It caught me off guard for a minute, seeing her like that, after all these years. Finally, I closed my gaping mouth and walked forward, hand extended. "Beverly, it has been a long time."

She stood neatly and put a cool hand in mine. "Three years." Precise, that was Beverly all over.

"You two know each other?" Ronnie asked.

I turned back to her. "Bev didn't mention that she knew me?" Ronnie shook her head.

I stared at the new woman. "Why didn't you mention it to Ronnie?"

"I did not think it necessary." Bev had to raise her chin to look me in the eye. Not many people have to do that. It's rare enough that I always find it an odd sensation, as if I should stoop down so we can be at eye level.

"Is someone going to tell me where you two know each other from?" Ronnie asked.

Ronnie moved past us to sit behind her desk. She tilted the chair slightly back on its swivel, crossed hands over stomach, and waited. Her pure grey eyes, soft as kitten fur, stared at me.

"Do you mind if I tell her, Bev?"

Bev had sat down again, smooth and ladylike. She had real dignity and had always impressed me as being a lady, in the best sense of the word. "If you feel it necessary, I do not object," she said.

Not exactly a rousing go-ahead, but it would do. I flopped down in the other chair, very aware of my jeans and jogging shoes. Beside Bev I looked like an ill-dressed child. For just a moment I felt it; then it was gone. Remember, no one can make you feel inferior without your consent. Eleanor Roosevelt said that. It is a quote I try to live by. Most of the time I succeed.

"Bev's family were the victims of a vampire pack. Only Beverly survived. I was one of the people who helped destroy the vampires." Brief, to the point, a hell of a lot left out. Mostly the painful parts.

Bev spoke in that quiet, precise voice of hers. "What Anita has left out is that she saved my life at risk of her own." She glanced down at her hands where they lay in her lap.

I remembered my first glimpse of Beverly Chin. One pale leg thrashing against the floor. The flash of fangs as the vampire reared to strike. A glimpse of pale, screaming face, and dark hair. The pure terror as she screamed. My hand throwing a silver-bladed knife and hitting the vampire's shoulder. Not a killing blow; there had been no time. The creature had sprang to its feet, roaring at me. I stood facing the thing with the last knife I had, gun long since emptied, alone.

And I remembered Beverly Chin beating the vampire's head in with a silver candlestick, while he crouched over me, breath warm on my neck. Her shrieks echoed through my dreams for weeks, as she beat the thing's head to pieces until blood and brain seeped out onto the floor.

All that passed between us without words. We had saved each other's lives; it is a bond that sticks with you. Friendships may fade, but there is always that obligation, that knowledge forged of terror and blood and shared violence, that never really leaves. It was there between us after three long years, straining and touchable.

Ronnie is a smart lady. She caught on to the awkward silence. "Would anybody like a drink?"

"Nonalcoholic," Bev and I said together. We laughed at each other, and the strain faded. We would never be true friends, but perhaps we could stop being ghosts to each other.

Ronnie brought us two diet Cokes. I made a face but took it anyway. I knew that was all she had in the office's little fridge. We had had discussions about diet drinks, but she swore she liked the taste. Liked the taste, garg!

Bev took hers graciously; perhaps that was what she drank at home. Give me something fattening with a little taste to it any day.

"Ronnie mentioned on the phone that there might be a death squad attached to HAV. Is that true?" I said.

Bev stared down at the can, which she held with one hand cupped underneath so it wouldn't stain her skirt. "I do not know positively that it is true, but I believe it to be."

"Tell me what you've heard?" I asked.

"There was talk for a while of forming a squad to hunt the vampires. To kill them as they have killed our . . . families. The president of course vetoed the idea. We work within the system. We are not vigilantes." She said it almost as a question, as if trying to convince herself more than us. She was shaken by what might have happened. Her neat little world collapsing again.

"But lately I have heard talk. People in our organization bragging of slaying vampires."

"How were they supposedly killed?" I asked.

She looked at me, hesitated. "I do not know."

"No hint?"

She shook her head. "I believe I could find out for you. Is it important?"

"The police have hidden certain details from the general public. Things only the murderer would know."

"I see." She glanced down at the can in her hands, then up at me. "I do not believe it is murder even if my people have done what the papers say. Killing dangerous animals should not be a crime."

In part I agreed with her. Once I had agreed with her whole-heartedly. "Then why tell us?" I asked.

She looked directly at me, dark, nearly black eyes staring into my face. "I owe you."

"You saved my life as well. You owe me nothing."

"There will always be a debt between us, always."

I looked into her face and understood. Bev had begged me not to tell anyone that she had beaten the vampire's head in. I think it horrified her that she was capable of such violence, regardless of motive.

I had told the police that she distracted the vampire so I could kill it. She had been disproportionately grateful for that small white lie. Maybe if no one else knew, she could pretend it had never happened. Maybe.

She stood, smoothing her skirt down in back. She sat her soda can carefully on the edge of the desk. "I will leave a message with Ms. Sims when I find out more."

I nodded. "I appreciate what you're doing." She might be betraying her cause for me.

She laid her purple jacket over her arm, small purse clasped in her hands. "Violence is not the answer. We must work within the system. Humans Against Vampires stands for law and order, not vigilantism." It sounded like a prerecorded speech. But I let it go. Everyone needs something to believe in.

She shook hands with both of us. Her hand was cool and dry. She left, slender shoulders very straight. The door closed firmly but quietly behind her. To look at her you would never know that she had been touched by extreme violence. Maybe that's the way she wanted it. Who was I to argue?

Ronnie said, "Okay, now you fill me in. What have you found out?"

"How do you know I've found out anything?" I asked.

"Because you looked a little green around the gills when you came through the door."

"Great. And I thought I was hiding it."

She patted my arm. "Don't worry. I just know you too well, that's all."

I nodded, taking the explanation for what it was, comforting crap. But I took it anyway. I told her about Theresa's death. I told her everything, except the dreams with Jean-Claude in them. That was private.

She let out a low whistle. "Damn, you have been busy. Do you think a human death squad is doing it?"

"You mean HAV?"

She nodded.

I took a deep breath and let it out. "I don't know. If it's humans, I don't have the faintest idea how they're doing it. It would take superhuman strength to rip a head off."

"A very strong human?" she asked.

The image of Winter's bulging arms flashed into my mind. "Maybe, but that kind of strength . . ."

"Under pressure, little old grannies have lifted entire cars."

She had a point. "How would you like to visit the Church of Eternal Life?" I asked.

"Thinking about joining up?"

I frowned at her.

She laughed. "Okay, okay, stop glowering at me. Why are we going?"

"Last night they raided the party with clubs. I'm not saying they meant to kill anyone, but when you start beating on people"—I shrugged—"accidents happen."

"You think the Church is behind it?"

"Don't know, but if they hate the freaks enough to storm their parties, maybe they hate them enough to kill them."

"Most of the Church's members are vampires," she said.

"Exactly. Superhuman strength and the ability to get close to the victims."

Ronnie smiled. "Not bad, Blake, not bad."

I bowed my head modestly. "Now all we got to do is prove it."

Her eyes were still shiny with humor when she said, "Unless of course they didn't do it."

"Oh, shut up. It's a place to start."

She spread her hands wide. "Hey, I'm not complaining. My father always told me, 'Never criticize, unless you can do a better job.' "

"You don't know what's going on either, huh?" I asked.

Her face sobered. "Wish I did."

So did I.

34

The Church of Eternal Life, main building, is just off Page Avenue, far from the District. The Church doesn't like to be associated with the riffraff. Vampire strip club, Circus of the Damned, tsk-tsk. How shocking. No, they think of themselves as mainstream undead.

The church itself is set in an expanse of naked ground. Small trees struggled to grow into big trees and shade the startling white of the church. It seemed to glow in the hot July sunshine, like a land-bound moon.

I pulled into the parking lot and parked on the shiny new black asphalt. Only the ground looked normal, bare reddish earth churned to mud. The grass had never had a chance.

"Pretty," Ronnie said. She nodded in the building's direction.

I shrugged. "If you say so. Frankly, I never get used to the generic effect."

"Generic effect?" she asked.

"The stained glass is all abstract color. No scenes of Christ, no saints, no holy symbols. Clean and pure as a wedding gown fresh out of plastic."

She got out of the car, sunglasses sliding into place. She stared at the church, arms crossed over her stomach. "It looks like they just unwrapped it and haven't put the trimmings on yet."

"Yeah, a church without God. What is wrong with this picture?"

She didn't laugh. "Will anybody be up this time of day?"

"Oh, yes, they recruit during the day."

"Recruit?"

"You know, go door to door, like the Mormons and the Jehovah's Witnesses."

She stared at me. "You've got to be kidding?"

"Do I look like I'm kidding?"

She shook her head. "Door-to-door vampires. How"—she wiggled her hands back and forth—"convenient."

"Yep," I said. "Let's go see who's minding the office."

Broad white steps led up to huge double doors. One of the doors was open; the other had a sign that read, "Enter Friend and be at Peace." I fought an urge to tear down the sign and stomp on it.

They were preying on one of the most basic fears of man—death. Everyone fears death. People who don't believe in God have a hard time with death being it. Die and you cease to exist. Poof. But at the Church of Eternal Life, they promise just what the name says. And they can prove it. No leap of faith. No waiting around. No questions left unanswered. How does it feel to be dead? Just ask a fellow church member.

Oh, and you'll never grow old either. No face-lifts, no tummy tucks, just eternal youth. Not a bad deal, as long as you don't believe in the soul.

As long as you don't believe the soul becomes trapped in the vampire's body and can never reach Heaven. Or worse yet, that vampires are inherently evil and you are condemned to Hell. The Catholic Church sees voluntary vampirism as a kind of suicide. I tend to agree. Though the Pope also excommunicated all animators, unless we ceased raising the dead. Fine; I became Episcopalian.

Polished wooden pews ran in two wide rows up towards what would have been an altar. There was a pulpit, but I couldn't call it an altar. It was just a blank blue wall surrounded by more white upsweeping walls.

The windows were red and blue stained glass. The sunlight sparkled through them, making delicate colored patterns on the white floor.

"Peaceful," Ronnie said.

"So are graveyards."

She smiled at me. "I'd thought you'd say that."

I frowned at her. "No teasing; we're here on business."

"What exactly do you want me to do?"

"Just back me up; look menacing if you can manage it. Look for clues."

"Clues?" she asked.

"Yeah, you know, clues, ticket stubs, half-burned notes, leads."

"Oh, those."

"Quit grinning at me, Ronnie."

She adjusted her sunglasses and did her best "cold" look. She's pretty good at it. Thugs have been known to shrivel at twenty paces. We would see how it worked on church members.

There was a small door to one side of the "altar." It led into a carpeted hallway. The air-conditioned hush enveloped us. There were bathrooms to the left, and an open room to the right. Perhaps this is where they had . . . coffee after services. No, probably not coffee. A rousing sermon followed by a little blood, perhaps?

The offices were marked with a little sign that said "Office." How clever. There was an outer office, the proverbial secretarial desk and etc. . . . A young man sat behind the desk. Slender, short brown hair carefully cut. Wire-frame glasses decorated a pair of really lovely brown eyes. There was a healing bite mark on his throat.

He rose and came around the desk, hand extended, smiling at us. "Greetings, friends, I'm Bruce. How may I help you today?"

The handshake was firm but not too firm, strong but not over-bearing, a friendly lingering touch, but not sexual. Really good car salesmen shake hands like that. Real estate brokers, too. I have this nice little soul, hardly used at all. The price is right. Trust me. If his big brown eyes had looked any more sincere, I would have given him a doggie biscuit and patted his head.

"I would like to set up an appointment to speak with Malcolm," I said.

He blinked once. "Have a seat."

I sat. Ronnie leaned against the wall, to one side of the door. Hands folded, looking cool and bodyguardish.

Bruce went back around his desk, after offering us coffee, and sat with folded hands. "Now, Miss . . ."

"Ms. Blake."

He didn't flinch; he hadn't heard of me. How fleeting fame. "Ms. Blake, why do you wish to meet with the head of our church? We have many competent and understanding counselors that will help you make your decision."

I smiled at him. I'll just bet you do, you little pipsqueak. "I think Malcolm will want to speak with me. I have information about the vampire murders."

His smile slipped. "If you have such information, then go to the police."

"Even if I have proof that certain members of your church are doing the murders?" A small bluff, otherwise known as a lie.

He swallowed, fingers pressing the top of his desk until the fingertips turned white. "I don't understand. I mean . . ."

I smiled at him. "Let's just face it, Bruce. You are not equipped to handle murder. It isn't in your training, now is it?"

"Well, no, but . . ."

"Then just give me a time to come back tonight and see Malcolm."

"I don't know. I . . ."

"Don't worry about it. Malcolm is the head of the church. He'll take care of it."

He was nodding, too rapidly. His eyes flicked to Ronnie, then back to me. He flipped through a leatherbound day planner on his desk. "Nine, tonight." He picked up a pen, poised and ready. "If you'll give me your full name, I'll pencil you in."

I started to point out that he wasn't using a pencil, but decided to let it slide. "Anita Blake."

He still didn't recognize the name. So much for me being the terror of vampireland. "And this is pertaining to?" He was regaining his professionalism.

I stood up. "Murder, it's pertaining to murder."

"Oh, yes, I . . ." He scribbled something down. "Nine tonight, Anita Blake, murder." He frowned down at the note as if there were something wrong with it.

I decided to help him out. "Don't frown so. You've got the message right."

He stared up at me. He looked a little pale.

"I'll be back. Make sure he gets the message."

Bruce nodded again, too fast, eyes large behind his glasses.

Ronnie opened the door, and I preceded her out. She brought up the rear like a bad-movie bodyguard. When we were out into the main church again, she laughed. "I think we scared him."

"Bruce scares easy."

She nodded, eyes shining.

The barest mention of violence, murder, and he had fallen apart. When he "grew up," he was going to be a vampire. Sure.

The sunshine was nearly blinding after the dimness of the church. I squinted, putting a hand over my eyes. I caught movement from the corner of my eye.

Ronnie screamed, "Anita!"

Everything slowed down. I had plenty of time to stare at the man and the gun in his hands. Ronnie smashed into me, carrying us both down and back through the church door. Bullets thunked into the door where I'd been.

Ronnie scrambled behind me, near the wall. I had my gun out and lay on my side pressed against the door. My heart was thundering in my ears. Yet I could hear everything. The wrinkle of my windbreaker was like static. I heard the man walk up the steps. The son of a bitch was gonna keep coming.

I inched forward. He walked up the steps. His shadow fell inside the door. He wasn't even trying to hide. Maybe he thought I wasn't armed. He was about to learn different.

Bruce called, "What's going on here?"

Ronnie yelled, "Get back inside."

I kept my eyes on the door. I would not get shot because ol' Bruce distracted me. Nothing was important but that shadow in the door, the halting footsteps. Nothing.

The man walked right into it. Gun in his hand, eyes searching the church. Amateur.

I could have touched him with the barrel of my gun. "Don't move." "Freeze" always sounds so melodramatic. Don't move, short, to the point. "Don't move," I said.

He turned just his head, slow, towards me. "You're The Executioner." His voice was soft, hesitant.

Was I supposed to deny it? Maybe. If he had come here to kill The Executioner, definitely. "No," I said.

He started to turn. "Then it must be her." He was turning towards Ronnie. Shit.

He raised his arm and started to point.

"Don't!" Ronnie screamed.

Too late. I fired, point-blank into his chest. Ronnie's shot echoed mine. The impact raised him off his feet and sent him staggering backwards. Blood blossomed on his shirt. He slammed into the half-opened door and fell flat on his back through it. All I could see were his legs.

I hesitated, listening. I couldn't hear any movement. I eased around the door. He wasn't moving, but the gun was still clutched in his hand. I pointed my gun at him and stalked to him. If he had so much as twitched, I would have hit him again.

I kicked the gun out of his hand and checked the pulse in his neck. Nada, zip. Dead.

I use ammunition that can take out vampires, if I get a lucky shot, and if they're not ancient. The bullet had made a small hole on the side it went in, but the other side of his chest was gone. The bullet had done what it was supposed to do; expand, and make a very big exit hole.

His neck lolled to one side. Two bite marks decorated his neck. Dammit! Bite marks or not, he was dead. There wasn't enough left of his heart to thread a needle. A lucky shot. A stupid amateur with a gun.

Ronnie was leaning in the doorway, looking pale. Her gun was pointed at the dead man. Her arms trembled ever so slightly.

She almost smiled. "I don't usually carry a gun during the day, but I knew I'd be with you."

"Is that an insult?" I asked.

"No," she said, "reality."

I couldn't argue with that. I sat down on the cool stone steps; my knees felt weak. The adrenaline was draining out of me, like water from a broken cup.

Bruce was in the doorway, ice pale. "He . . . he tried to kill you." His voice cracked with fear.

"Do you recognize him?" I asked.

He shook his head over and over again, rapid jerky movements.

"Are you sure?"

"We . . . we do not . . . condone violence." He swallowed hard, his voice a cracking whisper. "I don't know him."

The fear seemed genuine. Maybe he didn't know him, but that didn't mean the dead man wasn't a member of the church. "Call the police, Bruce."

He just stood there, staring at the corpse.

"Call the cops, okay?"

He stared at me, eyes glazed. I wasn't sure if he heard me or not, but he went back inside.

Ronnie sat down beside me, staring out at the parking lot. Blood was running down the white steps in tiny rivulets of scarlet.

"Jesus," she whispered.

"Yeah." I still held my gun loose-gripped in my hand. The danger seemed to be over. Guess I could put away the gun. "Thanks for pushing me out of the way," I said.

"You're welcome." She took a deep, shaky breath. "Thanks for shooting him before he shot me."

"Don't mention it. Besides, you got a piece of him, too."

"Don't remind me."

I stared at her. "You all right?"

"No, I'm well and truly scared."

"Yeah." Of course, all Ronnie had to do was stay away from me. I seemed to be the free-fire zone. A walking, talking menace to my friends and coworkers. Ronnie could have died today, and it would have been my fault. She had been a few seconds slower to shoot than I was. Those few seconds could have cost her her life. Of course, if she hadn't been here today, I might have died. One bullet in the chest, and my gun wouldn't have done me a hell of a lot of good.

I heard the distant whoop-whoop of police sirens. They must have been damn close, or maybe it was another killing. Possible. Would the police believe he was just a fanatic trying to kill The Executioner? Maybe. Dolph wouldn't buy it.

The sunshine pressed down around us like bright yellow plastic. Neither of us said a word. Maybe there was nothing left to say. Thank you for saving my life. You're welcome. What else was there?

I felt light and empty, almost peaceful. Numb. I must be getting close to the truth, whatever that was. People were trying to kill me. It was a good sign. Sort of. It meant I knew something important. Important enough to kill for. The trouble was, I didn't know what it was I was supposed to know.

35

I was back at the church at 8:45 that night. The sky was a rich purple. Pink clouds were stretched across it like cotton candy pulled apart by eager kids and left to melt. True dark was only minutes away. Ghouls would already be out and about. But the vampires had a few heartbeats of waiting left.

I stood on the steps of the church, admiring the sunset. There was no blood left. The white steps were as shiny and new as if this afternoon had never happened. But I remembered. I had decided to sweat in the July heat so I could carry an arsenal. The windbreaker hid not only the shoulder rig and 9mm, plus extra ammo, but a knife on each forearm. The Firestar was snug in the inner pant holster, set for a right-hand cross draw. There was even a knife strapped to my ankle.

Of course, nothing I was carrying would stop Malcolm. He was one of the most powerful master vampires in the city. After seeing Nikolaos and Jean-Claude, I'd say he ranked third. In the company I was judging him against, third wasn't bad. So why confront him? Because I couldn't think of what else to do.

I had left a letter detailing my suspicions about the church and everybody else in a safe deposit box. Doesn't everybody have one? Ronnie knew about it, and there was a letter on the secretary's desk at Animators, Inc. It would go out Monday morning to Dolph, unless I called up to stop it.

One attempt on my life and I was getting all paranoid. Fancy that.

The parking lot was full. People were drifting inside the church in small groups. A few had simply walked up, no cars. I stared hard at them, Vampires, before full dark? But no, just humans.

I zipped the windbreaker partway up. Didn't want to disturb services by flashing a gun.

A young woman, brown hair style-gelled into an artificial wave over one eye, was handing out pamphlets just inside the door. A guide to the service, I supposed. She smiled and said, "Welcome. Is this your first time?"

I smiled back at her, pleasant, as if I wasn't carrying enough weaponry to take out half the congregation. "I have an appointment to see Malcolm."

Her smile didn't change. If anything it deepened, flashing a dimple to one side of her lipsticked mouth. Somehow, I didn't think she knew I'd killed someone today. People don't generally smile at me when they know things like that.

"Just a minute; let me get someone to handle the door." She walked away to tap a young man on the shoulder. She whispered against his cheek and shoved the pamphlets into his hands.

She came back to me, hands smoothing along the burgundy dress she wore. "If you'll follow me?"

She made it a question. What would she do if I said no? Probably look puzzled. The young man was greeting a couple that had just entered the church. The man wore a suit; the woman the proverbial dress, hose, and sandals. They could have been coming to my church, any church. As I followed the woman down the side aisle towards the door, I glanced at a couple dressed in postmodern punk. Or whatever phrase is common now. The girl's hair looked like Frankenstein's Bride done in pink and green. A second glance and I wasn't sure; maybe the pink and green was a guy. If so, his girlfriend's hair was a buzz so close to her head, it looked like stubble.

The Church of Eternal Life attracted a wide following. Diversity, that's the ticket. They appealed to the agnostic, the atheist, the disillusioned mainstreamer, and some who had never decided what they were. The church was nearly full, and it wasn't dark yet. The vampires had yet to show. It had been a long time since I'd seen a church this full, except at Easter, or Christmas. Holiday Christians. A chill tiptoed along my spine.

This was the fullest church I'd been to in years. The vampire church. Maybe the real danger wasn't the murderer. Maybe the real danger was right here in this building.

I shook my head and followed my guide through the door, out of the church, and past the coffee klatch area. There really was coffee percolating on a white-draped table. There was also a bowl of reddish punch that looked a little too viscous to be punch at all.

The woman said, "Would you like some coffee?"

"No, thank you."

She smiled pleasantly and opened the door marked "Office" for me. I went in. No one was there.

"Malcolm will be with you as soon as he wakens. If you like, I can wait with you." She glanced at the door as she said it.

"I wouldn't want you to miss the service. I'll be fine alone."

Her smile flashed into dimple again. "Thank you; I'm sure it will be a short wait." With that she was gone, and I was alone. Alone with the secretary's desk and the leatherbound day planner for the Church of Eternal Life. Life was good.

I opened the planner to the week before the first vampire murder. Bruce, the secretary, had very neat handwriting, each entry very precise. Time, name, and a one-sentence description of the meeting. 10:00, Jason MacDonald, Magazine interview. 9:00, Meeting with Mayor, Zoning problems. Normal stuff for the Billy Graham of Vampirism. Then two days before the first murder there was a notation that was in a different handwriting. Smaller, no less neat. 3:00, Ned. That was all, no last name, no reason for the meeting. And Bruce didn't make the appointment. Methinks we have a clue. Be still, my heart.

Ned was a short form of Edward, just like Teddy. Had Malcolm had a meeting with the hit man of the undead? Maybe. Maybe not. It could be a clandestine meeting with a different Ned. Or maybe Bruce had been away from the desk and someone else had just filled in? I went through the rest of the planner as quickly as I could. Nothing else seemed out of the ordinary. Every other entry was in Bruce's large, rolling hand.

Malcolm had met with Edward, if it had been Edward, two days before the first death. If that was true, where did that leave things? With Edward a murderer and Malcolm paying him to do it. There was one problem with that. If Edward had wanted me dead, he'd have done it himself. Maybe Malcolm panicked and sent one of his followers to do it? Could be.

I was sitting in a chair against the wall, leafing through a magazine, when the door opened. Malcolm was tall and almost painfully thin, with large, bony hands that belonged to a more muscular man. His short, curly hair was the shocking yellow of goldfinch feathers. This was what blond hair looked like after nearly three hundred years in the dark.

The last time I had seen Malcolm, he had seemed beautiful, perfect. Now he was almost ordinary, like Nikolaos and her scar. Had Jean-Claude given me the ability to see master vampires' true forms?

Malcolm's presence filled the small room like invisible water, chilling and pricking along my skin, knee-deep and rising. Give him another nine hundred years, and he might rival Nikolaos. Of course, I wouldn't be around to test my little theory.

I stood, and he swept into the room. He was dressed modestly in a dark blue suit, pale blue shirt, and blue silk tie. The pale shirt made his eyes look like robin's eggs. He smiled, angular face, beaming at me. He wasn't trying to cloud my mind. Malcolm was very good at resisting the urge. His entire credibility rested on the fact that he didn't cheat.

"Miss Blake, how good to see you." He didn't offer to shake hands; he knew better. "Bruce left me a very confused message. Something about the vampire murders?" His voice was deep and soothing, like the ocean.

"I told Bruce I have proof that your church is involved with the vampire murders."

"And do you?"

"Yes." I believed it. If he had met with Edward, I had my murderer.

"Hmmm, you are telling the truth. Yet, I know that it is not true." His voice rolled around me, warm and thick, powerful.

I shook my head. "Cheating, Malcolm, using your powers to probe my mind. Tsk, tsk."

He shrugged, hands open at his sides. "I control my church, Miss Blake. They would not do what you have accused them of."

"They raided a freak party last night with clubs. They hurt people." I was guessing on that part.

He frowned. "There is a small faction of our followers who persist in violence. The freak party, as you call it, is an abomination and must be stopped, but through legal channels. I have told my followers this."

"But do you punish them when they disobey you?" I asked.

"I am not a policeman, or a priest, to mete out punishment. They are not children. They have their own minds."

"I'll bet they do."

"And what is that supposed to mean?" he asked.

"It means, Malcolm, that you are a master vampire. None of them can stand against you. They'll do anything you want them to."

"I do not use mind powers on my congregation."

I shook my head. His power oozed over my arms like a cold wave. He wasn't even trying. It was just spillover. Did he realize what he was doing? Could it actually be an accident?

"You had a meeting two days before the first murder."

He smiled, careful not to show fangs. "I have many meetings."

"I know, you are reeal popular, but you'll remember this meeting. You hired a hit man to kill vampires." I watched his face, but he was too good. There was a flicker in his eyes, unease maybe; then it was gone, replaced by that shining blue-eyed confidence.

"Miss Blake, why are you looking me in the eyes?"

I shrugged. "If you don't try to bespell me, it's safe."

"I have tried to convince you of that on several occasions, but you always played it . . . safe. Now you are staring at me; why?" He strode towards me, quick, nearly a blur of motion. My gun was in my hand, no thinking needed. Instinct.

"My," he said.

I just stared at him, quite willing to put a bullet through his chest if he came one step closer.

"You carry at least the first mark, Miss Blake. Some master vampire has touched you. Who?"

I let out my breath in one long sigh. I hadn't even realized I'd been holding it. "It's a long story."

"I believe you." He was suddenly standing near the door again, as if he had never moved. Damn, he was good.

"You hired a man to slay the freak vampires," I said.

"No," he said, "I did not."

It is always unnerving when a person looks so damn blasé while I point a gun at them. "You did hire an assassin."

He shrugged. Smiled. "You do not really expect me to do anything but deny that, do you?"

"Guess not." What the heck, might as well ask. "Are you or your church connected in any way to the vampire murders?"

He almost laughed. I didn't blame him. No one in their right mind would just say yes, but sometimes you can learn things from the way a person denies something. The choice of lies can be almost as helpful as the truth.

"No, Miss Blake."

"You did hire an assassin." I made it a statement.

The smile drained from his face, poof. He stared at me, his presence crawling along my skin like insects. "Miss Blake, I believe it is time for you to leave."

"A man tried to kill me today."

"That is hardly my fault."

"He had two vampire bites in his neck."

Again that flicker in the eyes. Unease? Maybe.

"He was waiting for me outside your church. I was forced to kill him on your steps." A small lie, but I didn't want Ronnie further involved.

He was frowning now, a thread of anger like heat oozing through the room. "I am unaware of this, Miss Blake. I will look into it."

I lowered my gun but didn't put it away. You can only hold a person at gunpoint so long. If they aren't afraid, and they aren't going to hurt you, and you aren't going to shoot them, it gets rather silly. "Don't be too hard on Bruce. He doesn't do well around violence."

Malcolm straightened, pulling at his suit jacket. A nervous gesture? Oh, boy. I'd hit a nerve.

"I will look into it, Miss Blake. If he was a member of our church, we owe you an extreme apology."

I stared at him for a minute. What could I say to that? Thank you? It didn't seem appropriate. "I know you hired a hit man, Malcolm. Not exactly good press for your church. I think you are behind the vampire murders. Your hands may not have spilled the blood, but it was done with your approval."

"Please, go now, Miss Blake." He opened the door as he said it.

I walked through, gun still in my hand. "Sure, I'll go, but I won't go away."

He stared down at me, eyes angry. "Do you know what it means to be marked by a master vampire?"

I thought a minute and wasn't sure how to answer it. Truth. "No."

He smiled, and it was cold enough to freeze your heart. "You will learn, Miss Blake. If it becomes too much for you, remember our church is here to help." He closed the door in my face. Softly.

I stared at the door. "And what is that supposed to mean?" I whispered. No one answered me.

I put away my gun and spotted a small door marked "Exit." I took it. The church was softly lit, candles maybe. Voices rose on the night air, singing. I didn't recognize the words. The tune was *Bringing in the Sheaves*. I caught one phrase: "We will live forever, never more to die."

I hurried to my car and tried not to listen to the song. There was something frightening about all those voices raised skyward, worshipping . . . what? Themselves? Eternal youth? Blood? What? Another question that I didn't have an answer to.

Edward was my murderer. The question was, could I turn him over to Nikolaos? Could I turn over a human being to the monsters, even to save myself? Another question that I didn't have an answer for. Two days ago I would have said no. Now I just didn't know.

36

I didn't want to go back to my apartment. Edward would be coming tonight. Tell him where Nikolaos slept in daylight or he'd force the information from me. Complicated enough. Now, I thought he was my murderer. Very complicated.

The best thing I could think of was to avoid him. That wouldn't work forever, but maybe I'd have a brainstorm and figure it all out. All right, there wasn't much chance of that, but one could always hope.

Maybe Ronnie would have a message for me. Something helpful. God knows I needed all the help I could get. I pulled the car into a service station that had a pay phone out front. I had one of those high-tech answering machines that allowed me to read my messages without having to go home for them. Maybe I could avoid Edward all night, if I slept in a hotel. Sigh. If I'd had any solid proof at all right that minute, I'd have called the police.

I heard the tape whir and click; then, "Anita, it's Willie, they got Phillip. The guy you was with. They're hurtin' him, bad! You gotta come—" The phone went dead, abruptly. Like he'd been cut off.

My stomach tightened. A second message came up. "This is you know who. You've heard Willie's message. Come and get it, animator. I don't really have to threaten your pretty lover, do I?" Nikolaos's laughter filled the phone, scratchy and distant with tape.

There was a loud click and Edward's voice came over the phone. "Anita, tell me where you are. I can help you."

"They'll kill Phillip," I said. "Besides, you aren't on my side, remember."

"I'm the closest thing you've got to an ally."

"God help me, then." I hung up on him, hard. Phillip had tried to defend me last night. Now he was paying for it. I yelled, "Dammit!"

A man pumping gas stared at me.

"What are you looking at?" I nearly yelled that, too. He dropped his eyes and concentrated very hard on filling his tank with gas.

I got behind the wheel of my car and sat there for a few minutes. I was so angry, I was shaking. I could feel the tension in my teeth. Dammit. Dammit! I was too angry to drive. It wouldn't help Phillip if I got in a car accident on the way.

I tried breathing deep gulps of air. It didn't help. I turned the key in the ignition. "No speeding, can't afford to get stopped by the cops. Easy does it, Anita, easy does it." I talk to myself every once in a while. Give myself very good advice. Sometimes I even take it.

I put the car in gear and drove out onto the road—carefully. Anger rode up my back and into my shoulders and neck. I gripped the steering wheel too hard and found that my hands weren't quite healed. Sharp little jabs of pain, but not enough. There wasn't enough pain in the whole world to get rid of the anger.

Phillip was being hurt because of me. Just like Catherine and Ronnie. No more. No freaking more. I was going to get Phillip, save him any way I could; then I was turning the whole blasted thing over to the police. Without proof, yeah, without anything to back it up. I was bailing out before more people got hurt.

The anger was almost enough to hide the fear behind it. If Nikolaos was tormenting Phillip for last night, she might not be too happy with me either. I was going back down those stairs into the master's lair, at night. Didn't seem real bright when you put it that way.

The anger was fading in a wash of cold, skin-shivering fear. "No!" I would not go in there afraid. I held onto my anger with everything I had. This was the closest I'd come to hate in a long time. Hatred; now there's an emotion that'll spread warmth through your body.

Most hatred is based on fear, one way or another. Yeah. I wrapped myself in anger, with a dash of hate, and at the bottom of it all was an icy center of pure terror.

37

The Circus of the Damned is housed in an old warehouse. Its name is emblazoned across the roof in colored lights. Giant clown figurines dance around the words in frozen pantomime. If you look very closely at the clowns, you notice they have fangs. But only if you look very closely.

The sides of the building are strung with huge plastic cloth signs, like an old-fashioned sideshow. One banner showed a man being hung; "The Death Defying Count Alcourt," it said. Zombies crawled from a graveyard in one picture; "Watch the Dead Rise from the Grave." A very bad drawing showed a man halfway between wolf and man shape; Fabian, the Werewolf. There were other signs. Other attractions. None of them looked very wholesome.

Guilty Pleasures treads a thin line between entertainment and the sadistic. The Circus goes over the edge and down into the abyss.

And here I go inside. Oh, joy in the morning.

Noise hits you at the door. A blast of carnival sound, the push and shove of the crowd, the rustling of hundreds of people. The lights spill and scream in a hundred different colors, all eye-searing, all guaranteed to attract attention, or make you lose your lunch. Of course, maybe that was just my nerves.

The smell is formed of cotton candy, corn dogs, the cinnamon smell of elephant ears, snow cones, sweat, and under it all a neck-ruffling smell. Blood smells like sweet copper pennies, and that smell mingles over everything. Most people don't recognize it. But there is another scent on the air, not just blood, but violence. Of course, violence has no smell. Yet, always here, there is—something. The barest hint of long-closed rooms and rotting cloth.

I had never come here before, except on police business. What

I wouldn't have given for a few uniforms right now.

The crowd parted like water in front of a ship. Winter, Mr. Muscles, moved through the people, and instinctively they moved out of his way. I'd have moved out of his way, too, but I didn't think I'd get the chance.

Winter was wearing a proverbial strongman's outfit. It had fake zebra stripes on a white background and left most of his upper body exposed. His legs in the striped leotard rippled and corded, like it was a second skin. His bicep, unflexed, was bigger around than both my arms. He stopped in front of me, towering over me, and knowing it.

"Is your entire family obscenely tall, or is it just you?" I asked.

He frowned, eyes narrowing. I don't think he got it. Oh, well. "Follow me," he said. With that he turned and walked back through the crowd.

I guess I was supposed to follow like a good little girl. Shit. A large blue tent took up one corner of the warehouse. People were lining up, showing tickets. A man was calling out in a booming voice, "Almost show time, folks. Present your tickets and enter. See the hanging man. Count Alcourt will be executed before your very eyes."

I had paused to listen. Winter was not waiting. Luckily, his broad, white back didn't blend with the crowd. I had to trot to catch up with him. I hate having to do that. It makes me feel like a child running after an adult. If a little running was the worst thing I experienced tonight, things would be just hunky-dory.

There was a full-size Ferris wheel, its glowing top nearly brushing the ceiling. A man held a baseball out to me. "Try your luck, little lady."

I ignored him. I hate being called little lady. I glanced at the prizes to be won. It ran long on stuffed animals and ugly dolls. The stuffed toys were mostly predators: soft plush panthers, toddler-size bears, spotted snakes, and giant fuzzy-toothed bats.

There was a bald man in white clown makeup selling tickets to the mirror maze. He stared at the children as they went inside his glass house. I could almost feel the weight of his eyes on their backs, like he would memorize every line of their small bodies. Nothing would have gotten me past him into that sparkling river of glass.

The Funhouse was next, more clowns and screams, the shooting whoosh of air. The metal sidewalk leading into its depths buckled and twisted. A little boy nearly fell. His mother dragged him to his feet. Why would any parent bring their child here, to this frightening place?

There was even a haunted house; it was almost funny. Sort of redundant, if you ask me. The whole freaking place was a house of horrors.

Winter had paused before the little door leading into the back areas. He was frowning at me, massive arms almost crossed over equally massive chest. The arms didn't quite fold right, too much muscle for that, but he was trying.

He opened the door. I went inside. The tall, bald man who had been with Nikolaos that first time was standing against the wall, at attention. His handsome, narrow face, the eyes very prominent because there was no hair, nothing much else to stare at, looked at me the way elementary school teachers look at troublemaking children. You must be punished, young lady. But what had I done wrong?

The man's voice was deep, faintly British, cultured, but human. "Search her for weapons before we go down."

Winter nodded. Why talk when gestures will do? His big hands lifted my jacket and took the gun. He shoved one shoulder so that I spun around. He found the second gun, too. Had I really thought they'd let me keep the weapons? Yes, I guess I had. Stupid me.

"Check her arms for knives."

Damn.

Winter gripped my jacket sleeves like he meant to tear them. "Wait, please. I'll just take the jacket off. You can search it, too, if you like."

Winter took the knives on my arms. The bald-headed man searched the yellow windbreaker for concealed weapons. He didn't find any. Winter patted my legs down, but not well. He missed the knife at my ankle. I had one weapon, and they didn't know it. Bully for me.

Down the long stairs and into the empty throne room. Maybe it showed on my face because the man said, "The master waits for us, with your friend."

The man led the way as he had down the stairs. Winter brought up the rear. Perhaps they thought I would make a break for it. Right. Where would I go?

They stopped at the dungeon. How had I known they would?
The bald-headed man knocked on the door twice, not too hard,
not too soft.

There was silence; then bright, high laughter drifted from inside.
My skin crawled with the sound. I did not want to see Nikolaos
again. I did not want to be in a cell again. I wanted to go home.

The door opened. Valentine made a hand-sweeping motion.
"Come in, come in." He was wearing a silver mask this time. A
strand of his auburn hair was stuck to the forehead of the mask,
sticky with blood.

My heart thudded into my throat. Phillip, are you alive? It was
all I could do not to yell out.

Valentine stepped against the door as if waiting for me to pass.
I glanced at the nameless bald man. His face was unreadable. He
motioned me ahead of him. What could I do? I went.

What I saw stopped me at the top of the steps. I couldn't go
farther. I couldn't. Aubrey stood against the far wall, grinning at
me. His hair was still golden; his face, bestial. Nikolaos stood in
a dress of flowing white that made her skin look like chalk, her
hair cotton-white. She was sprinkled with blood, like someone
had taken a red ink pen and splattered her.

Her grey-blue eyes stared up at me. She laughed again, rich
and pure and wicked. I had no other word for it. Wicked. She
caressed a white, blood-spattered hand against Phillip's bare chest.
She rolled her fingertip over his nipple, and laughed.

He was chained to the wall at wrist and ankle. His long, brown
hair had fallen forward, hiding one eye. His muscular body was
covered in bites. Blood rained down his tan skin in thin crimson
lines. He stared up at me from that one brown eye, the other hidden in his hair. Despair. He knew he had been brought here to
die, like this, and there wasn't a damn thing he could do about it.
But there was something I could do. There had to be. God, please
let there be!

The man touched my shoulder, and I jumped. The vampires
laughed. The man did not. I walked down the steps to stand a
few feet in front of Phillip. He wouldn't look at me.

Nikolaos touched his naked thigh and ran her fingers up it. His
body tightened, hands clenching into fists.

"Oh, we have been having a fine time with your lover here,"
Nikolaos said. Her voice was sweet as ever. The child bride incar-
nate. Bitch.

"He isn't my lover."

She pouted out her lower lip. "Now, Anita, no lying. That's no fun." She stalked towards me, slender hips swaying to some inner dance. She reached for me, and I backed up, bumping into Winter. "Animator, animator," she said. "When will you learn that you cannot fight me?"

I don't think she wanted me to argue, so I didn't.

She reached for me again, with one bloody, dainty hand. "Winter can hold you, if you like."

Stay still, or we hold you down. Great choices. I stayed still. I watched those pale fingers glide towards my face. I ground my fingernails into the palms of my hands. I would not move away from her. I would not move. Her fingers touched my forehead, and I felt the cool wetness of blood. She brushed it down my temple to my cheek and traced her fingers over my lower lip. I think I stopped breathing.

"Lick your lips," she said.

"No," I said.

"Oh, you are a stubborn one. Has Jean-Claude given you this courage?"

"What the hell are you talking about?"

Her eyes darkened, face clouding over. "Don't be coy, Anita. It does not become you." Her voice was suddenly adult, hot enough to scald. "I know your little secret."

"I don't know what you are talking about," I said, and I meant it. I didn't understand the anger.

"If you like, we can play games for a little while longer." She was suddenly standing beside Phillip, and I hadn't seen her move. "Did that surprise you, Anita? I am still master of this city. I have powers that you and your master have never even dreamed of."

My master? What the hell was she talking about? I didn't have a master.

She rubbed her hands along the side of his chest, over his rib cage. Her hand wiped away the blood to show the skin smooth and untouched. She stood in front of him and didn't come to his collarbone. Phillip had closed his eyes. Her head arched backwards, a glimpse of fangs, lips drawn back in a snarl.

"No." I stepped towards them. Winter's hands descended on my shoulders. He shook his head, slow and careful. I was not to interfere.

She drove her fangs into his side. His whole body stiffened, neck arching, arms jerking at the chains.

"Leave him alone!" I drove an elbow into Winter's stomach. He grunted, and his fingers dug into my shoulders until I wanted to scream. His arms enveloped me, tight to his chest, no movement allowed.

She raised her face from Phillip's skin. Blood trickled down her chin. She licked her lips with a tiny pink tongue. "Ironic," she said in a voice years older than the body would ever be. "I sent Phillip to seduce you. Instead, you seduced him."

"We are not lovers." I felt ridiculous with Winter's arms crushing me to his chest.

"Denial will not help either of you," she said.

"What will help us?" I asked.

She motioned, and Winter released me. I stepped away from him, out of reach. It put me closer to Nikolaos, perhaps not an improvement.

"Let us discuss your future, Anita." She began to walk up the steps. "And your lover's future."

I assumed she meant Phillip, and I didn't correct her. The name less man motioned for me to follow her up the stairs. Aubrey was moving closer to Phillip. They would be alone together. Unacceptable.

"Nikolaos, please."

Maybe it was the "please." She turned. "Yes," she said.

"May I ask two things?"

She was smiling at me, amused with me. An adult's amusement with a child who had used a new word. I didn't care what she thought of me as long as she did what I wanted. "You may ask," she said.

"That when we go, all the vampires leave this room." She was still staring at me, smiling, so far so good. "And that I be allowed to speak with Phillip privately."

She laughed, high and wild, chimes in a storm wind. "You are bold, mortal. I give you that. I begin to see what Jean-Claude sees in you."

I let the comment go because I felt like I was missing part of the meaning. "May I have what I ask, please?"

"Call me master, and you will have it."

I swallowed and it was loud in the sudden stillness. "Please . . . master." See, I didn't choke on the word after all.

"Very good, animator, very good indeed." Without her needing to say anything, Valentine and Aubrey went up the steps and out the door. They didn't even argue. That was frightening all on its own.

"I will leave Burchard at the top of the steps. He has human hearing. If you whisper, he won't be able to hear you at all."

"Burchard?" I asked.

"Yes, animator, Burchard, my human servant." She stared at me as if that was significant. My expression didn't seem to please her. She frowned. Then she turned abruptly in a swing of white skirts. Winter followed her like an obedient puppy on steroids.

Burchard, the once nameless man, took up a post in front of the closed door. He stared straight ahead, not at us. Privacy, or as close as we were getting to it.

I went to Phillip, and he still wouldn't look at me. His thick, brown hair acted like a kind of curtain between us. "Phillip, what happened?"

His voice was an abused whisper; screaming will do that to you. I had to stand on tiptoe and nearly press my body against his to hear him. "Guilty Pleasures; they took me from there."

"Didn't Robert try to stop them?" For some reason that seemed important. I had only met Robert once, but part of me was angry that he had not protected Phillip. He was in charge of things while Jean-Claude was away. Phillip was one of those things.

"Wasn't strong enough."

I lost my balance and was forced to catch myself, hands flat against his ruined chest. I jerked back, hands held out from me, bloody.

Phillip closed his eyes and leaned back into the wall. His throat worked hard at swallowing. There were two fresh bites on his neck. They were going to bleed him to death if someone didn't get carried away first.

He lowered his head and tried to look at me, but his hair had spilled into both eyes. I wiped the blood on my jeans and went back to stand almost on tiptoe next to him. I brushed the hair back from his eyes, but it spilled forward again. It was beginning to bug me. I combed my fingers through his hair until it stayed out of his face. His hair was softer than it looked, thick and warm with the heat of his body.

He almost smiled. His voice breaking as he whispered, "Few months back, I'd have paid money for this."

I stared at him, then realized he was trying to make a joke. God. My throat felt tight.

Burchard said, "It is time to go."

I stared into Phillip's eyes, perfect brown, torchlight dancing in them like black mirrors. "I won't leave you here, Phillip."

His eyes flickered to the man on the stairs and back to me. Fear turned his face young, helpless. "See you later," he said.

I stepped back from him. "You can count on it."

"It is not wise to keep her waiting," Burchard said.

He was probably right. Phillip and I stared at each other for a handful of moments. The pulse in his throat jumped under his skin like it was trying to escape. My throat ached; my chest was tight. The torchlight flickered in my vision for just a second. I turned away and walked to the steps. We tough-as-nails vampire slayers don't cry. At least, never in public. At least, never when we can help it.

Burchard held the door open for me. I glanced back at Phillip and waved, like an idiot. He watches me go, his eyes too large for his face suddenly, like a child who watches its parent leave the room before all the monsters are gone.

I had to leave him like that—alone, helpless. God help me.

38

Nikolaos sat in her carved wooden chair, tiny feet swinging off the ground. Charming.

Aubrey leaned against the wall, tongue running over his lips, getting the last bit of blood off them. Valentine stood very still beside him, staring at me.

Winter stood beside me. The prison guard.

Burchard went to stand by Nikolaos, one hand on the back of her chair.

"What, animator, no jokes?" Nikolaos asked. Her voice was still the grown-up version. It was like she had two voices and could change them with a push of a button.

I shook my head. I didn't feel very funny.

"Have we broken your spirit? Taken the fight out of you?"

I stared at her. Anger flared through me like a wave of heat. "What do you want, Nikolaos?"

"Oh, that's much better." Her voice rose and fell, a little-girl giggle at the end of each word. I might never like children again.

"Jean-Claude should be growing weak inside his coffin. Starving, but instead he is strong and well fed. How can this be?"

I didn't have the faintest idea, so I kept quiet. Maybe it was rhetorical?

It wasn't. "Answer me, A-n-i-t-a." She stretched my name out, biting off each syllable.

"I don't know."

"Oh, but you do."

I didn't, but she wasn't going to believe me. "Why are you hurting Phillip?"

"He needed to be taught a lesson, after last night."

"Because he stood up to you?" I asked.

"Yes," she said, "because he stood up to me." She scooted out of the chair and pattered towards me. She did a little turn so the white dress billowed around her. She freaking skipped over to me, smiling. "And because I was angry with you. I torture your lover, and maybe I won't torture you. And perhaps, this demonstration will give you fresh incentive to find the vampire murderer." Her pretty little face was turned up to me, pale eyes gleaming with humor. She was good.

I swallowed hard, and I asked the question I had to ask, "Why were you angry with me?"

She cocked her head to one side. If she hadn't been blood-spattered, it would have been cute. "Could it be that you do not know?" She turned back to Burchard. "What think you, my friend? Is she ignorant?"

He straightened his shoulders and said, "I believe that it is possible."

"Oh, Jean-Claude has been a very naughty boy. Giving the second mark to an unsuspecting mortal."

I stood very still. I was remembering blue, fiery eyes on the stairs, and Jean-Claude's voice in my head. All right, I had suspected it, but I still didn't understand what it meant. "What does the second mark mean?"

She licked her lips, soft like a kitten. "Shall we explain, Burchard? Shall we tell her what we know?"

"If she truly does not know, mistress, we must enlighten her," he said.

"Yes," she said and glided back to the chair. "Burchard, tell her how old you are."

"I am six hundred and three years of age."

I stared at his smooth face and shook my head. "But you're human, not a vampire."

"I have been given the fourth mark and will live as long as my mistress needs me."

"No, Jean-Claude wouldn't do that to me," I said.

Nikolaos made a small shrugging motion with her hands. "I had pressed him very hard. I knew of the first mark to heal you. I suppose he was desperate to save himself."

I remembered the echo of his voice in my head. "I'm sorry. I had no choice." Damn him, there were always choices. "He's been in my dreams every night. What does that mean?"

"He is communicating with you, animator. With the third mark will come more direct mind contact."

I shook my head. "No."

"No what, animator? No third mark, or no you don't believe us?" she asked.

"I don't want to be anyone's servant."

"Have you been eating more than usual?" she asked.

The question was so odd, I just stared for a minute, then I remembered. "Yes. Is that important?"

Nikolaos frowned. "He is siphoning energy from you, Anita. He is feeding through your body. He should be growing weak by now, but you will keep him strong."

"I didn't mean to."

"I believe you," she said. "Last night when I realized what he had done, I was beside myself with anger. So I took your lover."

"Please believe me, he is not my lover."

"Then why did he risk my anger to save you last night? Friendship? Decency? I think not."

All right, let her believe it. Just get us out alive, that was the goal. Nothing else mattered. "What can Phillip and I do to make amends?"

"Oh, so polite, I like that." She put a hand on Burchard's waist, a casual gesture like petting a dog. "Shall we show her what she has to look forward to?"

His whole body tensed as if an electric current had run through it. "If my mistress wishes."

"I do," she said.

Burchard knelt in front of her, face about chest level. Nikolaos looked over his head at me. "This," she said, "is the fourth mark." Her hands went to the small pearl buttons that decorated the front of the white dress. She spread the cloth wide, baring small breasts. They were a child's breasts, small and half-formed. She drew a fingernail beside her left breast. The skin opened like earth behind a plow, spilling blood in a red line down her chest and stomach.

I could not see Burchard's face as he leaned forward. His hands slid around her waist. His face buried between her breasts. She tensed, back arching. Soft, sucking sounds filled the room's stillness.

I looked away, staring at anything but them, as if I had found them having sex but couldn't leave. Valentine was staring at me. I stared back. He tipped an imaginary hat at me and flashed fangs. I ignored him.

Burchard was sitting beside the chair, half-leaning against it. His face was slack and flushed, his chest rising and falling in deep gasps. He wiped blood from his mouth with a shaking hand. Nikolaos sat very still, head back, eyes closed. Perhaps sex wasn't such a bad analogy after all.

Nikolaos spoke with her eyes closed, head thrown back, voice thick. "Your friend, Willie, is back in a coffin. He felt sorry for Phillip. We will have to cure him of such instincts."

She raised her head abruptly, eyes bright, almost glittering, as if they had a light all their own. "Can you see my scar today?"

I shook my head. She was the beautiful child, complete and whole. No imperfections. "You look perfect again, why?"

"Because I am expending energy to make it so. I am having to work at it." Her voice was low and warm, a building heat like thunderstorms in the distance.

The hair at the back of my neck crawled. Something bad was about to happen.

"Jean-Claude has his followers, Anita. If I kill him, they will make him a martyr. But if I prove him weak, powerless, they just fall away and follow me, or follow no one."

She stood, dress buttoned to her neck once more. Her cotton-white hair seemed to move as if a wind stirred it, but there was no wind. "I will destroy something Jean-Claude has given his protection to."

How fast could I get to the knife on my leg? And what good would it do me?

"I will prove to all that Jean-Claude can protect nothing. I am master of all."

Egocentric bitch. Winter grabbed my arm before I could do anything. Too busy watching the vampires to notice the humans.

"Go," she said. "Kill him."

Aubrey and Valentine stood away from the wall and bowed. Then they were gone, as if they had vanished. I turned to Nikolaos.

She smiled. "Yes, I clouded your mind, and you did not see them go."

"Where are they going?" My stomach was tight. I think I already knew the answer.

"Jean-Claude has given Phillip his protection; thus he must die."

"No."

Nikolaos smiled. "Oh, but yes."

A scream ripped through the hallway. A man's scream. Phillip's scream.

"No!" I half-fell to my knees; only Winter's hand kept me from falling to the floor. I pretended to faint, sagging in his grip. He released me. I grabbed the knife from its ankle sheath. Winter and I were close to the hallway, far away from Nikolaos and her human. Maybe far enough.

Winter was staring at her as if waiting for orders. I came up off the ground and drove the knife into his groin. The knife sank in, and blood poured out as I drew the blade free and raced for the hallway.

I was at the door when the first trickle of wind oozed down my back. I didn't look back. I opened the door.

Phillip sagged in the chains. Blood poured in a bright red flood down his chest. It splattered onto the floor, like rain. Torchlight glittered on the wet bone of his spine. Someone had ripped his throat out.

I staggered against the wall as if someone had hit me. I couldn't get enough air. Someone kept whispering, "Oh, God, oh, God," over and over, and it was me. I walked down the steps with my back pressed against the wall. I couldn't take my eyes from him. Couldn't look away. Couldn't breathe. Couldn't cry.

The torchlight reflected in his eyes, giving the illusion of movement. A scream built in my gut and spilled out my throat. "Phillip!"

Aubrey stepped between me and Phillip. He was covered in blood. "I look forward to visiting your lovely friend, Catherine."

I wanted to run at him, screaming. Instead, I leaned against the wall, knife held down at my side, unnoticed. The goal was no longer to get out alive. The goal was to kill Aubrey. "You son of a bitch, you fucking son of a bitch." My voice sounded utterly calm, no emotion whatsoever. I wasn't afraid. I didn't feel anything.

Aubrey's face frowned at me through a mask of Phillip's blood. "Do not say such things to me."

"You ugly, stinking, mother-fucking bastard."

He glided to me, just like I wanted him to. He put a hand on my shoulder. I screamed in his face as loud as I could. He hesitated for just a heartbeat. I shoved the knife blade between his ribs. It was sharp and thin, and I shoved it hilt deep. His body stiffened, leaning into me. Eyes wide and surprised. His mouth opened and closed, but no sound came out. He toppled to the floor, fingers grabbing at air.

Valentine was instantly there, kneeling by the body. "What have you done?" He couldn't see the knife. It was shielded by Aubrey's body.

"I killed him, you son of a bitch, just like I'm going to kill you."

Valentine jerked to his feet, started to say something, and all hell broke loose. The cell door crashed inward and smashed to bits against the far wall. A tornado wind blasted into the room.

Valentine dropped to his knees, head touching the floor. He was bowing. I flattened myself against the wall. The wind clawed at my face, tangling my hair in front of my eyes.

The noise grew less, and I squinted up at the door. Nikolaos floated just above the top step. Her hair crackled around her head, like spider silk. Her skin had shrunken against her bones, until she was skeletal. Her eyes glowed, pale blue fire. She started floating down the steps, hands outstretched.

I could see her veins like blue lights under her skin. I ran. Ran for the far wall, and the tunnel the ratmen had used.

The wind threw me against the wall, and I scrambled on hands and feet towards the tunnel. The hole was large, and black, cool air brushed my face, and something grabbed my ankle.

I screamed. The thing that was Nikolaos dragged me back. It slammed me against the wall and pinned my wrists in one clawed hand. The body leaned into my legs, bone under cloth.

The lips had receded, exposing the fangs and teeth. The skeletal head hissed, "You will learn obedience, to me!" It screamed in my face, and I screamed back. Wordlessly, an animal screaming in a trap.

My heart was thudding in my throat. I couldn't breathe. "Nooo!"

The thing shrieked, "Look at me!"

And I did. I fell into the blue fire that was her eyes. The fire burrowed into my brain, pain. Her thoughts cut me up like knives, slicing away parts of me. Her rage scalded and burned until I thought the skin was peeling away from my face. Claws scrapped the inside of my skull, grinding bone into dust.

When I could see again, I was huddled by the wall, and she was standing over me, not touching, not needing to. I was shaking, shaking so badly my teeth chattered. I was cold, so cold.

"Eventually, animator, you will call me master, and you will mean it." She was suddenly kneeling over me. She pressed her slender body over mine, hands pinning my shoulders to the floor. I couldn't move.

The beautiful little girl leaned her face against my cheek and whispered, "I am going to sink fangs into your neck, and there is nothing you can do to stop me."

Her delicate shell of an ear was brushing my lips. I sank teeth into it until I tasted blood. She shrieked and jerked away, blood running down the side of her neck.

Bright razor claws tore through my brain. Her pain, her rage, turning my brain into silly putty. I think I was screaming again, but I couldn't hear it. After a while I couldn't hear anything. Darkness came. It swallowed up Nikolaos and left me alone, floating in the dark.

39

I woke up, which was a pleasant surprise all on its own. I was blinking up into an electric light set in a ceiling. I was alive, and I wasn't in the dungeon. Good things to know.

Why should it surprise me that I was alive? My fingers caressed the rough, knobby fabric of the couch I was lying on. There was a picture hanging over the couch. A river scene with flatboats, mules, people. Someone came to stand over me, long yellow hair, square-jawed, handsome face. Not as inhumanly beautiful as he had been to me before, but still handsome. I guess you had to be handsome to be a stripper.

My voice came out in a harsh croak. "Robert."

He knelt beside me. "I was afraid you wouldn't wake up before dawn. Are you hurt?"

"Where . . ." I cleared my throat and that helped a little. "Where am I?"

"Jean-Claude's office at Guilty Pleasures."

"How did I get here?"

"Nikolaos brought you. She said, 'Here's your master's whore.' " I watched his throat work as he swallowed. It reminded me of something, but I couldn't think what.

"You know what Jean-Claude has done?" I asked.

Robert nodded. "My master has marked you twice. When I speak to you, I am speaking to him."

Did he mean that figuratively or literally? I really didn't want to know.

"How do you feel?" he asked.

There was something in the way he asked it that meant I shouldn't feel all right. My throat hurt. I raised a hand and touched it. Dried blood. On my neck.

I closed my eyes, but that didn't help. A small sound escaped my throat, very like a whimper. Phillip's image was burned on

216

my mind. The blood pouring from his throat, torn pink meat. I shook my head and tried to breathe deep and slow. It was no good. "Bathroom," I said.

Robert showed me where it was. I went inside, knelt on the cool floor, and threw up in the toilet, until I was empty and nothing but bile came up. Then I walked to the sink and splashed cold water in my mouth and on my face. I stared at myself in the mirror above the sink. My eyes looked black, not brown, my skin sickly. I looked like shit and felt worse.

And there on the right side of my neck was the real thing. Not Phillip's healing bite marks, but fang marks. Tiny, diminutive, fang marks. Nikolaos had . . . contaminated me. To prove she could harm Jean-Claude's human servant. She had proved how tough she was, oh, yeah. Real tough.

Phillip was dead. Dead. Try the word over in your mind, but could I say it out loud? I decided to try. "Phillip is dead," I told my reflection.

I crumbled the brown paper towel and stuffed it in the metal trash can. It wasn't enough. I screamed, "Ahhh!" I kicked the trash can, over and over until it toppled to the floor, spilling its contents.

Robert came through the door. "Are you all right?"

"Does it look like I'm all right?" I yelled.

He hesitated in the doorway. "Is there anything I can do to help?"

"You couldn't even keep them from taking Phillip!"

He winced as if I had hit him. "I did my best."

"Well, it wasn't good enough, was it?" I was still screaming like a mad person. I sank to my knees, and all that rage choked up my throat and spilled out my eyes. "Get out!"

He hesitated. "Are you sure?"

"Get out of here!"

He closed the door behind him. And I sat in the floor and rocked and cried and screamed. When my heart felt as empty as my stomach, I felt leaden, used up.

Nikolaos had killed Phillip and bitten me to prove how powerful she was. I bet she thought I'd be scared absolutely shitless of her. She was right on that. But I spend most of my waking hours confronting and destroying things that I fear. A thousand-year-old master vampire was a tall order, but a girl's got to have a goal.

40

The club was quiet and dark. There was no one there but me. It must have been after dawn. The club was hushed and full of that waiting silence that all buildings get after the people go home. As if once we leave, the building has a life of its own, if only we would leave it in peace. I shook my head and tried to concentrate. To feel something. All I wanted was to go home and try to sleep. And pray I didn't dream.

There was a yellow Post-it note on the door. It read, "Your weapons are behind the bar. The master brought those, too. Robert."

I put both guns in place and the knives. The one I had used on Winter and Aubrey was missing. Was Winter dead? Maybe. Was Aubrey dead? Hopefully. Usually it took a master vampire to survive a blow to the heart, but I'd never tried it on a five-hundred-year-old walking corpse. If they took the knife out, he might be tough enough to survive it. I had to call Catherine. And tell her what? Get out of town, a vampire is after you. Didn't sound like something she'd buy. Shit.

I walked out into the soft white light of dawn. The street was empty and awash in that gentle morning air. The heat hadn't had time to creep in. It was almost cool. Where was my car? I heard footsteps a second before the voice said, "Don't move. I have a gun pointed at your back."

I clasped my hands atop my head without being asked. "Good morning, Edward," I said.

"Good morning, Anita," he said. "Stand very still, please." He stood just behind me, gun pressing against my spine. He frisked me completely, top to bottom. Nothing haphazard about Edward; that's one of the reasons he's still alive. He stepped back from me, and said, "You may turn around now."

He had my Firestar tucked into his belt, the Browning loose in his left hand. I don't know what he did with the knives.

He smiled, boyish and charming, gun very steadily pointed at my chest. "No more hiding. Where is this Nikolaos?" he asked.

I took a deep breath and let it out. I thought about accusing him of being the vampire murderer, but now didn't seem to be a good time. Maybe later, when he wasn't pointing a gun at me. "May I lower my arms?" I asked.

He gave a slight nod.

I lowered my arms slowly. "I want one thing clear between us, Edward. I'll give you the information, but not because I'm afraid of you. I want her dead. And I want a piece of it."

His smile widened, eyes glittering with pleasure. "What happened last night?"

I glanced down at the sidewalk, then up. I stared into his blue eyes and said, "She had Phillip killed."

He was watching my face very closely. "Go on."

"She bit me. I think she plans on making me a personal servant."

He put his gun back in his shoulder holster and came to stand next to me. He turned my head to one side to see the bite mark better. "You need to clean this bite. It's going to hurt like hell."

"I know. Will you help me?"

"Sure." His smile softened. "Here I was going to cause you pain to get information. Now you ask me to help you pour acid on a wound."

"Holy Water," I said.

"It's going to feel the same," he said.

Unfortunately, he was right.

41

I sat with my back pressed against the cool porcelain of the bathtub. The front and side of my shirt was clinging to me, water-soaked. Edward knelt beside me, a half-empty bottle of Holy Water in one hand. We were on the third bottle. I had thrown up only once. Bully for me.

We had started with me sitting on the edge of the sink. I had not stayed there long. I had jumped, yelled, and whimpered. I had also called Edward a son of a bitch. He didn't hold it against me.

"How do you feel?" he asked. His face was utterly blank. I couldn't tell if he was enjoying himself or hating it.

I glared up at him. "Like someone's been shoving a red-hot knife against my throat."

"I mean, do you want to stop and rest awhile?"

I took a deep breath. "No. I want it clean, Edward. All the way."

He shook his head, almost smiled. "It is customary to do this over a matter of days, you know."

"Yes," I said.

"But you want it all in one marathon session?" His gaze was very steady, as if the question were more important than it seemed.

I looked away from the intensity of his eyes. I didn't want to be stared at right now. "I don't have a few days. I need this wound clean before nightfall."

"Because Nikolaos will come visit you again," he said.

"Yes," I said.

"And unless this first wound is purified, she'll have a hold on you."

I took a deep breath and it trembled. "Yes."

"Even if we clean the bite, she may still be able to call you. If she's as powerful as you say she is."

220

"She's that powerful and more." I rubbed my hands along my jeans. "You think Nikolaos can turn me against you, even if we clean the bite?" I looked up at him then, hoping to be able to read his face.

He stared down at me. "We vampire slayers take our chances."

"That wasn't a no," I said.

He gave a flash of smile. "It wasn't a yes, either."

Oh, goody, Edward didn't know either. "Pour some more on, before I lose my nerve."

He did smile then, eyes gleaming. "You will never lose your nerve. Your life, probably, but never your nerve."

It was a compliment and meant as one. "Thank you."

He put a hand on my shoulder, and I turned my face away. My heart was thudding in my throat until all I could hear was my blood pulsing inside my head. I wanted to run, to lash out, to scream, but I had to sit there and let him hurt me. I hate that. It had always taken at least two people to give me injections when I was a child. One person to man the needle and one to hold me down.

Now I held myself down. If Nikolaos bit me twice, I would probably do anything she wanted me to. Even kill. I had seen it happen before, and that vampire had been child's play compared to the master.

The water trickled down my skin and hit the bite mark like molten gold, scalding through my body. It was eating through my skin and bone. Destroying me. Killing me.

I shrieked. I couldn't hold it. Too much pain. Couldn't run away. Had to scream.

I was lying on the floor, my cheek pressed against the coolness of it, breathing in short, hungry gasps.

"Slow your breathing, Anita. You're hyperventilating. Breathe, slow and easy, or you're going to pass out."

I opened my mouth and took in a deep breath; it wheezed and screamed down my throat. I was choking on air. I coughed and fought to breathe. I was light-headed and a little sick by the time I could take a deep breath, but I hadn't passed out. A zillion brownie points for me.

Edward almost had to lie on the floor to put his face near mine. "Can you hear me?"

I managed, "Yes."

"Good. I want to try to put the cross against the bite. Do you agree or do you think it's too soon?"

If we hadn't cleansed the wound with enough Holy Water, the cross would burn me, and I'd have a fresh scar. I had been brave above and beyond the call of duty. I didn't want to play anymore. I opened my mouth to say, "No," but it wasn't what came out. "Do it," I said. Shit. I was going to be brave.

He brushed my hair away from my neck. I lay on the floor and pressed my hands into fists, trying to prepare myself. There is no real way to prepare yourself for somebody shoving a branding iron into your neck.

The chain rustled and slithered through Edward's hands. "Are you ready?"

No. "Just do it, dammit."

He did. The cross pressed against my skin, cool metal, no burning, no smoke, no seared flesh, no pain. I was pure, or as pure as I started out.

He dangled the crucifix in front of my face. I grabbed it with one hand and squeezed until my hand shook. It didn't take long. Tears seeped from the corners of my eyes. I wasn't crying, not really. I was exhausted.

"Can you sit up?" he asked.

I nodded and forced myself to sit, leaning against the bathtub.

"Can you stand up?" he asked.

I thought about it, and decided no, I didn't think I could. My whole body was weak, shaky, nauseous. "Not without help."

Edward knelt beside me, put an arm behind my shoulders and one under my knees, and lifted me in his arms. He stood in one smooth motion, no strain.

"Put me down," I said.

He looked at me. "What?"

"I am not a child. I don't want to be carried."

He drew a loud breath, then said, "All right." He lowered me to my feet and let go. I staggered against the wall and slid to the floor. The tears were back, dammit. I sat in the floor, crying, too weak to walk from my bathroom to my bed. God!

Edward just stood there, looking down at me, face neutral and unreadable as a cat.

My voice came out almost normal, no hint of crying. "I hate being helpless. I hate it!"

"You are one of the least helpless people I know," Edward said. He knelt beside me again, draped my right arm over his shoulders, grabbed my right wrist with his hand. His other arm encircled my waist. The height difference made it a little awkward, but he managed to give me the illusion that I walked to the bed.

The stuffed penguins sat against the wall. Edward hadn't said anything about them. If he wouldn't mention it, I wouldn't. Who knows, maybe Death slept with a teddy bear? Naw.

The heavy drapes were still closed, leaving the room in permanent twilight. "Rest. I'll stand guard and see that none of the bogeys sneak up on you."

I believed him.

Edward brought the white chair from the living room and sat it against the bedroom wall, near the door. He slipped his shoulder holster back on, gun ready at hand. He had brought a gym bag up from the car with us. He unzipped it and drew out what looked like a miniature machine gun. I didn't know much about machine guns, and all I could think of was an Uzi.

"What kind of gun is that?" I asked.

"A Mini-Uzi."

What do you know? I had been right. He popped the clip and showed me how to load it, where the safety was, all the finer points, like it was a new car. He sat down in the chair with the machine gun on his knees.

My eyes kept fluttering shut, but I said, "Don't shoot any of my neighbors, okay?"

I think he smiled. "I'll try not to."

I nodded. "Are you the vampire murderer?"

He smiled then, bright, charming. "Go to sleep, Anita."

I was on the edge of sleep when his voice called me back, soft and faraway. "Where is Nikolaos's daytime retreat?"

I opened my eyes and tried to focus on him. He was still sitting in the chair, motionless. "I'm tired, Edward, not stupid." His laughter bubbled up around me as I fell asleep.

42

Jean-Claude sat in the carved throne. He smiled at me and extended one long-fingered hand. "Come," he said.

I was wearing a long, white dress that had lace of its own. I had never dreamed of myself in anything like it. I glanced up at Jean-Claude. It was his choice, not mine. Fear tightened my throat. "It's my dream," I said.

He held out both hands and said, "Come."

And I went to him. The dress whispered and scraped on the stones, a continuous rustling noise. It grated on my nerves. I was suddenly standing in front of him. I raised my hands towards his slowly. I shouldn't do it. Bad idea, but I couldn't seem to stop myself.

His hands wrapped around mine, and I knelt before him. He drew my hands to the lace that spilled down the front of his shirt, forced my fingers to take two handfuls of it.

He cupped his hands over mine, holding them tight; then he ripped his shirt open using my hands.

His chest was smooth and pale with black hair curling in a line down the middle. The hair thickened over the flatness of his stomach, incredibly black against the white of his belly. The burn scar was firm and shiny and out of place against the perfection of his body.

He gripped my chin in one hand, raising my face towards him. His other hand touched his chest, just below his right nipple. He drew blood on his pale skin. It trickled down his chest in a bright, crimson line.

I tried to pull away, but his fingers dug into my jaw like a vise. I shouted, "No!"

I hit at him with my left hand. He caught my wrist and held it. I used my right hand to grip the floor and shoved with my knees. He held me at jaw and wrist like a butterfly on a pin. You can move, but you can't get away. I dropped to a sitting position, forcing him to strangle me or lower me to the ground. He lowered me.

I kicked out with everything I had. Both feet connected with his knee. Vampires can feel pain. He dropped my jaw so suddenly, I fell backwards. He grabbed both my wrists and jerked me to my knees, body pinned on either side by his legs. He sat in the chair, knees controlling my lower body, hands like chains on my wrists.

A high, tinkling laughter filled the room. Nikolaos stood to one side, watching us. Her laughter echoed through the room, growing louder and louder, like music gone mad.

Jean-Claude transferred both my wrists to one hand, and I could not stop him. His free hand stroked my cheek, smoothing down the line of my neck. His fingers tightened at the base of my skull and began to push.

"Jean-Claude, please, don't do this!"

He pressed my face closer and closer to the wound on his chest. I struggled, but his fingers were welded to my skull, a part of me. "NO!"

Nikolaos's laughter changed to words. "Scratch the surface, and we are all much alike, animator."

I screamed, "Jean-Claude!"

His voice came like velvet, warm and dark, sliding through my mind. "Blood of my blood, flesh of my flesh, two minds with but one body, two souls wedded as one." For one bright, shining moment, I saw it, felt it. Eternity with Jean-Claude. His touch . . . forever. His lips. His blood.

I blinked and found my lips almost touching the wound in his chest. I could have reached out and licked it. "Jean-Claude, no! Jean-Claude!" I screamed it. "God help me!" I screamed that, too.

Darkness and someone gripping my shoulder. I didn't even think about it. Instinct took over. The gun from the headboard was in my hand and turning to point.

A hand trapped my arm under the pillow, pointing the gun at the wall, a body pressing against mine. "Anita, Anita, it's Edward. Look at me!"

I blinked up at Edward, who was pinning my arms. His breathing was coming a little fast.

I stared at the gun in my hand and back at Edward. He was still holding my arms. I guess I didn't blame him.

"Are you all right?" he asked.

I nodded.

"Say something, Anita."

"I had a nightmare," I said.

He shook his head. "No shit." He released me slowly.

I slid the gun back in its holster.

"Who's Jean-Claude?" he asked.

"Why?"

"You were calling his name."

I brushed a hand over my forehead, and it came away slick with sweat. The clothes I'd slept in and the sheet were drenched with it. These nightmares were beginning to get on my nerves.

"What time is it?" The room looked too dark, as if the sun had gone down. My stomach tightened. If it was near dark, Catherine wouldn't have a chance.

"Don't panic; it's just clouds. You've got about four hours until dusk."

I took a deep breath and staggered into the bathroom. I splashed cold water on my face and neck. I looked ghost-pale in the mirror. Had the dream been Jean-Claude's doing or Nikolaos's? If it had been Nikolaos, did she already control me? No answers. No answers to anything.

Edward was sitting in the white chair when I came back out. He watched me like I was an interesting species of insect that he had never seen before.

I ignored him and called Catherine's office. "Hi, Betty, this is Anita Blake. Is Catherine in?"

"Hello, Ms. Blake. I thought you knew that Ms. Maison is going to be out of town from the thirteenth until the twentieth on a deposition."

Catherine had told me, but I forgot. I finally lucked out. It was about time. "I forgot, Betty. Thanks a lot. Thanks more than you'll ever know."

"Glad to be of help. Ms. Maison has scheduled the first fitting for the bridesmaid dresses on the twenty-third." She said it like it should make me feel better. It didn't.

"I won't forget. Bye."

"Have a nice day."

I hung up and phoned Irving Griswold. He was a reporter for the *Saint Louis Post-Dispatch*. He was also a werewolf. Irving the werewolf. It didn't quite work, but then what did? Charles the werewolf, naw. Justin, Oliver, Wilbur, Brent? Nope.

Irving answered on the third ring.

"It's Anita Blake."

"Well, hi, what's up?" He sounded suspicious, as if I never called him unless I wanted something.

"Do you know any wererats?"

He was quiet for almost too long; then, "Why do you want to know?"

"I can't tell you."

"You mean you want my help, but I don't get a story out of it."

I sighed. "That's about it."

"Then why should I help you?"

"Don't give me a hard time, Irving. I've given you plenty of exclusives. My information is what got you your first front page byline. So don't give me grief."

"A little grouchy today, aren't you?"

"Do you know a wererat or don't you?"

"I do."

"I need to get a message to the Rat King."

He gave a low whistle that was piercing over the phone. "You don't ask for much, do you? I might be able to get you a meeting with the wererat I know, but not their king."

"Give the Rat King this message; got a pencil?"

"Always," he said.

"The vampires didn't get me, and I didn't do what they wanted."

Irving read it back to me. When I confirmed it, he said, "You're involved with vampires and wererats, and I don't get an exclusive."

"No one's going to get this one, Irving. It's going to be too messy for that."

He was silent a moment. "Okay. I'll try to set up a meeting. I should know sometime tonight."

"Thanks, Irving."

"You be careful, Blake. I'd hate to lose my best source of front page bylines."

"Me, too," I said.

I had no sooner hung up the phone when it rang again. I picked it up without thinking. A phone rings, you pick it up, years of training. I haven't had my answering machine long enough to shake it completely.

"Anita, this is Bert."

"Hi, Bert." I sighed, quietly.

"I know you are working on the vampire case, but I have something you might be interested in."

"Bert, I am way over my head already. Anything else and I may never see daylight." You'd think Bert would ask if I was all right. How I was doing. But no, not my boss.

"Thomas Jensen called today."

My spine straightened. "Jensen called?"

"That's right."

"He's going to let us do it?"

"Not us, you. He specifically asked for you. I tried to get him to take someone else, but he wouldn't do it. And it has to be tonight. He's afraid he'll chicken out."

"Damn," I said softly.

"Do I call him back and cancel, or can you give me a time to have him meet you?"

Why did everything have to come at once? One of life's rhetorical questions. "Have him meet me at full dark tonight."

"That's my girl. I knew you wouldn't let me down."

"I'm not your girl, Bert. How much is he paying you?"

"Thirty thousand dollars. The five-thousand-dollar down payment has already arrived by special messenger."

"You are an evil man, Bert."

"Yes," he said, "and it pays very well, thank you." He hung up without saying good-bye. Mr. Charm.

Edward was staring at me. "Did you just take a job raising the dead, for tonight?"

"Laying the dead to rest actually, but yes."

"Does raising the dead take it out of you?"

"It?" I asked.

He shrugged. "Energy, stamina, strength."

"Sometimes."

"How about this job? Is it an energy drain?"

I smiled. "Yes."

He shook his head. "You can't afford to be used up, Anita."

"I won't be used up," I said. I took a deep breath and tried to think how to explain things to Edward. "Thomas Jensen lost his daughter twenty years ago. Seven years ago he had her raised as a zombie."

"So?"

"She committed suicide. No one knew why at the time. It was later learned that Mr. Jensen had sexually abused his daughter and that was why she had killed herself."

"And he raised her from the dead." Edward grimaced. "You don't mean . . ."

I waved my hands as if I could erase the sudden vivid image. "No, no, not that. He felt remorseful and raised her to say he was sorry."

"And?"

"She wouldn't forgive him."

He shook his head. "I don't understand."

"He raised her to make amends, but she had died hating him, fearing him. The zombie wouldn't forgive him, so he wouldn't put her back. As her mind deteriorated and her body, too, he kept her with him as a sort of punishment."

"Jesus."

"Yeah," I said. I walked to the closet and got out my gym bag. Edward carried guns in his; I carried my animator paraphernalia in it. Sometimes, I carried my vampire-slaying kit in it. The matchbook Zachary gave me was in the bottom of the bag. I stuffed it in my pants pocket. I don't think Edward saw me. He does catch on if a clue sits up and barks. "Jensen finally agreed to put her in the ground if I'll do it. I can't say no. He's sort of a legend among animators. The closest we come to a ghost story."

"Why tonight? If it's waited seven years, why not a few more nights?"

I kept putting things in the gym bag. "He insisted. He's afraid he'll lose his nerve if he has to wait. Besides, I may not be alive a few nights from now. He might not let anybody else do it."

"That is not your problem. You didn't raise his zombie."

"No, but I am an animator first. Vampire slaying is . . . a sideline. I am an animator. It isn't just a job."

He was still staring at me. "I don't understand why, but I understand you have to do it."

"Thanks."

He smiled. "Your show. Mind if I come along to make sure no one offs you while you're gone?"

I glanced at him. "Ever see a zombie raising?"

"No."

"You're not squeamish, are you?" I smiled when I said it.

He stared at me, blue eyes gone suddenly cold. His whole face became different. There was nothing there, no expression, except that awful coldness. Emptiness. I'd had a leopard look at me like that once, through the cage bars, no emotion I understood, thoughts so alien it might as well have inhabited a different planet. Something that could kill me, skillfully, efficiently, because that was what it was meant to do, if it was hungry, or if I annoyed it.

I didn't faint from fear or run screaming from the room, but it was something of an effort. "You've proved your point, Edward. Can the perfect-killer routine, and let's go."

His eyes didn't revert to normal instantly but had to warm up, like dawn easing through the sky.

I hoped Edward never turned that look on me for real. If he did, one of us would die. Odds are it would be me.

43

The night was almost perfectly black. Thick clouds hid the sky. A wind rushed along the ground and smelled of rain.

Iris Jensen's grave marker was smooth, white marble. It was a nearly life-size angel, wings outspread, arms open, welcoming. You could still read the lettering by flashlight: "Beloved daughter. Sadly missed." The same man who had had the angel carved, who sadly missed her, had been molesting her. She had killed herself to escape him, and he had brought her back. That was why I was out here in the dark, waiting for the Jensens, not him, but her. Even though I knew her mind was gone by now, I wanted Iris Jensen in the ground and at peace.

I couldn't explain that to Edward, so I hadn't tried. A huge oak stood sentinel over the empty grave. The wind rushed through the leaves and sent them skittering and whispering overhead. It sounded too dry, like autumn leaves instead of summer. The air felt cool and damp, rain almost upon us. It wasn't unbearably hot for once.

I had picked up a pair of chickens. They clucked softly from inside their crate where they sat near the grave. Edward leaned against my car, ankles crossed, arms loose at his sides. The gym bag was open by me on the ground. The machete I used gleamed from inside.

"Where is he?" Edward asked.

I shook my head. "I don't know." It had been almost an hour since full dark. The cemetery grounds were mostly bare; only a few trees dotted the soft roll of hills. We should have been seeing car lights on the gravel road. Where was Jensen? Had he chickened out?

Edward stepped away from the car and walked to stand beside me. "I don't like it, Anita."

I wasn't too thrilled either, but . . . "We'll give it another fifteen minutes. If he's not here by then, we'll leave."

Edward glanced around the open ground. "Not much cover around here."

"I don't think we have to worry about snipers."

"You said someone shot at you, right?"

I nodded. He had a point. Goosebumps marched up my arms. The wind blew a hole in the clouds and moonlight streamed down. Off in the distance a small building gleamed silver-grey in the light.

"What's that?" Edward asked.

"The maintenance shed," I said. "You think the grass cuts itself?"

"Never thought about it," he said.

The clouds rolled in again and plunged the cemetery into blackness. Everything became soft shapes; the white marble seemed to glow with its own light.

There was the sound of scrabbling claws on metal. I whirled. A ghoul sat on top of my car. It was naked and looked as if a human being had been stripped and dipped into silver-grey paint, almost metallic. But the teeth and claws on its hands and feet were long and black, curved talons. The eyes glowed crimson.

Edward moved up beside me, gun in his hand.

I had my gun out, too. Practice, practice, and you don't have to think about it.

"What's it doing up there?" he asked.

"Don't know." I waved my free hand at it and said, "Scat!"

It crouched, staring at me. Ghouls are cowards; they don't attack healthy human beings. I took two steps, waving my gun at it. "Go away, shoo!" Any show of force sends them scuttling away. This one just sat there. I backed away.

"Edward," I said, softly.

"Yes."

"I didn't sense any ghouls in this cemetery."

"So? You missed one."

"There's no such thing as just one ghoul. They travel in packs. And you don't miss them. They leave a sort of psychic stench behind. Evil."

"Anita." His voice was soft, normal, but not normal. I glanced where he was looking and saw two more ghouls creeping up behind us.

We stood almost back to back, guns pointing out. "I saw a

ghoul attack earlier this week. Healthy man killed, a cemetery where there were no ghouls."

"Sounds familiar," he said.

"Yeah. Bullets won't kill them."

"I know. What are they waiting for?" he asked.

"Courage, I think."

"They're waiting for me," a voice said. Zachary stepped around the trunk of the tree. He was smiling.

I think my mouth dropped to the ground. Maybe that was what he was smiling at. I knew then. He wasn't killing human beings to feed his gris-gris. He was killing vampires. Theresa had tormented him, so she had been the next victim. There were still some questions though, big ones.

Edward glanced at me, then back at Zachary. "Who is this?" he asked.

"The vampire murderer, I presume," I said.

Zachary gave a little bow. A ghoul leaned against his leg, and he stroked its nearly bald head. "When did you guess?"

"Just now. I'm a little slow this year."

He frowned then. "I thought you'd figure it out eventually."

"That's why you destroyed the zombie witness's mind. To save yourself."

"It was fortunate that Nikolaos left me in charge of questioning the man." He smiled when he said it.

"I'll bet," I said. "How did you get the two-biter to shoot me at the church?"

"That was easy. I told him the orders came from Nikolaos."

Of course. "How are you getting the ghouls out of their cemetery? How come they obey your orders?"

"You know the theory that if you bury an animator in a cemetery, you get ghouls."

"Yeah."

"When I came out of the grave, they came with me, and they were mine. Mine."

I glanced at the creatures and found that there were more of them. At least twenty, a big pack. "So you're saying that's where ghouls come from." I shook my head. "There aren't enough animators in the world to account for all the ghouls."

"I've been thinking about that," he said. "I think that the more zombies you raise in a cemetery, the greater your chances for ghouls."

"You mean like a cumulative effect?"

"Exactly. I've been wanting to talk this over with another animator, but you see the problem."

"Yes," I said, "I do. Can't talk shop without admitting what you are and what you've done."

Edward fired without warning. The bullet took Zachary in the chest and twisted him around. He lay face down, the ghouls frozen; then Zachary raised himself up on his elbows. He stood with a little help from an anxious ghoul. "Sticks and stones may break my bones, but bullets will never hurt me."

"Great, a comedian," I said.

Edward fired again, but Zachary darted behind the tree trunk.

He called, hidden from sight. "Now, now, no hitting the head. I'm not sure what would happen if you put a bullet in my brain."

"Let's find out," Edward said.

"Good-bye, Anita. I won't stay around to watch." He walked away with a troop of ghouls surrounding him. He was crouched in the middle of them, hiding I supposed from a bullet in the brain, but for a minute I couldn't pick him out.

Two more ghouls appeared around the car, crouched low on the gravel drive. One was female with the tatters of a dress still clinging to her.

"Let's give them something to be afraid of," Edward said. I felt him move, and his gun fired twice. A high-pitched squealing filled the night. The ghoul on my car leaped to the ground and hid. But there were more of them moving in from all sides. At least fifteen of them had been left behind for us to play with.

I fired and hit one of them. It fell to its side and rolled in the gravel, making that same high-pitched noise, like a wounded rabbit. Piteous and animal.

"Is there anyplace we can run to?" Edward asked.

"The maintenance shed," I said.

"Is it wood?"

"Yes."

"It won't stop them."

"No," I said, "but it will get us out of the open."

"Okay, any advice before we start to move?"

"Don't run until we are very close to the shed. If you run, they'll chase you. They'll think you're scared."

"Anything else?" he asked.

"You don't smoke, do you?"

"No, why?"

"They're afraid of fire."

"Great; we're going to be eaten alive because neither one of us smokes."

I almost laughed. He sounded so thoroughly disgusted, but a ghoul was crouching to leap at me, and I had to shoot it between the eyes. No time for laughter.

"Let's go, slow and easy," I said.

"I wish the machine gun wasn't in the car."

"Me, too."

Edward fired three shots, and the night filled with squeals and animal screams. We started walking towards the distant shed. I'd say maybe a quarter of a mile away. It was going to be a long walk.

A ghoul charged us. I dropped it, and it spilled to the grass, but it was like shooting targets, no blood, just empty holes. It hurt, but not enough. Not nearly enough.

I was walking nearly backwards, one hand back feeling Edward's forward movement. There were too many of them. We were not going to make it to the shed. No way. One of the chickens made a soft, questioning cluck. I had an idea.

I shot one of the chickens. It flopped, and the other bird panicked, beating its wings against the wooden crate. The ghouls froze, then one put its face into the air and sniffed.

Fresh blood, boys, come and get it. Fresh meat. Two ghouls were suddenly racing for the chickens. The rest followed, scrambling over each other to crack the wood and get to the juicy morsels inside.

"Keep walking, Edward, don't run, but walk a little faster. The chickens won't hold them long."

We walked a little faster. The sounds of scrambling claws, cracking bone, the splatter of blood, the squabbling howls of the ghouls—it was an unwelcome preview.

Halfway to the shed, a howl went up through the night, long and hostile. No dog ever sounded like that. I glanced back, and the ghouls were rushing over the ground on all fours.

"Run!" I said.

We ran.

We crashed against the shed door and found the damn thing padlocked. Edward shot the lock off; no time to pick it. The ghouls were close, howling as they came.

We scrambled inside, closing the door, for what good it would do us. There was one small window high up near the ceiling; moonlight suddenly spilled through it. There was a herd of lawnmowers against one wall, some of them hanging from hooks. Gardening shears, hedge trimmers, trowels, a curl of garden hose. The whole shed smelled of gasoline and oily rags.

Edward said, "There's nothing to put against the door, Anita."

He was right. We'd blown the lock off. Where was a heavy object when you needed it? "Roll a lawnmower against it."

"That won't hold them long."

"It's better than nothing," I said. He didn't move, so I rolled a lawnmower against the door.

"I won't die, eaten alive," he said. He put a fresh clip in his gun. "I'll do you first if you want, or you can do it yourself."

I remembered then that I had shoved the matchbook Zachary had given me in my pocket. Matches, we had matches!

"Anita, they're almost here. Do you want to do it yourself?"

I pulled the matchbook out of my pocket. Thank you, God. "Save your bullets, Edward." I lifted a can of gasoline in one hand.

"What are you planning?" he asked.

The howls were crashing around us; they were almost here.

"I'm going to set the shed on fire." I splashed gasoline on the door. The smell was sharp and tugged at the back of my throat.

"With us inside?" he asked.

"Yes."

"I'd rather shoot myself, if it's all the same to you."

"I don't plan to die tonight, Edward."

A claw smashed through the door, talons raking the wood, tearing it apart. I lit a match and threw it on the gasoline-soaked door. It went up with a blue-white whoosh of flame. The ghoul screamed, covered in fire, stumbling back from the ruined door.

The stench of burning flesh mingled with gasoline. Burnt hair. I coughed, putting a hand over my mouth. The fire was eating up the wood of the shed, spreading to the roof. We didn't need more gasoline; the damn thing was a fire trap. With us inside. I hadn't thought it would spread this fast.

Edward was standing near the back wall, hand over his mouth. His voice came muffled. "You did have a plan to get us out, right?"

A hand crashed through the wood, clawing at him. He backed away from it. The ghoul began to tear through the wood, leering at us. Edward shot it between the eyes, and it disappeared from sight.

I grabbed a rake from the far wall. Cinders were beginning to float down on us. If the smoke didn't get us first, the shed was going to collapse on top of us. "Take off your shirt," I said.

He didn't even ask why. Practical to the end. He stripped the shoulder rig off and pulled his shirt over his head, tossed it to me, and slipped the gun over his bare chest.

I wrapped the shirt over the tines of the rake and soaked it with gasoline. I set it on fire from the walls; no need for matches. The front of the shed was raining fire on us. Tiny burning stings like wasps on my skin.

Edward had caught on. He found an axe and started chopping at the hole the ghoul had made. I carried the improvised torch and a can of gasoline in my hands. The thought occurred to me that the heat was going to set the gasoline off. We weren't going to suffocate from smoke; we were going to blow up.

"Hurry!" I said.

Edward squeezed through the opening, and I followed, nearly burning him with the torch. There wasn't a ghoul for a hundred yards. They were smarter than they looked. We ran, and the explosion slammed into my back like a huge wind. I tumbled over into the grass, all the air knocked out of me. Bits of burning wood clattered to the ground on either side of me. I covered my head and prayed. My luck, I'd get caught by a flying nail.

Silence, or no more explosions. I raised my head cautiously. The shed was gone, nothing left. Bits of wood burned in the grass around me. Edward was lying on the ground, nearly touching distance from me. He stared at me. Did my face look as surprised as his did? Probably.

Our improvised torch was slowly setting the grass on fire. He knelt and raised it up.

I found the gasoline can unharmed and got to my feet. Edward followed, carrying the torch. The ghouls seemed to have fled, smart ghouls, but just in case . . . We didn't even have to discuss it. Paranoia, we had that in common.

We walked towards the car. The adrenaline was gone, and I was tireder than before. A person only has so much adrenaline; then you start running on numb.

The chicken crate was history; nameless bits and pieces were scattered around the grave. I didn't look any closer. I stopped to pick up my gym bag. It was untouched, just lying there. Edward moved ahead of me and tossed the torch on the gravel driveway. The wind rustled through the trees; then Edward yelled, "Anita!"

I rolled. Edward's gun fired, and something fell squealing on the grass. I stared at the ghoul while Edward pumped bullets into it. When I swallowed my heart back down into my chest, I crawled to the gasoline can and unscrewed it.

The ghoul screamed. Edward was driving the ghoul with the burning torch. I splashed gasoline on the cringing thing, dropped to my knees, and said, "Light it."

Edward shoved the torch home. Fire whooshed over the ghoul, and it started screaming. The night stank of burning meat and hair. And gasoline.

It rolled over and over on the ground trying to put out the fire, but it wouldn't go out.

I whispered, "You're next, Zachary baby. You are next."

The shirt had burned away, and Edward tossed the rake to the ground. "Let's get out of here," he said.

I agreed wholeheartedly. I unlocked the car, tossed my gym bag in the back seat, and started the car. The ghoul was lying on the grass, not moving, burning.

Edward was in the passenger seat with the machine gun in his lap. For the first time since I'd met him, Edward looked shaken. Scared, even.

"You going to sleep with that machine gun?" I asked.

He glanced at me. "You going to sleep with your gun?" he asked.

Point for Edward. I took the narrow gravel turns as quick as I dared. My Nova wasn't built for speed maneuvering. Having a wreck here in the cemetery didn't seem like a real good idea tonight. The headlights bounced over the tombstones, but nothing moved. No ghouls in sight.

I took a deep breath and let it out. This was the second attempt on my life in as many days. Frankly, I'd rather be shot at.

44

We drove in silence for a long time. It was Edward who finally spoke into the wheel-rushing quiet. "I don't think we should go back to your apartment," he said.

"Agreed."

"I'll take you to my hotel. Unless you have someplace else you'd rather go?"

Where could I go? Ronnie's? I didn't want her endangered anymore. Who else could I endanger? No one. No one but Edward, and he could handle it. Maybe better than I could.

My beeper trembled against my waist, sending shock waves all along my rib cage. I hated putting the beeper on silent mode. The damn thing always scared me when it went off.

Edward said, "What the hell happened? You jumped like something bit you."

I hit the button on the beeper, to shut it off and see who had called. The number lit up briefly. "My beeper went off on silent mode. No noise, just vibration."

He glanced at me. "You are not going to call work." He made it sound like a statement or an order.

"Look, Edward, I'm not feeling so hot, so don't argue with me."

I heard his breath ease out, but what could he say? I was driving. Short of drawing his gun and hijacking me, he was along for the ride. I took the next exit and located a pay phone at a convenience store. The store lot was fully lit and made me a wonderful target, but after the ghouls I wanted light.

Edward watched me get out of the car with my billfold gripped in my hand. He did not get out to watch my back. Fine, I had my gun. If he wanted to pout, let him.

I called work. Craig, our night secretary, answered. "Animators, Inc. May I help you?"

"Hi, Craig, this is Anita. What's up?"

"Irving Griswold called, says to call him back ASAP or the meeting's off. He said you'd know what that meant. Do you?"

"Yes. Thanks, Craig."

"You sound awful."

"Good night, Craig." I hung up on him. I felt tired and sluggish, and my throat hurt. I wanted to curl up somewhere dark and quiet for about a week. Instead, I called Irving. "It's me," I said.

"Well, it's about time. Do you know the trouble I've gone through to set this up? You almost missed it."

"If you don't quit talking, I may still miss it. Tell me where and when."

He did. If we hurried, we'd make it. "Why is everyone so hot to do everything tonight?" I said.

"Hey, if you don't want to meet, that's fine."

"Irving, I've had a very, very long night, so stop bitching at me."

"Are you all right?"

What a stupid question. "Not really, but I'll live."

"If you're hurt, I'll try to get the meeting postponed, but I can't promise anything, Anita. It was your message that got him this far."

I leaned my forehead against the metal of the booth. "I'll be there, Irving."

"I won't be." He sounded thoroughly disgusted. "One of the conditions was no reporters and no police."

I had to smile. Poor Irving; he was getting left out of everything. He hadn't been attacked by ghouls and almost blown up, though. Maybe I should save my pity for myself.

"Thanks, Irving, I owe you one."

"You owe me several," he said. "Be careful. I don't know what you're into this time, but it sounds bad."

He was fishing, and I knew it. "Good night, Irving." I hung up before he could ask any more questions.

I called Dolph's home phone number. I don't know why it couldn't wait until morning, but I had almost died tonight. If I did die, I wanted someone to hunt Zachary down.

Dolph answered on the sixth ring. His voice sounded gruff with sleep. "Yes."

"This is Anita Blake, Dolph."

"What's wrong?" His voice sounded almost alert.

"I know who the murderer is."

"Tell me."

I told him. He took notes and asked questions. The biggest question came at the end. "Can you prove any of this?"

"I can prove he wears a gris-gris. I can testify that he confessed to me. He tried to kill me; that I witnessed personally."

"It's going to be a tough sell to a jury or a judge."

"I know."

"I'll see what I can find out."

"We've almost got a solid case on him, Dolph."

"True, but it all hinges on you being alive to testify."

"Yeah, I'll be careful."

"You come down tomorrow and get all this information recorded officially."

"I will."

"Good work."

"Thanks," I said.

"Good night, Anita."

"Good night, Dolph."

I eased back into the car. "We have a meeting with the wererats in forty-five minutes."

"Why is it so important?" he asked.

"Because I think they can show us a back way into Nikolaos's lair. If we come in the front door, we'll never make it." I started the car and pulled out into the road.

"Who else did you call?" he asked.

So he had been paying attention. "The police."

"What?"

Edward never likes dealing with the police. Fancy that. "If Zachary manages to kill me, I want someone else to be looking into it."

He was silent for a little while. Then he asked, "Tell me about Nikolaos."

I shrugged. "She's a sadistic monster, and she's over a thousand years old."

"I look forward to meeting her."

"Don't," I said.

"We've killed master vampires before, Anita. She's just one more."

"No. Nikolaos is at least a thousand years old. I don't think I've ever been so frightened of anything in my life."

He was silent, face unreadable.

"What are you thinking?" I asked.

"That I love a challenge." Then he smiled, a beautiful, spreading smile. Shit. Death had seen his ultimate goal. The biggest catch of all. He wasn't afraid of her, and he should have been.

There aren't that many places open at one-thirty A.M., but Denny's is. There was something wrong with meeting wererats in Denny's over coffee and donuts. Shouldn't we have been meeting in some dark alley? I wasn't complaining, mind you. It just struck me as . . . funny.

Edward went in first to make sure it wasn't another setup. If he took a table, it was safe. If he came back out, it wasn't safe. Simple. No one knew what he looked like yet. As long as he wasn't with me, he could go anywhere and no one would try to kill him. Amazing. I was beginning to feel like Typhoid Mary.

Edward took a table. Safe. I walked into the bright lights and artificial comfort of the restaurant. The waitress had dark circles under her eyes, cleverly disguised by thick base, which made the circles look sort of pinkish. I looked past her. A man was motioning to me. Hand straight up, finger crooked like he was calling the waitress, or some other subservient.

"I see my party, now. Thanks anyway," I said.

The restaurant was mostly empty in the wee hours of Monday, or rather Tuesday morning. Two men sat at a table in front of the first man. They looked normal enough, but there was a sense of contained energy that seemed to spark in the air around them. Lycanthropes. I would have bet my life on it, and maybe I was.

There was a couple, male and female, sitting catty-corner from the first two. I would have bet money they were lycanthropes, too.

Edward had taken a table near them, but not too near. He had hunted lycanthropes before; he knew what to look for as well.

As I passed the table, one of the men looked up. Pure brown eyes, so dark they were almost black, stared into mine. His face was square, body slender, small build, muscles worked in his arms as he folded his hands under his chin and looked at me. I stared back; then I was past him and to the booth where the Rat King sat.

He was tall, at least six feet, dark brown skin, with thick, short-cut black hair, brown eyes. His face was thin, arrogant, lips almost too soft for the haughty expression he gave me. He was darkly handsome, strongly Mexican, and his suspicion rode the air like lightning.

I eased into the booth. I took a deep, steadying breath and looked across the counter at him.

"I got your message. What do you want?" His voice was soft but deep, without a trace of accent.

"I want you to lead myself and at least one man into the tunnels beneath the Circus of the Damned."

His frown deepened, forming faint wrinkles between his eyes. "Why should I do this for you?"

"Do you want your people free of the master's influence?"

He nodded. Still frowning.

I was really winning him over. "Guide us in through the dungeon entrance, and I'll take care of it."

He clasped his hands together on the table. "How can I trust you?"

"I am not a bounty hunter. I have never harmed a lycanthrope."

"We cannot fight beside you if you go against her. Even I cannot fight her. She calls to me. I don't answer, but I feel it. I can keep the small rats and my people from helping her against you, but that is all."

"Just get us inside. We'll do the rest."

"Are you so confident?"

"I'm willing to bet my life on it," I said.

He steepled his fingers against his lips, elbows on the table. The burn scar in his forearm was still there even in human form, a rough, four-pointed crown. "I'll get you inside," he said.

I smiled. "Thank you."

He stared at me. "When you come back out alive, then you can thank me."

"It's a deal." I held my hand out. After a moment's hesitation, he took it. We shook on it.

"You wish to wait a few days?" he asked.

"No," I said. "I want to go in tomorrow."

He cocked his head to one side. "Are you sure?"

"Why? Is that a problem?"

"You are hurt. I thought you might wish to heal."

I was a little bruised, and my throat hurt, but . . . "How did you know?"

"You smell like death has brushed you close tonight."

I stared at him. Irving never does this to me, the supernatural powers bit. I'm not saying he can't, but he works hard at being human. This man did not.

I took a deep breath. "That is my business."

He nodded. "We will call you and give you the place and time."

I stood up. He remained sitting. There didn't seem to be anything else to say, so I left.

About ten minutes later Edward got into the car with me. "What now?" he asked.

"You mentioned your hotel room. I'm going to sleep while I can."

"And tomorrow?"

"You take me out and show me how the shotgun works."

"Then?" he asked.

"Then we go after Nikolaos," I said.

He gave a shaky breath, almost a laugh. "Oh, boy."

Oh, boy? "Glad to see someone is enjoying all this."

He grinned at me. "I love my work," he said.

I had to smile. Truth was, I loved my work, too.

45

During the day I learned how to use a shotgun. That night I went caving with wererats.

The cave was dark. I stood in absolute blackness, gripping my flashlight. I touched my hand to my forehead and couldn't see a damn thing but the funny white images your eyes make when there is no light. I was wearing a hard hat with a light on it, turned off at present. The wererats had insisted on it. All around me were sounds. Cries, moans, the popping of bone, a curious sliding sound like a knife drawing out of flesh. The wererats were changing from human to animal. It sounded like it hurt—a lot. They had made me swear not to turn on a light until they told me to.

I had never wanted to see so badly in my life. It couldn't be so horrible. Could it? But a promise is a promise. I sounded like Horton the Elephant. "A person is a person no matter how small." What the hell was I doing standing in the middle of a cave, in the dark, surrounded by wererats, quoting Dr. Seuss, and trying to kill a one-thousand-year-old vampire?

It had been one of my stranger weeks.

Rafael, the Rat King, said, "You may turn on your lights."

I did, instantly. My eyes seemed to leech on the light, eager to see. The ratmen stood in small groups in the wide, flat-roofed tunnel. There were ten of them. I had counted them in human form. Now the seven males were fur-covered and wearing jean cutoffs. Two wore loose t-shirts. The three women wore loose dresses, like maternity clothes. Their black button eyes glittered in the light. Everybody was furry.

Edward came to stand near me. He was staring at the weres, face distant, unreadable. I touched his arm. I had told Rafael that I was not a bounty hunter, but Edward was, sometimes. I hoped I had not endangered these people.

"Are you ready?" Rafael asked. He was the same sleek black ratman I remembered.

"Yes," I said.

Edward nodded.

The wererats scattered to either side of us, scrambling over low, weathered flowstone. I said to no one in particular, "I thought caves were damp."

A smaller ratman in a t-shirt said, "Cherokee Caverns is dead cave."

"I don't understand."

"Live cave has water and growing formations. A dry cave where none of the formations are growing is called dead cave."

"Oh," I said.

He drew lips back from huge teeth, a smile, I think. "More than you wanted to know, huh?"

Rafael hissed back, "We are not here to give guided tours, Louie. Now be quiet, both of you."

Louie shrugged and scrambled ahead of me. He was the same human that had been with Rafael in the restaurant, the one with the dark eyes.

One of the females was nearly grey-furred. Her name was Lillian, and she was a doctor. She carried a backpack full of medical supplies. They seemed to be planning on us getting hurt. At least that meant they thought we would come out alive. I was beginning to wonder about that part myself.

Two hours later the ceiling dropped to a point where I couldn't stand upright. And I learned what the hard hats they had given Edward and me were for. I scraped my head on the rock at least a thousand times. I'd have knocked myself unconscious long before we saw Nikolaos.

The rats seemed designed for the tunnel, sliding along, flattening their bodies in a strange, scrambling grace. Edward and I could not match it. Not even close.

He cursed softly behind me. His five inches of extra height were causing him pain. My lower back was an aching burn. He had to be in worse shape. There were pockets where the ceiling opened up and we could stand. I started looking very forward to them, like air pockets to a diver.

The quality of darkness changed. Light—there was light up ahead, not much, but it was there. It flickered at the far end of the tunnel like a mirage.

Rafael crouched beside us. Edward sat flat on the dry rock. I joined him. "There is your dungeon. We will wait here until near dark. If you have not come out, we will leave. After Nikolaos is dead, if we can, we will help you."

I nodded; the light on my hard hat nodded with me. "Thank you for helping us."

He shook his narrow, ratty face. "I have delivered you to the devil's door. Do not thank me for that."

I glanced at Edward. His face was still distant, unreadable. If he was interested in what the ratman had just said, I couldn't tell it. We might as well have been talking about a grocery list.

Edward and I knelt before the opening into the dungeon. Torchlight flickered, incredibly bright after the darkness. Edward was cradling his Uzi that hung on a strap across his chest. I had the shotgun. I was also carrying my two pistols, two knives, and a derringer stuffed in the pocket of my jacket. It was a present from Edward. He had handed it to me with this advice: "It kicks like a sonofabitch, but press it under someone's chin, and it will blow their fucking head off." Nice to know.

It was daylight outside. There shouldn't be a vampire stirring, but Burchard would be there. And if he saw us, Nikolaos would know. Somehow, she'd know. Goosebumps marched up my arms.

We scrambled inside, ready to kill and maim. The room was empty. All that adrenaline sort of sat in my body, making my breathing too quick and my heart pound for no reason. The spot where Phillip had been chained was clean. Someone had scrubbed it down real good.

I fought an urge to touch the wall where he'd been.

Edward called softly, "Anita." He was at the door.

I hurried up to him.

"What's wrong?" he asked.

"She killed Phillip in here."

"Keep your mind on business. I don't want to die because you're daydreaming."

I started to get angry and swallowed it. He was right.

Edward tried the door, and it opened. No prisoners, no need to lock it. I took the left side of the door, and he took the right. The corridor was empty.

My hands were sweating on the shotgun. Edward led off down the right hand side of the corridor. I followed him into the dragon's lair. I didn't feel much like a knight. I was fresh out of shiny steeds, or was that shiny armor?

Whatever. We were here. This was it. I could taste my heart in my throat.

46

The dragon didn't come out and eat us right away. In fact, the place was quiet. As the cliché goes, too quiet.

I stepped close to Edward and whispered, "I don't mean to complain, but where is everybody?"

He leaned his back against the wall and said, "Maybe you killed Winter. That just leaves Burchard. Maybe he's on an errand."

I shook my head. "This is too easy."

"Don't worry. Something will go wrong soon." He continued down the corridor, and I followed. It took me three steps to realize Edward had made a joke.

The corridor opened into a huge room like Nikolaos's throne room, but there was no chair here. There were coffins. Five of them spaced around the room on raised platforms, so they didn't have to sit on the floor in the draft. Tall, iron candelabra burned in the room, one at the foot and head of each coffin.

Most vampires made some effort to hide their coffins, but not Nikolaos.

"Arrogant," Edward whispered.

"Yes," I whispered back. You always whispered around the coffins, at first, as if it were a funeral and they could hear you.

There was a neck-ruffling smell to the room, stale. It caught at the back of my throat and was almost a taste, faintly metallic. It was like the smell of snakes kept in cages. You knew there was nothing warm and furry in this room just by smell. And that really doesn't do it justice. It was the smell of vampires.

The first coffin was dark, well-varnished wood, with golden handles. It was wider at the shoulder area and then narrowed, following the contour of the human body. Older coffins did that sometimes.

"We start here," I said.

Edward didn't argue. He let the machine gun hang by its strap and drew his pistol. "You're covered," he said.

I laid the shotgun on the floor in front of the coffin, gripped the edge of the lid, said a quick prayer, and lifted. Valentine lay in the coffin. His scarred face was bare. He was still dressed as a riverboat gambler but this time in black. His frilly shirt was crimson. The colors didn't look good against his auburn hair. One hand was half-curled over his thigh, a careless sleeper's gesture. A very human gesture.

Edward peered into the coffin, gun pointed ceilingward. "This the one you threw Holy Water on?"

I nodded.

"Did a bang-up job," Edward said.

Valentine never moved. I couldn't even see him breathe. I wiped my sweating palms on my jeans and felt for a pulse in his wrist. Nothing. His skin was cool to the touch. He was dead. It wasn't murder, no matter what the new laws said. You can't kill a corpse.

The wrist pulsed. I jerked back like he'd burned me.

"What's wrong?" Edward asked.

"I got a pulse."

"It happens sometimes."

I nodded. Yeah, it happened sometimes. If you waited long enough, the heart did beat, blood did flow, but so slow that it was painful to watch. Dead. I was beginning to think I didn't know what that meant.

I knew one thing. If night fell with us here, we would die, or wish we had. Valentine had helped kill over twenty people. He had nearly killed me. When Nikolaos withdrew her protection, he'd finish the job if he could. We had come to kill Nikolaos. I think she would withdraw her protection ASAP. As the old saying goes, it was him or me. I preferred him.

I shook off the shoulder straps of the backpack.

"What are you looking for?" Edward asked.

"Stake and hammer," I said without looking up.

"Not going to use the shotgun?"

I glanced up at him. "Oh, right. Why not rent a marching band while we're at it?"

"If you just want to be quiet, there is another way." He had a slight smile on his face.

I had the sharpened stake in my hand, but I was willing to listen. I've staked most of the vampires that I've killed, but it never gets easier. It is hard, messy work, though I don't throw up anymore. I am a professional, after all.

He took a small case out of his own backpack. It held syringes. He drew out an ampule of some greyish liquid. "Silver nitrate," he said.

Silver. Bane of the undead. Scourge of the supernatural. And all nicely modernized. "Does it work?" I asked.

"It works." He filled one syringe and asked, "How old is this one?"

"A little over a hundred," I said.

"Two ought to do it." He shoved the needle into the big vein in Valentine's neck. Before he had filled the syringe a second time, the body shivered. He shoved the second dose into the neck. Valentine's body arched against the walls of the coffin. His mouth opened and closed. He gasped for air as if he were drowning.

Edward filled up another syringe and handed it towards me. I stared at it.

"It isn't going to bite," he said.

I took it gingerly between my thumb and the first two fingers on my right hand.

"What's the matter with you?" he asked.

"I'm not a big fan of needles."

He grinned. "You're afraid of needles?"

I scowled at him. "Not exactly."

Valentine's body shook and bucked, hands thumping against the wooden walls. It made a small, helpless noise. His eyes never opened. He was going to sleep through his own death.

He gave one last shuddering jump, then collapsed against the side of the coffin like a broken rag doll.

"He doesn't look very dead," I said.

"They never do."

"Stake their heart and chop off their heads, and you know they're dead."

"This isn't staking," he said.

I didn't like it. Valentine lay there looking very whole and nearly human. I wanted to see some rotting flesh and bones turning to dust. I wanted to know he was dead.

"No one has ever gotten up out of their coffin after a syringe full of silver nitrate, Anita."

I nodded but remained unconvinced.

"You check the other side. Go on."

I went, but I kept glancing back at Valentine. He had haunted my nightmares for years, nearly killed me. He just didn't look dead enough for me.

I opened the first coffin on my side, one-handed, holding the syringe carefully. An injection of silver nitrate probably wouldn't do me much good either. The coffin was empty. The white imitation silk lining had conformed to the body like a mattress, but the body wasn't there.

I flinched and stared around the room, but there was nothing there. I stared slowly upward, hoping that there was nothing floating above me. There wasn't. Thank you, God.

I remembered to breathe finally. It was probably Theresa's coffin. Yeah, that was it. I left it open and went to the next one. It was a newer model, probably fake wood, but nice and polished. The black male was in it. I had never gotten his name. Now I never would. I knew what it meant, coming in here. Not just defending yourself but taking out the vampires while they lay helpless. As far as I knew, this vampire had never hurt anyone. I laughed then; he was Nikolaos's protege. Did I really think he'd never tasted human blood? No. I pressed the needle against his neck and swallowed hard. I hated needles. No particular reason.

I shoved it in and closed my eyes while I depressed the plunger. I could have pounded a stake through his heart, but sticking a needle in him put cold chills down my spine.

Edward called, "Anita!"

I whirled and found Aubrey sitting up in his coffin. He had Edward by the throat and was slowly lifting him off his feet.

The shotgun was still by Valentine's coffin. Damn! I drew the 9mm and fired at Aubrey's forehead. The bullet tossed his head back, but he just smiled and raised Edward straight-armed, legs dangling.

I ran for the shotgun.

Edward was having to use both hands to keep himself from being strangled by his own weight. He dropped one hand, fumbling for the machine gun.

Aubrey caught his wrist.

I picked up the shotgun, took two steps towards them and fired from three feet away. Aubrey's head exploded; blood and brains spattered over the wall. The hands lowered Edward to the floor but didn't let go. Edward drew a ragged breath. The right hand convulsed around his throat, fingers digging for his windpipe.

I had to step around Edward to fire at the chest. The blast took out the heart and most of the left side of the chest. The left arm sort of hung there by strands of tissue and bone. The corpse flopped back into its coffin.

Edward dropped to his knees, breath wheezing and choking through his throat.

"Nod if you can breathe, Edward," I said. Though if Aubrey had crushed his windpipe I don't know what I could have done. Run back and gotten Lillian the doctor rat, maybe.

Edward nodded. His face was a mottled reddish purple, but he was breathing.

My ears were ringing with the sound of the shotgun inside the stone walls. So much for surprise. So much for silver nitrate. I pumped another round into the gun and went to Valentine's coffin. I blew him apart. Now, he was dead.

Edward staggered to his feet. He croaked, "How old was that thing?"

"Over five hundred," I said.

He swallowed, and it looked like it hurt. "Shit."

"I wouldn't try sticking any needles into Nikolaos."

He managed to glare at me, still half-leaning against Aubrey's coffin.

I turned to the fifth coffin. The one we had saved until last without any talk between us. It was set against the far wall. A dainty white coffin, too small for an adult. Candlelight gleamed on the carvings in the lid.

I was tempted to just blow a hole in the coffin, but I had to see her. I had to see what I was shooting at. My heart started thudding in my throat; my chest was tight. She was a master vampire. Killing them, even in daylight, is a chancy thing. Their gaze can trap you until nightfall. Their minds. Their voices. So much power. And Nikolaos was the most powerful I'd ever seen. I had my blessed cross. I would be all right. I had had too many crosses taken from me to feel completely safe. Oh, well. I tried to raise the lid one-handed, but it was heavy and not balanced for easy opening like modern coffins. "Can you back me on this, Edward? Or are you still relearning how to breathe?"

Edward came to stand beside me. His face looked almost its normal color. He took hold of the lid and I readied the shotgun.

He lifted and the whole lid slid off. It wasn't hinged on.

I said, "Shiiit!"

The coffin was empty.

"Are you looking for me?" A high, musical voice called from the doorway. "Freeze; I believe that is the word. We have the drop on you."

"I wouldn't advise going for your gun," Burchard said.

I glanced at Edward and found his hands close to the machine gun but not close enough. His face was unreadable, calm, normal. Just a Sunday drive. I was so scared I could taste bile at the back of my throat. We looked at each other and raised our hands.

"Turn around slowly," Burchard said.

We did.

He was holding a semiautomatic rifle of some kind. I'm not the gun freak Edward is, so I didn't know the make and model, but I knew it'd make a big hole. There was also a sword hilt sticking over his back. A sword, an honest-to-god sword.

Zachary was standing beside him, holding a pistol. He held it two-handed, arms stiff. He didn't seem happy.

Burchard held the rifle like he was born with it. "Drop your weapons, please, and lace your fingers on top of your heads."

We did what he asked. Edward dropped the machine gun, and I lost the shotgun. We had plenty more guns.

Nikolaos stood to one side. Her face was cold, angry. Her voice, when it came, echoed through the room. "I am older then anything you have ever imagined. Did you think daylight holds me prisoner? After a thousand years?" She walked out into the room, careful not to cross in front of Burchard and Zachary. She glanced at the remains in the coffins. "You will pay for this, animator." She smiled then, and I had never seen anything more evil. "Strip them of the rest of their weaponry, Burchard; then we will give the animator a treat."

They stood in front of us but not too close. "Up against the wall, animator," Burchard said. "If the man moves, Zachary, shoot him."

Burchard shoved me into the wall and frisked me very thoroughly. He didn't check my teeth or have me drop my pants, but that was about it. He found everything I was carrying. Even the derringer. He shoved my cross into his pocket. Maybe I could tattoo one on my arm? Probably wouldn't work.

I went out to stand with Zachary, and Edward got his turn. I stared at Zachary. "Does she know?" I asked.

"Shut up."

I smiled. "She doesn't, does she?"

"Shut up!"

Edward came back, and we stood there with our hands on top of our heads, weapons gone. It was not a pretty sight.

Adrenaline was bubbling like champagne, and my pulse was threatening to jump out of my throat. I wasn't afraid of the guns, not really. I was afraid of Nikolaos. What would she do to us? To me? If I had a choice, I'd force them to shoot me. It had to be better than anything Nikolaos had in her evil little mind.

"They are unarmed, Mistress," Burchard said.

"Good," she said. "Do you know what we were doing while you destroyed my people?"

I didn't think she wanted an answer, so I didn't give her one.

"We were preparing a friend of yours, animator."

My stomach jerked. I had a wild image of Catherine, but she was out of town. My god, Ronnie. Did they have Ronnie?

It must have showed on my face because Nikolaos laughed, high and wild, an excited tittering.

"I really hate that laugh," I said.

"Silence," Burchard said.

"Oh, Anita, you are so amusing. I will enjoy making you one of my people." Her voice started high and childlike and ended low enough to crawl down my spine.

She called out in a clear voice, "Enter this room now."

I heard shuffling footsteps; then Phillip walked into the room. The horrible wound at his throat was thick, white scar tissue. He stared around the room as if he didn't really see it.

I whispered, "Dear God."

They had raised him from the dead.

47

Nikolaos danced around him. The skirt of her pastel pink dress swirled around her. The large, pink bow in her hair bobbed as she twirled, arms outstretched. Her slender legs were covered in white leotards. The shoes were white with pink bows.

She stopped, laughing and breathless. A healthy pink flush on her cheeks, eyes sparkling. How did she do that?

"He looks very alive, doesn't he?" She stalked around him, hand brushing his arm. He drew away from her, eyes following her every move, afraid. He remembered her. God help us. He remembered her.

"Do you want to see him put through his paces?" she asked.

I hoped I didn't understand her. I fought to keep my face blank. I must have succeeded because she stomped over to me, hands on hips.

"Well," she said, "do you want to watch your lover perform?"

I swallowed bile, hard. Maybe I should just throw up on her. That would teach her. "With you?" I asked.

She sidled up to me, hands clasped behind her back. "It could be you. Your choice."

Her face was almost touching mine. Eyes so damned wide and innocent that it seemed sacrilegious. "Neither sounds very appealing," I said.

"Pity." She half-skipped back to Phillip. He was naked, and his tanned body was still handsome. What were a few more scars?

"You didn't know I was going to be here, so why raise Phillip from the dead?" I asked.

She turned on the heels of her little shoes. "We raised him so he could try to kill Aubrey. Murdered zombies can be so much fun, while they try to kill their murderers. We thought we'd give him a chance while Aubrey was asleep. Aubrey can move if you disturb him." She glanced at Edward. "But then you know that."

"You were going to let Aubrey kill him again," I said.

She nodded, head bobbing. "Mmm-uh."

"You bitch," I said.

Burchard shoved the rifle butt into my stomach, and I dropped to my knees. I panted, trying to breathe. It didn't help much.

Edward was staring very fixedly at Zachary, who was holding the pistol square on his chest. You didn't have to be good at that range or even lucky. Just squeeze the trigger and kill someone. Poof.

"I can make you do whatever I please," Nikolaos said.

A fresh spurt of adrenaline rushed through me. It was too much. I threw up in the corner. Nerves and being hit very hard in the stomach with a rifle. Nerves I'd had before; the rifle butt was a new experience.

"Tsk, tsk," Nikolaos said. "Do I frighten you that much?"

I managed to stand up at last. "Yes," I said. Why deny it?

She clapped her hands together. "Oh, goody." Her face shifted gears, instant switch. The little girl was gone, and no amount of pink, frilly dresses would bring her back. Nikolaos's face was thinner, alien. The eyes were great drowning pools. "Hear me, Anita. Feel my power in your veins."

I stood there, staring at the floor, fear like a cold rush on my skin. I waited for something to tug at my soul. Her power to roll me under and away. Nothing happened.

Nikolaos frowned. The little girl was back. "I bit you, animator. You should crawl if I ask it. What did you do?"

I breathed a small, heartfelt prayer, and answered her. "Holy Water."

She snarled. "This time we will keep you with us until after the third bite. You will take Theresa's place. Perhaps then you will be more eager to find out who is murdering vampires."

I fought with everything in me not to glance at Zachary. Not because I didn't want to give him away, I would do that, but I was waiting for the moment when it would help us. It might get Zachary killed, but it wouldn't take out Burchard or Nikolaos. Zachary was the least dangerous person in this whole room.

"I don't think so," I said.

"Oh, but I do, animator."

"I would rather die."

She spread her arms wide. "But I want you to die, Anita, I want you to die."

"That makes us even," I said.

She giggled. The sound made my teeth hurt. If she really wanted to torture me, all she had to do was lock me in a room and laugh at me. Now that would be hell.

"Come on, boys and girls, let's go play in the dungeon." Nikolaos led the way. Burchard motioned for us to follow. We did. Zachary and he brought up the rear, guns in hand. Phillip stood uncertainly in the middle of the room, watching us go.

Nikolaos called back, "Have him follow us, Zachary."

Zachary called, "Come, Phillip, follow me."

He turned and walked after us, his eyes still uncertain and not really focused.

"Go on," Burchard said. He half-raised the rifle, and I went.

Nikolaos called back, "Gazing at your lover; how nice."

It wasn't a long enough walk to the dungeon door. If they tried to chain me to the wall, I'd rush them. I'd force them to kill me. Which meant I'd better rush Zachary. Burchard might wound me or knock me unconscious, and that would be very, very bad.

Nikolaos led us down the steps and out into the floor. What a day for a parade. Phillip followed, but he was looking around now, really seeing things. He froze, staring at the place where Aubrey had killed him. His hand reached out to touch the wall. He flexed his hand, rubbing fingers into his palm as if he was feeling something. A hand went to his neck and found the scar. He screamed. It echoed against the walls.

"Phillip," I said.

Burchard held me back with the rifle. Phillip crouched in the corner, face hidden, arms locked around his knees. He was making a high, keening noise.

Nikolaos laughed.

"Stop it, stop it!" I walked towards Phillip, and Burchard shoved the gun against my chest. I yelled into his face, "Shoot me, shoot me, dammit! It's got to be better than this."

"Enough," Nikolaos said. She stalked over to me, and I gave ground. She kept walking, forcing me to back up until I bumped against the wall. "I don't want you shot, Anita, but I want you hurt. You killed Winter with your little knife. Let's see how good you really are." She strode away from me. "Burchard, give her back her knives."

He never even hesitated or asked why. He just walked over to

me and handed them to me, hilt first. I didn't question it either.
I took them.

Nikolaos was suddenly beside Edward. He started to move
away. "Kill him if he moves again, Zachary."

Zachary came to stand close, gun out.

"Kneel, mortal," she said.

Edward didn't do it. He glanced at me. Nikolaos kicked him in
the bend of the knee hard enough to make him grunt. He dropped
to one knee, and she grabbed his right arm and tugged it behind
his back. One slender hand grabbed his throat.

"I'll tear out your throat if you move, human. I can feel your
pulse like a butterfly beating against my hand." She laughed and
filled the room with warm, jostling horror. "Now, Burchard, show
her what it means to use a knife."

Burchard went to the far wall, with the door above him at the
top of the steps. He laid the rifle on the floor, and unbuckled his
sword harness, and laid that beside the rifle. Then he drew a long
knife with a nearly triangular blade.

He did some quick stretches to limber his muscles, and I stood
staring at him.

I know how to use a knife. I can throw well; I practice that.
Most people are afraid of knives. If you show yourself willing to
carve someone up, they tend to be afraid of you. Burchard was
not most people. He went down into a slight crouch, knife held
loose but firm in his right hand.

"Fight Burchard, animator, or this one dies." She pulled his
arm, sharp, but he didn't cry out. She could dislocate his shoulder, and Edward wouldn't cry out.

I put the knife back in its right wrist sheath. Fighting with a
knife in each hand may look nifty, but I've never really mastered
it. A lot of people don't. Hey, Burchard didn't have two knives
either. "Is this to the death?" I asked.

"You will not be able to kill Burchard, Anita. So silly. Burchard
is only going to cut you. Let you taste the blade, nothing too
serious. I don't want you to lose too much blood." There was
an undercurrent of laughter in her voice, then it was gone. Her
voice crawled through the room like a fire-wind. "I want to see
you bleed."

Great.

Burchard began to circle me, and I kept the wall at my back. He
rushed me, knife flashing. I held my ground, dodging his blade,

and slashing at him as he darted in. My knife hit empty air. He was standing out of reach, staring at me. He had had six hundred years of practice, give or take. I couldn't top that. I couldn't even come close.

He smiled. I gave him a slight nod. He nodded back. A sign of respect between two warriors, maybe. Either that, or he was playing with me. Guess which way I voted?

His knife was suddenly there, slicing my arm open. I slashed outward and caught him across the stomach. He darted into me, not away. I dodged the knife and stumbled away from the wall. He smiled. Dammit, he'd wanted to get me out in the open. His reach was twice mine.

The pain in my arm was sharp and immediate. But there was a thin line of crimson on his flat stomach. I smiled at him. His eyes flinched, just a little. Was the mighty warrior uneasy? I hoped so.

I backed away from him. This was ridiculous. We were going to die, piece by piece, both of us. What the hell. I charged Burchard, slashing. It caught him by surprise, and he backpedaled. I mirrored his crouch, and we began to circle the floor.

And I said, "I know who the murderer is."

Burchard's eyebrows raised.

Nikolaos said, "What did you say?"

"I know who is killing vampires."

Burchard was suddenly inside my arm, slicing my shirt. It didn't hurt. He was playing with me.

"Who?" Nikolaos said. "Tell me, or I will kill this human."

"Sure," I said.

Zachary screamed, "No!" He turned to fire at me. The bullet whined overhead. Burchard and I both sank to the floor.

Edward screamed. I half-rose to run to him. His arm was twisted at a funny angle, but he was alive.

Zachary's gun went off twice, and Nikolaos took it away from him, tossing it to the floor. She grabbed him and forced him against her body, bending him at the waist, cradling him. Her head darted downward. Zachary shrieked.

Burchard was on his knees, watching the show. I stabbed my knife into his back. It thunked solid and hilt-deep. His spine stiffened, one hand trying to tear out the blade. I didn't wait to see if he could do it. I drew my other knife and plunged it into the side of his throat. Blood poured down my hand when I took the knife out. I stabbed him again, and he fell slowly forward, face down on the floor.

Nikolaos let Zachary drop to the floor and turned, face blood-stained, the front of her pink dress crimson. Blood spattered on her white leotards. Zachary's throat was torn out. He lay gasping on the floor but still moving, alive.

She stared at Burchard's body, then screamed, a wild banshee sound that wailed and echoed. She rushed me, hands outstretched. I threw the knife, and she batted it away. She hit me, the force of her body slamming me into the floor, her scrambling on top of me. She was still screaming, over and over. She held my head to one side. No mind tricks, brute strength.

I screamed, "Nooo!"

A gun fired, and Nikolaos jerked, once, twice. She rose off me, and I felt the wind. It was creeping through the room like the beginnings of a storm.

Edward leaned against the wall, holding Zachary's dropped gun.

Nikolaos went for him, and he emptied the gun into her frail body. She didn't even hesitate.

I sat up and watched her stalk towards Edward. He threw the empty gun at her. She was suddenly on him, forcing him back into the floor.

The sword lay on the floor, nearly as tall as I was. I drew it out of its sheath. Heavy, awkward, drawing my arm down. I raised it over my head, flat of the blade half resting on my shoulder, and ran for Nikolaos.

She was talking again in a high, sing-song voice. "I will make you mine, mortal. Mine!"

Edward screamed. I couldn't see why. I raised the sword, and its weight carried it down and across, like it was meant to. It bit into her neck with a great wet thunk. The sword grated on bone, and I drew it out. The tip fell to scrape on the floor.

Nikolaos turned to me and started to stand. I raised the sword, and it cut outward, swinging my body with it. Bone cracked, and I fell to the floor as Nikolaos tumbled to her knees. Her head still hung by strips of meat and skin. She blinked at me and tried to stand up.

I screamed and drove the blade upward with everything I had. It took her between the breasts, and I stood running with it, shoving it in. Blood poured. I pinned her against the wall. The blade shoved out her back, scraping along the wall as she slid downward.

I dropped to my knees beside the body. Yes, the body. She was dead!

I looked back at Edward. There was blood on his neck. "She bit me," he said.

I was gasping for air, having trouble breathing, but it was wonderful. I was alive and she wasn't. She fucking wasn't. "Don't worry, Edward, I'll help you. Plenty of Holy Water left." I smiled.

He stared at me a minute, then laughed, and I laughed with him. We were still laughing when the wererats crept in from the tunnel. Rafael, the Rat King, stared at the carnage with black-button eyes. "She is dead."

"Ding dong, the witch is dead," I said.

Edward picked it up, half-singing, "The wicked old witch."

We collapsed into laughter again, and Lillian the doctor, all covered with fur, tended our hurts, Edward first.

Zachary was still lying on the ground. The wound at his throat was beginning to close up, skin knitting together. He would live, if that was the right word.

I picked my knife up off the floor and staggered to him. The rats watched me. No one interfered. I dropped to my knees beside him and ripped the sleeve of his shirt. I laid the gris-gris bare. He still couldn't talk, but his eyes widened.

"Remember when I tried to touch this with my own blood? You stopped me. You seemed afraid, and I didn't understand why." I sat beside him and watched him heal. "Every gris-gris has a thing you must do for it, vampire blood for this one, and one thing you must never do, or the magic stops. Poof." I held up my arm, dripping blood quite nicely. "Human blood, Zachary; is that bad?"

He managed a noise like, "Don't."

Blood dripped down my elbow and hung, thick and trembling over his arm. He sort of shook his head, no, no. The blood dripped down and splatted on his arm, but it didn't touch the gris-gris.

His whole body relaxed.

"I've got no patience today, Zachary." I rubbed blood along the woven band.

His eyes flared, showing white. He made a strangling noise in his throat. His hands scrabbled at the floor. His chest jerked as if he couldn't breathe. A sigh ran out of his body, a long whoosh of breath, and he was quiet.

I checked for a pulse; nothing. I cut the gris-gris off with my knife, balled it in my hand, and shoved it in my pocket. Evil piece of work.

Lillian came to bind my arm up. "This is just temporary. You'll need stitches."

I nodded and got to my feet.

Edward called, "Where are you going?"

"To get the rest of our guns." To find Jean-Claude. I didn't say that part out loud. I didn't think Edward would understand.

Two of the ratmen went with me. That was fine. They could come as long as they didn't interfere. Phillip was still huddled in the corner. I left him there.

I did get the guns. I strung the machine gun over my shoulders and kept the shotgun in my hands. Loaded for bear. I had killed a one-thousand-year-old vampire. Naw, not me. Surely not.

The ratmen and I found the punishment room. There were six coffins in it. Each had a blessed cross on its lid and silver chains to hold the lid down. The third coffin held Willie, so deeply asleep that he seemed like he would never wake. I left him like that, to wake with the night. To go on about his business. Willie wasn't a bad person. And for a vampire he was excellent.

All the other coffins were empty, only the last one still unopened. I undid the chains and laid the cross on the ground. Jean-Claude stared up at me. His eyes were midnight fire, his smile gentle. I flashed on the first dream and the coffin filled with blood, him reaching for me. I stepped back, and he rose from the coffin.

The ratmen stepped back, hissing.

"It's all right," I said. "He's sort of on our side."

He stepped from the coffin like he'd had a good nap. He smiled and extended a hand. "I knew you would do it, ma petite."

"You arrogant son of a bitch." I smashed the shotgun butt into his stomach. He doubled over just enough. I hit him in the jaw. He rocked back. "Get out of my mind!"

He rubbed his face and came away with blood. "The marks are permanent, Anita. I cannot take them back."

I gripped the shotgun until my hands ached. Blood began to trickle down my arm from the wound. I thought about it. For one moment, I considered blowing his perfect face away. I didn't do it. I would probably regret it later.

"Can you stay out of my dreams, at least?" I asked.

"That, I can do. I am sorry, ma petite."

"Stop calling me that."

He shrugged. His black hair had nearly crimson highlights in the torchlight. Breathtaking. "Stop playing with my mind, Jean-Claude."

"Whatever do you mean?" he asked.

"I know that the otherworldly beauty is a trick. So stop it."

"I am not doing it," he said.

"What is that supposed to mean?"

"When you have the answer, Anita, come back to me, and we will talk."

I was too tired for riddles. "Who do you think you are? Using people like this."

"I am the new master of the city," he said. He was suddenly next to me, fingers touching my cheek. "And you put me upon the throne."

I jerked away from him. "You stay away from me for a while, Jean-Claude, or I swear . . ."

"You'll kill me?" he said. He was smiling, laughing at me.

I didn't shoot him. And some people say I have no sense of humor.

I found a room with a dirt floor and several shallow graves. Phillip let me lead him to the room. It was only when we stood staring down at the fresh-turned earth that he turned to me. "Anita?"

"Hush," I said.

"Anita, what's happening?"

He was beginning to remember. He would become more alive in a few hours, up to a point. It would almost be the real Phillip for a day, or two.

"Anita?" His voice was high and uncertain. A little boy afraid of the dark. He grabbed my arm, and his hand felt very real. His eyes were still that perfect brown. "What's going on?"

I stood on tiptoe and kissed his cheek. His skin was warm. "You need to rest, Phillip. You're tired."

He nodded. "Tired," he said.

I led him to the soft dirt. He lay down on it, then sat up, eyes wild, grabbing for me. "Aubrey! He . . ."

"Aubrey's dead. He can't hurt you anymore."

"Dead?" He stared down the length of his body as if just seeing it. "Aubrey killed me."

I nodded. "Yes, Phillip."

"I'm scared."

I held him, rubbing his back in smooth, useless circles. His arms hugged me like he would never let go.

"Anita!"

"Hush, hush. It's all right. It's all right."

"You're going to put me back, aren't you?" He drew back so he could see my face.

"Yes," I said.

"I don't want to die."

"You're already dead."

He stared down at his hands, flexing them. "Dead?" he whispered. "Dead?" He lay down on the fresh-turned earth. "Put me back," he said.

And I did.

At the end his eyes closed and his face went slack, dead. He sank into the grave and was gone.

I dropped to my knees beside Phillip's grave, and wept.

48

Edward had a dislocated shoulder and two broken bones in his arm, plus one vampire bite. I had fourteen stitches. We both healed. Phillip's body was moved to a local cemetery. Every time I work in it, I have to go by and say hello. Even though I know Phillip is dead and doesn't care. Graves are for the living, not the dead. It gives us something to concentrate on instead of the fact that our loved one is rotting under the ground. The dead don't care about pretty flowers and carved marble statues.

Jean-Claude sent me a dozen pure white, long-stemmed roses. The card read, "If you have answered the question truthfully, come dancing with me."

I wrote "No" on the back of the card and slipped it under the door at Guilty Pleasures, during daylight hours. I had been attracted to Jean-Claude. Maybe I still was. So what? He thought it changed things. It didn't. All I had to do was visit Phillip's grave to know that. Oh, hell, I didn't even have to go that far. I know who and what I am. I am The Executioner, and I don't date vampires. I kill them.